DESTINY FINDS YOU

TYGARYA SAGA
BOOK ONE
by
ANNETTA LINCOLN

I0650820

DEDICATION

To all those fantasy readers who like a strong female lead,
who swears and drinks a lot, kicks ass and takes no prisoners.
This one is for you.

WARNING

Set in a medieval dystopian fantasy world with magic
Mentioned throughout this series are several triggers including;
A lot of swearing
Violence
Intimidation
Gas-lighting
Submission
Assault
Fettering
Whipping
Gagging
Forced Proximity

PART I

LITTLE CAT AND HER WHITE KNIGHT

ANTYN'S
PROPHECY COLLECTION

*"Seek the White Rose
among dangerous thorns"
"The Dragon's son
with the power of
the White Rose
will some day
Rule the World"
- excerpts from
Collection of Prophecy*

Map of Arial

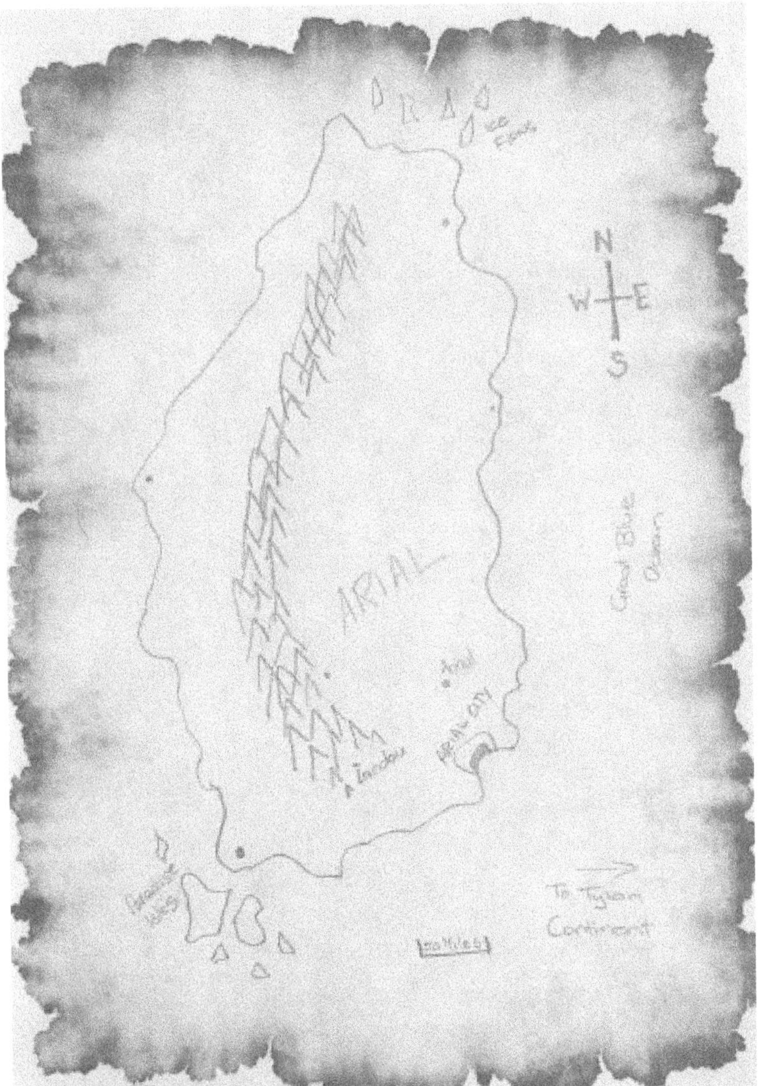

1

The morning had dawned bitterly cold with a thick frost on the ground in the harbour side capital city of Arial. No decent person was up and about yet, however there were still people out this chilly morning. Their poorly clothed bodies shivering beneath the rags they wore; their fingers and toes beginning to freeze numb. A small group of five they were, just underfed youngsters ranging in age from ten through to fifteen years. They were standing just inside a smelly wet alleyway waiting for any unaware passers-by that looked like they could be carrying something, anything, of worth.

Across the street, they are watching intently into a low window where an elderly man was stoking the fire against the cold dawning day.

"This is ridiculous!" A fiery young girl in her early teens exclaimed suddenly as she rubbed her hands together and blew on them trying to warm them up.

She would be a very pretty girl, not that anyone would be able to notice unless they really paid attention. Dressed as she was in a ragged skirt and dirty linen blouse. Her uncut waist length ash blond hair, which was tied back with a piece of twine, was so dirty and knotty it resembled old straw and was stuffed inside a cheese cutter hat. Her face was hidden underneath months of dirt, as they all were. It was her eyes that gave her away, huge irises of blue that changed with her mood from ice blue to an intense vivid sky blue – hues very rarely seen in humans here so she seldom let them be noticed. They were the scourge of any city; the unwanted and orphaned children of the poor, left to survive the only way they could – in the clutches of the gangs and the greedy.

"How can we be expected to pick people's pockets when I can't even feel my own fingers?" The young girl complained to her fellow thieves.

"That may be but we have to try, Tyg, or..." A boy known as Dane tried to reply. He was roughly the same age as Tyg and also her best friend.

"This is crazy! We'll just end up getting ourselves caught if we try anything with our fingers frozen numb. I'm going back to the Hut" Tyg interrupted Dane, cutting him off. He shook his head at the hot head girl.

"Barion will skin you alive if you go back empty handed" Dane tried to press the issue.

"Better skinned and warm." Tyg said with a grin then turned and started walking down the alleyway leaving the others grumbling with confusion unable to decide what to do, stay or follow.

As she reached the other end of the alley and prepared to cross the street she heard the others come up behind her. She smiled to herself and turned to face them.

"See sense did youse?" She asked smugly.

"I don't know about sense but we can't let you go back to face Barion by yourself, better to do it as a group." Dane replied matter-of-factly.

"Why? I'm not scared of him! He's a spineless weasel that just carries out someone else higher up's orders." The disgust in Tyg's voice all too apparent.

"Shhh!" Dane tried to quiet her as they all looked around suspiciously. "If Barion hears you talking like that he'll do worse than skin you, he'll have you shipped out to some slave auction."

"Pah! I'd like to see him try!" Tyg exclaimed indignantly as Dane shook his head giving up. "Come on, let's go!" Tyg said and headed off across the street and down another alley as the others scuttled along after her, their feet freezing in the squelching melt of last night's snow as it turned to slush in the drizzle that was just starting to fall.

After turning down several alleys, keeping off the main streets and out of sight, they arrived at a dingy no-exit. The only feature a large iron door in the gloom in the back wall. Tyg banged her fist on it for admittance, three solid knocks. In the middle of the door a small flap opened revealing a hard pair of eyes staring down at them.

"What are you lot doing back already? You can't possibly have picked every pocket in this filthy city so quickly, now shove off and get back to work!" A gruff voice to match the eyes staring at them, growled through the door.

"Just let us in Caern, please?" Dane asked as he stepped in front of Tyg taking the lead. "It's too cold out this morning. Besides, there is no one up yet and our fingers are frozen anyway. We couldn't pick a pocket if we tried. Come on, open the door. It's freezing out here, please."

The hard eyes regarded them all a moment, then just as Tyg was about to say something the eyes looked down at Dane again.

"You realise that you're going to have to explain yourself to Barion if I let you in?"

"Yes, yes. Just open the door." Dane replied stepping on Tyg's foot to prevent her from answering and saying something they would all regret.

"Alright then, in ya come young'uns."

As Caern unlocked the heavy iron door Tyg leaned over Dane's shoulder and whispered in his ear. "If you ever do that again I'll ram a knife between your ribs."

3

Dane turned with a shocked expression to see Tyg staring at him, her large eyes a deathly pale blue. Tyg swept past him bumping his shoulder and disappeared through the door. Dane stood dumbly watching after her still too shocked to speak when a strong hand clasped his shoulder.

"Just let it go Dane, you know what she's like when she gets in a mood about something."

Dane looked up into the face of his friend Pete, who smiled at him with an understanding look.

"Yeah, I know..." Dane replied with a sigh as they both turned and entered the low dark room beyond.

Stepping inside Tyg looked around the interior which opened up onto a large dimly lit room – like a warehouse – with a large open fire burning invitingly in the middle. Several people were milling around, some talking fervently in small groups, and some sitting at tables gambling and drinking – even at this early hour. Some were dozing wherever they could in corners on piles of worn cushions or make shift beds and old couches. In most instances money seemed to be changing hands and deals are being done, gambling, drinking and general rowdy behaviour. Directly across from the entrance, far to the back, was another door that led to an office, the master's office – Barion. The door heavily guarded by a large burly man who, it seemed to Tyg, was completely covered in wiry black hair. He was also covered in numerous weapons.

As Tyg moved towards the fire pit she stretched her hands out to warm them up, just as a weedy pale little man approached her.

"What are you doin' 'ere child?" He asked of Tyg in a slithery whiney voice. As Tyg turned towards him the others of her group caught up to her and also start warming their hands by the fire.

The man watched with interest. "Ah, mutiny is it, children?" He asks of all of them in that same whiney voice. "And, let me guess just who the ring leader is in this mutiny, hmm?" He continued fixing a stare once again upon Tyg who was looking at him with an intense dangerous look, her eyes blazing with an ice blue fire.

"You know your problem Grak? You have nothing better to do than annoy us 'children' because all the other adults can't stand the mere sight of you." Tyg stated, placing her hands on her hips and facing Grak full on as he inhaled sharply with shock. "Why don't you do everyone a favour and go outside in the freezing cold, lie down in some filthy gutter somewhere and die!" Tyg spat out the last word like venom. A few nearby men snickered as they overheard.

"Why you little wench!" Grak yelled, his pride hurt and struck Tyg with a back handed blow across the face, causing her hat to fly off her head and her long hair to tumble down her back. "You will learn to be more respectful of your elders!"

Tyg staggered back momentarily her hand going to her flaming cheek, feeling the heat of the sting knowing there was going to be a welt there. She looked up at Grak with a deadly stare as her wrath exploded.

"Right, that does it!" Tyg growled like a demon as she launched herself at Grak. She ran into him pushing him in the chest toppling him off balance and sent him crashing to the floor. Tyg jumped on top of him and proceeded to rain a flurry of punches about his head and face as he tried to protect himself with his arms up, screaming pitifully.

"Help, help me! Get her off me!" Grak wailed as people started to gather around. "Get this little freak off me!"

Dane and Pete stepped forward quickly and grabbed Tyg under the arms and dragged her off while she screamed profanities that would make a sailor blush. Several other people were laughing and snickering at the scene, a voice even joked that Grak was finally getting what he deserved. A small group of men stood off to one side, whispering and looking at Tyg with an evil intent since her hat fell off and her long hair was revealed.

Meanwhile, the bodyguard at Barion's door discreetly knocked on it to get Barion's attention then opened the door slightly, ducking his head in and saying two words. "Trouble boss."

With Dane and Pete finally managing to get Tyg off Grak and holding her back as she struggled to release their grip, the door to Barion's office opened. He stepped out and took in the scene quickly with his alert, beady eyes. A small man, with a tired expression, he winced as he saw Grak coming to his feet dabbing at his scratched face and of the young girl Tyg – never out of trouble – being held back by her friends as she struggled and hurled abuse at Grak.

Barion sighed, wiping a hand over his face. He hated having to deal with these situations. As he quietly closed the door to his office he glanced at his guard giving him a look of unfelt thanks. The guard grinned back at him. Barion sighed again and walked towards where a large mob was beginning to gather. Some people turned noticing him, followed by his huge guard and skulked away quickly.

"Enough!" Barion yelled in a surprisingly strong and commanding voice. The room was hushed to silence as everyone's focus turned to him. All except for Tyg, who didn't appear to have heard him over her own raging as she continued to rant and swear, struggling against her friends' hold.

Dane whispered quickly in her ear as Barion just glared at her, his face starting to turn an unsavoury red. She went quickly silent as she looked over to him her eyes going wide as she realised the whole room was silent but her.

"What the hell is going on out here, it sounds like market day down at the wharves?" Barion said in a strong authoritative tone, his eyes fixed on Tyg.

"She attacked me Barion, Sir, look..." Grak jumped in from beside Barion, holding up his arms and pointing to the scratches on them and his bloodied nose. "I've warned you about her before, she's rabid and should be put down like a rabid dog."

Grak suddenly ducked behind Barion as Tyg went berserk again struggling to get free of her friends vice like grips, as they struggled to hold her back. She had always been freakishly strong for a girl, rivalling even the likes of Dane and Pete, both big boys.

"Enough, I said!" Barion yelled at her again. Tyg quieted down and looked sullenly at the floor as Barion calmed his voice and asked of her. "Is what he says true?"

"Well, does it look like it's true?" Tyg answered indignantly her voice full of sarcasm.

"Don't make things any worse for yourself, Tyg." Dane said quickly as he saw Barion starting to lose his patience. "Just tell him what happened, please."

"Yes, a wise boy. I suggest you take his advice girl and stop the smart comments and do as you have been instructed and tell me what happened here." Barion said in a no-nonsense tone.

"But, I told you what happened Barion, Sir, you needn't ask this feral animal." Grak said from behind Barion, his voice whiny and subservient.

"Grak?" Barion said, wearily wiping his hand over his face.

"Yes, Sir?" Grak asked, eager to please.

"Shut up." Barion said dismissively, causing Grak to grumble to himself, fold his arms and sulk. Barion turned back to Tyg. "Well?"

"Well, he came up to me wanting to know why I was here and when I told him to mind his own business he struck me across the face, so I retaliated." Tyg shrugged and folded her arms defiantly as her friends hesitantly let her go.

"Hmm, I see." Barion sighed, looking closely at the red mark on Tyg's cheek, a testament to her story. "But, what exactly are you doing here, you're supposed to be out on the streets earning your keep by now?"

"Yeah, well...it's too cold." Tyg replied flatly. "Our fingers are frozen and it makes them clumsy and slow, we can't pick pockets with frozen fingers so we decided it was better to come back and warm them up."

"We decided?" Barion commented sardonically, looking bemused as he looked around at the others of the group standing a short way off.

"Yeah, that's right, we all decided." Dane stepped forward with Pete nodding behind him.

Barion smiled to himself to see the kids sticking together, but Grak pushed forward again.

"What about what she did to me?"

"Grak, I thought I told you to shut up? It sounds to me like you got exactly what you deserved." Barion grumbled, rounding on him. "Now, go away and stop whining at me." Barion then looked around the room taking in everyone in the crowd who was standing around watching the proceedings. "In fact, you can all get out and earn me some money and stop standing around here, this isn't a free house. Now go!" Barion raised his voice. "Out!" Everyone suddenly jumped into action at Barion's order and started scrambling around trying to look busy. Barion turned back to address Tyg.

"This is not the first time you have come to my attention girl, but, I expect this to be the last." Barion said it with that same authoritative tone, but then stopped and regarded her more closely. "I fear however, that it won't be the last time will it?" He asked rhetorically then changed tact. "How old are you?"

Tyg looked at him nervously and shrugged. "About thirteen I think." Tyg didn't want to know why he was asking.

Barion seemed deep in thought. "Perhaps a little young yet, but it would certainly get you out of my hair..." He muttered mostly to himself.

"Wait a minute..." Tyg interrupted knowing what was coming next and getting very nervous.

Barion looked her full in the face. "You know your time here is nearly up."

"I will not be a whore!" Tyg said defiantly, crossing her arms, but the words came out quiet, almost a whisper as a little fear crept in.

"You will be and do exactly what I see fit." Barion retorted stepping up close to her. "You cause any more trouble here and I will be straight round to Rose's with you, do we understand each other?" He asked, his tone deathly quiet.

Tyg looked at him stunned silent, her eyes like saucers and now an intense cornflower blue.

"Good." Barion said as he turned from her and walked back to his office. He shuddered like a chill breeze had just passed through him, he never liked dealing with that strange girl.

"Are you okay, Tyg?" Dane asked quietly, he had never seen Tyg scared silent before.

Tyg turned to look at him. "I can't let that happen, I need to do something, I need to get myself a dagger. I need to learn to defend myself properly." She turned and started walking off back towards the door heading back outside. As she walked she started tucking her hair up inside her hat once more.

Once outside Dane caught up with her again.

"Tyg, surely there are other alternatives." Dane said as he follows her.

"Like what?" She asked him. "You heard him, once more in trouble and I'm off to Rose's. I can't let that happen...I won't!" Tyg

9

was definitely spooked. "First man that comes at me is going to get a dagger in his heart!"

Dane knew what she meant, he knew there was no way she would stay out of trouble, and people were beginning to notice her – men were beginning to notice her. Dane worried about what could happen to Tyg if she was ever found to be alone. He wished his friend was a male, then everything would be different. Suddenly Dane had an idea.

"Why not disappear into the shadows, lay low for a while." Dane suggested. Tyg stopped walking and turned to listen. "You could start dressing differently, look more like a guy, perhaps you could go unnoticed and..."

"Pretend to be a guy..." Tyg muttered to herself, interrupting Dane. She looked at him with a smile on her face. "You're brilliant Dane!"

2

Tyg thought hard about it and decided the best thing to do was to cut her hair and start strapping her chest tight with fabric. She started dressing like a boy in long linen pants and a tunic over a white linen shirt. But, the problem was nothing could disguise her face or her eyes, so if someone looked closely enough they would still know who she was even though she kept a long fringe to cover her face as much as she possibly could. She decided that something more drastic was going to have to be sacrificed to prevent her life going down a path she would rather kill herself than go down.

Tyg got herself a dagger and started practising with it every day while the others stood in the alleyways waiting for crowds in which to disperse and use their light-fingered talents.

Dane was surprised at how fast she got good at throwing her dagger at targets.

"Wow, Tyg. That's amazing, you can almost hit the target every single time now."

"Yeah, but I need to be able to hit the dead centre every single time." Tyg said frustrated at herself.

"Why?" Dane asked, a little cautiously.

Tyg wiped a hand over her forehead. "Because, Dane, I am changing my career path." She declared with a grin. "You know those guys in black that stay at the warehouse sometimes?"

"From the Assassin's Guild?" Dane baulked.

"Yeah, them. Well, next time they are in the warehouse I intend to try and get a job with them."

"You're not serious?" Dane stared hard at Tyg as she threw her dagger again, this time it hit the bull's-eye. She turned and grinned back at Dane, happy with herself. He wondered if she realised that of anyone, those men would have her bent over and at their mercy faster than she could blink.

"Deadly." She answered, satisfied with her decision.

A week later Tyg got her chance. She was sitting not far from the group of men that had caught her attention. She sat quietly in a corner unnoticed but watching and studying the men. Something about these men intrigued Tyg, almost like fate was trying to push her in their direction. Nothing else seemed to matter to her, she had to get in with them. They were a nasty group of men and most of Barion's workers kept away from them. Tyg wondered if she was with these men if others would also stay away from her. Assassins, mercenaries, cutthroats for hire. These were some of the names whispered around the Hut about these men. What fascinated Tyg about them though was their weapons and the skill with which they seemed to use them, they were the best of the best, so went their fearsome reputations.

Right now they were in the midst of a competition. Whoever could hit the bull's-eye the most times in a row on the target drawn on the wall won the rights to an expensive bottle of whisky. Tyg had overheard them earlier when they arrived. How their leader: an evil looking man called Palin, had stolen it from a house of one of their clients. Tyg knew what they meant by 'client' and she knew the man wasn't going to miss the bottle.

Palin was winning, which was no surprise. You didn't become leader of a group such as these without being the best among them. They had all been drinking and Palin was now shouting at them for a decent competitor to step forward.

"Can no one beat me? Come on you bunch of worthless dogs, someone must be able to hit that target more than my six times in a row?" Palin was swinging the bottle of whisky in front of their faces.

"Yeah, but you haven't finished yet, since you haven't missed yet, so you say six now but what's it gonna be in the end, Palin?" One guy with a nasty scar down his left cheek asked as the rest laugh.

"No fair, you know you can't be beaten." Another young man with blond curls called out.

"Bah! How am I ever going to find myself a worthy apprentice...I ain't getting any younger." Palin roared.

The man with the scar laughed loudly and clapped Palin on the back. "Neither am I, old friend. I think we're about the same age, I think I'm a bit past becoming your apprentice."

That made them all laugh.

Tyg saw her opportunity, so she quickly tucked her hair up inside her cap and stood up.

"I can throw a dagger just as good as you." She announced proudly.

The group stopped laughing and all turned to stare at what they thought was a young boy – Tyg's height often lent people to jump to that conclusion, at already five foot seven inches tall she wasn't the normal height for a female, and was the same height as most men in Arial. The group fell into fits of laughter, cajoling and carrying on about the insolent thief wanting to become Palin's apprentice and beat him at throwing daggers. It was a huge joke to them all, except Palin. He wasn't laughing, instead he was regarding the dirty young wretch standing in front of him with curiosity. Palin held his hand up and the group fell silent.

"Well, boy, you think you can hit that bull's-eye there?" Palin asked, pointing at the target.

"I don't think, I know I can." Tyg answered confidently, her eyes blazing ice blue, as she pulled her dagger out of her belt and threw it without a second glance at the target. It hit solidly dead centre of the target. The men all stared from the target to Tyg, their faces showing surprise. Palin started clapping in a mocking manner, causing Tyg's eyes to flash indignantly.

"Well done, boy, I think you definitely have talent." He said as he walked over to the target and pulled Tyg's dagger out of the wall. He walked over to her and walked a slow circle around her looking her up and down. "How old are you boy?" He asked, stopping in front of Tyg again and scowling down at her. Palin stood about five inches taller than her.

"About fifteen, I suppose." Tyg said with a shrug. Palin grunted and handed back her dagger.

"Now let's see you do that again, boy, and I'll consider you for my apprentice."

Tyg took a deep breath concentrating on the target, this was it, her one chance to move up and out of Barion's clutches. Tyg threw the dagger and watched it like it was in slow motion as it spun through the air and once more it hit home, in the exact same mark she had landed the dagger the first time. This surprised even Palin, who stared at her a long moment while the others all cheered for Palin's new apprentice. One walked over and handed Tyg a mug of ale and clapped her on the back, which nearly sent her reeling forward as she quickly clasped hold of her hat to stop it from falling off her head. Palin grabbed her arm and threw the mug of ale back at the man covering him in the frothy liquid.

"No apprentice of mine is going to be corrupted by the likes of you lot!" Palin shouted as he led Tyg a few yards off and sat her down heavily on an upturned keg. He shouted so that the men could hear. "Now, you will sit here and watch these drunkards and learn that if I ever see you in a state like that I'll string your guts out to dry." He grabbed Tyg by the shirt and pulled her face close to his as he bent down towards her. "Understand!"

The men all laughed, yelling that Palin was being unfair to the poor boy. Meanwhile, Palin was now whispering to Tyg, his eyes locked on hers. "I know who you are, girly, and this is a dangerous game you're playing. I want you to come see me tomorrow morning at dawn. Now, as soon as the gang's attention on you is gone, make sure you disappear again...like you were before."

"You knew I was there?" Tyg said a little in awe of Palin's knowledge of her.

He didn't answer but turned and joined the men, grabbing up the whisky bottle and opening it to the cheers of the group. He started handing it around. Tyg took her chance and slipped quietly away.

The next day Tyg returned to the same place at dawn to find most of the men from last night asleep in drunken stupors, fallen where they had stood, some on the floor wrapped in blankets with women. Tyg grit her teeth at the sight. Palin was sitting sharpening a dagger on a whetstone. He looked up at her, put his whetstone away, and with dagger in hand walked past her without a word. He turned back to look at her, his face saying everything – he expected her to follow – then he turned and continued to walk away.

Tyg almost had to run to catch up. She followed him through the streets and into an old disused warehouse. Once there he turned on her, grabbing her by the front of her shirt again and tossing her to the ground, causing the hat on her head to fall off, leaving her hair to tumble down around her face and to her shoulders, it had grown quickly.

"Do you even realise what could have happened if even one of those men had done the same to you and they all realised you're a girl?" Palin shouted at her.

Tyg didn't understand why he was so angry. As she stood up and dusted herself off she didn't quite know what to say. Then her own anger took over as she saw his condescending expression.

"I know! That's why I came to you! I have practised and practised throwing my dagger till I can hit the mark nearly every time, but that wouldn't help me fight off any of those men – or any men. I want to learn from you, so I can defend myself."

Palin laughed. "Defend yourself?" He scoffed.

Tyg's eyes flashed. "I know what happens to every young girl in the Hut around my age, even younger, I don't want to be raped! I don't intend to have that happen to me ever, and I have no intention of becoming a whore like they all do, broken and lost! I'll kill any man before any of them ever touch me!" Tyg took in a deep breath as she shook with emotion, calming herself and looked at the floor. "I am willing to give myself to you, for your protection from others – if you're willing to teach me everything you know." She swallowed hard before looking up at him.

Palin stared at her a moment, seeing her eyes go from that blazing ice blue to a calm sky blue, he had seen her before in the Hut. He knew she had a reputation as being the best pickpocket around, as well as the nastiest piece of meat available too. He knew she had stealth and cunning and was extremely agile and strong. He had even heard of her choking out a boy a couple of years older than her, by holding him up off his feet against a wall. He knew some more unsavoury types were also starting to look at her with great interest. She was special and Palin knew it.

He was suddenly determined that wasn't going to happen to this girl. He could use her skills in his group. He had, had definite plans for a woman in his group for some time. And, she definitely seemed to have some natural talent and a desire to learn. He also knew she was right, once with him no one would dare try and touch her again.

"I don't sleep with children, girly, I'm not like that." He answered solemnly to her. "But, you're right I could use you...but it's not going to be easy."

"I know that." Tyg muttered.

"I expect you to learn how to fight, hand to hand, with daggers, with swords, with sticks and staffs. Am I getting through...?"

"Yes."

"Are you prepared to kill someone? Do you have any idea what it's like to take another's life?"

"Not yet, but I'm prepared to if that's what you ask of me."

"Hmm." Palin appraised her with a smile. "Can you read and write?"

Tyg was a bit surprised at the sudden direction change his questioning had taken. "A little bit, when I was at the orphanage, they taught us enough they said."

Palin snorted his disapproval of such places. "I bet they did."

He handed her a small book, it had a soft red leather cover and looked old and tatty. "Try and read this, you need to be able to read before we go any further." Palin explained looking down on her.

"Read, why?" Tyg asked as she took the small book and stared at it, opening it slowly to peer inside.

"Because, girly, you need to be able to follow instructions written down." Palin said his impatience running out. "Now, I don't want to hear you question me again, or by the gods, I will strike you down."

Tyg looked up at him and nodded her subservience to him, knowing she had agreed to give herself to him in which ever fashion he so chose, she was his to do with as he wanted.

Palin looked at her a moment longer to make sure she stayed silent, then continued. "This will be your training ground, I expect you to be here every day at dawn, is that understood?"

Tyg nodded again, smiling. When Palin saw her smile he grimaced as he saw the radiance it gave her young face. 'It may take more than my reputation to keep some men at bay when you're older.' He thought to himself, but hopefully, by then her own reputation would be enough.

"This life is not easy, girly, are you sure this is what you want?"

"Yes." Tyg answered with no hesitation. "By the way, my name is Tyg."

"I know what your name is. I needed to remind you of who you are though and calling you girly, I think does it." It was Palin's turn to smile as Tyg looked at him, she was about to say something when she noticed his fist curl tight at his side. Tyg took a deep breath and nodded.

"Good, I'm glad to see you are able to control that waspish tongue of yours. I'm not above hitting you if that is what it takes for you to learn." His gruff voice was menacing.

Tyg glared up at him, her eyes blazing and opened her mouth to say something again, but closed it again and remained silent.

"Good." Palin said, then held his hand out to her as he stared at her intensely. "So, are you with me, Tyg?"

Tyg stared at him in shock then smiled and took his hand and shook it. "Yes, I'm with you, Palin."

Palin laughed. "Yes, well I know all about you, your reputation around Barion's Hut precedes you. You were right to seek help to defend yourself for what you know is coming."

Tyg swallowed hard at the way Palin stared at her when he said it. It was clear he had heard other men talk about her, it made her nervous as she stood in front of him. Palin smiled a tight grimacing smile. "Your first lesson starts now, how to see an attack coming and prepare to defend against it..." With that, Palin sprung forward, launching himself at Tyg, grabbing her shoulders and tossing her to the ground. Tyg landed hard and gasped for breath for a few seconds. When she finally turned towards Palin she found him standing over her with his hand outstretched offering to help her up. "This time you will anticipate the attack and step back to defend against it."

3

Tyg spent the next several months meeting Palin in the warehouse every morning and training. The warehouse was decked out like an obstacle course and Tyg trained like an acrobat, learning to climb, jump, flip and land correctly using mounds of hay and shipping crates. She learnt how to fight with daggers, swords, sticks and hand to hand. She was surprised how naturally it all came to her, like the knowledge was inside her how to fight and it was just being let out of its cage. She thrived learning all the skills required.

Palin was surprised at how ferocious and formidable a fighter she became so quickly, She was immensely strong, freakishly strong, like she wasn't human. He recognised her sociopathic nature and nurtured it, keeping her away from people as much as possible, isolating her and focusing her mind to only what he wanted. He even went so far as to move her to a little bedsit where she could stay, safe from the Hut and the people there. His only concern was the fact that she was still under Barion's jurisdiction as part of the Thieves' Guild. He was going to have to change that soon, but that meant introducing her to the people of the Assassin's Guild, which he wasn't sure she was quite ready for, maturity wise. He decided he needed a test of her abilities.

"I've got a job for you." Palin said as they sat down for a breather during one of her training sessions. "I know you're not actually officially part of the Assassin's Guild yet, but see this as a test."

"A job?" Tyg said excited. "An actual job...like to kill someone?"

"Don't get too excited, you're not killing anyone...yet." Palin chuckled.

"Oh, okay." Tyg seemed disappointed which unnerved Palin a bit. He coughed.

"All in good time...let's just start off slow, okay..."

Tyg smiled at him and he winced. "So what do you want me to do?"

"Retrieve something."

Tyg frowned. "Burgle someone you mean?"

Palin shrugged. "Take back something that belongs to me."

"You can't get it back yourself?"

"Enough of the questions." Palin growled. Tyg pressed her mouth together and looked at the floor.

"The place is guarded, and I believe they are expecting me to try something so they are all on high alert..." Palin regarded Tyg a moment. "There could be trouble if you are found out...you may have to fight your way out...or..."

Tyg looked up at him. "Or?" She raised an eyebrow at him, she didn't like the way he had said it.

"They will be surprised you're a girl...you could use that hesitation..."

Tyg frowned, settling an icy stare at him.

He grinned. "Use what you have available to you, Tyg, its survival."

"Okay..." Tyg said dubiously. "So what is it I'm getting back for you?"

"A contract."

"A contract?"

Palin growled. "That's what I said...look the names on that bloody contract are very important...this could save a lot of people from being killed...cause if that contract gets used in the wrong hands there will be a cleansing..."

Tyg looked at him with an eyebrow raised. "A cleansing?"

Palin gave her a very grumpy and vile look. "The names on that contract will have to be taken out to avoid the authorities getting their hands on them."

"Is your name on that contract?"

Palin stared at her but didn't answer.

Tyg smiled. "Consider it done."

Palin smiled back. "Good girl." He raised his fist in her direction and she bumped it with hers.

"I've got this, Palin." Tyg said. "For you."

It seemed pretty straightforward from the instructions Palin had given her. He had gone over and over them for a full day until he had been satisfied she knew exactly what to do. Which had annoyed her to no end.

Now, she found herself outside the grounds of a large manor house on the outskirts of the city. She peered over the block wall and studied the house. It was an hour after dark and it had been determined that the Lord would be in his dining room with his family having dinner. Tyg could see the light shining out of several downstairs rooms. She glanced up and saw no light coming from upstairs.

She crept over the wall and made her way round the lawns to the other side of the house and looked up at the balcony that supposedly led to the master bedroom, where the safe was supposed to be. Just then she heard someone approaching. She scowled and darted off into the darkness and climbed up a large oak tree that stood proud in one corner of the grounds.

She could make out the figure of a man, by the lantern he carried, walking around the perimeter of the house walking two rather large and mean looking dogs. 'Damn it.' Tyg thought, Palin was right the Lord was expecting trouble. She saw another man appear from the other direction with two more dogs. They meet in the middle and conversed a moment before turning around and walking back along their routes again.

Tyg waited a moment then jumped down and adjusted the coat that Palin had given her to wear, it was a bit small and tight, but it was black. She checked her daggers were clear in their scabbards and then quickly and silently ran across the lawns and jumped up, vaulting off a large ornamental urn and diving sideways to grab the railing of the balcony. She hauled herself up and over and sat down in the darkness as she heard the dog handlers coming back once again.

Once they had gone she tried the balcony doors. Locked. She dug into her pocket and took out two small slim metal tools and stuck them into the basic lock and jiggled and manipulated the lock until she heard the bar slide over and click. She grinned as she put the tools back in her pocket and opened the door and slipped inside. It was almost pitch black in the bedroom, Tyg could make out basic shapes of a bed, chair and drawers ...basic bedroom stuff. She glanced around and could see doors leading to another room. She had been told to look for this and made her way over to it. A dressing room, something she had never heard of before, but apparently the desired thing. A room to get dressed in seemed absurd to her, couldn't you get dressed anywhere, why did you need a special room. She opened the door and crouched down just inside and again reached into her pockets. She drew out a small candle and a box of matches but just as she was about to light it she heard the strike of a match from behind her. She turned to see a man sitting in the chair, lighting a candle that was on the table next to him. He was middle aged, very slim - almost gaunt and had a very cruel looking grin on his face.

"Well, well...just as I had almost given up hope, here you are."

Tyg straightened and placed a hand on a dagger.

"Who the hell are you?" She snarled at him, she knew it wasn't the Lord. She had been given his description and he was the complete opposite of this guy.

"Who I am is of no concern to you, but to say I have been hired by Lord Maton to keep something he has acquired secure."

Tyg grinned. "I'm obviously in the right room then."

The man raised his eyebrows and smirked. "Insolent thief aren't you." He casually put a cigarette in his mouth and lit it with a match. Tyg knew she could have had a dagger at his throat the minute he looked down at the match box, but she felt like playing with this guy a bit longer, he seemed so sure of himself. She folded her arms and leaned against the doorframe watching him. He again raised his eyebrows in surprise as he exhaled the smoke.

"Take your time..." Tyg muttered.

"Lower your hood and remove your mask."

Tyg hesitated and grimaced when she saw his smug grin return. She lowered her hood and pulled the scarf from her face. He squinted at her, then grabbed the candle and held it up, his eyebrows for the third time rising in surprise.

"You're a girl?"

Tyg grinned and shrugged. "What difference does that make?"

He stood up, cigarette hanging from his mouth, and walked to the door. As he went to open it Tyg's dagger was at his throat as she came up behind him and grabbed his arm. "I wouldn't do that if I were you."

She dragged him back to the chair and pushed him down in it. He frowned. "How are you so strong?" He muttered around the cigarette.

"For a girl, you mean?" Tyg sneered at him. "Where's the contract?"

The man laughed and took a draw from the cigarette, removing it from his mouth. "You think I know...I was just told that you people had been led to believe it was in a safe in this room, that this is where you would head." He laughed again as Tyg scowled. They had been fed false information, what the hell was she to do now?

"If you don't know where it is, then you're of no further use to me." Tyg muttered and held her dagger up.

He looked at her shocked. "Now wait a minute...you couldn't possibly...you're a girl."

Tyg came round the back of the chair, her dagger resting on the man's throat. "What the hell has that got to do with anything?" Tyg growled in his ear, sick of hearing the same thing from this guy over and over.

"You can't kill me..." He sneered. "Girls can't do that sort of thing..."

"Girls can't...maybe..." Tyg breathed. "But I'm not just any girl..."

Tyg covered his mouth as he went to scream out and slit his throat. She walked back round the chair and stared at the dead man for a moment. She felt strangely detached. She had expected to feel...something....at killing her first person...remorse....grief...happiness even....but she felt nothing. She shrugged and grabbing the candle she went into the dressing room to see if there was a safe in there at all. After searching for several minutes through the vast quantities of clothes...she got it now about the need for a dressing room...she found nothing. Damn. She pondered what to do next.

She looked down and saw the blood on her hands. She grimaced then wiped it off on the duvet. It didn't seem to want to come off very easily. 'Damn it.' Tyg thought, why were these the small details you're never bloody told about?

She went to the door and put her ear to it. She was sure there was no one directly outside the door. The man had spoken confidently and she was sure if someone outside had heard they would have come in by now. She opened it slightly and looked out. She saw no one and the whole floor was in darkness, so she walked out onto the landing and padded across to another door, opened it and went inside. A kid's room. A plan formed in her mind.

It was about two hours later, Tyg was lying on the bed, when a lady came in holding a candle and the hand of a child about six years old. Tyg sprang up before the lady could even register surprise enough to scream and closed the door behind her.

"Sit on the bed." Tyg growled. "I'm not going to hurt you."

Tyg had repositioned her scarf over her face and pulled her hood back up, so the lady and small child were terrified as all they saw were Tyg's ice blue eyes. The kid started to cry. 'Good, let him cry.' Tyg thought. 'Means I won't have to wait as long for someone to come looking.'

Tyg was leaning on the wall by the door, waiting as the lady of the house and her child huddled on the child's bed, she was trying to get the child to stop crying, when the door opened and a middle aged slightly overweight man in fine clothes came huffing into the room.

"What's the boy's problem?" He asked gruffly as his wife stared at him in horror. He heard the door close behind him and when he turned and saw a pair of ice blue glowing eyes staring at him out of the blackness he fell to his knees, suddenly a blubbering mess.

"Oh, please don't hurt us...please, I have what you want, just don't hurt my family."

"You had a mercenary waiting for me, you set me up to go to the wrong room." Tyg growled as she advanced on the man. He made her sick just looking at him grovelling.

His eyes went wide. "Did you kill him?"

"Yes, I did."

"Oh, dear Gods, please don't hurt us."

"Stop saying that." Tyg growled. "I'm not going to hurt you...just give me what I want."

"Okay...okay...I'm going to have to go downstairs to get it...it's in the drawing room."

"Hmm, and you think I'm going to let you go down there and alert whoever else you have down there..."

"Come with me...let my family go...they won't cause any trouble...I promise."

Tyg looked from man to woman and back again. She didn't believe the woman would have the courage to alert anyone. "Does the bedroom door lock?"

"Ah, yes..."

"Get me the key..." Tyg looked at the woman when she said it. The woman slowly got up and went over to the boy's small dresser and opened a little drawer under the mirror. She took out the key and walked like a scared rabbit towards Tyg holding it out to her. Tyg could see the woman shaking. Tyg took the key from her. "Thank you." She said making the woman look shocked to hear manners from a burglar. She retreated back to her son.

"Get up." She said to the man and stepped behind him, poking a dagger into his ribs. "Open the door, and any sound out of you and you die, got it?"

"Got it." He stammered as he opened the door and stepped out with Tyg right behind him. She locked the door and put the key in her pocket and slowly let Lord Maton walk down the hall towards the staircase. She halted him at the top and leaned over the banister to look down. Seeing and hearing no one she prodded Lord Maton to continue. At the bottom of the stairs he walked along the hall towards the front of the house. Tyg heard someone coming and grabbed Lord Maton and pulled him into the nearest open doorway, clamping a hand over his mouth. It was a reception room. She waited and heard a couple of servants chatting as they walked down the hall with the dishes from dinner, then proceeded with Lord Maton to the drawing room. Once in there Tyg closed and locked the door and leaned against it.

"Get the contract." Tyg ordered. "And hurry the fuck up!" She was starting to get nervous that her luck was going to start running out.

Lord Maton hurried over to a bookcase and took a large volume off the shelf, placing it on the floor he opened it to reveal the fact that it was hollow inside, a false book. He took out some papers that were folded up inside and handed them up to her. Tyg stepped forward and took them. Stuffing them inside her shirt she stared at the Lord. "If these are the wrong papers and not the contract I was sent to get, I will come back and kill your entire family...do you understand?" Her eyes blazed.

Lord Maton nodded his head. "Yes...they are the right ones, I promise."

"Get up." Tyg ordered him. "We are going back upstairs."

"What? Why? Please...there's no one here...only the men outside with the dogs and the one waiting in the room..."

"Really?" Tyg asked dubiously. "This place was supposedly well guarded."

"That man...the one you killed...he was supposed to kill whomever came in...I don't understand why...how..." He trailed off under Tyg's scrutiny. She knew why he hadn't managed to kill her...because he found out she was a girl. Just like what Palin said. Tyg grinned to herself.

"Just get moving..." Tyg growled. She felt better now, knowing she only had to worry about the men outside.

They were halfway up the stairs when the butler spotted them. He called out causing Tyg to flinch. "Damn it." She muttered as she quickly pushed Lord Maton up the stairs and along the hall, unlocking the door she pushed him into the room and closed and locked the door behind them.

Lady Maton was still sitting on the bed with her son curled up in her lap. Lord Maton went to them and put his arms around them both. Banging started on the door with demands it be unlocked immediately.

"What are you going to do now?" Lord Maton asked quietly.

"Leave of course." Tyg grunted as she went to the window and opened it wide. She climbed onto the sill and looked down, directly below was lawn. Perfect. She looked back at the Lord and his family and tossed him the key then back flipped out the window.

She ran quickly knowing the men with dogs would be after her soon. She heard the barking as the dogs were obviously released and was relieved when she reached the stone wall and jumped up onto it, looking back once she jumped and flipped over onto the ground on the other side and took off into the darkness.

It was after midnight when she finally got back into the city and wondered if Palin would want to know she was back now or in the morning. She made her way to the warehouse just to be sure he wasn't waiting there for her.

She grimaced when she walked in to find him pacing. He turned and stared at her.

"Tyg! What the fuck, I thought something had gone wrong."

"Something did go wrong." Tyg muttered as she pulled the papers from inside her shirt and handed them to him.

He looked at the papers in her hand. "You still got the contract?" He walked over to the light of the lantern and held the papers up at an angle so he could read them. Tyg watched hoping they were the right ones. Palin seemed satisfied and tucked them away. "So, what went wrong?"

"Where do I start?" Tyg said and then told him everything that happened. He was shocked that she had killed the mercenary but more shocked by the blasé way she retold the fact and held her hands up showing the red stains still round her fingernails and in the creases of her hands.

"Right, well follow me, we have to go..."

"Go?" Tyg said thinking her job was surely finished.

"To make sure this contract doesn't fall into the wrong hands again."

Tyg rolled her eyes and stuffed her hands in her pockets and followed Palin out as he picked up the lantern, extinguished it and carried it out with him.

They entered a dark strange house in the far south quarter, somewhere Tyg felt uncomfortable being. Even the docks were better than this area. Palin lit the lantern and put it in the window and sat down on a musty old couch in the derelict lounge room. Tyg stood to the side, looking around not wanting to touch anything. Her eyes settled on the long black smudge on the wall where water had been dripping down the wall for years.

"Why the fuck are we here, Palin?"

"Just wait." He muttered. "Sit down, take a nap...it could be a long wait and since it's already past midnight you better get some sleep...I still expect you back at the warehouse in the morning."

"What the fuck? Don't I deserve a day off...or at least a sleep in?"

"No, if you can't handle it, go back to the Hut." Palin growled.

"That was completely unnecessary." Tyg scowled and folded her arms.

"Hmm, perhaps that was a bit harsh...but seriously Tyg, try and get some sleep."

Tyg sat down next to Palin and leant her head back and relaxed, closing her eyes. Palin looked at her a moment then sat forward and took out a pack of cards from his pocket and started playing a game of solitaire on the dusty table.

"When do you sleep?" Tyg asked him without opening her eyes.

"After your training session at the warehouse, when you go back to being a pickpocket."

Tyg opened her eyes and sat up. "You're fucking kidding me?"

"Why would I?" Palin said amused as he stared at his cards.

"Mother..."

"Tyg!" Palin growled.

Tyg collapsed back again and closed her eyes. "So when I'm finally free of Barion and the Hut, is that when I sleep too?"

Palin shrugged. "Most likely, we do most of our work at night."

"And when is that going to be, Palin?"

"Soon, Tyg....soon." Palin smiled to himself. "This is the first step to that."

It was half an hour later when Palin heard someone come through the door. He elbowed Tyg who sat up her eyes blazing and her hand going to her dagger.

Palin looked at her startled. "Really?" He questioned harshly. "Get up, he's here, cover yourself."

Tyg stood up and pulled her hood up and pulled her scarf back over her face and stood behind Palin who remained sitting on the couch.

A heavily robed man entered and went to the window and removed the lantern, placing it on the table, then lowered his hood as he sat down in the musty chair opposite the couch.

"Palin, good to see you." The man muttered as Tyg's eyes went wide. Lord Kor sat in front of her in all his dashing finery.

"Lord Kor." Palin said back.

"Do you have it?"

"Yes." Palin handed the contract over to Kor, who opened it, read it quickly and then placed it on the table. "Good, destroy it."

Palin took out a box of matches and lit one, touching it to the papers catching them alight and threw them into the old fireplace.

Kor looked up at Tyg. "Is this the one you spoke of?"

"Yes."

"And they got the papers?"

"Yes."

Kor smiled at her. "Please remove your hood, I wish to meet this mysterious girl."

Tyg looked at Palin as she had seen him flinch. "Do it." He muttered.

Tyg lowered her hood and pulled her scarf down.

"Tyg, is it?" Kor regarded her with interest, a languid smirk on his handsome face. She was surprised at how young he appeared to be, and he was quite handsome.

"Yes." Tyg muttered, not liking the scrutiny.

"Thank you for your service, you did well. I hope I can rely on your talents in the future."

"That is determined by me, Kor." Palin growled.

"Indeed, okay well...job well done...contract destroyed...have a good night." Kor stood up, pulled his hood up and left.

Palin sat in silence for a couple of minutes while Tyg stared at the door wondering what the hell just transpired, then he stood up.

"Right, we can go now."

4

Palin finally decided now was the time to tell Tyg about the Guild and what they did.

"Let me explain a few things about how we operate around here." Palin said sitting down and motioning for Tyg to do the same. She sat down heavily, glad of the rest after a hard workout. "As you know my men, and me, take care of certain people that get in the way of others, for a price."

"You're assassins." Tyg said matter-of-factly.

"Yes, but it is a lot more complicated than that, it is only one part of what I do and what I co-ordinate."

Tyg sat up straight, interest lighting a fire in her eyes.

"The government turn a blind eye to our activities as long as we stay fairly discreet and don't get too greedy. In turn we help them to get certain information they need to keep control. All in all it works very well." Palin said to her in hushed tones.

"So you help the government to stay in power?" Tyg asked a little in awe.

"You could say that?"

"What if you don't like the government?" Tyg asked thinking.

Palin squinted at her with interest. "What do you mean?"

"What I mean is, wouldn't you sort of have control over who is in Government? Because you could just feed the wrong information to a government you didn't like to discredit them and help a government you like to get into power." Tyg explained.

"You're extremely perceptive for someone so young...and a girl?" Palin answered, his turn to be awed.

"I take offense to that." Tyg said disgruntled, folding her arms.

"You're a thief and a beggar and you take offense to that?" Palin laughed.

Tyg grit her teeth becoming annoyed. "Just because I'm a girl has nothing to do with intelligence."

Palin held his hands up in mock surrender. "Well, I've never come across an overly intelligent woman before so I guess there's no evidence to confirm or deny that statement. Although, you do seem to have brains beyond your years like you have been schooled, but I know you haven't."

"I will be that evidence." Tyg said confidently. "Wait and see."

"I like your tenacity, Tyg, but to get back to what you were saying...it's not as simple as controlling the government, because you forgot one thing."

"What's that?"

"The government is run and decided on by the council, the Lords who own this land, and they never change. It is them that request our aid from time to time."

"Request?" Tyg asks smiling.

"That's what we like to call it." Palin also smiled.

"Okay, so the government don't know about you then...only the Council?"

"Actually, only a small number of the Council know about our arrangement and who they are stays with me, unless I decide someone else needs to know."

"Like Lord Kor..." Tyg said smugly.

"Don't ever utter that name again, do you hear me!" Palin growled.

"So, why are you telling me this?"

"Because you are nearly ready to join the fold. My only concern is the trouble that seems to follow you around like a puppy."

"I can't help that." Tyg said defensively.

"Quite, that's why I think it's time for you to leave the Hut. It's time to set you on another path, one where your talents will be better served to my requirements. It's time to let everyone know who you work for now."

"And what path is that exactly?"

"One that gives you access to the sort of information we gather to give to the Council."

"So, I'm to be a spy?"

"Not in so many words, we have a system. I have another assignment for you." Palin looked hard at Tyg. "Can you handle that?"

"Yes, of course I can."

"Are you ready to get serious blood on your hands? Are you with me, Tyg?"

"Yes. I'm with you, Palin." Tyg smiled sardonically, Palin always asked that question before starting anything.

"Good, well then I think it's about time to shed this petty thief and make it quite clear to everyone at Barion's just who you are under the protection of."

"About time." Tyg said relieved to finally be accepted by Palin and be safe, and a little shocked to find out just how powerful a man Palin really was. It was no wonder when he entered the Hut people got out of his way.

"Follow me." Was all he said to Tyg as he got up and walked off out of the warehouse and headed down the street. Tyg ran after him, tucking her hair up into her cap. It had now grown back to half way down her back after the year with Palin, because Palin had refused her to cut it anymore.

She followed him for several blocks when he stopped suddenly causing Tyg to almost run into him as he rounded on her. He pointed to a doorway. "Inside."

5

As Tyg stepped inside a strong smell of cheap perfume invaded her nostrils, she stopped in the doorway as she realised what sort of place this was, as a young woman in a scarlet dress walked up. Palin pushed her the rest of the way in.

"Palin, darling, long time no visit." The young woman pouted at him as she curled her hands around his arm and draped herself over him. She looked at Tyg then. "What do you have here? He's a little young to become a man yet, don't you think?" She giggled at her own joke. As she squinted for a closer look her mouth twisted. "He's very pretty..."

Palin laughed and reach forward grabbing Tyg's cap and tore it off her head.

"Oh!" The girl exclaimed in surprise. "It's a girl? Well, she's still too young to be in here, no matter how tall she is." The young woman looked Tyg up and down her frame that was now five foot nine, most women in Arial were at most five foot four. The people of Arial were a race short in stature.

The look Tyg gave Palin made him laugh even harder as Tyg fought to try and keep her mouth shut. Her eyes betrayed her feelings by turning a cold ice blue fire. Her mind was a turmoil of emotions, she thought Palin had just sold her out, but then Palin got his laughter under control and started to explain, holding up his hand to Tyg in mock surrender. Tyg hadn't even realised she had drawn her dagger. Tyg looked around the room, there were a few customers with ladies and everyone was looking at her.

"Put that thing away...in fact give it to me." Palin, quick as lightning grabbed the dagger from Tyg and placed it in his belt.

"The next time you ever draw a dagger on me, girly, you had better know you can win." Palin growled at Tyg then turned to the young woman who was looking at Tyg with a mortified expression.

"I want you to take good care of her and give her a bath and some new clothes."

That was it, Tyg couldn't keep her mouth shut any longer.

"I am not wearing clothes like that!"

Suddenly Tyg was on the ground. Palin had back handed her causing her to collapse. The heat in her cheek flaring as Tyg struggled back to her feet. Palin was holding the young woman back with a large forearm, as she wanted to go to Tyg's aid.

"Your quick tongue is going to be the death of you, girly!" Palin said. "Or the death of me."

"What is going on here?" A very stern voice pierced the chaos.

Palin turned to face the owner of the establishment. As Tyg looked up to see a middle aged woman with dark hair shot through with grey and rouged cheeks. Her eyes, however, still looked youthful and intelligent. Her dress is full skirted and of a red and black patterned fabric, the bustier however left nothing to the imagination.

She eyed Tyg with a contemptuous stare, then turned to Palin, waiting for an answer to her question.

"Madam Rose, I am requiring your services of a different matter, I need you to do a little of your magic on her." Palin said indicating Tyg, who was now standing at her full height with her arms folded.

"Her? I didn't even recognise her as a 'her'." Madam Rose said as she approached Tyg and grabbed her chin.

"That's the problem, she's been hiding herself as a boy."

"I can understand that." Madam Rose interrupted coldly.

"Ah...yes, well, now she is under my protection and I want her to look like what she is without fear." Palin said folding his arms.

Tyg looked across at him with a new found respect, almost making her eyes well up with tears. Madam Rose and the girls all looked at him in much the same way.

"Your protection?" Madam Rose asked.

"Yes, she works for me now." Palin said gruffly trying to stamp out the gushy looks.

Madam Rose looked at Palin a moment, something vast seemed to pass between them, and then she turned back to Tyg, still holding her chin. As she looked into Tyg's eyes she bit her lip. "How old are you?" Rose asked softly as she turned Tyg's head this way and that, glancing at her face in different lights.

"I don't know, about sixteen, I guess?" Tyg was feeling very awkward under all the scrutiny.

"Sixteen? I thought you said you were fifteen?" Palin asked.

"It's been another six months, Palin, I don't know for sure. We didn't celebrate birthdays at the orphanage or at the Hut, so I just lost track. The matron there could probably tell you." Tyg shrugged.

"I doubt that." Rose scoffed. She turned back to Palin as she dropped Tyg's chin finally and briefly grabbed Tyg's shirt pulling it in around her body tightly, noticing how Tyg has been concealing her womanly body by wrapping bandages around her chest tightly. "You do know what you're going to uncover, don't you?"

It was Palin's turn to shrug as Tyg looked from one to the other not sure what Rose was talking about.

"Very well." Rose said resigned. "But I will not be held responsible."

"I'm not asking you to be. I'll be back in a couple of hours." Palin said back then turned to Tyg pointing a finger at her, then closing his fist. "No smart comments and do as you're told, got it?"

Tyg nodded and turned to Rose, who had her hand outstretched to her.

"Come." Tyg took Rose's hand and Rose walked her through a doorway at the back of the room, with the other young woman in tow.

"Madam, I would be happy to do this for you." The young woman offered.

"Excellent Bella, take good care of her, you heard she is under Palin's protection." She turned to look at Tyg again. "You sure you know what you're doing, child? Seeking protection from a man like him?"

"He's teaching me everything he knows about defending myself and killing people who get in my way." Tyg answered coldly, sneering slightly.

Rose and Bella both looked at her with surprise then turned to look at each other. "And, how's that going for you?" Rose asked raising an eyebrow.

"Very well, thank you." Tyg answered with a big grin.

"Well, perhaps you do know what you're getting yourself in to." Rose said finally. "Follow Bella to the baths and I will see you once you're clean and clothed."

"I don't want to dress like that." Tyg said for a second time.

"Of course not, Sweetie. I will dress you like the rest of your new family. Don't you worry, I know what you wear will need to be practical." Rose said with a laugh. "I will find something and place it in my office for when she is ready to dress." Rose said then to Bella, who nodded, and placing a hand on Tyg's shoulder Bella steered her down the hallway to the baths.

Half way down the hall Tyg's stomach gave a very loud rumble. Tyg sighed in embarrassment as Bella turned Tyg to face her.

"When was the last time you had a decent meal?" Bella asked, a smile on her lips.

"Ah, well..." Tyg thought long and hard about the question. "Well, I can't say I remember ever having a decent meal, but the last meal I had would be the day before yesterday. I had a half bowl of soup that was left by a guy at the Lion Inn when he was sitting outside. I managed to swipe it off the table before anyone saw." Tyg explained, her stomach grumbling again at the thought of food.

"That's appalling." Bella said naively. Tyg almost said to her that what Bella did for food was appalling, but managed to keep her mouth shut. Palin would be pleased, Tyg thought to herself.

"Come on, we will go to the kitchen and get you something to eat first, I think?" Bella announced and turned to head back down the hallway to a small kitchen at the rear of the building. As they entered the rudimentary kitchen Bella indicated for Tyg to sit at a small wooden table at which there was four chairs. It was by the fire that had a small flame stirring in it keeping a pot of stew heated, which was hanging over the top. Bella disappeared into the larder, shortly returning with a wooden board that had a couple of chunks of fresh bread, and some cheese on it. She also had a glass of milk. She deposited all of it in front of Tyg, who stared at it. Tyg couldn't believe this wasn't a dream and didn't want to touch it, fearing it would disappear.

"Well? Eat up. I'll go get your bath ready, I won't be long." Bella said with an encouraging smile and disappeared out the door.

The moment she was gone Tyg took a huge bite of the cheese followed by the bread, still slightly warm. Her eyes closed in ecstasy. She suddenly heard soft tinkling laughter. Tyg froze and opened her eyes to see another young woman standing in the doorway, an amused expression on her face as she watched Tyg engulfing the food. Tyg, slightly embarrassed dropped the bread back down on the board and gulped down several mouthfuls of milk trying to clear her mouth to speak.

"No, don't stop. I'm sorry I didn't mean to laugh." The young woman said. "You just reminded me of myself when I first came here. My name's Tess, Bella got called away so I'll help you from here." She walked forward and grabbed Tyg's chin wiping it on a corner of her skirts, where the milk had run down Tyg's chin.

"There that's better, just try to slow down a bit or you will give yourself a stomach ache." Tess sat down at the table opposite Tyg and smiled her encouragement. A pretty young woman not much older than Tyg, Tyg wondered how she ended up here. Tyg returned the smile and slowly picked up a piece of cheese popping it into her mouth and chewing it slower.

"That's better, you'll enjoy it better that way." Tess grinned then stood up again. "You finish eating and I'll go see to your bath, I won't be long. Just stay here, don't go wandering off." Tyg nodded at Tess and Tess left. Tyg continued eating until it was all gone, then leaned back in the chair to wait for Tess to return.

After a short while, Tess returned to find Tyg dozing in the chair, her hands laced over her now full belly. Tess smiled and shook her head at the skinny waif.

"Tyg...Tyg, wake up." Tess said gently.

"Huh, what?" Tyg jumped awake her hand going for her dagger, which wasn't there. Suddenly realising where she was she relaxed as she looked at Tess's startled face. "Sorry." Tyg said lamely looking down at her hands.

"Ah, your bath is ready...follow me." Tess replied a smile returning to her warm face as she indicated the door.

Back down the hallway they approached the end door, opening it Tess indicated for Tyg to go inside.

"This way." Tess said as she led her into a small room in which stood a cast iron tub filled with steaming hot water, around the tub lay a variety of small glass bottles and vials filled with different scents and oils. Tyg suddenly felt very dirty and started stripping off her clothes before Tess even had a chance to close the door.

"Do you need any help?" Tess asked as she started picking up the strewn clothes.

"Look after this?" Tyg asked as she handed Tess the little red book that Palin had given her, one day she knew she had to give it back, once she could read every word with no difficulty. Tess nodded and placed it into a large pocket in her skirt. Tyg stepped up onto a small wooden step and stepped over into the bath. A deep sigh escaped Tyg's lips as she immersed herself up to the neck in the hot water. Tess noticed Tyg wasn't skinny or a waif, but muscular and lean.

"Could you tell me which scent is the best?" Tyg finally asked as she peered over the edge of the tub at the array of bottles.

"I like this one the best." Tess replied as she picked up a small purple bottle containing some oil. "It smells like the wild flowers you might find in the meadows, would you like to try it?" Tess asked.

As Tyg nodded Tess pulled the cork out and dropped five drops of the sweet scented oil into the water. "That's all you need, not much." Tess explained as a lovely fresh summer smell filled the air. Both Tess and Tyg inhaled it deeply and sighed.

"I love it, do you like it?" Tess asked.

"It's perfect, Tess, thanks." Tyg replied dreamily, her eyes closing and a soft smile on her face.

Tess studied the young girl's face and bit her lip as she saw for the first time the real beauty of a woman of high-born breeding, she wondered how this girl came to be a street urchin.

Tyg opened one eye and peered at Tess, who was staring open mouthed at her. "What?" Tyg asked beginning to feel uncomfortable.

"Oh, nothing. I'm sorry I was miles away. It's the scent it makes me dream of the country side." Tess promptly lied to cover her discovery. "Sorry, I'll leave you to enjoy your bath and go get some more hot water."

Tess scurried quickly out the door as Tyg watched her leave, feeling like there was more to her staring than Tess let on. She shrugged to herself setting it from her mind, and sunk back down into the bath and closed her eyes in bliss.

Tess returned later with a large jug of steaming water in her arms. She poured it into the tub, injecting new warmth into the cooling water, waking Tyg from her doze. Tyg opened her eyes and looked at Tess, a curious look on her face as she noticed a small bag under Tess's arm. Tess smiled at her and placed the empty jug on the ground and then pulled over a chair and placed the bag on her lap as she sat. Tyg sat up leaning over to get a better look as Tess held up an assortment of scrubbing brushes, hairbrushes, soap and loofahs and deposited them on the floor in front of the tub.

"Here, take these and start scrubbing." Tess handed Tyg a scrubbing brush, cloth and soap. "I'll do your hair."

As Tess started lathering up Tyg's hair with a shampoo that smelt divinely of coconut, Tyg started to wash herself clean. Months of dirt, and her old life, fell away as she scrubbed. Tess started to hum a tune familiar to Tyg and she joined in, adding an accompaniment to Tess that the girl has never heard before. Tess stopped humming and listened to the beautiful heart wrenching tune that Tyg was now singing, amazed at the levels and the complicated cadences of the tune, that to her was always a simple child's song. Tess suddenly knew that this girl was no simple pick pocket.

Tyg stopped suddenly aware that Tess was no longer humming, or scrubbing. She turned to look at Tess who was standing behind her, tears standing in her eyes as she looked down on Tyg.

"What's wrong? I'm sorry, I didn't mean to interrupt. I just knew the song and added the rest, I didn't mean to..." Tyg said worried that she had made Tess cry.

"It's not that, Tyg, it's just so beautiful. I've never heard it that way before, it moved me...that's all. You can interrupt my humming whenever you like if you sing like that, where did you learn it?" Tess replied embracing Tyg's wet soapy head in a quick reassuring hug.

"I don't actually know?" Tyg said, brushing Tess away from her. She didn't like to be touched. "It just came to me when you started humming, that I had heard that tune before somewhere." Tyg answered confused, wondering just how she did know it.

"Well, maybe your mother used to sing it to you when you were a babe?" Tess said resuming her scrubbing of Tyg's hair.

"No, my mother died giving birth to me, it could have been my aunt? She took care of me as a babe...until..." Tyg fell silent. She didn't really know why she had been given suddenly to an orphanage at four years old and no longer remembered anything about her aunt or what may have happened to her.

"That's bound to be it." Tess replied cheerfully encouraging Tyg to smile. "Now time to rinse, stand up."

Tess walked around the tub and grabbed the jug she bought the water in with, then standing on the chair she dunked the jug into the water filling it and looked down at Tyg still lying in the tub.

"Come on, don't be shy...I've seen it all before...stand up so I can rinse you off."

Tyg slowly stood, feeling self-conscious in her clean nakedness. Just then Tess emptied the jug over Tyg's head, expelling all the soap from her hair. Tess repeated the rinsing several more times until she was satisfied that all the soap had gone. She then stepped down from the chair and fetched a rough towel which she held open for Tyg to step into.

"I don't know why you're so shy about your body, Tyg. You have a wonderful figure...I wish I had a figure like that." Tess compared her own short, slightly dumpy figure with the athletic, muscular hour glass figure of Tyg, as she stepped out of the tub and wrapped the towel around her.

"You try going for days without food but still having to walk miles around the city looking for your next meal ticket, you would probably look skinny like me." Tyg replied with a smile. "Not to mention training with Palin, every day."

Tess returned her smile and nodded. "You're probably right, Tyg, sorry. I didn't mean to bring back those memories for you."

"Memories? They're not memories, Tess...I'm talking about this morning." Tyg answered bemused.

"Ah, well that petty thief life, I think, may have just left you behind...or you left it behind would be more accurate." Tess replied with a laugh.

"Hmm, perhaps." Tyg replied soberly.

Tess sensing Tyg's mood shift, tried to change the subject.

"Now, shall we go see what Madam Rose has found for you to wear?"

Tess handed Tyg some clean underwear to put on and a robe, then they made their way down the hall and up the stairs to Tess's room.

6

Tess's room was a very simple one, with a small bed in one corner, covered with a crisp white sheet of stiff linen and a small woollen blanket folded at the bottom. A small table beside it held a candlestick with a candle stub still in it and a book, paper and quill and inkpot. A chest pushed against one wall held most of her possessions and a table and chair was against the opposite wall, on it another candle and an array of sewing equipment and scissors.

"Stay here." Tess said as she scurried away to grab Tyg's new clothes from Madam Rose's room, which was a beautiful pale blue dress, the same colour as Tyg's eyes.

Tyg looked at it with distaste. "It's a dress."

"Yes...Rose wants you to wear it, she said she insists."

Tyg scowled but grabbed the dress. As Tyg put it on she looked down at herself. "It's a bit big?"

"No problem." Tess said as she went to the table and grabbed a jar full of pins.

Tyg stood waiting, knowing Tess was obviously in her element as she hovered over her sewing kit. Tess turned, her mouth full of pins and told Tyg to stand very still, almost incoherently through the pins. She started humming again as she worked her way around the dress pinning and tucking. After a few minutes she stood up and stretched, checking that everything looked okay.

"That's about it I think, okay...I'll need you to take it off now. You can throw that blanket around you, while you wait, if you get cold." Tess pointed to the blanket on the end of her bed then started undoing the ties at the back of the dress and helped Tyg out of it. Tyg put the robe back on then grabbed the blanket and put it around her shoulders, as Tess set to work humming to herself absorbed in what she was doing. Sensing the need to be quiet, Tyg sat on the end of the bed and waited patiently, remembering the times when she had to wait quietly in the shadows waiting for a mark.

After a while Tyg inched her way up the bed until she was sitting next to the small table. She lifted the book and opened it, looking at the contents with bored disinterest. It was a book of sketches of dresses with notes beside them about fabric, colour, stitching etc. She put the book back down and looked at the paper, which was also covered with the same drawings of people wearing fine gowns.

"Finished!" Tess suddenly said, causing Tyg to just about jump out of her skin. She turned to Tess who was holding the dress up, studying it.

"Well, it's about time." Tyg grumbled, standing up and walking over to Tess, taking the dress and putting it on.

"Yeah, sorry, you must have got bored. I don't notice the time when I'm sewing. I love it." Tess replied beaming with pride as she tied the back of Tyg's dress pulling it tight and admired her handy work. As Tyg turned to face her she looked up at Tyg's face.

"Oh my." Tess exclaimed as she looked upon the face of an angel.

"What is it? Is something wrong?" Tyg asked looking down on herself.

"No, quite the opposite, Tyg, you are quite beautiful. I feel that Rose is in for quite a shock when she sees you."

"You're just saying that." Tyg said blushing, and tucking her hair behind her ears feeling strangely self-conscious.

"No, actually I'm not, now we just need to do something with your hair, sit down." Tess pointed to the chair. As Tyg sat Tess again started rummaging through all the stuff on the table, she pulled out a few hair pins and a string of seed pearls. "Lovely, these will be perfect." Tess said to herself as she went to her chest, opened it and retrieved a hairbrush.

"I don't think we really need to go that far, do we?" Tyg scoffed.

"Yes, as a matter of fact, I think we do." Tess replied as she started brushing through Tyg's wealth of silver blond, long hair, experimenting with different ways of piling it on top of Tyg's head.

"But..." Tyg tried to disagree but got shushed to silence and told to keep still. Tyg sighed and gave in to Tess's manipulations of her hair.

After several minutes Tess finally stepped back rubbing her sore arms.

"Done! You look absolutely regal, Tyg. Are you sure you're from the streets?"

"Since I was eight years old." Tyg replied.

"Well, you're not now, come on let's show you to Rose."

"Ah, sure, but what about my feet?" Tyg held up a foot to show they were bare.

"Oh, I forgot about your feet...um....let's see...you may fit my good shoes?" Tess rummaged through her chest and came up with a pair of white satin court shoes, which she put on Tyg's extended feet, then pulled Tyg up to standing.

"They're a little big but they won't fall off will they?" Tess asked.

"No, they feel okay." Tyg replied. "But, I still don't get what this is all about?" Tess nodded and laughed as she led Tyg out of her room and down the stairs.

Stopping outside the door closest to the main entrance foyer Tess told Tyg to wait as she knocked softly. A voice called out to enter and Tess opened the door a crack and slipped through. Tyg heard voices softly talking and then Tess returned to the door sticking her arm through, grabbing Tyg's hand and pulling her through into a large room consisting of several lush divans and couches and also an elaborately carved desk with very neat piles of paper on it. Seated behind that desk was Rose, a very shocked look on her face as a giggling Tess pushed Tyg forward and announced her.

"Madam Rose I give you her lady, Tyg.

Tyg looked round scowling at Tess's mischievous face as she heard herself called a lady, but the scraping of the chair across the floor as Rose stood caused Tyg to look back at Rose.

"Oh, my, dear child." Rose struggled to talk. "You have quite taken my breath away...never in a million years would I have expected such a beautiful butterfly to come out of such an ugly cocoon." Rose walked around the desk and came up to Tyg, who standing now at five feet nine inches, she had finally stopped growing, was a good six inches taller than Rose. She walked around Tyg looking her up and down, shaking her head in disbelief. As she came once again to the front she looked full at Tyg's face, taking in her pale, almost translucent, blue eyes, her alabaster skin, the high cheek bones, the pert nose and the sculptured chin. She sat back on the edge of her desk, her face full of thought.

"You, my child, are a jewel."

"It was all Tess, really." Tyg said feeling very uncomfortable under all the scrutiny.

"Yes, Tess has indeed done a wonderful job, but I feel that her job was most easy." Rose chuckled.

"Indeed it was, Madam, as soon as the dirt washed off, there she was." Tess replied still giggling. Tyg turned and scowled at her again.

"Tyg, I need a serious word with you dear, please sit down."

"Okay..." Tyg said a bit suspiciously.

"There's just something I feel obliged to check on before sending you off with Palin." Rose said as she sat down behind her desk again.

"I already told you, I know what I'm doing."

"No, not that, dearest...but you'll be with men...I was wondering if you were...well...have you got your womanly flow yet?'

"My what?"

Tess jumped in. "Some people call it Moon-flow or monthly flow."

"Oh that...yes...I started a couple of years ago...although I guess with not eating regular...it's not regularly every month either."

"Oh, okay, well I just wanted to check you knew what it was and how to handle it because you can't ask men like Palin about these things."

Tyg laughed. "No, I suppose not. I can see his face now." They all laughed, then Tyg added. "I had help from a couple of the women that hung round the Hut at the time, but thanks for your concern."

"Quite, well just remember I'm here if you ever need a woman to talk to."

"Thank you." Tyg said genuinely surprised.

"Okay, Tess, I need you to put that dress into a bag for Tyg to take with her." Rose then turned back to Tyg "And, Tyg...you can now change into these..."

Rose bent down and grabbed a handful of clothing and put them on the desk. Tyg got up and stepped forward and looked through the pile, a large grin appearing on her face. Leather pants, black to the knee boots and a black linen shirt.

"Sent from Palin, who should be here soon to collect you." Rose continued.

"Thank you, Rose." Tyg said happy at the real clothes she now got to wear.

"Come on, Tyg." Tess said as she hurried Tyg out of the room and back to hers to change.

Back in Tess's room as Tyg was putting the linen shirt on Tess screwed her nose up. The leather pants were a bit tight.

"What?" Tyg said regarding her curiously.

"I don't think Palin allowed for your womanly curves." Tess giggled. Tyg frowned.

"Oh, I think we can do better than just that frumpy shirt." Tess said as she got up and went to her chest and started rummaging around in it again. She procured a black corset belt which she wrapped around Tyg's waist over the shirt, pulling it tight and completely changing the look. Tess stood back and looked admiringly.

"That's much better." She grinned as Tyg looked over herself standing there in black leather and boots, she reached up and undid the first couple of buttons on the shirt and looked at how the corset belt accentuated her bosoms, the V-neck of the shirt unbuttoned teasing cleavage.

"Now you get it." Tess grinned, "Now your hair." Tess said as she started to take down what she already done and started braiding up the sides and teasing up the middle, letting it all fall down her back from a high ponytail. The effect was striking and dangerous.

"You look like a warrior princess." Tess said as she clapped her hand. "Let's go back to Rose's office so we can wait for Palin."

"Okay." Tyg said smiling. "And, thank you."

"No problem, I had fun." Tess said with a friendly smile.

As they returned to Rose's office Palin was already there waiting, sitting on the side edge of Rose's desk with his right leg crooked up on the desk with his arms folded looking down on Rose who was seated behind her desk. As the door opened Rose's eyes widened and Palin turned towards the door, dropping his leg to stand, but sat back down on the desk in shock as he saw Tyg.

"Bloody hell." Palin whispered as he dragged a hand over his eyes, pinching the bridge of his nose and shaking his head. "What have I done?" He exclaimed in a muttered tone to himself.

"I did try to warn you." Rose said as she stood up and walked around the desk to Palin, dropping a hand on his shoulder. "Wait till you see her in that dress." Rose chuckled to herself. Palin raised his head and cursed at the woman.

"You're enjoying this far too much." Palin growled.

"Is there a problem?" Tyg asked them, putting one hand on her hip.

"No problem, dear." Rose said amused. "Now how about we get you a cloak or something?" She looked at Tess.

"Good idea." Palin muttered as Tess handed Tyg her bag with her dress in it and left to find a cloak for Tyg.

"Right then, let's go. Thank you for your help." Palin said to Rose as he got up and strode to the door.

"I'll send my bill round." Rose said to Palin's back making him stop and turn with a questioning look, then he cursed again and turned back. As he past Tyg he stopped a moment and looked her full in the face.

"Are you quite ready to face the world looking like that?" Palin asked her.

Tyg looked down at herself then back to Palin "With you beside me, yes." Tyg said plainly.

"Hmm." Palin grunted as he held something out to Tyg. "You're going to need this."

Tyg looked down and saw her dagger in his upturned hand.

"Thanks." Tyg said with a grin and put it into her belt.

Palin turned and left the room. Tyg threw her bag over one shoulder and followed him out, followed by Rose who whispered to her. "You look beautiful, Tyg, you take care of yourself."

Tyg turned her head and smiled at Rose. "I will."

Tess was coming back down the hall carrying a heavy black woollen cloak with a large hood, and draped it over Tyg's shoulders. Palin reached out and flicked the hood up as well.

"Better." He muttered then turned to Rose. "We'll leave by the back entrance." He announced and walked off through the kitchen and out the back door and onto a side street.

He glanced at Tyg as she stepped out. "Ready to go to the Hut?" Tyg just grinned.

7

As Tyg entered the warehouse that was known as the Hut, walking behind Palin, she noticed people looking and starting to mutter to each other.

Palin marched straight through the warehouse to Barion's door. The guard gave Palin a nod in greeting and looked at Tyg suspicious for a moment.

"Lower your hood." He ordered gruffly.

Palin nodded his consent and Tyg lowered her hood.

The guard looked surprised then laughed. "Oh, this is too good." He exclaimed as Tyg grinned at him. He banged on the door and opened it a crack to poke his head in. Palin indicated for Tyg to put the hood back up as he looked around the warehouse seeing everyone looking and talking.

"Go in." The guard said as he opened the door all the way.

As Palin walked in with Tyg behind him, Barion looked up from where he was perusing a pile of jewellery using a loupe to check the quality of the merchandise.

"Palin, how goes it?" Barion said cheerfully, then the smile slid off his face as Tyg once again lowered her hood and stared at Barion with a vicious grin. "What the fuck is going on here? What is she doing with you? And, why is she dressed like that?" Barion's eyes bulged out of his head.

"I've come to let you know, Barion, that Tyg is changing Guilds, she works for me now."

Barion stood up. "Like fuck, Palin! She's the best I've got out there."

Palin folded his arms. "Well, perhaps you should have protected her better."

Tyg was biting her tongue wanting to speak, but Palin had ordered her not to say anything unless asked a question. Barion fixed Palin with a hard look.

"So explain to me how this..." He waggled his finger from Palin to Tyg and back. "...came about?"

"She applied to be my apprentice and proved it with showing her knife throwing skills, so I took her on and trained her."

"How long has this 'training' been going on?" Barion sneered.

"About a year." Palin stepped closer to the desk and leaned his knuckles on it. "I'm willing to pay you."

Barion's eyes lifted and moved to Tyg, he saw her expression as she stared at Palin's back.

"Of course you are...but you didn't warn her, did you?" Barion laughed and collapsed back in his chair and regarded Palin. "To be honest, Palin, I would be glad to have her out of here. She's nothing but trouble." His eyes glanced at Tyg again. "Although, I can see this year with you has finally shut that dangerous mouth of hers." Barion indicated for Palin to sit.

"Indeed." Palin conceded as he sat down. He never looked at Tyg and had instructed her to stay behind him, so expected her to. "Price, Barion...I don't have all day."

Barion squinted his eyes. "It's got to be gold, Palin." He said as he again appraised Tyg's new look.

"Gold? Seriously?" Palin scoffed. "No pick pocket is worth gold coins."

"No, but I can see how she is going to be an absolute asset on your team, so I think she's worth at least two gold."

"Two!" Palin spluttered in outrage. Tyg folded her arms with a bitter twist to her mouth. She couldn't believe Palin was actually buying her from Barion!

"Yes, two." Barion said smugly.

Palin grinned and took two gold coins out of his pocket and threw them on the desk as he stood up. "Fine, Barion...I was willing to pay four."

"Fuck you, Palin." Barion said as he grabbed the two coins and flinched at the news he had short changed himself.

"Pleasure doing business with you, Barion." Palin said as he turned to the door to leave. "Oh, and just for your peace of mind, if you had refused to sell her...Kor has interest in this happening." Barion paled slightly as his eyes narrowed. As Palin's hand touched the door knob he heard Barion speak to Tyg.

"Are you sure this is what you want, Tyg?"

"Yes, Barion, it is." Tyg answered confidently.

"You know you can no longer come here, I don't want you here again."

"But..."

"Tyg!" Palin growled making Tyg go silent.

"No friends you have made here can know...you leave here it's like you died...got it?" Barion said mercilessly.

Tyg looked at the floor. "Got it."

She turned and as Palin opened the door she walked out of the office after him. As they were walking across the warehouse Tyg had to talk.

"Why did he do that? You lot come in here all the time."

Palin shrugged. "He's pissed at losing you."

"But, he was losing me anyway, he said as much to me, that I was getting too old."

Just then a couple of men blocked their exit.

"Where do you think you're going with her?" One guy asked Palin. Tyg looked up suddenly realizing she hadn't raised her hood upon leaving Barion's office.

Palin gave Tyg a look to keep quiet and turned back. "I'd say that's none of your business, friend."

"I'm not your friend, Palin, but I had been planning on being hers." Tyg shuddered at the thought.

"So, you know who I am?" Palin asked curiously.

"Yeah, I know who you are, doesn't give you the right to be taking her anywhere."

"Oh, I have every right...she belongs to me."

"What? Bullshit!" The men looked at each other then back to Palin, their faces showing their outrage.

"Barion and I just finished negotiations and settled on a price. So unless you have four gold to buy her off me I suggest you get out of my way." Palin growled as he stepped up to the man, flicking his coat back to free access to his sword.

The guy baulked at the price and was suddenly less sure of himself seeing Palin go for his sword, his mate was already backing up.

"This isn't over, sweet cheeks." The guy said to Tyg, who was standing with her arms folded, mainly to keep herself under control as she was shaking with rage.

Palin looked at her impressed she was keeping quiet and then barged past the man and headed for the door with Tyg right behind him.

"Well done, Tyg." Palin praised her. "You see how you can avoid trouble if you just keep your mouth shut."

"Yes, Palin." Tyg said sullenly, she hated everything that just happened and was so full of rage she felt like she was going to burst.

Palin stopped and turned to face her. "Are you alright?"

"No, Palin, I'm not." Tyg said through gritted teeth, her eyes blazing.

"Ah." Palin guessed what she might be feeling after witnessing herself get sold to him and him mention the price to those men.

"How about we go to the obstacle course, let you let off some steam."

"Great idea." Tyg said still gritting her teeth.

"I can see what you mean about defending yourself, do you know those men?"

"Not really, no."

"Hmm, can I give you a tip, Tyg?"

"A tip?" Tyg looked sideways at Palin as they walked.

"Something I've noticed about you, that if you work on it and use it, can speak more than words in a situation like that."

"Really...?" Tyg said coolly. "...not sure where this is going, but what's that?"

"Your eyes, Tyg."

"My eyes?" Tyg laughed. "Got to say, that's not what I thought you were going to say."

"Ha!" Palin replied as they reached the warehouse where Tyg did her training. As they went inside Palin continued. "You are aware your eyes are like nothing seen before?"

Tyg shrugged. "People mention them, yeah, mainly to call me a freak."

"And are you aware of how they change colour with your moods."

Tyg looked at him. "Is that how you know when I'm about to..." Tyg looked shocked. "You cheat."

Palin laughed. "It's one indication, when you focus on your opponent they do change colour, but when you get mad, like before, they look like they're on fire, like ice on fire."

"I can't help that."

"I'm not asking you to stop it, I'm telling you to make it define you."

"What?" Tyg asked confused.

"Your eyes, Tyg, they pierce the soul...you have a habit of looking away...don't. Hold your opponents gaze, use it to your advantage. It will stop any opponent in their tracks and that hesitation...that is your advantage."

8

"You said you had an assignment for me?" Tyg asked Palin the next day when they met at the warehouse.

"Yes, I did." Palin said, sitting down. "But this is a very secretive mission, Tyg, no one must know about it...no one."

Tyg shrugged. "Who the hell would I tell?"

Palin smiled slightly, she was right, he was the only person she had any real contact with these days.

"Not even the Guild knows about this, Tyg."

"Really? Well that's just peaked my curiosity."

"We are going to have to travel to Annul, we leave tomorrow morning at first light."

"Annul? Seriously? I've never been out of Arial City." Tyg was astonished and excited."

"It's not a sight-seeing holiday...it's a mission...in and out unseen, that's the plan."

"Oh, that's a shame." Tyg frowned. "So what is it exactly that I'm doing?"

"Ending a monster's life." Palin said bitterly.

Tyg stared at him. "A monster?"

"I'll tell you more once we're on the road, now go home, get some sleep, it's going to be a long two days there and back."

☬

"Would you sit still?" Palin growled. "That horse is going to throw you off."

"I've never been on a bloody horse before, Palin...I would rather walk, it's so bumpy it hurts."

Palin laughed. "Wait till the day after we get back."

"What does that mean?"

"You'll get it when you get it." Palin said cryptically still laughing to himself.

"Okay..." Tyg said dubiously. "So can you tell me about what we're doing now?"

"Sure..." Palin said glancing sideways at her. "We are going to kill Lord Ardmond Guilliano."

"Kill a Lord! Fucking hell, Palin...is that why this is so secret?"

"Kind of, this is a personal vendetta to me, I'm paying a life debt forward for someone who meant a lot to me."

"Oh..." Tyg said looking at him strangely, the way he said it seemed to tell her not to press him for details.

"So, what has this Lord Ardmond done?"

Palin looked around. "Let's stop for something to eat." He led his horse over to a nearby tree and then sat down under its shade and took an apple out of his bag and threw it at Tyg as she walked over leading her horse. Tyg caught the apple and sat down cross-legged on the grass, looking at Palin, still waiting for him to answer her question.

Palin took out another apple and bit into it. He chewed it a moment and caught Tyg's questioning look. He sighed.

"Lord Ardmond is a monster, in the true sense of the word, Tyg. He has very particular tastes that most people would find abhorrent, but because he's almost the most powerful man in Annul he gets away with it, people know and they enable him and look the other way...it's disgusting."

Tyg looked at the ground. "Do I want to even know what you're talking about?"

Palin looked at her and clenched his jaw. "No, but you'll hear it anyway...it's important that you know just how crucial it is that this man dies tonight."

"Tonight."

"It's the only chance we are going to get, after tonight he will become the most powerful man in Annul and will become untouchable."

"Shit."

"He is planning a coup tonight, sending out his best men to kill the Lord Mayor. That's why tonight is best for us, because he will be leaving himself open."

"I get it." Tyg smiled faintly as she looked at the ground and drew in the dirt with a stick. "So tell me then..." Tyg grit her teeth.

"He likes virgins, Tyg...and the younger the better."

Tyg looked up at Palin her eyes blazing. "Fucking hell." She breathed. "Don't worry, Palin. That man dies tonight...if it's the last thing I fucking do on this earth! I won't let you down."

"I knew you wouldn't." Palin said quietly watching her as her eyes turned completely black momentarily and she stood up, grabbing the reins of her horse. His jaw clenched at the sight and he let out a bitter breath.

"I'm itching to get there now..." Tyg growled as she jumped up on her horse. Palin scrambled up and jumped up on his horse as Tyg took off at a gallop. He saw her unsteadily holding herself on the horse for the first few yards but then adjusted and suddenly became a natural horseman. Palin smiled to himself. Natural swordsman, natural horseman, natural born killer.

"So this is the place huh?" Tyg asked looking at the large house behind its gates. "I thought you said the Lord's men would be gone."

"The main ones should be, these are just lackeys."

Tyg looked at Palin. "I really hope you're right, Palin."

Palin looked at her solemnly. "So do I, now put your hood up, let's go."

Palin brought Tyg to the gates of Lord Guilliano's house. When the guard looked under Tyg's hood and saw a pretty young girl he grinned and let Palin in. As they rode their horses up to the house they noticed some men sitting on the steps and leaning on the wall.

"Halt right there." One of them stood up. "State your business."

"I have a gift for Lord Ardmond Guilliano."

"Well, the Lord is with his wife at present, how about we have a look..."

Tyg lowered her hood and jumped off the horse, hitching it to the post. She walked up to the bottom of the steps, stopped and smiled beautifully up at them.

"Well now..." He muttered smiling back as the others stood up with interest. He looked at Palin. "You can leave now."

"I don't think so, that's my merchandise."

"Hmm, well go wait at the gate...we'll send her out once we're finished with her." He saw the frown of doubt on Palin's face. "Don't worry, we'll just warm her up for the Lord, we won't spoil her." He grinned viciously and licked his tongue over his teeth.

Palin took one last look at Tyg, giving her a warning shake of his head as he saw her eyes had gone ice blue before he turned and fled back to the gate, with the intention of killing the two men there leaving Tyg an escape route.

Tyg pressed her mouth together and took a deep breath in through her nose, slowly releasing it, trying to stay calm. Her eyes betrayed her however as they shone that telling cool ice blue. The man came up and grabbed her chin.

"You're something rather special ain't ya girl...pretty eyes you have...ain't never seen anyone with eyes like those before."

"Nor hair that colour." Another man said as he stepped forward. "Perhaps we better not touch this one...seems she might be one of those special cases."

"Hmm, but it's not normal for them to come here...somethings not right." The man holding her chin said as he looked into her eyes. Tyg smiled and watched as his face went from smiling evilly at her to abject horror as her eyes dilated to black before him. Blood suddenly spurted out of his mouth as he staggered back his hand dropping down to the dagger that Tyg was holding and shoving up through his stomach up under his ribs until it found his heart.

"Oh, I'm extra special." Tyg breathed at him in a snarl. She lifted him up on the blade of the dagger and walked him up the stairs and then kicked his body backwards at the next guy who ran at her. He caught the dead body awkwardly falling down entangled in it. This slowed the other two down as they had to jump over him, giving Tyg time to flick her dagger into her left hand. She grinned at them. One guy hesitated as the other one drew his sword but then fell with a throwing knife in his eye. The other got a throwing knife in his chest. He staggered backwards and fell over the guy that was just managing to get to his feet.

Tyg ran inside and shut the door. She was just locking it when she heard a gasp behind her. She turned and saw the maid standing there holding a tray. She dropped it in her fright and screamed. Tyg's face was splattered with blood from where the man had coughed it out at her. She wiped her face and stalked up to the maid.

"Where is Lord Ardmond Guilliano?"

"Ah, he just ran up the stairs...with his family...please don't kill me."

"I'm not going to kill you, show me where he is."

Tyg drew her sword and turned back to the door as it broke open and the two guys rushed in. Tyg jumped and landed both feet into the chest of the first guy through the door, causing him to crash back into the second guy and they both fell down in the doorway. Tyg stuck her sword into the first and leaned over the second guy as he was trapped under the now dead body. She grinned at him, as she leaned heavily on her sword through the other man's chest, He lay paralysed with fear as he looked into her black eyes.

"What sort of devil are you?"

"A devil come for a monster." Tyg said to him as she placed her dagger, in her left hand, against his throat. "And all his cohorts."

His eyes went wide as she slit his throat. She watched with a detached morbid curiosity as the light went out of his eyes. She stood up and turned slowly back to the terrified maid who was still standing, watching - unable to move in her fear.

"Move." Tyg growled.

The maid didn't move. Tyg walked up to her and grabbed her shoulder shoving her forward towards the stairs "I said move!"

The maid trembled as she tried to get her legs to move up the stairs and along the hall. She stopped at the end of the hall and pointed to a door.

"In there..."

Tyg looked at her and smiled. "Thank you...you may go." The maid stared wide eyed at her then fled.

Tyg looked at the door a moment then with all her strength kicked at it, aiming for just below the doorknob where the lock was. The wood splintered and the door swung open with a crash.

Tyg heard screaming, yelling and crying. A cacophony of sounds that shouldn't be there. She closed her eyes a moment and snarled. His family.

She opened her eyes as she walked into the room. Focusing on a horrible looking man with red hair and a rashy red face that was hiding behind his equally ugly looking wife and two boys.

"You fucking coward." Tyg growled at him as she approached. He was in the corner of the room, beside the dresser and was holding onto his family for dear life, making sure they stayed in front of him. He stared at her with conflicting emotions.

"You're a woman...no...a girl!"

"A virgin girl....you like what you see?" Tyg snarled at him through bared teeth. He baulked and shrank behind his family.

Tyg sheathed her sword and dagger and lunged forward grabbing the wife and pulling with all her strength. The woman came free with Tyg and Tyg held her a moment looking at her terror before letting her go. "Go, you're free."

The woman stared at Tyg and ran back to her husband. Tyg stared at her unbelieving.

"What the fuck are you doing? Do you know what your husband has been doing to countless young girls?"

The wife sneered at her, her eyes suddenly vicious.

"Fucking hell, you do know. What the fuck!" Tyg breathed out incredulously.

Tyg suddenly realised that the wife knew about it all along and that as long as she was rich and allowed to spend money on whatever she wanted and hold power over the city of Annul as that monster's wife she didn't care what he did to any poor kids.

Tyg shook with rage. She took out her dagger and advanced on the woman and grabbed her hair and pulled her once more away from her family. She screamed and grabbed at Tyg's hand and kicked and struggled against her, but Tyg's strong vice grip wasn't letting go. She threw the woman against the side of the bed.

"How the hell can you live with yourself knowing what he does to young girls...children...no older than yours?" Tyg screamed at her. Lady Guilliano couldn't speak, her eyes were focused solely on the dagger in Tyg's hand as she clutched the folds of her dress to herself.

"You're more of a monster for allowing it than he is for doing it!" Tyg calmed herself and leaned over the Lady. "What if you had daughters instead of sons?" The Lady's eyes went wide and her lip started to quiver. "Think about that." Tyg stood up, drew her sword and stuck it through the woman's heart, to the screams of terror from her sons. She looked straight into her eyes as they locked together, like she was looking straight into her soul. Tyg felt nothing but rage. She turned to Lord Ardmond.

"Last chance to let your sons live" Tyg snarled at him as she could hear people yelling downstairs.

"Please..." The Lord begged.

"Get up." Tyg ordered.

Lord Ardmond stood up, his sons clinging to him crying at the death of their mother.

"Get over to that desk and write a confession of what you have been doing and where you keep those poor girls."

Lord Ardmond, shaking violently walked over to the desk and sat down as Tyg went to the door and closed it then shoved all her weight behind the dresser, moving it in front of the door. The children stared at her wondrously.

"You're so strong." One of them muttered. The other one clouted his brother to silence as they stood next to their father as he was scribbling on a piece of paper. "Hurry up." Tyg said as she snatched the oldest boy from his father and held him from behind, her dagger at his throat. "I need to get more ink..." Lord Ardmond said as he opened a drawer and made out like he was searching through it looking for another ink pot. He suddenly threw a small knife at Tyg. It hit his own son in the stomach, Tyg let go of him as he cried out. Lord Ardmond seemed unremorseful and held another knife up in his own defence. Tyg looked at Lord Ardmond surprised, clenching her teeth in annoyance.

"Your family mean nothing to you."

The younger son looked terrified and ran to the door trying to move the dresser and get out, or let the people on the other side in. He was screaming for help. Tyg threw a dagger at him. It struck him handle first in the temple and he collapsed, silent. Tyg walked up to Lord Ardmond and grabbed the wrist of the hand holding the knife and wrenched the knife from his hand. She grabbed his other arm and twisted it round behind his back and forced him face down on the desk.

"Write the damn letter." She growled at him. "At least save your sons."

He lifted his head slightly and grabbed the pen, dipping it in the ink pot and scribbled on the paper. Tyg watched over his shoulder, which took him by surprise.

"Yes, I can read...so don't try to just scribble crap." Lord Ardmond looked at her chagrined and wrote the letter of confession.

The people on the other side of the door were starting to break through, so Tyg couldn't waste any more time. Enough of the letter was written to get the confession she wanted.

Without any further waiting Tyg pulled Lord Ardmond back, dragging him by his hair to next to his wife and slit his throat. She walked over to the eldest boy and picked his body up, carried him to the bed and laid him on it. She removed the dagger from his stomach and pressed his own hands down hard to the wound and closed his eyes. He scrunched them shut, his lip trembling. She picked up the younger boy who was still unconscious, breathing shallow, a small trail of blood coming from his temple. She lay him down next to his brother unsure if the older boy was going to make it.

She went to the window and opened it and climbed out, jumping to the ground as she saw some men yell out and come running. She drew her sword, borrowed from Palin. An arrow slammed into her shoulder throwing her back a step. She growled and grabbed the arrow pulling it out of her flesh and threw it on the ground. That made the two men hesitate and Tyg heard them mutter to each other. She advanced on them at a run and as they ran at her she jumped into the air and somersaulted over their heads, rolling over the ground and back up and running. She had to get back to her horse that was at the entrance. She felt another arrow whiz past her shoulder and she flinched. She made it to the corner of the building and ducked round.

She saw her horse and another man standing in front of it. She kept running knowing the other two weren't far behind her. She was going to have to take them all down somehow, she couldn't afford for them to follow her.

As she reached the man by her horse she clashed swords with him and turned him round so she was sheltered by him from anymore arrows. One whizzed past and she cursed. She caught the man's sword with her own again as he frantically tried to hack and chop at her. She smiled at his lack of training as she drove her dagger into his ribs and kicked him backwards. She jumped up on her horse and turned it, dug her heels in hard, gripping onto its sides with her thighs for dear life as it reared up at the two men approaching. They staggered back from the hooves and as its legs hit the ground the horse was off in a panicked gallop.

She could hear the two men shouting curses and promises for revenge as the servants ran out of the house shouting too.

As she reached the gates they stood open, two dead bodies were on the ground and she galloped through knowing Palin was on the road waiting about fifty yards further on.

Tyg saw a figure sitting on a horse in the moonlight and as she came up on them they called out.

"Tyg, thank the Gods, what took you so long?" Palin held his horse steady as Tyg reined in next to him.

"There was a minor complication." Tyg grimaced.

"What sort of minor complication?"

"He knew I was coming."

"What?"

"Well, he didn't know *I* was coming, but he was certainly expecting someone, those guys at the door were trained, not very well...but they were trained. One got me with an arrow."

"Shit, I was afraid of that...are you okay? So what happened?"

"Yes, I'm fine, I pulled it out, it's nothing, but when I got to him the fucking coward was hiding behind his family."

"Fuck!" Palin growled. "This was the only chance we would ever have to get him."

"Don't worry, I got him." Tyg smiled.

"What? You just said..." Palin stared at her.

"I got him, okay...let's get going..."

"Wait a minute, Tyg. What are you saying...his wife? His children?"

"Got in the way and I dealt with it and finished the job *you* wanted me to do."

"Fucking hell, Tyg, you killed his family!" Palin looked at her horrified.

"You told me to kill him no matter what...I had no choice...besides his wife knew everything. I don't know about his kids."

"But..." Palin suddenly realised what he had created and fell silent, this was the outcome he had wanted all along.

"Why are we debating this? The job is done...let's go!"

Once they were back out on the road Palin took a moment to scrutinise what Tyg had said had happened. She had told him everything blow by blow once they were sure they had gotten away. He had serious doubts about what he had done, what he had encouraged. He wondered now if he was going to be able to continue to control her. What if she flipped out one time and turned on him? Could he stop her now? He realised his mistake in keeping her away from people, although she seemed to prefer it, he should have forced her to interact with people and learn some moral compass. He frowned and turned to her.

"Tyg, how are you feeling?"

Tyg turned to look at him with a raised eyebrow. "I told you I'm fine, would you stop asking?"

"I have to...what you did...it has to have some effect on the soul..." Palin pushed.

Tyg's eyes changed colour to ice blue. He knew he was starting to piss her off. "It hasn't affected my soul...I doubt I even have one."

"To even say that statement means you've obviously been affected by it." Palin said frustrated. "Don't you see that?"

Tyg stared at him. "I don't want to talk about this anymore Palin, I did what you asked."

"I know, and now I'm regretting asking you, it was wrong of me."

"What is the point of dwelling on that? The deed is done, you can't change it, so move on...that's what I'm doing...if you'll let me."

Palin pressed his mouth together as Tyg turned away and moved her horse into a canter. He was going to have to change a few things once they got back to Arial, he could see that now.

9

Six months passed in the blink of an eye as Tyg continued to do the odd jobs for Palin while continuing her training and living by herself in the small bedsit. She still hadn't met any of the Assassin's Guild and Palin had told her he wanted to keep her under wraps for the time being so she could continue to walk around easily.

As Tyg walked into the warehouse for training one sunny morning, she found four men there waiting for her.

"Well, finally." One said as they all stood up from the various places they had been lounging. Tyg looked at each of them in turn and drew her dagger.

"Oh, good. She wants to play." Said one particularly ugly man with a large scar running across his face, through his eye which was white and blind. He was the closest one to her and lunged at her. She jumped sideways towards his blind side and kicked his knee out from underneath him. As he fell she grabbed him by the hair on top of his head and went down with him, controlling the fall, crouching behind him. As she brought her dagger around to his throat she paused as the other men froze. She grinned a vicious grin at them as she slit the man's throat.

"Fucking hell, bitch!" One man swore as he ran forward, Tyg was quickly on her feet and backed up to a large wooden crate as the man went to his fellow, who was gurgling as his life ebbed away. The man stood up and turned to Tyg.

"That was my brother, you whore!"

"Like I give a shit?" Tyg said back to him as she appraised the three men stalking towards her.

"We are gonna fuck you up." One of the other men said.

Tyg's eyes had become a cool ice blue and her pupils had dilated so there was only the thinnest ring of ice blue fire around the large inky blackness. As her eyes settled on the man he hesitated slightly. That gave Tyg the opening she needed as she launched across the two meter gap between them. She leapt now, going feet first, she landed and slid between the man's legs as he stood with his legs apart, braced for the impact that didn't come. Instead, as Tyg slid between his legs she raised her dagger and cut deep into the man's thigh severing his artery. As he went down on his knees crying out Tyg swung round and came deftly back to her feet. Now, facing the other two as they turned around. They were now all yelling.

'The noise should definitely bring someone curious surely?' Tyg thought. 'And, where the hell is Palin?' Tyg looked around her and turned and jumped up onto another large wooden crate, then up onto a second one piled up. Trying to separate the men, she looked down on the two men and smiled.

"Fuck! Get up there!" The first guy yelled at the other one, as he grabbed a plank of wood. The other guy started climbing up. Tyg looked at where the first guy was standing and leapt off the crates, doing a sideways flip to land on the ground about two meters from the first guy. He closed the gap extremely fast, faster than Tyg anticipated and he clocked her with the wood across the head. Tyg crumpled to the ground seeing stars. She lost her dagger in the impact and was now grabbed by her braid and was being hauled by it into the middle of the floor, as the other guy jumped down and followed, laughing.

"We'll teach you, bitch. Kill two of our mates!"

"My brother!" The first guy said as he let go of Tyg's hair and stepped over her. Leaning down he went to punch her in the head, but Tyg reached up and grabbed his belt, pulling him off balance and sending him toppling over the top of her.

As she tried to scramble to her feet, the second guy was on her. He had a dagger and as she fought against him for it he plunged it into her side, just as she kicked him in the groin sending him staggering back. Tyg scrambled backwards on her right side, her hand going to the dagger in her left side. The first man suddenly stepped over her again and knelt down, sitting on her stomach as he pushed her hand away and grabbed the dagger hilt himself, twisting it. Tyg screamed as he laughed.

"How do you like that, bitch!" He said, but suddenly he was silent. Tyg looked up to see him sitting there, stunned. An arrow protruding from his eye. As he toppled sideways off Tyg, the other man also fell with an arrow in his shoulder. Tyg looked back and saw Palin, standing in the doorway, with a couple of his men. One of which was holding a bow.

"Tyg! Bloody hell!" Palin called out as he ran over to her.

The other two guys went to the fallen men and made sure they were dead, if they weren't they finished them off, but kept the one with the arrow in his shoulder alive.

"Palin!" Tyg breathed. "Am I glad to see you?"

"That's an understatement, I'm sure, sorry it took so long. These guys had planned this...hold on..." Palin said as he grabbed the dagger and pulled it out of Tyg's side. He took his shirt off and scrunched it up, pushing it hard against the wound. "Keep pressure on it, Tyg, I'll get you out of here."

He picked Tyg up then and carried her out of the warehouse, as a couple of others arrived to take care of the scene and the guy who was still alive. Palin, with his two men both following, ran up the side streets and back alleys to Rose's. He charged in the back door, breaking the lock. As one of his men swept the kitchen table clear, he lay Tyg down on it. A startled young woman was standing at the bench.

"Get Rose." Palin yelled to her.

She stood frozen to the spot. One of Palin's men grabbed her by the arm and led her to the interior door. "Go!" He said as the girl fled.

Tyg was trying to sit up. "I'm fine, Palin, really."

"Like fuck you are, Tyg!" Palin said as he put a large hand on her shoulder and held her down. He was surprised at the strength Tyg still had left as she pushed his hand off her shoulder and sat up. She felt woozy and put a hand to her head. She felt the stickiness of blood by her temple from where the plank of wood had hit her.

"Tyg, for fuck's sake, keep still or you'll bleed out, that knife wound is fucking deep." Palin said, just as Rose came hurrying into the room, with the young girl behind her. She looked at the shirtless Palin, then saw Tyg sitting on the kitchen table covered in blood.

"Oh, dear mercy." She cried as she came over to Tyg and lifted her shirt to better see the wound. She turned and looked balefully at Palin.

"It wasn't my fault." He said. "Some guy stabbed her with a knife...a trap."

"Really?" Rose said her eyes wide. "Well, I need to get these clothes off her so, you men can go wait outside...Ruby, dear, get Palin a shirt...and Tyg too."

"Yes, ma'am." The girl said as she hurried off. Palin and his men went out to wait in the alley.

As Rose stripped Tyg's shirt off and looked at the wound, she glanced up at Tyg.

"It's already stopped bleeding, so it couldn't have been too deep. I'll just give it a clean to get rid of all this blood, so I can see exactly what I'm dealing with."

Rose went and retrieved a bucket of water and dipped a rag into it and started washing the area clean. The girl, Ruby walked through with the shirts, then Rose sent her to get bandages from her office down the hall. The more Rose washed the wound clean the more her face looked shocked. Tyg was watching her intently.

Rose looked up at her face. "How is this possible?"

"I heal fast."

"That isn't even possible, there isn't a wound here, just a red scar?"

"You can't tell anyone, Rose."

"What?" Rose looked at Tyg in awe.

"I mean it, not Palin, not anyone. Just bandage it up and act like it's still there, okay...please?"

"Why?" Rose stuttered.

"Look, Rose. If Palin, or anyone, was to find out about how fast I heal...do you know how he would use that to his advantage...he already suspects because in training I get bruised and scraped up, but he's noticed how the next day they're gone. If he knew how fast a stab wound can heal..."

"I understand, child." Rose said gently. "I don't understand IT, but I understand what you're saying...but, what are you?"

"I'm a girl...who heals fast...and that is all, Rose...nothing else."

"Okay." She said unconvinced, just as another girl entered with the bandages. It was Tess.

"Oh my goodness! Tyg, are you okay! When Ruby said you were here and injured, I just had to come see you."

"Thanks, Tess." Tyg smiled. "I'm fine."

"Oh Tyg, you always say that..." Tess smiled.

"Thank you, Tess, you can go now." Rose said.

"Thank you." Tyg said to the girl as she scampered from the room.

Rose dressed the now healed wound, as Tyg used the wet rag to clean the blood off her face and hands. Once she was dressed and sitting at the table, Rose put more water in a kettle on the log stove and started making tea.

"I don't want tea."

"Nonsense, a good strong tea with lots of sugar in it, that's exactly what you need right now, Tyg, you're shaking like a leaf."

Tyg looked at her hands. They were trembling, but it wasn't from what Rose thought. It was rage seething inside her.

Rose went to the back door. "You can come back in now, Palin."

"Bout fuckin time." He muttered as he brushed past Rose and looked at Tyg. "I am so sorry, Tyg." He said as he sat down at the table.

"What happened?" Tyg asked.

"It was a set-up. I'm trying to find out now, who was behind it."

"A set up?" Tyg said surprised. She had thought those men had perhaps just seen her enter the warehouse before and wanted to have their way, but now. "They were sent to kill me?" Tyg asked through teeth gritted with rage.

"Oh, by the gods!" Rose said as she overheard.

Palin turned to stare at Rose. One of Palin's men stepped up to her.

"I'll finish the tea, Ma'am." He said as a cue for Rose to take her leave. Rose nodded and gave Tyg a brief smile.

"Thank you, Rose. I don't know how to thank you enough." Tyg said full of meaning.

"Take care of yourself, child, you're special." Rose said then, causing Palin to frown as Rose left the room. The other of Palin's men closed the door and stood in front of it.

"What was that about?" Palin asked suspiciously.

Tyg shrugged, then changed the subject. "Who the fuck wanted me dead?"

"We don't know that for sure, I'm looking into it." Palin explained. "All I know is that I got a note to say you needed me over at the docks at some address...when I went there, two men were there to keep me busy. I managed to fight them off, grabbed Stills and Luke here, and came as fast as I could. I knew it was going to be a trap waiting for you. I'm sorry I got there too late to stop it." Palin wiped a hand over his face. "How is it?"

"It's fine, Palin. I'll be fine...thanks to him." Tyg glanced at Stills, with the bow and quiver strapped to his back. He turned from where he was pouring the tea and gave her a curt salute.

"The bow is something I may need to learn..." Tyg said half to herself.

"Well, Stills here would be the one to teach you." Palin said then, making Stills stare at him as he brought the teapot over to the table. Palin caught the look and laughed.

"Don't panic, Stills. She's a very quick study."

"So I've heard." He muttered, glancing briefly at her with a strange look as he went back over to the bench and leaned back on it, folding his arms and crossing his feet.

Palin poured a cup of tea out from the teapot and deposited it in front of Tyg.

"Sugar." Tyg said.

"What?"

"Sugar, Rose says I need to have it sweet."

Stills stepped over and put the sugar bowl on the table, giving her that strange look again, then resumed his position.

"Thanks." Tyg said as she plopped three sugar cubes into the tea in front of her. "I want the fucker, Palin." Tyg stated coldly, staring at her cup.

"I know, Tyg. We'll get him for you." Palin said as he stood up. "On that note, I had better go...I'm leaving Stills and Luke with you."

"I don't need nursemaids, Palin, I'm fine."

"They're not nursemaids. Tyg. Their job is to stop you from rampaging off on your own looking for vengeance."

Tyg looked up at Palin surprised. He was looking down on her with a grin on his face. Tyg smiled back at the fact he knew her so well.

"You know me too well." She said as she glanced at Stills and then at Luke. Stills smiled a beaming smile at her and Luke winked.

"They're two of my best men, Tyg, don't be stupid." Palin ordered. "Head back to the Hide after your tea." Palin gave both his men a long look then left.

Stills came over and sat down at the table grabbing an apple from the bowl. "So you're the famous apprentice we keep hearing about?" Crunching on the apple, juice running down his chin. Tyg looked at him. He wasn't very old, maybe only a couple of years older than her, and was good looking but with that cock-sure attitude of someone who knows he is.

"Hardly famous." Tyg muttered as she sipped her tea.

"Well, I've never had a hit put out on me."

"That would be infamous." Luke chimed in from the door, where he was still standing with his huge arms folded. He was middle aged and very grumpy looking with a full beard, flecked with grey.

"What?" Stills said as Tyg looked at him with a frown.

"Infamous, famous but in a bad way." Luke said as he drew a toothpick out of his pocket and stuck it in his mouth.

"Ha! Perfect, yeah." Stills laughed. Tyg downed her tea with a grimace at his laughter and stood up.

"Let's go." She said sourly.

"Hang on a minute." Luke said as he opened the door and disappeared into Rose's establishment.

"What is he doing?" Tyg asked standing, waiting by the back door.

Stills was still sitting eating his apple. He shrugged. "Who knows, probably booking a girl for later?"

Tyg gave him a flat look. He grinned and shrugged again as he wiped the juice from his chin with the back of his hand. "What? Some guys have to, that's why these girls are here."

"But, not you, I bet?"

"Well, no I don't." Stills said awkwardly, then looked at Tyg grinning roguishly. "I do just fine."

Luke appeared again carrying a cloak and threw it at Tyg.

"Put this on." He said. "Better you're not seen and recognised right now."

"Good thinking." Stills said. "See that's why he's here."

As Tyg put the cloak on, she looked at Stills with a frown. "So, why are you here?" She snapped.

Luke laughed and clapped Stills on the shoulder as he walked past him to the door.

"She's got you there." Luke opened the door for Tyg and then followed her out as Tyg pulled up her hood. Stills came sauntering out the door last, throwing the apple core on the street.

"Isn't it obvious, I'm the hero here..."

10

As they walked off heading for Palin's Hide Stills caught up to Tyg with a casual jog, falling into step with her. "So, I can see why Palin kept you to himself for so long." He said glancing at her with an amused grin. Tyg ignored him and just kept walking.

"Shut up, Stills." Luke growled.

"What?" Stills acted like he was confused, then laughed. "Well, you have to admit, Luke, if she was a he and nowhere near as cute looking, we would have meet her well before now...just saying."

Tyg stopped and faced Stills. "That's not the reason my identity was kept secret."

"Keep moving." Luke said gruffly.

"Fair enough." Stills said amused as they continued walking.

They completed the rest of the walk in silence, coming up to a tenement house and entering after Luke knocked and spoke to whoever came to the door.

Inside things were pretty basic. A couple of men were there playing cards in the front room. They stopped and stared as Tyg entered and lowered her hood.

"How about we go into the kitchen?" Stills said, looking at the looks on the other guys faces with a smug grin.

"Good idea." Luke said. "I'll stay here a moment, fill these guys in."

Stills led Tyg to the kitchen at the back and sat down at the small table.

"I'm not sure what's here, but make yourself a tea or coffee, whatever. Make yourself at home."

Tyg sat down and rubbed her eyes. "Got anything stronger?"

Stills grinned at her. "Like what?"

"Anything alcoholic, right now, I'm not fussy."

"How old are you?"

"Old enough to fuckin' drink." Tyg answered making him laugh.

"Okay." Stills got up and looked around. He went into a bottom cupboard and pulled out a bottle of volka, he showed it to Tyg. "This do?"

"Perfect." Tyg said with a smile, as Stills poured two glasses of it and came back to the table.

"So, Stills is a weird name?" Tyg said as she downed the volka in one swig.

"Is it?" Stills said with a shrug. "No weirder than yours and mine's a nickname at least." He grabbed the bottle and refilled her glass.

"Are you making fun of my name?" Tyg asked bewildered as she gulped half the second glass back too.

"Weren't you doing the same to me?" Stills laughed. He had perfect teeth, perfect mouth, and dazzled when he laughed like that.

"No." Tyg frowned at him. "I guessed it was a nickname. I was curious what it meant, where it came from, is all?"

"Okay, sorry." Stills said as he leaned back in his chair and put his feet up on the table. "It's because of the bow. People say I hit moving targets...people...like they are standing still...get it?"

"Yeah, I get it...makes perfect sense." Tyg laughed making Stills chuckle too. "So are you really that good with a bow?"

"If I do say so myself." Stills said smirking.

"So, would you consider teaching me?"

"If we ever get the time together...sure, why not?" Stills shrugged. "Can't say it wouldn't be a pleasure to get to know YOU better."

Tyg was just taking a sip of her drink and froze, looking at him as she slowly lowered the glass back to the table. He was looking at her with a smirk, his eyes sparkling. As their eyes met his took on an intense smoulder, but then he blinked and raised his glass to his lips, blocking his eyes from view. When he lowered it Tyg was looking at her glass, deep in thought.

"Well, this is exciting." He said looking around the room for something to do. "Do you play cards?"

Tyg shook her head as she rested her chin in her hand, her elbow on the table and blinked slowly.

"Are you okay?" Stills asked with concern. "I mean, I know you just got stabbed and everything but you look..."

"I think Rose put something in my tea." Tyg said with a frown.

"Oh, shit." Stills said sitting up. "She could have told us, you probably shouldn't have had that volka then." He got up and went to the door, opened it and called out for Luke.

He was there is seconds. "What is it?"

"We're gonna need a bed."

"What the fuck?" Luke replied as he pushed past Stills in the doorway. He saw Tyg was asleep at the table.

"Rose put something in her tea. It's made her sleep." Stills muttered.

"Oh..." Luke laughed. "For a second then I thought..."

Stills laughed awkwardly and raked a hand through his unruly hair. "I fucking wish, mate. Not even I work that quick and this chick may just be out of my league."

"Wow, out of your league?"

"Yeah, alright, shut up." Stills pouted and looked away. He was known in the Guild as the pretty boy who could land any woman he wanted.

"Okay, I'll carry her upstairs, you go ahead and check Palin's room, and I'll put her in there."

"Right." Stills said as he led the way upstairs as Luke gently lifted Tyg in his arms and followed.

When Tyg woke, she startled and sat up looking around. She noticed Stills was sitting in a chair in the corner snoozing himself. She was in a strange room, on a strange bed with her cloak and boots removed.

'At least nothing else is removed.' Tyg thought to herself. She slowly remembered what had happened then and sat up. She glanced to the window and guessed it must now be late afternoon. She looked back to Stills. She appraised him as he slept. He was the best looking guy Tyg had ever seen, and to be able to look at him without any hindrance made her curious. She sat up a bit more, leaning over, her teenage girl mind taking over. He was definitely only in his early twenties, if that. With shoulder length brown hair which he tucked behind his ears. He was maybe a couple of inches taller than her, six feet she guessed. Lean and muscular and had some interesting tribal tattoos on his arms. His skin was of a hue that made him look tanned all the time and his face was blemish free, chiselled with a scruffy growth on his chin. Suddenly Tyg saw a slow grin spread over his mouth, which made Tyg realise he wasn't sleeping at all.

"Like what you see?" He said without even opening his striking pale hazel eyes, then he slowly opened them to reveal that smoulder she had seen earlier. He had long thick black lashes that made the paleness of his eyes stand out and made them extra expressive and he knew how to work it.

Tyg blushed and looked away embarrassed. "Sorry, I didn't mean to..."

"Don't apologise. I did the same to you while you slept." Stills confessed as he sat up and rubbed his face with his hands.

"You what?" Tyg said shocked, sitting up with her feet on the floor.

"Relax, there was nothing inappropriate. Palin would have my head."

"I would have your head." Tyg said as she leant down off the bed and grabbed her boots and started pulling them on. "Did you remove my boots?"

"No." Stills chuckled at her nervous behaviour, seeing her for the pretty teenage girl she was underneath the hard killer reputation she had already. "Luke did, but listen...stop that and stay there...I'll go get you something to eat." Tyg paused and sat back up.

Stills got up, stretched his back out and walked over to the door. When he opened it Tyg noticed another guy standing outside it, guarding. He turned and looked in the room seeking out Tyg, he grinned. Stills pushed him back into the hall and closed the door. Tyg heard them through the door.

"Back up Jons!" Stills growled.

"Why do you get the fun job?" Jons whined.

"Because I'm more trustworthy than you, deviate." Stills said then. "Leave the door closed and just do your job."

"Alright, alright. No need to be cranky."

"I'm just getting food, I'll be straight back...I warn you."

"I said alright...geeze." Jons sounded exasperated. "Calm down."

Tyg smiled to herself as she heard Stills. 'So, he's trustworthy...good to know.' She thought.

11

When the door opened again it was Palin who entered, followed by Stills with a plate of dried fruit, bread, cheese and some dried meat. He also had a mug of water which Tyg took gratefully and downed a third of it instantly.

"Sorry, it's not volka." Stills said cockily. Tyg glared at him.

Palin sat in the chair in the corner and crossed an ankle over his thigh and waited while Stills gave Tyg the plate of food and turned to leave.

"Please stay." Tyg said to him. He turned surprised and glanced at Palin.

Palin shrugged. "Whatever."

Stills looked at Tyg "Are you sure?"

Tyg looked at him and smiled as she chewed, she nodded. She found herself quite liking the guy.

Palin frowned as Stills closed the door and leaned on the door frame folding his arms and crossing his ankles like he had in Rose's kitchen. He gave Tyg a beaming smile. Tyg looked down at her plate, bashful.

Palin coughed. "Really?" He said. "Can we get to business now?" He looked from Tyg to Stills and back again still frowning. Tyg scowled at him, Stills just grinned wider.

"We got some information out of the one Stills shot in the shoulder. Seems they weren't there to actually kill you. They were there just to send a message...apparently."

"What sort of message exactly?" Tyg asked as she saw out of the corner of her eye Stills start scratching his jaw.

"We're still getting that out of him. He's proving to be a very worthy opponent, but my guess is someone has found out the identity of my little cat and wanted to show me they knew by incapacitating you for a while. Which, I guess they succeeded."

"I'm fine, Palin."

"You can't possibly be, Tyg." Palin scoffed. "Anyway, I'm going to speak to Barion because I've decided to try keep you there with him for a while."

"What? I'm not going back to the warehouse."

"No, of course not. I didn't mean the warehouse. I meant his house."

"What?" Tyg gaped at him, speechless.

"Where he lives. It's a better part of town, patrolled more by the City Watch."

"So, what's that got to do with me?"

Palin shrugged. "Perhaps, a step in the right direction." He said vaguely.

Tyg looked at him confused and went to speak. "No, Tyg. I've made my decision." Palin said it with that hardly veiled threat of violence. Tyg looked at him a moment then downcast her eyes and played with the fruit on her plate.

"Fine, but at least give me a shot at that guy you're torturing."

"Not a chance!"

Tyg fixed Palin with a baleful stare. "Why the fuck not?"

"No, Tyg!"

"He's the one that stuck me, Palin. I want a chance to return the favour."

Palin wiped a hand over his face, then looked at Stills. "What do you reckon?"

Stills shrugged. "If it was me? Eye for an eye." Stills glanced at Tyg, as Palin leaned back in his chair, and winked at her. Tyg grinned at him, showing her perfect teeth. He, in turn, gave her a very sultry look as they continued to stare at each other. Tyg blushed and looked away just as Palin stood up, having missed the exchange.

"I'll sleep on it."

"Palin, please." Tyg implored him.

"I said, I'll sleep on it!"

"Where exactly?" Stills asked amused. "Since this little minx seems to have stolen your bed."

"What?" Tyg said shocked and stood up.

"Its fine, Tyg, sleep here. I'll sleep down the hall. I'd rather you were in a lockable room anyway."

Palin said as he grabbed a key off the drawers and held it up.

"You're going to lock me in?"

"No, he is." Palin said as he handed the key to Stills.

Stills looked shocked and looked about to refuse it, but saw the look on Palin's face. He was staring straight at Stills when he continued. "Since you seem to like having Stills around, he can be your minder until all this is over."

"Boss, I don't think..." Stills protested as Tyg yelled at Palin in protest too.

"I don't pay you to think." Palin said to Stills then rounded on Tyg. "And, as for you, do you need another lesson in how to take orders?" Palin had clenched his fist.

Both Tyg and Stills quietened and looked sullenly at each other, then at the floor.

"Good." Palin said and left the room, smiling to himself.

"Well that's great news!" Stills said as he put the key into his pocket.

"I'm sorry, really I am, because I'm fine." Tyg said sullenly, still pushing food around her plate.

"No, I mean, it's really great news." Stills said laughing as he leaned over, grabbed a piece of dried meat from Tyg's plate then collapsed into the armchair.

"Really?" Tyg said dubious.

"Yeah, perhaps I'll get to teach you to shoot arrows after all." He grinned as he chewed.

"Huh, okay." Tyg said slightly confused. "But, how does locking me in work though?"

"How do you mean exactly?"

"Well, you're hardly going to stay in here for the night, locked in with me." Tyg explained smugly. "And, as soon as you leave and lock the door I'll be leaving too...out the window."

Stills looked at her for a long moment, scratching his chin. "Is that so...?" He muttered darkly.

Tyg was pleased with herself, knocking Stills off his ego perch for a moment, as she tucked back into her food.

"Oh! I get it now. Palin called you his 'Little Cat'...for cat burglar, huh?" Stills laughed. "Well, little cat, where is it you want to go so badly?"

Tyg shrugged. "Back to my place."

"And, where is that exactly?"

"I have a little bedsit close to the east market square."

"Shit! Your own place?" Stills said surprised. "Well, aren't you the lucky one."

"Not really...you haven't seen it." Tyg smiled wanly and took a drink of water.

"Well, it's not dark yet...maybe we can go there now, pick up your stuff...sounds like you're not going to be needing it anymore."

Tyg looked shocked at the implication. "Not going to need it...but...my cat?"

Stills burst out laughing causing Tyg to scowl and blush at the same time. "This is about a pet cat?"

"What's so funny?"

"Nothing...nothing." Stills said calming himself down with a sigh. "You didn't strike me as the type to care about some mangy feline?"

"I love cats actually." Tyg said tartly.

"Okay, well let's go see to your cat then." Stills said getting up and going to the door. He took the key out and locked it.

"What are you doing?"

"There are four men plus Palin downstairs. If you want to go, out the window really is your best option."

"But, you've locked the door...?"

"And?" Stills smirked, folding his arms.

"And! They'll think you're in here with me, with the door locked?" Tyg was blushing again.

"But, I am?" Stills looked at her with that smouldering gaze.

"Well, I know you are, but they'll think...." Tyg was really blushing now and her eyes were starting to blaze.

"Who cares what they think, little cat?" Stills decided to stop torturing her, even though he loved watching her blush. He went and opened the window. He extended his hand to her as he sat on the window sill, half in, half out.

"So? Are you coming?"

Tyg looked at the door for a moment, then quickly put her boots and cloak on and brushed Stills hand away, as he grinned and crawled through the window and out onto the small ledge. He inched across it towards the drain pipe, then scaled down it to the ground. Tyg watched him, as she sat on the window ledge, her legs dangling free. She regarded Stills amused as he looked up at her and motioned for her to hurry. He looked up and down the side alley the window opened on to.

Tyg slipped off the window ledge, flipped and landed on her feet almost right beside Stills. As she straightened up from the impact she turned and looked at Still's amazed face. She smiled smugly, raised her hood and turned without a word and walked off.

"What the fuck?" Stills whispered and ran to catch up. "What the hell was that?" Stills asked Tyg as he came up beside her.

"What was what?" Tyg asked back coyly, shooting him a sideways glance from under her hood.

"That jumpy, flippy thing you just did?" Stills said amazed. "That was some tricky move."

Tyg shrugged. "I've always been able to jump and flip...agility...one of the reasons Palin has me working for him."

"Yeah, I can see..." Stills muttered as he scratched his jaw in thought.

They covered a couple of blocks and then entered a back alley behind another tenement. Tyg went up to a door and took a key out of her back pocket. She unlocked the door. At the same moment a small tabby cat suddenly appeared and started meowing at Tyg's feet. As she opened the door and went in the cat bolted inside first. Tyg turned in the doorway, to Stills.

"Come in." She said with a smile as she went over to a small table and grabbed the matches to light the lantern, as it was already dark and gloomy in the no window, one roomed bedsit.

Tyg sat on the small bed and stroked the cat as Stills came in and closed the door. He sat down in the one chair.

"See what I mean?" Tyg said with a grimace.

"Hmm, still at least it's your own place."

"Yeah, I suppose."

Tyg took out some cheese and dried meat from her pocket and started feeding it to the waiting hungry cat.

"When did you take that?" Stills said surprised. Tyg gave him a flat look. "Oh..." Stills said then as his mind clicked. "That's right you worked as a pickpocket first."

Tyg smiled a small grin in acknowledgement as Stills glanced up at her. "So is it true what I've heard about you?" He asked then.

"Well, I don't know what you've heard...or from where?" Tyg scowled.

"The guys talk of Palin's apprentice. They say you came up to them in Barion's warehouse and threw a dagger at a target...got the bull's eye twice in a row?'

"Yeah, that's true."

"So is it also true that Palin got you to do the Mandos contract?" Stills glanced up under his brows.

Tyg looked at him uncomfortably. Stills saw her expression and laughed. "Don't worry, little cat, we work for the same guild, the whole divulge secrets on threat of death is basically our guild motto, but we can talk about such things to each other."

"Is that so?" Tyg said sceptically. "Besides, I'm not part of the Guild...yet."

"It is, and you basically are if you've been working for Palin for so long now...trust me. Besides, you've basically already told me it was you by your reactions."

"Hmm." Tyg snorted

"And, I heard about those guys you killed in that alleyway a couple weeks back." Stills said sitting up.

"Did you now...?" Tyg said darkly.

"Yeah, of course...everyone did...but only we know it was you who did it."

"We?"

"The Guild, little cat."

"My name's Tyg." Tyg said it as a drawn out sigh.

"Yeah, but I like little cat." Stills eyes smouldered again as he appraised her. "I would have killed those guys too, you know?"

Tyg looked up at him and caught his gaze. She stopped breathing for a second then managed to tear her eyes away from his. "Good to know, because all the people walking past the alley, hearing that poor girl's screams, all did nothing." Tyg was looking down at the cat and suddenly picked it up, hugging it to her chest and kissing it on the head as it purred. She suddenly looked so young and vulnerable to Stills. He scratched his chin again.

"It's a cruel world we live in." He muttered. "What made a pretty little thing like you want to join the Assassin's Guild for fuck's sake?"

"The alternative was far worse." Tyg shrugged. "Besides, it seems I have a knack for killing people." Tyg looked up at Stills then, her eyes had changed colour and were blazing with intensity. Stills swallowed hard at the gaze and looked away. Tyg smiled to herself remembering what Palin had told her about her eyes.

"Shit, Tyg!" Stills said suddenly using her real name again. "That's a neat trick with the eyes."

"Beats the look you keep giving me, huh?"

Stills laughed. "Ah, fuck...you got me there. Force of habit I'm afraid." He rubbed the back of his neck.

Tyg had gotten up and grabbed a bag and was throwing some clothes in it and other stuff from round the room.

"Force of habit?" She glanced at him as she leaned round him to grab some stuff off the table. He saw her eyes had gone back to the pretty sky blue they had been before. He scratched his jaw.

"Ah, yeah...see a pretty girl...you know...what I mean is...when I see a girl I like...that I...ah...fuck..." Stills rubbed his eyes and gave up trying to explain since he was just making a dick out of himself. When he looked at Tyg she was standing looking at him amused.

"It's okay, I get it."

"Sorry." Stills said quietly, feeling awkward in front of a girl for the first time ever.

"Don't be." Tyg said swinging her bag up and over her shoulder. "I actually don't mind it. I'm just not used to not minding it, that's making it confusing." Tyg actually blushed again.

Stills leaned back on an elbow on the table and grinned. "Well, I'll be damned." He felt much better again, knowing Tyg obviously liked him too. But, then her eyes flashed.

"Just don't get too sure of yourself." She said as she glanced at him up and down, then she grabbed the cat under one arm. "Ready to go?"

Stills was still grinning and stood up, blew the lantern out and turned to Tyg with a devilish grin. "Sure thing, little minx."

Tyg frowned. "Really?"

"Yes, really." He smouldered.

Tyg rolled her eyes and turned to the door, but Stills jumped over and grabbed the heavy bag off her.

"Let me take that for you."

"Oh, so you're a gentleman now?" Tyg looked up at him puzzled.

Stills opened the door and stepped halfway out, turned and winked at her. "I always have been...remember?"

Tyg blushed again as she remembered when she woke up and studied him. She shook her head.

"You're incorrigible, that's what you are." She said as they stepped out and Tyg locked the door.

"Wow, big words now, is it?" Stills was still looking devilish.

"Oh, for fuck's sake, shut up before I shut you up!" Tyg growled under her breath.

Stills laughed, and so did Tyg. She decided she liked Still's company a lot.

When they came back to Palin's hideout Stills looked up at the window.

"Ah...didn't really think this through..."

Tyg laughed and handed him the cat, then took off her cloak and handed that to him too.

"Well, you've obviously got a plan?" He said as he watched her back up to the other side of the alley and flatten her back against the stone building on that side. Tyg looked up at the window, then down, took a deep breath and sprinted across the alley and ran up the wall far enough that she could grab hold of the windowsill and pull herself up and inside. Then, she came back, leaning out the second storey window with a grin, she held out her hands. Stills shook his head amazed and struggled to hold the cat up. Tyg shook her head, trying to be quiet. "Put the cat down." She mouthed. "Throw the bag."

Stills put the cat down and it looked up at Tyg, as she patted the windowsill. It nonchalantly jumped up onto the tiny edges of the bricks and was soon sitting on the sill next to Tyg.

Stills was highly amused by the proceedings and chucked the bag up so Tyg could catch it. Then it was his turn. He jumped a couple of times trying to reach Tyg's hands and missed. Then on the third try he felt the vice like grip of Tyg's hand around one wrist and Tyg dragged him up to where he could grab the window ledge. As she stepped back to allow him room to clamber in, he let out an explosive breath.

"Fuck! That was...exhilarating!" He said as he swept his hands through his hair.

Tyg sat on the bed and laughed as she pet the cat.

"Gods, you're strong, Tyg. I really didn't think you would be able to lift me up."

"No problem." Tyg said with a shy smile. They were back in the locked room and she didn't know what that meant.

Stills sat in the chair and rubbed his face as Tyg got up and lit the candles in the sconces around the room. He watched her as she turned and caught him staring, his eyes smouldered at her.

"You're doing it again." Tyg said with a bashful smile.

"I know." Stills said back with a disarming grin. "You're amazing, Tyg, you know that?"

"No, I'm not...I'm just who I am."

Tyg opened the bag and rustled around in it, pulling out a hair brush and some other stuff and laying them out on the bed. She looked up at Stills. "Any chance of getting some water in that jug over there?"

"Sure, of course...I'll be right back." Stills grabbed the water jug off the dresser and taking the key out of his pocket, unlocked the door. He stopped, put the jug down and went to the window. He pulled it shut and locked the latch. He looked at Tyg with another sultry gaze. "Stay put, little minx." He said as he grabbed the jug and slipped out the door, locking it behind him.

Tyg laughed and once he was gone she pulled her boots off and hung her cloak and sat cross-legged on the bed. She grabbed her braid and started undoing it, shaking her hair loose, then started brushing it.

Tyg heard a commotion downstairs, with raucous laughter. She then heard thumping up the stairs and the key in the lock. As Stills opened the door and walked in he froze for a moment, staring at Tyg with her hair down as she was slowly drawing the brush through it. She was looking at him with an eyebrow arched.

"What's all the noise out there?"

"Oh...that...nothing." Stills said as he closed the door and put the water jug on the dresser.

"Really? Nothing?" Tyg lowered the brush and regarded him.

"Ah...just the boys...you know...being boys."

Tyg scowled. "I told you what would happen if you locked us both in."

"And, I told you not to worry about it." He snapped sulkily.

Tyg looked at him unconvinced as he sat back in the chair and then reached into his shirt and pulled out a hip flask.

"I got this though..." He grinned that disarming smile.

"What is it?" Tyg asked as she smiled. Stills looked at her, with her hair down and sitting on the bed the way she was. He swallowed hard and tried to focus on what his job was.

"It's Volka, of course." He took a swig then held it out to Tyg.

"Excellent." Tyg said as she crawled across the bed towards him and held her hand out to take the hip flask.

"Fuck, Tyg, don't do that." Stills blinked and rubbed his face, as Tyg took a swig of the Volka.

"Do what?"

Stills looked intently at her. "Do you really have no idea of the impact you have, looking like that. With your hair down and crawling across the bed like that. Fuck girl, you're not making this easy on a poor guy." He rubbed the back of his neck, feeling awkward again.

Tyg looked shocked and handed the hip flask back, then retreated back up the bed and sat on the pillows drawing her knees up.

"I'm sorry...I didn't..." Tyg looked mortified and glanced down at the cat, now asleep on the bed and blushed with embarrassment.

"Yeah, I know you didn't. But, you should...you need to....ah, forget it."

"What?"

"Don't worry. A conversation for another day, perhaps." Stills decided to not push it. Tyg was frowning at him. "Look it's late, so I'll give you space to do whatever you plan to do with that..." He indicated the water jug. "...and I'll let you get some sleep. Palin said he wants you back training first thing tomorrow, since jumping in and out of windows, you're obviously not aggrieved by your wound at all."

Tyg went pale. "Fuck, he said that? He knew?"

"Yeah, sure did...and clouted me round the head for letting you go."

"Gods! I'm so sorry Stills, really I am."

"No worries." He stood up and went to the door, but looked back. "It was worth it!" His eyes sparkled. "I'll be back in a bit later."

"You're planning on sleeping in here, then?"

"I wasn't, but now Palin finds it so amusing he's making me."

"Oh, shit, I'm sorry." Tyg frowned.

"Stop saying you're sorry." Stills smiled and left the room.

Tyg stared at the door a long time, then got up and poured the water into the ceramic bowl that was next to the jug, using a cloth that had been in her bag she wiped her face, round her neck, down her cleavage and then wiped her arms and hands clean. She removed her dagger belt and put it on the floor beside the bed. She pulled her socks off her feet, then washed them too. She then blew the lights out leaving only one, by the chair. She hesitated a moment, then decided to remove her leather pants as well, she really didn't want to sleep in them. She climbed into the bed and threw a blanket and pillow over to the chair. She suddenly felt exhausted after the events of the day and she still had lingering effects of Rose's tea. She curled up under the blankets and was soon dozing.

She heard the lock and door open later, but kept her eyes closed as the door closed and locked again. She heard Stills coo at the cat a moment, then sit in the chair.

For several minutes all she could hear was his rustling around trying to get comfortable, tossing around and muttering to himself. Tyg opened her eyes and sat up.

"If you promise to continue to be a gentleman and keep your hands to yourself, there is another side of this bed that I'm not using."

Stills stared at her in the gloom, she smiled. "I trust you." She lay back down and closed her eyes with a smile. She heard Stills get up, blow out the candle and come round the bed. He clambered in the other side, after removing his boots and sighed blissfully as he relaxed.

"Better?" Tyg muttered, keeping her back to him.

"Much, thank you."

"No problem."

"Good night, Tyg." Stills whispered then.

Tyg smiled to herself, hearing him say her name. "Good night, Stills."

"Stefan."

"Good night, Stefan." She whispered back, grinning to herself like a fool as her heart thumped.

12

Tyg woke first and the room was washed in early morning light. She turned over and looked at Stills face as he was sleeping facing her direction. She rested her head back on the pillows and smiled to herself. This was a completely new experience for her, waking up next to someone. Even though they hadn't even accidently touched or bumped each other all night, thanks to the cat sleeping between them, Tyg still found it an amazing feeling to wake up and see Stills lying asleep next to her.

As she lay there just watching him sleep, she found herself wondering what it would be like to actually kiss a guy. She felt her cheeks warm at the thought. She had never even given herself a moment to even consider it before, but she had to admit now, lying here, she was feeling very attracted to this young, good looking rogue.

Just then his eyes flickered open and he looked straight at her across the pillows.

"Good morning." He said with a smile as he noticed in the slowly increasing light, her luminous eyes looking back. Luckily for Tyg he couldn't see her blushing in the wane light.

"Morning." Tyg said back. "Sleep well?"

"Yes, thank you, much better than if I'd stayed in that chair."

They just looked into each other's eyes for a long moment. As Tyg bit her lip and rolled it through her teeth Stills blinked and quickly sat up, raking his hands through his hair.

"We better get moving." He said, sounding a little flustered, but didn't make a move off the bed.

Tyg sighed. "I know...but..." She faltered, not knowing if she should finish her sentence. She had wanted to say she was enjoying lying there looking at him. She blushed at the mere thought. Stills looked down at her and saw her blush this time.

"But?" He asked amused.

Tyg sat up. "Nothing." She grabbed her leather pants from the end of the bed and dragged them under the blankets to put them on and keep her dignity. Stills scrambled out of the bed in a panic, he hadn't noticed her pants there in the dark.

"Fuck girl, you're not dressed under there?" He faced the wall. "You're going to give me a freaking heart attack."

"Sorry...I'm still wearing underwear, I'm not completely...you know..." Tyg said as she slipped out of the bed while his back was turned and pulled her pants up over her hips, did up the buttons and her belt buckle, tying the string from her dagger sheath around her thigh. "I just couldn't sleep in them, it's too uncomfortable."

"You could have warned me."

"Really? I thought it better you didn't know."

Tyg saw him look at the ground and rub the back of his neck. "You're probably right." He chuckled hoarsely.

"You can turn around." Tyg said as she grabbed her hair brush and quickly brushed her hair out then grabbed her hair tie and pulled it all back into a high ponytail, then plaited it. She then grabbed some socks out of her bag and pulled them on and finally her boots. Stills had turned and was leaning on the wall with his ankles crossed watching her amused.

"Ready to go?" He asked, as he bent down to put his own boots on.

"One sec." Tyg said as she opened the window and tipped the water from the basin out, poured some fresh water into it and splashed her face with it.

"What about my stuff?" Tyg asked, looking up at where Stills was once again leaning on the wall, smiling.

"Palin said to leave it here for now, even the cat."

"Okay then, let's go."

Stills went to the door as Tyg pulled her cloak on. He opened it for her, then locked it again behind them. Tyg followed him downstairs and back into the kitchen. All seemed quiet and she wondered if anyone else was up yet. Stills grabbed his coat and bow and quiver.

"We'll get something to eat from the market on the way. I've got a few coins and I'm sure Palin will reimburse me as a work expense."

Tyg laughed, a genuine musical laugh that made Stills go weak at the knees. He scratched his jaw in thought. "Good luck with that." Tyg said still laughing.

"Quite amused by that, huh?" Stills laughed too. "Come on then, to your new training location."

"New?"

"Well, the other one is now compromised, isn't it? So..."

"Oh, yeah, I guess so."

"Ready to go learn how to shoot arrows?" Stills said as she past him in the doorway. Tyg faltered and glanced up at him. His eyes were once again smouldering.

"Serious?"

"Sure, why not." He shrugged and gave her a dashing smile.

"Okay, archery is all about posture, so you need to stand more like this..."

Stills explained as he came up behind her and grabbed her shoulders, pulling them back, as he kicked her feet out wider. He then grabbed her hands, putting his arms around her and guided them with his. Tyg looked sideways at him, pulling her head away slightly as he looked over her shoulder. He glanced at her and she raised an eyebrow at him. She could feel the hardness of his chest against her back.

"What?" Stills asked with a small frown.

"Nothing." Tyg replied, biting her lip. Her heart was thumping in her chest at having him so close.

Stills grinned and went back to looking at the target. "Are you concentrating?"

"It's a bit hard too." Tyg muttered.

Stills chuckled a sexy little rumble in his throat as he drew the bow up with her and notched the arrow.

"Just lightly otherwise it won't release right, now pull it back...fingertips...breathe...."

The arrow went flying and to Stills surprise it actually hit the target, but just barely.

"Not bad, now try it on your own." He said, stepping away.

Tyg went to notch another arrow, but when she pulled it back Stills was suddenly right behind her again. He placed a hand on her stomach, causing her to tense and draw it in.

"That's better...but breathe, relax your shoulders." He instructed. "Now do it." He kept his hand round her on her stomach, his chest against her back, as she drew the arrow back and let go.

The arrow hit the target closer to the bull's eye this time.

"Great shot! You sure you haven't done this before?" He said encouragingly.

Tyg turned in his arms and looked at him, lowering the bow. Stills looked her in the eye, going silent.

"Gods, I wish I could kiss you right now." He breathed.

Tyg smiled and lifted her face and kissed him, a quick teasing kiss on the lips. He looked at her surprised for a moment. He had expected her to scowl and possibly punch him. Then his eyes smouldered as he held her gaze. He reached up with one hand and ran it up her cheek and round the side of her head as he tightened the grip on her waist with the other and kissed her back. He licked his tongue across her lips and her mouth opened. They kissed passionately for several seconds.

Stills pulled away, stepping back and shaking his head. "Stop! We can't do this, Palin will kill me!"

Tyg watched him turn away and walk over to a crate and sit down looking perturbed. He raked a hand through his hair and looked up at her with his eyes still dark and smouldering. Tyg placed a hand on her hip as the other clenched the bow.

"Oh, you say stop, but then continue to look at me like that? Do you know that is the first time I've ever kissed anyone?"

Stills stared at her. "What!?"

"Yeah, and of everyone, I chose you. It might not mean much to you, I'm sure you've kissed heaps of girls, but kissing you means something to me."

"Fuck, Tyg, it's not that." Stills sighed, looking away darkly. "I never thought you would ever want to kiss me. I knew you didn't...wouldn't..." He sighed again and rubbed the back of his neck. "I'm a bit speechless to be fair. But, I took this job on, minding you, with very explicit instructions from Palin not to touch you."

"Argh!!" Tyg growled, her eyes blazing ice blue fire. She grabbed an arrow, lifted the bow, notched it, pulled back and released it all in the blink of an eye. The arrow hit the target dead centre.

Stills stood up. "How the fuck!?" He stared at her, as Tyg rubbed her eyes, alleviating her dull headache. "How the hell did you do that?"

Tyg looked at the target, then at Stills, and shrugged. "I always seem to be able to focus better when I'm angry."

"What are you angry at now?" Palin said as he walked in.

Stills baulked at the sight of him, thinking how close it had been to him catching them kissing.

Tyg grinned a vicious grin, her eyes still blazing, but now full of meaning as she looked at Stills. He couldn't help but wink back and give her a goofy grin.

Palin was looking at the target. "Told you she was a quick study." He said rubbing his chin thoughtfully. He turned and appraised the two of them. "So, why are you angry?"

"It's nothing, Palin, we'll discuss it later." Tyg said as she walked off to retrieve the arrows from the target on the far side of the warehouse.

"Hmm, you're not upsetting her, I hope?" Palin said to Stills as Stills sat back down. "I set you the task of minding her because she seemed to like you."

"Really?" Stills looked at Palin surprised.

"Yeah, well, she doesn't like too many people, so I thought it might keep her calm, you know?"

"I've heard, but...it's kinda back fired on you, to be honest." Stills grimaced and looked up.

"Really?" Palin looked hard at Stills, who looked nervous. "Oh, I see. I thought I saw a spark."

"Are you fucking kidding me, you set this up?"

"Stills...you're both young, her especially. She needs a bit of fun. She's always so goddamned serious, it's unnerving. Have fun with this thing you have going on...yes I noticed...it might just help to soften her a bit."

"But, you told me..."

"Absolutely! A bit of harmless flirtation, whatever, but don't go any further. Keep it light-hearted. Otherwise things will just end up even more complicated."

Stills rubbed his face. "Fuck's sake, Boss, you're asking a hell of a lot...I actually really like her."

Palin laughed. "Of course you do, everyone does. Difference is she actually likes you...fuck knows why. So, just take it slow okay?"

"What's so funny?" Tyg asked as she wandered back over and put the arrows in the quiver.

"Nothing." Palin said turning to her. "Well? What are you doing standing there? You're supposed to be training...so train!"

Tyg clamped her mouth shut firmly, then stalked off again, rolling her shoulders, warming them up. She jumped and grabbed hold of a rafter and started doing chin ups.

Palin glanced sideways at Stills. "You sure you want to get involved with that?"

Stills chuckled, his eyes still a little wild. "Ha! Yeah, she's bloody strong for a woman."

"For a woman?" Palin laughed again. "She's stronger than most men I know."

Stills looked at him and saw he was serious. "Gods, what have you done?" Stills muttered to himself, looking at the roof.

"You can go while we train." Palin said to him.

"Can I watch?"

"You sure you want to?"

"Yeah...why?"

"No reason..." Palin said walking off chuckling to himself.

As Palin walked over to where Tyg was, carrying a large bag, she noticed and hauled herself up to sit on the beam of the rafters, grinning down at him.

"Get down here!" Palin yelled in good humour.

Tyg sat back hooking the beam with her knees and leaned backwards. She hung upside down looking at him. Palin grabbed two sticks out of the bag and screwed them together to make a long staff, which he threw on the ground, then took out another two short sticks and held them up to her.

"Sticks again?" Tyg asked bored.

"You need to fight with whatever is handy, more than likely it will be sticks, like that guy got you with the plank of wood...need I remind you."

"Fine." Tyg said resigned as she released her legs from the beam and did a 180 in the air, grabbing the sticks in each hand and landing lightly on the ground in front of Palin, bending her knees to absorb the shock.

"Fucking hell!" They both heard Stills exclaim. As they both turned to him, Palin frowned as Tyg grinned, her eyes blazing.

"If you can't keep quiet I'll have you train with her."

"No, Palin." Tyg said uneasy.

"What? Afraid of hurting him?"

"Now, wait a minute..." Stills exclaimed again.

"Ha! Now you've hurt his pride." Palin laughed as he picked up a small shield and a wooden practise sword.

Stills watched fascinated as Tyg attacked, jumped, twirled and twirled the sticks round. Then she threw the sticks into the air and grabbed the staff and started twirling that, attacking Palin with amazing speed and agility.

He stared wide eyed as he suddenly realised what Palin was doing. He was training up the perfect killing machine and being a beautiful young woman, no one would ever see it coming. He frowned, he didn't know how he felt about that, especially given his own increasing feelings about her. He felt a jolt of protectiveness and grimaced at himself. "Fuck..."

Palin called a halt and grabbed a water flagon out of the bag and threw it at Tyg. She drank from it, wiping her mouth with the back of her hand, then handed it back. She went back to practising with the staff on her own, as Palin made his way over, sweaty and exhausted, to sit down next to Stills.

Stills watched Tyg doing her dance with the staff, her motions were so fluid and easy, it was mesmerising to watch. He swallowed hard. Palin laughed at him.

"Second thoughts?"

"Fuck, Boss. You're creating a killing machine? Out of her? Fuck's sake...is that fair on her?"

"She gave herself to me to do with as I wished...this is my wish, besides there's things about her you don't know." Palin growled.

Stills stared at him a moment, seeing the obsession in his eyes and shook his head.

"I think it best if I do go..." He stood up.

Palin looked at him. "Okay, be back here in half an hour. I've got a surprise for her and want you there."

"Of course." Stills looked curious but didn't ask.

As Stills went to leave Tyg stopped and looked at him.

"You're leaving?"

"I'll be back shortly." Stills said uncomfortably, stuffing his hands in his pockets.

Tyg gave him a dazzling smile. "Okay...good....bye then." She said as she turned and picked up the wooden sword and started to practise with that. He watched a moment as she showed the same amazing skill with that as she had done with the staff and the short sticks. He turned, feeling sad for her and wandered off.

Once Stills had left Palin strode over to Tyg. She stopped and lowered the sword, seeing him. He stood in front of her, hands on his hips.

"There's something I've been meaning to ask you...about that stab wound...show me the scar." He growled the order at her. Tyg baulked. "Now Tyg!"

Tyg pulled her shirt up to show Palin the fact that there was no scar to show him, her eyes were on the ground, her mouth pressed into a hard line. She knew this day would come and she wasn't sure how she felt about it.

"Explain this to me."

"What?"

"Don't play coy with me. I pulled that dagger out myself...I know how deep it was. Where the fuck is the scar, where is anything?"

"I don't know." Tyg answered evasively.

"What do you mean, you don't know! Wounds like that can't just disappear."

Tyg sighed and sat down on the ground. "Give me a knife." She muttered.

"What? Why?" Palin asked.

"Just give me a damn knife, Palin."

Palin drew his dagger from his belt and handed it hilt first to Tyg. She stared up at him for a moment. He saw sadness in her eyes.

"Tyg?" He asked.

"Before I show you this, Palin, please promise me you'll never tell anyone, and never purposely put me in harm's way?"

"What?"

"Promise me, Palin, I need to trust you."

"Okay, Tyg. I promise."

"Promise what?"

Palin sighed. "I promise to not tell anyone or put you purposely in harm's way."

Tyg regarded him, gauging his sincerity a moment. Then her eyes went ice blue and she took the dagger and sliced it across her forearm, cutting it open deep, right in the fleshy part before the elbow on the inside.

"What the hell!" Palin gasped, more at the fact that she didn't even flinch.

The cut bled for several seconds, then stopped. A clear fluid replaced it and before Palin's eyes the wound sealed itself shut, becoming a red swollen scar. After several minutes the scar had receded and disappeared completely. Palin fell to his knees as he watched Tyg's wound heal itself.

He looked up at her face. "I knew you were special Tyg, but this....this is a fucking miracle."

Tyg just looked at him silent.

"Do you know what you are?" Palin asked her wide eyed.

"Nothing, Palin. I'm nothing."

"No, no, you are something, Tyg. You're like the next stage of human...evolved."

"Don't be daft." Tyg scoffed as she handed his dagger back to him and stood up.

Palin stood up too. "I'm serious, Tyg. You master every weapon, you're as strong as an ox. You can heal superfast and don't even scar. Your eyes change colour. No one else is like you."

"You can't tell anyone, Palin."

"Oh, I won't, Tyg, don't worry. Your secret is safe with me, as long as you're with me, Tyg."

Tyg looked hard at Palin.

"Are you with me, Tyg?" Palin held his fist out.

Tyg grinned to herself then bumped Palin's fist with hers. "I'm with you, Palin."

Palin then grabbed Tyg and pulled her into a rough embrace. Tyg was surprised and didn't know how to react. "You've become like a little sister to me, Tyg. No harm will come to you on my watch, just stay loyal to me."

"Thank you, Palin." Tyg breathed a little shocked.

"Although, I do have a surprise for you." Palin said then.

Tyg looked at him serious. "I have one for you too. What is it?"

"You first." Palin said knowing what was coming.

"Okay." Tyg said suddenly shy. "It's about Stills."

"Let me stop you right there, Tyg...I'm happy for you, okay, I've seen the looks, if you like him, good for you, and it's about time you didn't take life so serious."

Tyg was looking at him shocked.

"But, promise me to take things slow, don't go rushing into anything."

"Okay, Dad" Tyg smiled as Palin laughed. "So, what's my surprise?"

"It's time for you to formally join the Guild." Palin stated smiling.

"Join the Guild?" Tyg sounded surprised and joyed.

"You're no longer my apprentice, Tyg, I think you've more than proven that. It's time to take the Oath."

"Wow...okay."

"But, there's an initiation first."

"Initiation?"

"Nothing you can't handle."

Stills wandered back in, looking at the two of them.

"Finished then?" He asked.

"Yes, we have somewhere to be." Palin said

"Oh?" Stills enquired, looking at Tyg, she was grinning from ear to ear. "Something happy obviously."

Tyg stepped over to him and hugged him. Stills looked up at Palin who just smiled at him and turned to pack the bag up. Stills smiled too and hugged Tyg back.

"I'm finally going to take the Oath and become part of the Assassins Guild properly."

"Is that so?" Stills looked back at Palin surprised. "And the initiation?"

"That's where we're going now." Palin answered.

"Have you told her what's involved, Palin?" Stills said wrapping his arms tighter around her, feeling strangely protective of her all of a sudden.

Palin growled. "It's Boss to you, Stills, remember your place."

Stills looked at the ground as Tyg stepped back looking at the two of them confused. "Fucking hell!" Stills said exasperated.

"What's wrong? I thought you would be happy for me?" Tyg said looking at him as he raked his hands through his hair and rubbed his eyes.

"Happy for you...what gave you that idea?" Tyg looked shocked and a little disappointed. "Did Palin tell you what this initiation entails?"

"Well, no, not yet...but I trust him."

"That's the surprise, Stills, perhaps you should trust me a little more where Tyg is concerned...now let's go." Palin growled again. Tyg bounded out of the warehouse, as Stills looked hard at Palin as he passed him.

"I really hope you know what you're doing."

"Just wait and see, Stills." Palin said laughing and clapped Stills on the shoulder.

13

They went down to the docks and entered a warehouse down there. It appeared to be closely guarded. As Tyg followed Palin in, she was holding hands with Stills, which raised more than a few eyebrows of the other men who were gathered there.

Tyg's eyes went wide as she saw who was waiting for her in the middle of the room. Strung up as he was by his wrists, shirtless and covered with blood, was the man who had stabbed her. Tyg looked at Palin surprised they had kept the guy this long.

"See I told you it would be a good surprise." Palin said grinning.

Stills scratched his jaw and let go of Tyg's hand. She turned to him with an eyebrow arched.

"You're on your own now, Tyg...good luck." He said with a smile. "But I know you won't need it." He stroked a finger down her cheek and then walked off to where a group of men were standing. They clapped him on the back and muttered and laughed. He stood with them, his hands stuffed in his pockets, a look of deep concern on his face.

Tyg was staring at the man in chains. Her eyes were now blazing.

"Let him down!" Palin ordered. Someone released the chain where it was secured over at the wall, and the man fell to the ground. Another man walked over and undid the cuffs holding him.

Tyg knew what this was and grinned viciously, stepping forward. Palin put an arm out to stop her.

"Wait!" He ordered. Tyg froze, but her eyes never left the man's face as he scrambled up to standing and saw her. He looked around realising himself what was happening, then turned back to her and grinned viciously back at her, spitting blood out. Someone threw the man a sword. He picked it up and tested its weight, then turned to Tyg.

"Come on then bitch, let's finish this."

Palin drew his own sword and held it out to Tyg. She glanced at it, then up at Palin. As she took the sword from him, she twirled it, threw it in the air and caught it, spinning it round expertly, as she stepped forward towards the man.

He looked shocked at her sword skill for a moment but then screamed and charged at her, swinging blindly. Tyg saw his attack like it was slow motion. Her eyes dilated so there was no colour at all just inky blackness. As he charged she deftly sidestepped and slashed him across the arm. She turned, spinning the sword, as the man grabbed his arm with a grunt and turned to face her again.

Tyg was looking at him with a hideous snarl, showing her teeth. He saw the sharp canines and the black eyes and felt terror. "I'm going to kill you, you fucking freak!"

Tyg just stood up, dropping the sword low, as if inviting him to try. The men circled round them were all cheering her. The man lunged forward again, this time Tyg brought her sword up to meet his. As they clashed he slid his blade down to hook the hilts together, trying to wrestle Tyg's sword from her grasp. He leaned over the blades and head butted her in the mouth, causing Tyg's lip to split and blood to drip down her chin. She pushed him back, breaking the sword lock and kicked him in the stomach sending him reeling back, tripping and falling over. He scrambled away as Tyg went to jump on him, and managed to get back to his feet. He back pedalled several steps and came up against the wall of men, they pushed him back into the circle. As Tyg advanced on him, she placed the sword tip first into the wood of the floor and advanced on him with no weapon. The men around her went crazy. Tyg's sole focus however was on the man in front of her. The man that had stabbed a dagger into her side, deliberately twisted it to make her feel excruciating pain.

"Fuck you, bitch!" He screamed as he lunged at her again, swinging the sword haphazardly. Tyg ducked and stepped in close, turning round she slammed her back into the man's chest even as she grabbed his sword arm. Then she bent over and flipped the man over her, as he crashed to the ground, Tyg wrenched the sword from his grasp. He lay winded on the ground for a few seconds as Tyg walked over to where she had left her sword and pulled it out of the floor boards. Now with a sword in each hand, she turned back to the man and walked up to him. He was lying on the floor, scrambling backwards, watching her approach, as she spun both blades round, as easy in her left as it was in her right. She liked the feeling of two swords. She stepped over him and put the two swords crossed over each other at his neck. He raised his eyes and spat at her. Tyg uncrossed the swords, slicing them both across the man's throat, nearly decapitated him. The men around her went crazy whooping and clapping. Palin came over and put a hand on her shoulder. Tyg flinched and stepped back, lifting the swords.

"Tyg!" Stills called out. Tyg blinked then, her eyes coming into focus and returning to normal. She looked down at the dead man, then threw the swords on the ground. Palin picked his sword up, cleaned it and sheathed it. Stills grabbed her round the neck with one hand and pulled her into his chest. He kissed her head. "It's over, Tyg, relax now."

Tyg looked up at him and smiled. Palin stepped back over and clapped her on the back.

"I knew Stills would come in handy." He said laughing. "Come on, it's Oath time."

As they stepped over to where a table had been set up she noticed a short sword lying there, a new one, with a black leather handle and silver cross piece. Palin stood before her and indicated for her to kneel.

As she sank to her knees before him, he looked at the crowd of his men.

"Tyg has completed the initiation, what say you all, are you all agreed that she has passed?"

Hoots and hollers and cheering replied.

"Good." Palin looked down on Tyg. He drew his sword and pointed it at her. "On this sword do you swear fealty to the Assassin's Guild and to me, its leader."

"Yes, Palin." Tyg answered.

"Do you swear, on threat of death, to never speak of our Guild or the secrets held within?"

"I swear, Palin, on threat of death, to serve you and the Guild, and never to speak of it to anyone."

Tyg reached out and placed her hands under the blade and then bowed her head down and kissed the blade.

"Welcome to the Assassin's Guild, Tyg." Palin sheathed his sword and then turned and grabbed the other sword off the table. He pulled it out of its sheath and held it out in two hands to Tyg.

"For you, as your passage into the Guild." Palin smiled at her as she looked shocked and took the sword in two hands. Other men started crowding round her, clapping her on the back and welcoming her in. She staggered to her feet feeling overwhelmed by them all. Stills suddenly barged through, pushing them all back.

"That's enough of that, give her some room." He growled at them in an annoyed tone.

Tyg smiled at Stills who handed her the sheath for the sword. Tyg put it away and put it back on the table, someone then shoved a tankard in her face.

"Drink up!"

Tyg took it gratefully and drowned it in one go to more cheers. Stills shook his head and leaned his hip on the table as Tyg turned and sat down on it.

"You okay, little cat?" Stills asked smiling.

"Yeah, just a bit overwhelmed, I'm not used to crowds."

"You did good today." Stills smouldered as he looked at her. "Want to get out of here?"

Tyg looked up at his gaze. "Can we?"

"They'll all be drunk in no time and won't even notice you're gone, trust me."

"Okay"

Stills waved at someone, and Tyg noticed Luke and another guy come over.

"We're getting out of here, coming?"

"Yeah sounds good." Luke said.

The other guy looked at Tyg, holding his hand out. "I'm Bron."

Tyg smiled at him. "Hi." She said awkwardly as she shook his hand, then dropped it. Stills grabbed her hand, pulling her up, as she grabbed the sword.

"Come on let's go."

14

"Ah, guys...I don't really think I should go in there?" Tyg hesitated in front of the tavern.

"Nonsense, you're one of us now, and we go where we want." Luke said brusquely.

"But, there's a reason I don't go into places like this."

"So, just put your hood up, it'll be fine." Stills said encouragingly.

Tyg shrugged and pulled her hood up and followed Stills, Luke and Bron into the semi crowded but quiet Inn. As they sat down in a quiet corner Tyg noticed the guys getting stares and people muttering.

"Wow, okay. You guys get a similar reaction."

Stills shrugged. "Just ignore it." Stills seemed to notice someone he recognised and groaned. "Oh, shit."

The other guys laughed as a girl's shrill voice called out. "Stills! Is that you?"

"Have you not sorted that chick out yet?" Luke asked.

"What's this?" Tyg asked as she watched the young doe-eyed girl approaching. She was pretty but nothing special, with her shoulder length brown hair. Her bust was shoved up by a corset worn over her very low cut blouse.

"Still's admirer, she's been bugging him for months. He hasn't got the balls to tell her he's not interested." Luke explained as Bron chuckled.

"Yeah, poor Stills, too good looking for his own good."

Tyg looked sideways at him as he squirmed uncomfortably.

"Shut up, guys." He whispered hoarsely.

Tyg grinned to herself as she reached into her hood and purposely pulled a length of hair forward that had loosened and come out of her braid earlier and started playing with it. The girl bounced over full of exuberant energy.

"It's been so long, gorgeous, what have you been doing?" Tyg felt a pang of jealous hatred when the girl called Stills gorgeous.

"Not much." Stills replied annoyed.

The girl then noticed Tyg playing with her hair, but couldn't quite see her face. She frowned and put her hands on her hips. The other guys were watching amused.

"And who is this?" The girl asked indignantly. Luke and Bron wooed and turned away laughing.

Stills choked. "Ah..."

Tyg stood up and at the same time pulled her hood down. She leaned over the table across the front of Stills and held her hand out to the girl, beaming a truly beautiful smile at her as she locked eyes with her.

"Tyg...and you?" Tyg asked of the girl, who was now standing staring open mouthed at Tyg, then at Stills, who had folded his arms and was grinning amused looking at Tyg, then the girl looked back to Tyg.

"Ah...I'm Tania...nice to meet you, my Lady." The girl said as she quickly took Tyg's hand and curtsied.

Luke and Bron roared with laughter as the girl blushed and then fled, tears in her eyes. Tyg sat back down, smirking and took a sip of her drink.

"Satisfied?" Stills asked as the other guys continued to laugh.

"She just did you a favour, Stills." Bron said.

"What did I do?" Tyg asked, looking at Stills.

"You know exactly what you did, young lady." Stills berated her. "That was cruel."

"Oh, come on, Stills, give Tyg a break. You couldn't stand that girl and Tyg had all the right to put the strumpet in her place." Luke said.

Stills rubbed his eyes. "Shut up, guys."

"Why? This is too good." Luke chuckled.

"Did you see her face when she saw Tyg's?" Bron asked laughing.

Tyg smiled wanly at Stills. "I'm sorry. I didn't mean to really...just...when she called you, gorgeous..."

Stills looked at her amazed. "What? You were jealous? You?" Stills sat forward, facing Tyg.

Tyg gave him a strange look and blushed slightly. Stills laughed then and hooked an arm around Tyg's neck, pulling her to him and kissing her on the head.

"Oh no! She's still watching..." Luke said.

"Oh, poor girl, she's completely heartbroken now." Bron added.

"Would you guys shut up now?" Tyg said in a low growl. They both went silent and regarded Tyg for a second, then both grabbed their tankards and drank, looking elsewhere.

Stills laughed again, keeping his arm around Tyg's shoulders and shuffling his chair closer. "Oh, you listen to her." He said to them as they both grimaced. Bron pulled a deck of cards out of his pocket and changed the subject.

"Cards anyone?" He turned to Luke, prompting him to play to get rid of the awkwardness.

Tyg laughed and shook her head as she leaned deeper into Stills side.

"No, you guys go ahead." Stills said, kissing and nuzzling Tyg's hair, then laying his cheek on her head.

"Yeah, you've got your hands full." The guys both laughed again and turned their attention to each other and the cards.

Stills and Tyg sat that way while they drank their drinks and watched the card game. Tyg was more than comfortable in Stills arms and he didn't want any reason to let go of her.

When the food arrived however, they sat up. Tyg was famished after all the training then the initiation. They all tucked into the food with a fervour.

"I'll be back." Bron said then, getting up and heading out the door that went to the latrines out the back.

When he came back he looked wary. "I think we may have a problem."

"What now?" Luke asked.

"Little Tania is stirring up trouble...I knew she was mental."

"What?" Stills said shocked. "What the hell is she doing?"

"If she can't have you, no one can." Tyg muttered.

"Clever girl." Luke growled. "I would say Tyg's got it in one."

"Fuck's sake...it's not like I ever even led her on or anything?" Stills said rubbing his eyes.

"Like I said...mental." Luke said, tapping the side of his head.

"So, what's she doing exactly?"

"Not sure...I just heard some muttering about Tyg and you out back." Bron explained.

"I told you I shouldn't have come in here." Tyg said standing up.

Stills grabbed her arm and pulled her back down. "Just sit down, Tyg."

"Yeah, it's actually safer now to stay in here, they won't do anything inside the Inn." Luke said.

"Should I go get back up?" Bron asked, still munching on bread.

Stills looked at Tyg. "No, we don't need any back up."

Tyg looked back at him and blinked, looking away. She knew what he meant.

"Stay here, I'm going to see if I can diffuse this situation first." Stills got up.

"How exactly?" Tyg asked arching an eyebrow at him.

"Just stay calm, little cat, and stay here." Stills said as he smiled at her then walked off through the Inn to the bar. Within seconds Tania had manoeuvred her way to the bar and was beside Stills. Tyg was watching intently as Stills was talking to the girl. Tyg could tell by the body language things weren't going well. Tyg noticed a group of guys watching the exchange intently.

Tyg stood up.

"Tyg, don't get involved." Luke growled.

Tyg turned her eyes to Luke with an eyebrow raised.

"Seriously, Tyg. He needs to sort this himself."

"Yeah, he created the mess." Bron agreed.

"How did he create this mess exactly?" Tyg faced them her eyes blazing. "He did nothing to encourage her right? He just stayed polite?"

"Well, yeah, but we all knew she was nuts. He should have shut her down the first time she tried to flirt with him."

Tyg laughed. "Guess his ego wouldn't let him."

Luke and Bron laughed. "Exactly, so leave him to deal with it."

Tyg looked back at Stills and Tania at the bar, she had started to raise her voice. Tyg frowned, and dropped her cloak on the bench.

"Oh, shit." Luke muttered, rubbing his forehead.

Suddenly Tania raised her hand to slap Stills across the face, but instead she found her wrist being held in the vice like grip of Tyg, as Tyg's face suddenly filled her vision. Tania stared petrified at Tyg's eyes.

"Enough, Tania. You're just making a fool of yourself now." Tyg growled at her. Stills went to grab Tyg's shoulder to pull her back but Tyg pushed Stills in the chest with her other hand, sending him staggering back a few steps.

"Tyg, calm down." Luke said as he stepped over to the bar.

Tania's eyes were welling with tears. "You're hurting me." She wailed.

"Right, and no one is going to do anything about it...because I'm a woman, hurting a woman, not working as you planned, huh?"

"What?" Stills said looking around Tyg at Tania's face. "You were trying to get me to hit you?"

Tania was wailing now. "Yeah, to give these other guys the excuse to beat you up, isn't that right, Tania?" Tyg said her name in a guttural growl.

"Hey, take it outside, whores!" The Innkeeper bellowed at them. Then he looked at Tyg. He saw the way she was dressed, the dagger and sword on her belt, the same as the men standing around her. "What the fuck is going on here?" He demanded.

"Tyg, let her go." Stills whispered in her ear as he stood behind her.

Tyg's eyes slid to the Innkeeper as she let Tania's wrist go. "What did you call me?"

"Ah...nothing...sorry, but I think you should all leave."

"Good idea." Luke said, shoving Tyg's cloak into her chest, causing her to grab it.

"Back up Stills...Luke...those guys are waiting for any chance to defend her honour...isn't that right? You manipulative little bitch?" Tyg said deathly quiet.

"Hey, what's going on here, you putting your hands on that woman?" A large bearded man said striding over followed by a few of his drunken mates.

Tyg looked at Tania, then at Stills, with a satisfied smirk at being proved right. She turned and looked at the bearded man in front of her.

"Which woman?" She asked sweetly.

"Ah..." The guy couldn't really say Tania as Tyg was standing between her and Stills. "...either of you?"

"Well, for one...he can put his hands wherever he likes on me...and two...as for her, he wouldn't touch her with a barge pole."

Luke and Bron both stifled laughs as Stills eyes just about popped out of his head.

"What do you mean by that exactly?" The guy wasn't about to give up.

"You know exactly what I mean." Tyg stepped up to him, her eyes still blazing.

"Oui! You lot! I said no trouble." The Innkeeper said as he came back over. "And, I thought I already told you lot to get out?"

"Just leave it man, you got played." Stills muttered to the guy as his fellows all started backing off.

"Is that right?" He turned to Stills with a smirk.

"Oh, fuck's sake." Stills said standing up straight.

Tyg however grabbed Tania by the arm and threw her in front of the bearded man. "Tell him." Tania looked nervous. "Tell him." Tyg's voice went vicious.

"Alright, she's right...sorry...he hasn't laid a finger on me."

"Good." Tyg said satisfied as the bearded man looked at Tania with a frown. "Let's go."

Tyg turned and put her arm around Stills waist and walked him out the door, followed by Luke and Bron, who were soon falling over laughing as they stepped out.

"By the Gods, Tyg! You know how to show a guy a good night out, that was fantastic!" Bron laughed. "But how did you know?"

Tyg shrugged. "I'm a woman, I figured out her game."

"We better get moving before those dickheads come out." Luke said with a grin.

"I wish they would." Tyg muttered, then she turned to Stills. "You're quiet, did I do wrong?"

"No, Tyg." Stills said as he stepped closer to her and put his hand on the side of her face, bowed his head down and kissed her.

"Fuck, Stills, you've got a death wish." Luke muttered, not knowing of Palin's consent.

"Not at all." Stills grinned as he put his arm around Tyg's shoulders and walked off with her up the street.

15

When they arrived back at the Hide Palin was there playing cards with a couple of other men. They were all semi drunk and smoking cigars. As Tyg and Stills walked down the hall they heard Palin bellow out.

"Tyg! Get in here."

Tyg flinched and changed course and walked into the front living room. Stills followed along behind, hands in his pockets. He leaned on the side of the couch with his hip as Tyg walked up in front of the chair Palin was sitting in and looked at him with an eyebrow raised.

"There she is..." One guy said as the other one muttered something inaudible and whistled softly making Stills frown at him.

Palin scowled at her. "You're supposed to be laying low, where the fuck have you been?"

Tyg shrugged "Getting something to eat."

"With who?" Palin looked at Stills who grinned at him.

"Stills, Luke and Bron...why?"

"Hmm. Good crew...might be able to work with that..." Palin seemed lost in his own thoughts for a moment.

"So is that it?" Tyg glanced at the two men that were both grinning at her, she scowled at them, her eyes blazing, making them both look away.

Palin smiled. "No, I have a bet going that only you can sort out for me."

"Are you serious?" Tyg sighed. "More of this shit?" Stills frowned not knowing what was going on and scratched his chin.

"Come on...it's only an informal bet with these guys."

"Fine." Tyg rolled her eyes and turned to look at the two assassins properly. "So who am I contesting?"

"Both of them."

"At the same time?" Tyg sneered sarcastically making Palin roar with laughter.

"Wow, cocky much?" One guy said.

"Me first..." The other of them said.

"And you are?" Tyg asked folding her arms.

"Jared...and he's Brax."

"Nice to meet you." Brax said grinning.

"They were impressed with the way you handled your initiation."

Tyg scoffed. "Killing a sleep deprived tortured man isn't exactly hard."

"Wow, she is confidant." Jared said.

Palin laughed and Tyg's gaze slid to him. "So best over the kitchen table, I'm guessing." Tyg smiled and walked off as Palin, Jared and Brax all stood up, gathering up their stuff. Tyg grabbed Stills hand and dragged him behind her down the hall to the kitchen.

"What the fuck is going on?" Stills demanded. Tyg looked at him with an eyebrow raised.

"Jealous already?" Tyg asked chuckling. "It's an arm wrestle, calm down. It's something Palin likes to put me through from time to time for his own amusement."

"You're kidding? He makes money off you? That's deplorable."

Tyg looked at Stills amused. "He makes money off all of us."

"Well, yeah, I guess so...but this is exploitation." Stills said unhappy about it.

"Careful, you don't want Palin to hear you."

As they entered the kitchen Tyg sat down at the table and leaned back in the chair hooking an arm around the decorative knob on the chair's back. Stills leaned against the bench folding his arms and crossing his feet as was his habit. Tyg smiled at him.

"What?" He said, slightly grumpy.

Tyg shrugged. "I don't know...I just like the way you stand like that."

"Really..." Stills said smiling and smouldered at her with his pale hazel eyes twinkling darkly.

Tyg blushed slightly as the others walked in. Stills chuckled. "And I like that..." He said meaning her blush. "...it's cute."

"Cute?" Jared said over hearing. "Gods, this boy has it bad!" He clapped Stills on the shoulder.

"Hey! Don't call me boy, Jared, I'm not much younger than you!" Stills grumbled rubbing his shoulder.

"Yeah, maybe...but look at that adorable youthful face of yours." Jared teased as he grabbed Stills by the cheeks with one hand and squeezed them.

Stills pushed him away. "Knock it off!"

"He's just jealous." Brax muttered. "Because he looks so old and haggard for his age."

"Well, now he has two things to be jealous of Stills for." Palin laughed as he sat down at the table and leaned back in his chair putting his feet on the table. "Stills here, is dating my wee cat, with my permission. I feel like a proud father." He chuckled to himself.

Both Jared and Brax stared at Palin, then Stills, then Tyg.

"Can we get this over with?" Tyg said sounding bored. "And can someone get me a drink?"

"Here..." Brax handed over an earthenware jug.

Tyg sniffed it and cringed. "What is it?"

"Rum."

"No thanks." Tyg shuddered. "It smells awful."

Stills suddenly put a bottle of Volka on the table, the same one he had found the day before. Now half empty. "She likes Volka." He said with a grin and a wink.

Tyg grinned back. "Thank you, Stefan."

"Stefan!" Palin exclaimed. "First name basis, this is serious." He said joining in on teasing Stills.

Palin, Jared and Brax all laughed, causing Stills to retreat again to leaning on the kitchen bench in the background. Tyg noticed he was blushing now.

"Shut up, guys!" Stills grumbled.

"Yeah, shut up and hurry up." Tyg said sitting up and putting her elbow on the table and flexing her hand. "I don't have all day." Tyg grabbed the volka bottle, pulled the cork out with her teeth and drank from it.

"Got somewhere to be?" Palin asked.

"Aren't I moving today?" Tyg asked him.

"Nope, not today. Barion said to take you over to meet his wife tomorrow for brunch."

"His wife?" Tyg was surprised.

Jared suddenly grabbed Tyg's hand in his and slammed it on the table. "Got ya! That was easy." He laughed jovially.

Tyg's eyes blazed and she stared at him. "Not funny."

"Actually, hilarious!" Brax joined in. Tyg rolled her eyes.

"Gods! I hate drunk people."

"How can you say that when, I've heard, you drink like a fish?" Brax asked, indicating the volka bottle in her hand.

Tyg grinned. "Want a drinking contest?"

"Ha! Anytime light weight." Brax said, he was quite burly and confidant he could hold his liquor quite well.

"Not right now, one competition at a time." Palin said. "Show your money."

Jared and Brax both put their hands in their pockets and started shelling out coins onto the table. Tyg sat bored taking another swig from the bottle, drumming her fingers on the table.

"Right, all this says she can't beat both of us." Jared said as Palin looked over the mass of bronze and copper coins on the table.

"So weakest first, is it?" Tyg said staring at Jared, her eyes glowing faintly.

"What the fuck... you cheeky bitch." Jared snorted then smiled. "I like you..." Stills frowned darkly and shifted his weight.

"She's got a point though..." Brax laughed.

"Shut up, Trog!" Jared grumbled.

"Hurry up already." Tyg groaned and reset her elbow on the table, holding her hand up. Jared took it in his and set his elbow on the table.

"Okay..." Palin put his hand over the top of theirs. "...on my count."

Tyg was looking at Jared's face intently. He was looking at their hands. He glanced up and she locked eyes with him. He couldn't look away as Tyg smiled at him. Stills didn't like the look of that smile, it seemed too friendly for his liking.

"Three...two...one...go!" Palin called.

Tyg slammed Jared's hand onto the table, then let go and sat back, taking a sip from the bottle again.

"Wait! What the fuck!" Jared exploded as Brax laughed. "She distracted me with those bloody eyes!"

Stills smiled to himself, now he understood.

"I want another go." Jared moaned.

"No way! You heard the countdown, not our problem if you weren't ready." Palin laughed. "Ha! You got beaten by a sixteen year old girl."

Tyg glanced over at Stills, who frowned at hearing that. "Seventeen." Tyg corrected.

"What?" Palin questioned. "How come every time your age comes up in conversation it changes?"

"Because it only seems to come up in conversation once a year."

"Hmm." Palin grunted dubiously. "Right...next! Swap seats."

Brax practically pushed Jared out of the chair in his hurry for his turn. Tyg looked at him amused, he caught the look. "I can't wait to hold your hand, little cat."

"Watch it." Tyg scowled at him.

Brax grinned and put his elbow on the table and waggled his fingers at her. "Come on, hold hands with me, sweetheart." Tyg grit her teeth.

"Knock it off, Brax." Stills growled behind him. Tyg looked up at Stills, her eyes blazing. He frowned at her then shrugged. Brax just laughed.

"Whoa, steady there mate..." Jared said draping his arm round Stills' shoulders. Stills struggled to get him off but Jared hooked his arm around Stills' neck. Tyg slid her eyes back to Brax and put her elbow on the table clasping hands with him. He pulled her hand towards his mouth and kissed it, grinning at her. Tyg snarled at him as Palin grabbed their hands and set them ready.

"On my count." Palin said. Tyg and Brax were already looking at each other. Tyg could see Brax wasn't going to be fooled as easily. He was at least twice her size, but Tyg pulled the sleeve of her shirt up to her shoulder, showing her arm muscles, which were now starting to pop due to the strain each of them was holding as Palin held them steady. Brax glanced at her bicep and frowned.

"Three...two...one...go!" Palin released their hands and they stalemated in the middle with even pressure.

Brax grit his teeth and tried to budge Tyg's arm. She relented a little making him grin, but then she applied more pressure and swung their arms back in her favour.

"Fuck Brax, come on!" Jared shouted, still with his arm around Stills' neck.

"How are you so strong?" Brax breathed through his gritted teeth. Tyg smiled and brought the volka bottle to her lips. Palin chuckled.

"Shit, she's not even trying..." Stills muttered as Jared stepped forward. Stills ducked his head and got out of Jared's hold.

"Brax, she's making a fool out of you." Jared growled.

"Shut up!" Brax said concentrating as he managed to pull back the advantage.

"Yes, that's good, Brax, keep it going...keep the pressure on!" Jared started coaching and cheering him on.

Stills looked at Palin's face and saw quiet confidence. Stills frowned and resumed his stance on the kitchen bench. Tyg glanced up at him and smiled. Stills smouldered back with a smirk.

"Tyg!" Palin said annoyed. "Do you mind actually concentrating?"

Brax had got Tyg's hand to within an inch of his victory. Tyg rolled her eyes. "Oh, alright." She said and applied some real pressure, her bicep bulged and veins popped out as she mercilessly pushed Brax's hand slowly all the way back to her side as he strained and started to sweat.

"Fuck!" Brax yelled, making his frustration work for him as he pushed back a little again. He then leaned forward and licked Tyg's hand. Tyg growled as she lost momentum. Jared laughed.

"Finish this." Palin said crossly.

Tyg glanced at him and grinned then suddenly her eyes went black and she heaved her full strength against Brax's arm and slammed his hand onto the table.

"You fucking cheat." Tyg muttered as she grinned in triumph, then took a big swig of the volka and stood up.

"Fuck!" Brax groaned as he cradled his hand a moment.

"Oh, man!" Jared said in despair as Palin scooped the coins up laughing.

Tyg went to leave.

"Where are you going?" Palin asked.

"To my room..."

"My room." Palin reminded her. Tyg crossed her arms and raised an eyebrow. "Fine...go." Palin said as he put the coins in his pocket.

"What? You're not even going to give her a share of the winnings?" Stills asked as he stepped forward.

"Leave it." Tyg muttered as she walked off.

Palin stared at Stills balefully as Stills frowned again, then followed Tyg out.

"Ha! Whipping boy!" Brax teased.

"Yeah, who wears the pants?" Jared called out as Stills slammed the door behind him to laughter. Tyg was in the hall, leaning on the wall waiting. He stepped over to her.

"You waiting for me?" He asked frowning.

Tyg smiled. "Of course, you've got the key...remember?"

"Huh, yeah." Stills took the key out of his pocket and handed it to her. Tyg took it with a questioning look.

"I'm going for a walk." Stills said as he stuffed his hands into his pockets and headed for the front door. Tyg watched him for a moment frowning. As he reached the door and opened it Tyg couldn't hold back her confusion.

"Did I do something wrong?"

Stills halted and turned back to her. "No, not you...I realise you're not in a situation to argue with Palin. Ha! Neither am I, but..."

"So you're mad at Palin?"

"So should you be..." Stills said, perturbed. "Why aren't you?"

Tyg smiled and looked at the floor, then back up at Stills. She walked up to him. "Palin does split the money with me, but he doesn't give it to me directly, is all." She whispered.

"And you trust him?"

"Of course."

"Alright, well I'm sorry then." Stills scratched the back of his neck awkwardly.

Tyg smiled weakly. "Enjoy your walk." She turned and walked back down the hall and up the stairs.

Stills stood in the doorway conflicted, then closed it and went into the living area and got himself a drink.

16

He sat on the couch and put his feet up on the low table in front. He could hear Palin and the others laughing and drinking. He thought about going back and joining them but he wasn't in the mood.

He heard the front door open and glanced up at the open door where he could see the hallway.

"Luke?" Stills said.

"Hey man, what you up to?"

"Well, not much...it's only been like...an hour since we left you guys. Where's Bron?"

"Outside, where's Palin?"

"In the kitchen." Stills sat up. "What's happening?"

"Follow me." Luke said as he went through to the kitchen. Stills got up and followed. Palin looked up as they entered. Palin, Brax and Jared had resumed their card playing. "We've got a problem, Boss."

"What?"

"Same one as before."

Stills grimaced. "Tyg?" He asked.

"Yeah, there's still someone out there asking questions about her."

"How do you know this?" Palin asked.

"Bumped into Jon from the Hut. He mentioned someone had been skirting around the Thieves' Guild asking questions about a white haired teenaged girl with blue eyes."

"Shit." Palin looked at Stills. "Where is she?"

"Upstairs."

"You're sure about that?"

Stills grimaced. "Not really...." He turned and ran off up the stairs and banged on the locked door of Palin's room. No answer. "Damn it!"

Stills sprinted back down the stairs and out the back door, dodging past Luke and Palin who were standing waiting. He looked up once he was in the alley, at the window and saw it open.

"Fuck!" Stills yelled as Palin walked out the back door, strode up to him and punched him in the side of the head. Stills staggered back.

"You bloody idiot!" Palin roared and hit him again, getting his nose. "You had one fucking job!"

Luke stepped in before Palin hit him again.

"I'm sorry, I didn't really think she would take off." Stills said wiping his bleeding nose.

"I told you she wouldn't let this go...she's just been biding her time...but she doesn't realise there are professional squads after her...she'll get into a fight even she can't win." Palin growled furious.

"Okay, where would she go?" Luke asked.

"Fuck knows!" Palin said frustrated. "She could be anywhere in this fucking city."

Stills looked up. "Maybe we should start at the warehouse where she was training?"

Palin scowled at him. "I've a good mind to chuck you out of the Guild!"

Stills swallowed worried. "Let me find her, please Boss"

"We can all look for her." Jared said from the doorway.

"Right...split up...Stills and Luke...Jared and Brax..."

"Bron is out front too." Luke added.

"He can go with me..." Palin said.

Tyg had entered Palin's room feeling a bit out of sorts. She knew Stills had reacted badly to her age and the fact Palin liked to make money off her arm wrestling people. Was he having second thoughts? She knew kissing him that morning had been a risk but she didn't think him being upset could impact on her this much. She sat on the bed and looked at the window. Since Stills obviously wasn't going to check on her any time soon...

As she entered the alleyway she made her way over to her old warehouse training ground. As she pulled the door back and stepped into the gloom she looked around remembering the last time she was in there.

She grimaced as she walked up to the spot where her blood still stained the floor boards. How was she going to find out anything? Wait...They were still looking for her weren't they? Isn't that why she was supposed to still lie low?

She walked out of the warehouse and boldly walked down the middle of the street, her long braid of silver blond hair uncovered by a hood. She made her way down the streets towards the lower city levels near the docks. If anyone dodgy was lurking about they would be down there.

Tyg looked at the sun. She had maybe three more hours of daylight left. She didn't want to risk getting caught at night. If she didn't draw anyone out in that time she would return to the Hide.

It only took one hour of walking around to get noticed by the right people. Tyg was aware of being followed. She grinned and walked down an alleyway. Two men suddenly appeared on either side of her, blocking her way. Big burly men with tattoos. Tyg suddenly felt an explosion of pain in her back just below her right shoulder. She was forced to her knees as another crack hit her back again. The two men laughed and grabbed her arms, hauling her to her feet, as a third man came from behind her and walked in front of her vision. He was tall and slim and wore a long black coat with blood red lining that flashed in your vision as he walked. His long black hair was half tied back and knotted at the back of his head, his eyes dark and vicious. He would have been quite handsome except for the pure evil caste to his sharp features. He was holding a long bull whip, curling it up around his arm as he smiled viciously at her.

"Got ya!" Redcoat said mercilessly as Tyg struggled to get free of the other two's grip on her arms. She kicked out sideways into one man's knee, causing him to lose balance as his leg buckled underneath him. Tyg wrenched her arm free and brought it straight round into the second man's face, making him stagger back with a broken nose.

"Fuck!" Redcoat yelled as he flicked his whip free again and lashed it out at Tyg again. She put her arm out to shield her face and the whip curled around her arm. A tug of war ensued between Redcoat and Tyg. She grabbed the whip with her other hand and dug her heels in and grit her teeth.

"How are you so fucking strong, bitch!" Redcoat growled surprised.

It didn't take long, however, for the other two men to jump on her again and they grappled her to the ground.

"Get her hands and feet tied." Redcoat ordered as he walked behind her again, flicking his whip out. Tyg was on her knees, being held firmly by the other two men, as they gripped her shoulders. Her arms were bound with rope by the wrists and elbows in front of her, and her ankles were bound.

Redcoat crouched down behind her and leaned forward towards her ear as he flicked her braid forward over her shoulder. "So you like to kill women and children, do you? What sort of monster are you?"

"That man was the fucking monster!" Tyg growled. The boy must have died and they have blamed me.

"He was our bread and butter." Redcoat stated then stood up and walked off a few steps. "Hold her still."

Tyg felt the same flash of pain in her back again as Redcoat started whipping her. Tyg grit her teeth as she felt the whip ripping through her shirt and biting into her flesh again. She grunted at the pain.

"Oh, you're tough, but no one holds out against a whip for too long...I want to hear you scream, bitch."

Tyg growled. "Fuck you!"

She felt another explosion of pain and struggled against the two men holding her shoulders. She was thankful for her fast healing making each lash slightly more bearable. Tyg yelled out in anger, shaking, mad at herself for her situation as the whip struck again.

The men all laughed and Redcoat walked back up behind her and grabbed her by her braid pulling her head back.

"Five lashes and not a single scream...I'm going to enjoy breaking you." He said as he tied a gag around her mouth. "Let's go, boys, we can't linger here." Redcoat pulled Tyg backwards by the hair a couple of yards then one of them picked her up over his shoulder.

Tyg struggled against the guy, making him slow down as they tried to run from the alleyway.

"Keep still, bit..."

Tyg was suddenly thrown to the ground, the wind knocked out of her. She heard her name being screamed by someone. Dazed she looked up and saw the man that was carrying her lying face down not moving. The other two guys were stopped a few yards off. Redcoat was shouting.

"Damn you, you bastard!" He yelled to someone behind Tyg that she couldn't see. "This isn't over!"

Tyg saw an arrow hit the second guy and he lurched and fell, but Redcoat dragged him to his feet and they disappeared round a corner. A figure came into Tyg's view and chased them...was that Luke?

"Tyg...fucking hell...are you okay?" Someone asked as they grabbed her and helped her to sit up, ripping the gag from her mouth.

Tyg looked up into the face of Stills. She smiled sadly at him once the gag was gone and shook her arms and hands out as Stills cut the ropes. He helped her to her feet and wrapped his arms around her.

"I'm so glad I found you. What were you thinking? You could have been killed. You're not invincible you know? You need to stop being so reckless." Stills berated her. Then he suddenly realised she had wrapped her arms around him and was clinging to him strongly, her head buried in his chest...she was crying silently. He wondered if she had ever cried before. He lowered his head to hers.

"It's okay, Tyg. I've got you now...it's over...we can go home." Stills whispered softly. Tyg shook her head against his chest. "Okay, not yet then. We'll just stay here till you're ready..."

Luke appeared at the end of the alley. Stills waved him away. Luke nodded his head and left to go find the others.

"Tyg?" Stills said softly. "Are you really okay...?"

Tyg looked up at him, her large luminous eyes watery and full of misery. Stills felt his heart tearing, looking at her face. There was the teenage girl he had seen only glimpses of up until now. Tyg let him go long enough to wipe her face. She took a deep breath but wrapped her arms around him again.

"I don't want to let you go right now." Tyg muttered. "But I'm fine...I just...I learnt a valuable lesson today...and my pride's taken a bit of a hit." Tyg chuckled ashamed.

"Are you serious? You were nearly killed, and you're talking about lessons and pride?" Stills said incredulously "Look at your shirt...its covered in blood. I mean what did they do?"

"That one guy...in the coat with the red lining....he had a whip."

"He whipped you?" Stills pulled her further into him. "Gods, Tyg...I'm sorry."

"What are you sorry for? It was my own stupid fault."

"I should never have left you alone, it was my job to protect you and I failed."

Tyg looked up at him again. "Don't blame yourself."

"I don't know what I would have done if I hadn't found you, Tyg." Stills met her gaze and stroked the side of her face, wiping away some dirt and tears.

"Seems I owe my life to you twice now." Tyg said smiling, then kissed him on the lips.

"Yes, you do...so let me care for you, okay? No more running off on your own."

"Okay." Tyg agreed as Stills leaned in and kissed her again deeper and more meaningful this time.

"Come on, let's get your back looked at."

"Its fine, Stills, I have a gift."

"A gift?"

"I heal really fast..."

Stills looked at Tyg's back, although her shirt was ripped and blood soaked her back showed only a few red marks. "Bloody hell, is this why Palin took you on?" Stills grit his teeth.

"He didn't know."

"But, he does now?"

"Yeah, the dagger wound."

"Fuck, I kind of forgot about that."

Tyg chuckled. "Yeah, it's completely healed, no scar.

Stills looked wide eyed at her. Tyg stepped away from him looking at the ground. "Let me guess, you're about to ask me 'what am I', right?" She said bitterly.

Stills grit his teeth, then he stripped off his bow and quiver and his sword belt, then removed his coat. He put it around Tyg's shoulders. "I don't care what you are...I just care, okay?" He bopped her on the nose and grinned. Tyg smiled and pushed her arms through the sleeves as Stills picked up his stuff again. "Are you ready to go back yet?"

"No...can we just walk..."

"Sure thing, little cat." Stills put his arm round her shoulders and walked her out of the alleyway and down the street. "Let's get something to eat, huh?"

"And drink?"

Stills laughed. "And she's back." Tyg smiled weakly. "I know just the place..." Stills said then and changed course heading up a different street and away from their usual side of the city.

17

He took her through to an area of the city she had rarely been. It was middle class, lots of merchants had their homes here. Stills led her to a small corner pub called The Stag and Hind. When they entered Stills led her over to a little quiet nook. There weren't many people in there and that suited Tyg just fine.

"What do you want?" Stills asked her as she sat down on the long bench against the wall. She was still feeling quite shaken by what happened and was more quiet than usual.

"Anything as long as its alcohol." Tyg muttered and propped her head up on her hand, her elbow on the table. "But, not rum."

"Okay." Stills laughed. "And something to eat?"

"If I have to..."

"I think it would be a good idea."

"Whatever you say my white knight." Tyg looked up at him, her eyes glowing slightly and smiled fondly at him.

Stills looked at her a moment. "The little cat and her white knight...sounds like the start of a great fairy tale." He laughed as he bent over and kissed her cheek.

"I'll let you know as the story progresses whether it's a fairy tale or not." Tyg smiled back at him.

"Ha! Okay then..." Stills wandered off to get the food and drinks ordered. Tyg looked around the place. It seemed so clean compared to taverns by the docks. It even had little vases with daises in them on the tables. Tyg took a daisy out of the vase and played with it, twirling it round in her fingers. Tyg heard a couple of people say hello to Stills like he was a local. He came back and sat beside her on the bench seat, putting his arm around her and pulling her into him protectively.

"Please tell me this isn't your favourite place for bringing girls?" Tyg asked teasingly.

"Ah, well...."

Tyg chuckled. "It's okay, you don't have to answer...I know you've had girls before. Gods, the other guys never seem to shut up about it."

"Hmm." Stills rubbed the back of his neck embarrassed. "But you're the most beautiful girl I've ever been on a date with."

Tyg sat up. "Is this a date?"

"Of course it is...I'm buying you dinner, plying you with alcohol." Stills laughed when he saw the shock on her face. "Don't worry, little cat, you're in safe hands."

Tyg looked away. "I know."

The serving girl brought over a tankard of ale and a bottle of red wine with a glass. Tyg looked at Stills shocked. "Red wine? You're spoiling me now."

"Well, after the day you've had. Besides that, we are still celebrating your acceptance to the Guild."

"Thank you." Tyg said. "Could you take me somewhere else after this...?"

"Sure where?"

"A bath house?"

"Oh...ah...okay. Maybe we should get you a change of clothes first?" Tyg screwed her face up. "Oh! That's adorable." Stills laughed.

"What?"

"That look, scrunching up your little nose." Stills bopped her nose. "Adorable."

"Shut up."

Stills laughed and took a long draught from his tankard as the serving girl brought their food to them. It was thick crusty bread and ham hock stew. After the first mouthful Tyg realised she did need food and ate it with gusto.

"See, you're looking better already." Stills said.

"Can I ask a favour?"

Stills looked at Tyg. "What is it?"

"Don't tell Palin about the situation you found me in, please." Tyg seemed quite distraught about it.

"Well, it might be too late for that, depends on if Luke has told him yet."

"Oh, that's right...Luke was there too."

"It's okay to fuck up every now and then you know, Tyg, that's how we learn."

"That's very grown up of you." Tyg smiled then looked away. "But, not the philosophy of Palin."

"Yeah, I get that too...he expects perfection...I've already come up against his fists today." Stills muttered.

"What!" Tyg spun on him.

Stills rubbed his jaw. "Yeah, he gave me a couple of whacks to the head for losing you." He saw Tyg's face change and clenched his jaw. "I'm fine, no need to worry...I deserved it."

"No! You don't!" Tyg growled. "I'm sorry I caused that."

"Don't be sorry, Tyg. It's fine...I told you that already." Stills scooped her into his arms and held her against his chest.

The serving girl came over with a fresh tankard of ale and put it on the table. She regarded the two of them and smiled.

"You've done good there, Stills." She said. "She's beautiful and you make a really cute couple."

Tyg lifted her head and looked at the woman. She seemed to be older, not a girl at all. Her hair braided into twin plaits made her appear younger at first glance, but she was probably in her thirties.

"Thanks Ma..." Stills said flushed. Tyg looked at him shocked. "Ma?"

The woman and Stills both laughed. "Oh, no...not that...it's short for Matilda...goodness no!" Matilda exclaimed.

"Oh...so does Stills come here often then?"

"Ah..." Matilda looked at Stills and flushed.

"We've already been through this, Tyg." Stills muttered, bopping her on the nose again.

"Hmm..." Tyg grunted at him, then turned back to Matilda. "So could you recommend a good bath house in this area?"

Matilda looked surprised a moment at the question. "Ah, sure...probably the best bet for a young girl like yourself at this time of the evening would be to come upstairs with me and let me sort you one here."

"Really, you would do that?" Tyg asked surprised.

"Wow, Ma...that's a great offer." Stills said also surprised.

"No worries, it would definitely be safer.....that's all."

"Yeah definitely...what do you say, Tyg?" Stills asked encouragingly.

"Sure, sounds good...but aren't you busy down here?"

"Not really tonight." Matilda said looking around. "You stay here and wait while I get it filled...finish your food and drink."

"I'm going to need a new shirt as well..." Tyg muttered a bit ashamed.

"Oh! Okay....well I'm sure we can find something for you to wear, at least until you get home."

"Thank you so much, Ma." Stills said smiling at her.

"Yes, thank you." Tyg smiled.

"No problem, I'm just happy for Stills, here." Matilda said as she walked off.

"Well, that worked out well...how's that fairy tale going, little cat?" Stills asked as he pulled her closer into him again.

"So far so good." Tyg said and kissed his cheek, then lay her head on his chest again.

"Maybe we should stay here the night?" Stills muttered, half to himself.

"What?" Tyg looked up at him. He looked at her with that smoulder for a second, then blinked and looked away smiling.

"Not what I meant..." Stills explained. "But you obviously don't want to go back to the Hide tonight."

"Not really..."

"So, while you have your bath I can go back, get your clothes and tell Palin that you're found and safe and where you are..."

"Sounds like a plan." Tyg smiled a genuinely happy smile, warming Stills' heart to see it. She straightened her right leg and dug into the pocket of her pants and pulled out the key, holding it out to Stills.

"But, you have to promise me you'll stay put, little cat." Stills said sternly as he took the key.

"Of course, my knight." Tyg grinned.

By the time Stills returned to the little corner pub Tyg was upstairs in a room for the night. He knocked on the door. Tyg opened it and let him in. She was wrapped in a blanket off the bed, her hair was still damp and she had a brush in her hand that Matilda had given her.

"I got your stuff and fed your cat." Stills said as he placed her bag on the bed, then sat down beside it and looked up at her. She was frowning at him, her eyes blazing. He knew what she was looking at. "It's fine, little cat." He grimaced as he touched the split in his eyebrow from where Palin had hit him again.

"Tell me what happened..." Tyg said quietly as she sat on the bed and drew her legs up underneath her, settling the blanket round her bare feet. Stills got a flash of naked thigh.

He stood up flushing. "You're naked?"

"No." Tyg said amused. "Not entirely...but I've been waiting for you to get back."

"Shit, little cat." Stills rubbed the back of his neck. "Should I leave then...while you get dressed?"

"Just let me put a shirt on, I'm not sleeping in leather pants."

"Huh...okay..." Stills turned his back as Tyg dug into her bag and found a clean shirt and cropped singlet that she wore underneath, which she put on, dropping the blanket so it was tucked in round her waist.

"Okay...now tell me what happened."

Stills glanced over his shoulder and clenched his jaw, than sat back on the bed.

"Palin wasn't happy that I didn't insist on you going straight back there and he was even less happy when I told him you wanted to stay the night here."

"So he hit you again?"

Stills shrugged. "I was expecting it."

"That doesn't make it right."

"No...but he's the Boss and after threatening to chuck me out of the Guild...well...this is easier to accept."

"He did what?" Tyg growled.

"He's the Boss, Tyg and I did fuck up."

"Yeah, so did I..."

"That's why you won't go back?"

"Who wants to go somewhere they know they'll get beaten..."

"I doubt he would hit you..."

Tyg regarded him with an eyebrow raised. "I know he will."

"What for? Nearly getting killed?"

"Exactly." Tyg grimaced.

"You're kidding?" Stills looked at her face. "You're not kidding...fucking hell."

"And you didn't come back alone, did you?"

"Ah...no." Stills said with a wry smile. "Bron is here as well as Jared." Stills rolled his eyes.

Tyg grinned. "Jared likes giving you a hard time, huh?"

"He's a pillock!"

Tyg laughed. "So what are they doing?"

"Just watching the place. I told Palin about the guy in the black coat with the red lining. Don't worry, Luke hadn't mentioned anything, he had waited for us to get back. So Palin doesn't know any of those details. Only that we found you in an altercation with that guy and his cronies."

"Thank you." Tyg said bitter sweet as she shuddered at the memory.

"I imagine there are more of the Guild outside watching the place, but Palin is wanting you back at the Hide as soon as it's light."

"Hmm." Tyg muttered and shuffled her feet under the covers and threw the blanket down as she lay down and put her head on the pillow, lying on her side. She curled herself into a ball.

Stills awkwardly scratched his chin and looked around the simple but clean room. "I would go and let you sleep..." Tyg looked up at him without moving. "...but Palin ordered me not to leave your side for any reason until I hand you to him tomorrow."

"Hand me to him?" Tyg grimaced.

"His words, not mine."

"So what if I go to the bathroom, you going to follow me there too?"

"Tyg..." Stills sat forward leaning his elbows on his knees and glanced sideways at her. "...Don't make this any harder than it already is."

Tyg smiled and looked away, closing her eyes. "Guess we'll cross that bridge when we come to it then..."

"Hmm." Stills grunted as he grabbed the extra blanket Tyg had tossed and pulling his boots off he lay down on the floor. Tyg sat up slightly and peered over the edge of the bed. Stills had his arms under his head and he glanced up at her. He smiled. "You look like a puppy dog with those big eyes peering over the edge like that."

"What are you doing?"

"Going to sleep, isn't that what you're doing?"

"So, now we're officially dating you can't sleep next to me?"

"Ah...technically I am next to you..." Stills said coyly, crossing his ankles.

"You know what I mean." Tyg sat up a bit more and glared down on him. "You don't need to sleep on the hard floor."

"Probably best that I do." Stills said smiling and closed his eyes as a lock of her hair fell and touched his face.

"You have a blanket, you can lie on top of the covers and be comfortable. Stop being such a jackass and get up here!" Tyg growled.

Stills opened one eye and peered at her. He unfolded his arms and touched the lock of hair, curling it round his finger. "Okay, just stop looking down on me like that, it's too adorable."

Tyg smiled and shuffled back to the other side of the bed against the wall and lay her head down, as Stills got up and lay on the bed next to her. Tyg was looking at him, smiling, as he looked at the ceiling.

"Stop it, Tyg." He said, then turned his head and regarded her quietly.

"Thank you for everything you've done for me today, White Knight."

Stills turned onto his side facing her and reached out a hand. He flicked her hair back off her face. "That's quite alright, little cat. Now get some sleep." He bopped her nose. Tyg grinned and suddenly kissed him on the lips then turned over to face the wall.

"Good night, Stefan."

Stills smiled to himself. "Good night, Tyg." He turned over and blew the candle out.

Sometime during the night Tyg woke up. She sat up startled looking around in the darkness. Stills was awake instantly.

"What's wrong?" He asked also sitting up. It was very dark in the little room and Stills could only just make out Tyg's outline.

"I had a bad dream." Tyg shuddered. "I'm fine...go back to sleep."

Stills lay back down. "Are you sure?" He wondered if it had been about the man in the red lined coat.

"Yes..." Stills didn't think it sounded very convincing.

"You want me to hold you? No funny stuff...I promise." Tyg suddenly pushed up against him and he moved his arm so she could snuggle into his side, her head on his chest. He lowered his arm round her and pulled her into him. "Better?"

"Yes, thank you."

"No need to thank me, you can use me any time you need, what are White Knights for." Stills chuckled. "Good night again, Tyg."

"Night." Tyg whispered smiling happily to herself.

18

When Tyg woke in the morning she was on her side facing the wall. Stills was behind her, pressed up against her back, his arm over her protectively. Tyg smiled to herself. This was amazing, she had never woken up in someone's arms before and she liked how much better she slept being held by someone. She didn't want this to come to an end, so she closed her eyes again and wrapped Stills' arm up in hers hugging it to her chest. She was aware that it meant his hand was touching her breast, but she didn't care.

Stills groaned a little in his sleep at the movement and brushed her breast with his hand cupping and cradling it as he slept. Tyg smiled to herself, enjoying the strange intimacy without Stills being aware of what he was doing.

"As nice as this is, we need to get up." Stills whispered in her ear.

Tyg blushed but didn't move. "Damn, you always manage to do that." Tyg muttered.

Stills chuckled and nuzzled into the back of her neck, kissing her, causing goose bumps on her flesh. Then he took his arm back and sat up. He shuffled back and leaned his back on the wall. Tyg rolled over onto her other side and put her head on his thigh. He looked down at her shocked for a moment then smiled and played with her hair. He had to keep reminding himself of her sexual innocence.

"Still don't want to go back, huh?"

"Not at all...and worse I have to go to Barion's today. I hate that man."

"He's the jeweller, who runs the Hut, yeah?"

"What? A jeweller...I don't know, but he runs the Thieves' Guild."

"Right...good side job...convenient."

"Yeah, I suppose...I always wondered what he did with the jewels."

Stills looked at the little window in the room and saw that it was getting light. "We really need to be going, Tyg."

"Just a few more minutes...he's already angry, what's being a bit late going to do...?"

"Best not to poke a bear."

Tyg looked up at Stills smiling at the strange comment. She shuffled up a bit so her head was on his chest. She put her arm around him and clung to him. Stills grit his teeth as he gently held her head.

"Tyg, I'm going to find that guy in the coat and I'm going to whip the flesh from his bones and then I'm going to fill him full of arrows."

Tyg sat up and turned her body to face him, curling her legs up and pulled the blanket up. Her face showed her surprise. "My White Knight." She breathed as she crashed her mouth to his and kissed him as she wrapped her arms around his neck.

He wrapped his arms around her and kissed her back. He rolled them over on the bed so he was lying on top of her.

Just then someone banged on the door.

"Get up, lovebirds, we have to go!" It was Bron's voice.

Stills looked down at Tyg and smiled and grimaced at the same time. "Just as well I suppose..." He said and climbed off her and got up. He started putting his boots on. "I'll wait for you downstairs." He glanced back at her. She was sitting up looking at him, a pink blush on her cheeks as the sun started filtering in the small window.

As he stood up Tyg reached up and grabbed his arm. He turned back and saw Tyg was kneeling on the bed. Lucky her shirt just covered her modesty as she pulled him down and kissed him again. He resisted the temptation of pushing her down on her back again and stepped back, bopping her nose.

"Fucking hell, little cat...get dressed before you get into some serious trouble." He said his eyes smouldering intensely at her. He shook his head to clear his thoughts and chuckled as he left the room.

Tyg grinned. Whatever this day brings at least it started well, she thought as she got up.

As they entered the Hide Palin was waiting for them in the front room. He had been looking out the window so as soon as they stepped in, he called out.

"In here, now!"

Tyg flinched against Stills side. As they stepped into the front room Palin frowned at Stills.

"You can wait in the hall, this is between me and her." Palin growled.

Stills stepped away from Tyg and back pedalled out of the room, closing the door. Tyg stood in front of Palin, her hands in her pockets and her head down. So she wasn't expecting the back hand when it hit. She staggered sideways and pulled her hands out of her pockets just as Palin struck her again. She staggered again and fell to her knees. She tasted blood.

"What the hell were you thinking?" Palin yelled at her as she looked up at him, her eyes blazing. He hit her again. "Don't fucking look at me like that, girly!"

Tyg flinched as he called her that, it had been months since he had called her that. "I'm sorry Palin...I just..."

He went to strike her again but stopped when he saw her flinch. He realised she was just going to let him keep hitting her, even though she had the strength and training to stop him. He lowered his hand and scowled. "Damn it, Tyg....I could have lost you."

"I know...but, this is all my own doing, it's because of the Guilliano job, that guy with the coat said as much."

"Hmm, that guy is Raven and he's part of the Annul branch of the Guild."

"What!"

"They were a squad, Tyg...they would have killed you...eventually...he has a bloody nasty reputation."

Tyg grimaced at what Raven had said about breaking her. "Yeah, I got that much."

"Good, so perhaps you'll behave yourself for fucking five minutes and let the grownups deal with this?" Palin growled. "He's obviously gone rogue so I need to set up a meeting with his Guild."

Tyg bowed her head. "Yes, Boss."

Palin turned and walked back to the chair he had been sitting in and sat down heavily. "Get up for fuck's sake." Tyg clambered to her feet. "Go and get cleaned up...have you eaten yet?" Tyg shook her head. "Right, meet me in the kitchen with that bloody Stills after then."

"Okay." Tyg said meekly as she went to the door and opened it. She turned in the doorway and looked back at Palin, he was staring at her with a strange look on his face. "I'm really sorry..."

"Pah!" Palin growled. "Go, damn it."

As Tyg stepped back into the hallway she put her hand to her mouth. It came away bloody.

"Fuck, Tyg...are you okay?" Stills asked as he stood up from where he had been leaning on the wall.

"I'm fine." Tyg said as she pushed past him and went towards the stairs. He grabbed her arm and pulled her backwards into him, wrapping his arms around her.

"He shouldn't have hit you. Hitting women is wrong."

"Is killing them?" Tyg said bitterly but she relaxed into him.

"To be honest I don't know the moral rules on women hurting women, but men shouldn't." He tried to make light of the situation. Tyg turned round to look at him, an eyebrow raised.

"I guess that's why I'm here..."

The door to the front room suddenly opened and Palin was standing there staring at them. His eyes went dark seeing Tyg in Stills embrace, but Stills quickly stepped back away from her.

"I thought I told you to go get cleaned up." Palin growled.

"I was just going..." Tyg rolled her eyes causing Palin to step up to her and raise his hand. Stills growled and suddenly his hand wrapped around Palin's wrist. Tyg's eyes went wide as Stills and Palin locked eyes.

"Enough of hitting her, for fuck's sake..." Stills muttered.

Palin blinked and pulled his arm back. "Both of you better get the fuck out of my sight right the fuck now!"

Stills clenched his jaw as Tyg grabbed his hand and pulled him down the hall and up the stairs to Palin's room.

Palin stood a moment with his arms crossed as he watched them disappear up the stairs, then shook his head. He hadn't expected Stills to fall so hard and so fast for the girl.

"What the fuck was that?" Tyg admonished Stills once they were in the bedroom.

"Fuck, I don't know...instinct took over." Stills looked bewildered.

Tyg looked at him with wide eyes. "Don't do that." She turned away and walked over to the dresser. "I can fight my own battles."

"I know that...but you wouldn't with him...would you? You're happy to just let him hit you." Stills said frustrated. "Well, I'm not!"

Tyg poured some water into a bowl and grabbed a cloth and cleaned the blood off her face. She looked up at him as she wiped her chin, and smiled at him. "You know the whole white knight thing was a joke...I didn't mean for you to take it seriously."

Stills grimaced and sat down in the chair in the corner and sighed. "Like I said, I don't know what came over me." He went quiet and watched Tyg as she finished cleaning her face, then got a brush and started brushing her hair, pulling it up into a ponytail then braiding it.

"You've got blood on your shirt." Stills muttered then.

"What?"

"There's blood on your shirt." Stills indicated at a couple of drops of blood.

Tyg looked down and swore then pulled the shirt off and threw it on the bed and started rummaging in her bag for a clean one. Stills grit his teeth and looked away.

"Fuck, little cat, you need to stop doing shit like that, okay?"

Tyg looked up at him surprised, then smirked. "You just had your hand on one this morning pretending to be asleep, you perv."

Stills looked back at her shocked as she pulled a clean shirt up over her head. He took the moment to appraise her flat stomach and smooth fair skin. The singlet she was still wearing covering her breasts. As she poked her head through and pulled the shirt down she glanced up at him, looking at him under her lashes. Stills was smouldering darkly at her again.

"And, it was delightful, little cat, a wonderful way to wake up."

Tyg walked over to him as he leaned back in the chair looking up at her. Something had changed in her. She didn't seem so nervous about intimacy around him now. He grit his teeth as she climbed into his lap and wrapped her arms around his neck. He locked eyes with her.

"We're supposed to be taking this slow. I didn't think it would be me reminding you of that." He said to her as she smiled beguilingly at him.

"Shut up." Tyg whispered and kissed him, forcing her tongue into his mouth. He wrapped his arms around her and kissed her back as smells of bacon cooking wafted up from the kitchen. They looked at each other as the smells hit their nostrils and Stills stomach growled. Stills grinned.

"I'm famished, I don't know about you."

"Palin did say to get cleaned up and go to the kitchen and bring you."

"Palin's cooking?"

"Yeah, I think so..."

Stills struggled up to his feet causing Tyg to stand. "I'm not missing his cooking..."

"He's good at cooking?"

"Breakfasts he is..." Stills grinned. "Come on..."

"But what about what just happened with him..."

Stills smiled knowingly at Tyg. "You think we all don't have our disagreements?" Tyg looked at him blankly. "The thing with arguments, Tyg, is to forgive after things are said otherwise they fester." He looked at her strangely. "You really don't know much about human interaction do you?"

Tyg flinched. "It was best I kept mostly to myself growing up."

"Well, little cat...I'm here now..." Stills grabbed her gently round the head and pulled her into him and kissed her forehead. "Come on, I'm starving..."

As they walked into the kitchen Palin was fussing round the coal range, he had several pans on the go and suddenly the house was full of men.

"Word gets around..." Stills said smiling and leaned against the wall as all the chairs were already taken.

Tyg walked up behind Palin and wrapped her arms around him, hugging him tightly. "I'm sorry, Palin."

He froze and looked shocked, then turned slightly and reached out and hooked her neck with his arm and hugged her back.

"Its fine, Tyg, just learn the lesson and move on."

Tyg smiled. Stills was right. She glanced up at Stills and he winked at her. All the other guys in the room were looking at her with wide eyes. She smiled shyly and walked into Stills, who wrapped his arms around her protectively smirking at all the others.

Brax stood up. "Here, kitty cat, have my seat." He said cheerfully. He then got barraged with comments concerning his arm wrestle loss to her the day before.

Tyg smiled and grabbed Stills hand and pushed him into the seat then sat on his lap.

"Hey, no fair, you could have sat on my knee." Brax complained.

"Knock it off, Brax." Stills said amused.

"The chair was nearly breaking under you as it was..." Tyg muttered at him, causing everyone in the room to roar with laughter, except Brax who folded his arms and grumbled to himself. Stills realised then that Tyg was more than capable of holding her own.

Palin started putting plates of food on the table and the guys tucked into it.

Tyg grabbed a piece of bacon and ate it watching with disgust at the table manners of them all as it seemed like some sort of competition to see who could eat the most in the shortest amount of time. Tyg reached out for another piece of bacon before it was all gone. Palin rapped her on the back of the hand with his spatula.

"Don't forget you've got a brunch to go to."

Tyg scowled at him and stuck the bacon in her mouth. "How could I forget?"

He looked at her. "Look, I know you don't like Barion and to be frank he doesn't much like you either, but..."

"What? Who doesn't like our kitty cat?!" Brax growled from across the table making Stills frown at him. Palin gave him a look to shut up and continued.

"...it's for the best right now that you go stay over there, trust me."

"Where's she going?" Jared asked then, causing Palin to roll his eyes and address the room.

"Tyg is none of any of you lots business, okay."

"No, we just spent hours searching for her yesterday cause she was a Guild member in trouble..." Jared growled back, causing Tyg to choke on her food shocked.

"I'm sorry." She mumbled.

"Sorry my arse!" Brax said. "You're a Guild member now, we would all die for you, got it!" He looked at her then at Palin.

Palin rubbed his eyes and shrugged. "Fuck's sake." He muttered as he realised what Brax was saying.

"I don't know what to say..." Tyg blushed.

"You're family now, Kitty cat, got it." Brax said to her smiling. She looked around at the other men, they were all looking at her. She looked down at the table. Stills squeezed her waist encouragingly.

"That's enough, guys...fuck. All of your ugly faces looking at her is enough to give anyone nightmares." Stills said.

"Ha! Yeah we all know yours is the only face she wants to see right now..." Brax huffed. Bron came up and whacked him over the head.

"Enough man, fuck's sake."

Tyg got up. "I'm going to get ready to leave..." They could all see her awkwardness and Stills stood up as well, standing behind her.

As she left the room Stills stopped and looked at Jared and Brax. "Good going." He growled then slammed the door shut.

"What did I say?" Brax asked causing Bron to whack him again.

Palin sighed. "She doesn't do well in groups..." He muttered and sat down and helped himself to food. "She'll get over it...but will you lot?"

"What's that supposed to mean?"

"Ha!" Palin just laughed. "Forget it."

19

Tyg stepped up to the door of a white stone house in a long line of white stone houses similar to the tenement housing in Palin's area but white, and clean. With street lighting and wrought iron balustrades with shiny black doors and brass knockers.

"Shit, Barion lives here?"

"Hmm." Palin grunted.

"Why the fuck does he spend all his time at the Hut then?"

"Because that's where he earns his money..." Palin muttered. "Come on..."

Palin walked up and knocked on the door. It opened to reveal the face of a middle aged woman with straw coloured hair. She was a decent looking woman, but tiny and smiled openly and friendly at them.

"Palin." She greeted him, causing Tyg to raise an eyebrow not realising they already knew each other.

"Mae, nice to see you." Palin returned, then turned sideways on the doorstep. "This is Tyg." He said. Tyg lifted her hood and let it fall behind her and smiled awkwardly at the woman in front of her.

"Hi." Tyg muttered.

Mae's eyes had gone wide. "Oh my, you better come in child, quickly."

She ushered them in. "Just put your things down here and we can sort that later, please come into the front room....Barion is waiting."

Tyg scowled and Palin looked at her. "Knock it off! He's saving your arse."

"At what cost?" Tyg asked causing Palin to look at her surprised. "There's always a cost with Barion...remember..." She said bitterly recalling the day Palin had to pay Barion money for her.

"Fuck's sake, let it go." Palin growled as they stepped into the front room. "And keep your mouth shut."

Barion was standing in front of his chair waiting for them to enter. Mae walked in and indicated for Palin and Tyg to sit down on the couch that faced Barion.

"Palin, good to see you again." Barion said with a grin as Palin walked up to him and shook his hand.

"Barion, thanks for this." Palin said casually and sat down. Tyg sat down next to him, crossing her legs and folding her arms.

"Tyg." Barion said coolly.

Tyg smiled at him but said nothing. Barion frowned then grinned as he sat down.

"So what have you gone and done now?" Barion asked then.

Tyg grit her teeth as Palin sat forward. "That doesn't matter to you, Barion."

"Really? Is my life in danger and that of my wife's by her being here?"

Palin shrugged. "Your life is in danger regardless, just by your own job description, so nothing in your life will change with her being here for a while." Palin muttered. "Stop trying to get a rise out of her...we have already discussed this. And as I have informed you, Kor wants her on this side of the city."

Barion was staring at Tyg with an amused expression. "I just needed to know that she had a grip on her temper these days...I don't need that sort of psychotic behaviour under my roof, I need to be able to sleep at night."

Palin smiled and glanced at Tyg. "She's all good." Tyg looked at him and smiled a sarcastic grin at him. Palin laughed. "See."

"Hmm, well any indiscretion, any at all...just once and she's out of here...got it."

"Got it."

Tyg looked at Mae who had sat down in a chair on the other side of Barion, she was staring at Tyg with a whimsical look on her face. Tyg raised an eyebrow at her and stared back, her eyes changing colour to ice blue.

"Oh my..." Mae breathed. Barion looked over at her and noticed Tyg's expression.

"I warned you." He said to Mae.

"Dearest, you did not warn me at all...you did not tell me that she was an angel."

Tyg baulked and looked at Palin panicked. "Calm down Tyg, it's just a compliment..."

Palin turned to Mae. "She doesn't do well with compliments."

"What on earth do you mean?" Mae said standing up and coming over to Tyg and taking her hand. "What have you been doing with this girl, locking her in a box?"

Palin frowned. "She doesn't like people, it's her own choice to stay away from them." Mae looked doubtfully at Palin.

"Well, we will have to change that...I think you would be perfect for my new adventure."

"Your new adventure?" Tyg muttered taking her hand back from Mae with disgust.

Barion laughed. "Oh, Mae, I think you are barking up the wrong tree there...this girl is borderline sociopathic, I don't think she would go well in any of your ventures."

"Maybe, it's just what she needs..." Palin muttered.

Tyg turned to him and her eyes blazed. "Like fuck, Palin!"

"Oh, there she is, finally!" Barion said leaning back in his chair.

"Tyg!" Palin growled.

"No way, Palin. I am not staying quiet while these people talk about me like I'm some sort of social experiment."

"Oh dear, no that's not it at all, sorry, you have misunderstood me." Mae uttered franticly.

"Leave it, Mae." Barion said grumpily. "Show her to her room...Palin and I need to talk."

Tyg stood up staring at Barion causing him to swallow hard. Tyg grinned then followed Mae out.

In the hall Tyg picked up the wicker basket that had her cat in it. Mae looked at it shocked.

"Oh, you have a cat...I don't think Barion likes cats..."

"Well, I don't like Barion, yet here we are..." Tyg sneered, then saw the shocked look on Mae's face. Tyg sighed. "I'm sorry, look I'll keep him in my room, he will go in and out the window, Barion will never see him. He's a good mouser..."

"Okay..." Mae said as she took the basket letting Tyg pick up her bags and followed Mae up the stairs to her new room.

Tyg was surprised at the space in it, and the fact that she had a double bed all to herself. She smiled to herself. She could get used to this.

She opened the window that opened out to the main street and then opened the basket, letting her cat out. He jumped onto the windowsill and looked out at the street washing a paw casually.

"Your cat seems to be right at home." Mae said amused.

"Yeah, he's used to moving around with me."

"How long have you had him?"

"Ah, maybe a year or so..."

"What's his name?"

"He doesn't have one..."

"You've never named him?"

"He's not a pet...it's hard to explain...he's a companion, it would be wrong to name him."

Mae looked at Tyg like she was weird but then changed the subject.

"Okay well, let me show you the rest of the house and then we can take the pastries and tea into the front room, the men are hopefully finished with their talk..."

Tyg rolled her eyes. "I'm sorry about all this."

"Oh, don't be child...it will be nice to have another woman in the house." Mae smiled friendly.

"Ah, well...you do know what I do, right?"

"I know enough not to ask questions, dear, and that is enough." Mae indicated the fact that Tyg was wearing black and carrying weapons.

Tyg smiled. "Okay."

The brunch had gone awkwardly and Palin had finally left followed very quickly by Barion. Tyg went up to her room and was standing looking out the window when she saw a familiar figure walking up the street. She grinned and raced down the stairs in time to hear the knock at the door.

Tyg beat Mae to the door and opened it, pulling Stills inside. Mae looked surprised as she stood in the hallway and looked at the tall, lean, good looking man wearing a black military style waistcoat and coat, armed to the hilt, standing in her house. Tyg turned to Mae.

"This is Stills...you'll be seeing him a lot."

Tyg pulled him into the front room and closed the door.

"Hey, Tyg," Stills said amused looking at her surprised. "Getting settled in..."

Tyg rolled her eyes. "I suppose so...I don't really know what I'm supposed to do here."

"Well, I can help with that...I am here to take you over to the warehouse."

Tyg smiled and wrapped her arms around Stills waist. He wrapped his arms around her and kissed her forehead. "I missed you." Tyg muttered into his chest.

He leaned back making her look up at him, "I missed you too, little cat." He kissed her lips and she pressed her body against him kissing him back eagerly. "Come on, we have to go."

"Alright...but do I tell Mae or not? I don't know..."

Stills looked at Tyg strangely for a moment. She really didn't have any idea about social interactions. "Yes, Tyg...let her know you'll be back at dusk."

Tyg smiled at him. "Okay..."

Tyg wandered down the hall while Stills waited at the door. She found Mae in the kitchen peeling potatoes. She stopped and gave Tyg a pleasant smile.

"I'm going out....ah...work...be back at dusk."

"Thank you, Tyg, I'll see you then, I'm making potato gratin for dinner."

"I don't know what that is...but okay."

"Will your friend join us for dinner?"

Tyg frowned. "I don't know..."

Mae smiled. "Shall we ask him then?"

Tyg shrugged as Mae wiped her hands on her apron and walked out into the hallway. Stills straightened as he saw her approach with Tyg behind her looking strangely at him.

"Ma'am." Stills said politely.

"Hello, just call me Mae, you are close to Tyg?" Stills looked over Mae's shoulder and saw Tyg scowling. Stills grinned.

"Yes, I'm her boyfriend." Stills laughed when he saw Tyg's face as her eyes widened, but blazed at him.

"Oh, I see..." Mae said just as surprised.

"Alright, that's enough...this is really no one's business." Tyg said tartly as she barged past the both of them and opened the front door. Stills laughed again and grabbed Tyg's wrist firmly.

"Easy there, little cat, put a damn hood on before you go outside."

Tyg hesitated and stepped backwards a step looking at him. "Ah...yeah...right, hang on." Tyg raced up the stairs to her room to grab her coat.

"So, will you be coming back here for dinner?" Mae was asking Stills as Tyg came back down the stairs.

Stills smiled. "Depends, are you a good cook?"

Mae grinned. "Yes, actually I am."

"Then, if Tyg wants me here, I'll be here."

"Of course I want you here..." Tyg smiled as she put an arm around his waist. Mae looked at the two of them and smiled.

"Lovely couple..." She muttered. Stills chuckled.

"You're not the first person to say that." He said amused as he cradled Tyg's head with his hand and kissed her hair. "Come on we have to go....nice to meet you, Mae."

"Till tonight then, you two." Mae said as they walked out onto the street, Tyg pulling her hood up.

They kept to the side streets and alleys so they weren't too noticeable as they made their way over to the warehouse.

"She seems nice..." Stills said.

"Too nice." Tyg muttered.

"How can someone be too nice?" Stills asked confused.

Tyg shook her head and shrugged. "I don't know, I'm just not used to people being nice I guess, not without them wanting something....especially her being Barion's wife."

"I'm nice to you, and don't want anything." Stills said smiling.

Tyg stopped walking and smirked at him. "You do want something..."

Stills turned back and smouldered at her. "Well, perhaps I do...someday." He turned and kept walking. Tyg watched his back for a moment and smiled to herself then ran to catch up, grabbing his arm with hers and hugging it.

Stills looked sideways at her. "If you want my opinion, I think Mae seems pretty genuine."

20

As Tyg entered the warehouse with Stills she saw Luke and Bron were there, sitting on a couple of crates. Bron had a lute and was strumming it casually. Tyg raised an eyebrow.

"What are you guys doing here?"

"Waiting for you..." Bron said with a grin, looking at Stills. "Did you not tell her?"

"No, I thought it best to wait." Stills said glancing sideways at Tyg

"What the fuck is going on here?" Tyg asked, her eyes going ice blue.

"Palin has decided to try and team us up."

"Us..." Tyg said looking at Luke and Bron.

"Oh, come on..." Luke said. "We're not that bad....are we?"

Tyg smiled. "No, I guess not, I could think of worse..."

"Like?" Bron pressed grinning. Stills jumped up on a large crate facing her and smirked. Tyg could see she was not going to get any support from him in this. Tyg screwed her face up at him. He grinned at her.

"Brax and Jared." Tyg shrugged causing them all to laugh.

"Good answer." Stills said reaching out for her and pulling her over to him.

"So, you play the lute? That's surprising..." Tyg said to Bron, who strummed it at her grinning.

"Name a tune."

Tyg shrugged. "I have no idea..."

"Okay, how about this one..." Bron started playing a light jingle about hay girls at harvest time.

Tyg scowled at him. "How about The Ballad of Jonquil Boates." Stills interjected.

Bron changed the tune and started playing the slower tune of the ballad.

"Oh, I know this..." Tyg said as she leaned back on the crate between Stills open knees as he put his arms around her shoulders. She started to sing the ballad.

All three guys stared at her as she sang, with wonder in their eyes. Stills clenched his jaw and stared over her shoulder at the other two guys.

Bron and Luke looked at him. Stills tried to communicate to Bron to stop playing, but Bron just shook his head and looked away ignoring him. Stills frowned. He didn't want these guys looking at Tyg the way they were right now, it was making him angry and jealous. He knew it was unreasonable, she was only singing but...he was relieved when the song finished.

"Fucking hell, Tyg, that was amazing!" Bron said as Luke clapped and cheered.

"I had no idea you could sing like that, little cat." Stills whispered in her ear.

"Well you wouldn't...but now you do." Tyg said turning to look at him amused.

"I guess so..." Stills said smouldering at her as she put her hands on his thighs and reached up on her toes and kissed him.

"Sing another one..." Luke said, nudging Bron.

"What about the one about Highwayman Jack?" Bron started playing the tune. Tyg looked at Stills and smiled at him as his eyes darkened but Luke stood up and pulled her away from Stills and sat her down next to Bron.

"Sing not kiss." Luke laughed.

"Who got to decide that exactly...?" Stills muttered folding his arms. He went quiet as Tyg started singing the song.

Tyg was halfway through the song when Palin stormed in.

"What the fuck is going on in here?" He stared at Tyg who immediately shut up, her eyes wide.

"We were just passing the time with a song or two." Luke said shrugging.

Palin growled. "Every passer-by on the fucking street is stopping to listen to her fucking sing."

"Well, yeah they probably would, she's got an amazing voice..." Bron said as he put the lute down. They had all noticed Tyg's reaction and how she had slowly stood up and retreated into the arms of Stills, looking at Palin with great concern. Stills was frowning concerned as he wrapped his arms around her protectively. "What's the problem, Boss?"

"The problem is you're causing us to be noticed...and what is one thing she is NOT supposed to be doing?" Palin was raging. "Plus, she knows she is not supposed to sing!"

"I'm sorry." Tyg muttered.

"No, we're sorry, Boss, we kind of made her do it."

"You made her do it?" Palin folded his arms.

"Yeah, well...it was either sing or we had to watch her kissing Stills, which would you prefer?" Bron said grinning.

"Shut the fuck up." Stills muttered.

Palin looked at the four of them and smirked, rubbing his eyes. "Fuck's sake, I'm working with complete morons."

"But at least we're all bonding well..." Bron grinned.

"Take the advice of your bond mate, Bron and shut the fuck up!" Palin muttered. "I need to talk to Tyg."

He indicated with his head for her to follow him over to the other side of the warehouse. Tyg glanced up at Stills and then wandered off. Stills frowned and scratched his jaw.

"I have to warn you." Palin said as Tyg walked up to him. "Mae, it seems, has her sights set on you joining her little venture, and apparently Kor thinks it's a good idea too, so..."

"Wait a minute..." Tyg scowled. "I work for you...not Mae...not Kor."

"Yes, well, as I have explained to you, certain people are involved in the information we gather..." Tyg folded her arms. "You are going to open new avenues for getting that information."

"Do I really want to know where this is heading?"

"Probably not." Palin scoffed. "However, I just wanted to warn you that when you get back to Barion's you're going to have it suggested to you..."

"And I have to say yes..."

"Yes."

"Is that an order?"

"Yes."

Tyg's eyes blazed and Palin frowned. "Tyg, don't look at me like that, do as you are told. Oh, and you're going to have the chance to sing..."

"What the fuck..." Tyg growled.

"I thought you would be happy about that, since you didn't seem to have a problem singing to them."

"I am not singing in front of people!"

"You'll do as you are told." Tyg stared at him. "Don't look at me like that, Tyg." Palin warned with a growl again.

Tyg looked away. "Are we done here?"

"No, we are not...I have made contact with the Annul Guild...unfortunately Raven hasn't gone rogue..."

"What?"

"They are adamant that a meeting must be held, they want to discuss your validity being in the Guild here."

"Can they do that?"

"No, not really." Palin said. "The Guilliano murders happened before you joined so were done outside of Guild knowledge, but because it involved children, they want to seek that you are handed over to them as they have a contract out for you."

"Do they have any proof?"

"None, other than your description."

"Fuck, so what now?"

"I'm going to ignore it for now, and think on it...if I have to hold a meeting with my Guild and tell them what's going on, it's going to come out that you were responsible for the murders..."

Tyg looked at the ground. "You've dug me a hole, Palin."

"Don't worry, Tyg, just stay low...I've got your back, don't worry...I'll sort this...just because you look like you do, is no evidence that you were in Annul...all I need is to create you an alibi."

"It better be a bloody good one..."

"Don't worry, Tyg." Palin held his fist out and Tyg begrudgingly touched it with hers.

They turned just as Jared and Brax walked in the warehouse with two more guys wearing the same black ensemble that said they were assassins.

"What's all this?" Tyg muttered to Palin as they walked back towards where Bron, Luke and Stills were sitting.

"They are just reporting in, Tyg...go back to your boyfriend." Palin muttered back. Tyg looked sharply at him with an eyebrow raised, but then grinned and wandered back to where Stills was still sitting on top of the shipping crate. He had been watching them the whole time but now he scowled at Jared and Brax. Tyg jumped up onto the shipping crate beside Stills. He smiled at her and put his arm around her shoulders pulling her into him and kissed her hair.

"You okay, little cat?" He asked as Jared, Brax and the two others walked over to where Palin was waiting for them.

"Yeah, fine." Tyg muttered.

Stills angled his head to look at her face. "Are you sure?"

"Yes, I've just been told I have to do something for Mae...that's all."

"Oh, what's that?"

Tyg looked at him a little surly. "Do I ask you about your assignments?"

"Sorry..." Stills said frowning. "I didn't realise..."

Tyg smiled. "That's okay." She leaned over quickly and kissed him on the lips. "Are we okay?"

Stills looked at her with that smoulder, his pale hazel eyes glittering in the gloom. "Of course we are...why wouldn't we be?"

Tyg shrugged. "I don't know...I'm just not very good at this..."

Stills laughed. "Oh, little cat...you're doing just fine...just..."

"What?"

"Just try not to get yourself into any more life threatening situations..."

"I'm an assassin...it kinda comes with the territory..."

"No, it doesn't...plan and take no risks...little cat."

"Is that like a motto?" Tyg smiled.

"It shall be your motto, from now on, okay?" Stills bopped her on the nose and laughed. He wrapped Tyg up in his arms and held her.

Brax and Jared wandered over, while Palin was still talking to the other two.

"Hi there, kitty cat. How's about a cuddle for Braxy, hmm."

"Whoa, dude!" Jared cringed as Stills scowled darkly at him.

Tyg sat up, pushing Stills back and jumped down off the crate and walked up to Brax smiling.

"Sure, Braxy, why not..." Tyg held her arms out as Stills growled something under his breath and Jared just about tripped over his own feet. Her eyes were blazing ice blue fire.

Brax grinned and walked in towards Tyg, she grabbed his shoulders and brought her knee up into his groin. Brax doubled over in pain and Tyg hammered her fists on his back, forcing him to his knees, she jumped behind him and grabbed his hair pulling his head back as she held her dagger to his throat.

"Tyg!" Palin shouted from across the room and came running as Stills jumped off the crate and stood in front of her.

"Tyg, steady on...let him go..." Stills talked in a calm voice.

Jared was doubled over laughing, not realising the danger Brax was now in. Luke and Bron had stood up bewildered and the other two guys were standing behind Palin with their arms folded.

"What the fuck, Tyg, I was joking..." Brax mumbled, barely wanting to breathe.

"Tyg! Let him go!" Palin shouted.

Tyg looked at him and his blood went cold. Her eyes were black. Stills walked up to her and put his hand on her arm holding the dagger.

Tyg flinched and looked at him as he moved her hand from Brax's throat, her eyes wavered back to blue and she blinked at him.

"What are you doing?" Tyg growled at Stills, but he wrapped his arms around her then and hugged her. Her eyes went wide and she dropped the dagger. "That's my little cat." Stills whispered and tucked her head under his chin and held her until she calmed down.

"Thank buggery..." Brax snorted as he clambered away from her. "She needs a fucking cage, Palin!"

Palin stared at Brax. "Your mouth needs one! What happened to she's a member of the Guild...would you treat another member like that!"

"Well...I...." Brax stuttered then looked down ashamed. "I'm sorry, I was only joking."

"It gets a little thin after a while, Brax." Stills growled.

Tyg was just staring at everyone. She had never had anyone stand up for her like this before...she had always fought her own battles. She really didn't know how to take this.

"Take her away from here, Stills...now. Luke, Bron...go with them."

"Okay." Luke said.

"Come on, baby girl...let's go." Stills breathed in her ear, turning her round and leading her to the door.

21

Stills looked at Luke and Bron as they stood out on the street. "Can you guys make yourselves scarce for a minute?"

"Sure." Luke said and patted Bron on the shoulder. They pulled back and followed along a few yards behind as Stills and Tyg walked down the street. He still had his arm around her shoulders and she had put her arm around his waist.

"You want to explain to me what just happened in there?" Stills asked.

Tyg grimaced looking at the ground. "I wanted it to stop, I was sick of him constantly coming on to me like he did...that's the sort of shit I used to get in the Hut! I didn't think I would still get it now."

"I'm sorry." Stills said then. "I should have spoken to him sooner."

"Why?" Tyg looked up at him confused.

"Because..." Stills gave her a funny look.

Tyg looked at him perplexed. "I don't get it? Why is it your problem to sort out? And don't try and use any excuse to do with that White Knight stuff, I can fight my own battles."

Stills grimaced. "You don't have to, I'm here by your side as your boyfriend, or whatever you want to call me." Stills stopped walking and turned her to face him. "I care for you, and you should always know that you can tell me when anything is annoying you like that...I can help." Stills looked hard at her. "Were you seriously going to kill him?"

Tyg frowned. "I don't know...I don't think so...I just wanted him to get the message to stop."

"Well, I think he has definitely got that message." Stills laughed and embraced her once again. "So what should we do with our bit of free time?"

"Free time?"

"Well, that's to say we are out here while you cool off..."

"Oh, I see..." Tyg looked around and then smiled. "Can we go to the market?"

Stills smiled down at her and nodded. "Sure, let's go to the market, but just keep your hood up okay?"

They wandered through the various stands and food stalls. Stills bought Tyg and him a candied apple each and they sat on some hay and listened to the gypsy band playing. Tyg was watching the gypsy dancers in their long flowing skirts and the delicate crocheted shawls they had tied around their waists with little silver bells, so when they shook their hips it added to the music being played.

"Where do you get shawls like that?" Tyg asked Stills.

He stared at her a moment. "You like them?"

"Yeah, I do, I like the little musical noise they make when the girls move..."

"Really?" Stills looked at her surprised.

Tyg looked at him and grinned. "Surprised, huh?"

"Yeah, I gotta say I am..."

"You don't think I would suit one?"

"I think you would suit one too well" Stills gave her a roguish lop-sided grin.

Tyg leaned over and gave him a slow lingering kiss on the lips, causing Luke and Bron to wander over.

"Geeze you guys just can't control yourselves, can you?" Bron mumbled as he sat down next to Stills, looking around vigilantly.

"You're causing a sight, and you're not supposed to be...if Palin saw you guys kissing in public like that he would thrash both of you." Luke berated them as he stood with his hands on his belt.

"Sorry." Tyg said blushing and hiding her face in the depths of her hood.

"Look I get it...young love and all that...but not here, not right now with everything going on to do with you, okay guys?" Luke said smiling understandingly down at them.

"Gods, you sound like our father, or something." Stills muttered but winked at Tyg when she looked up at him.

"Think of me as the voice of reason." Luke laughed. "Come on, let's keep moving."

As Tyg and Bron stood up Stills looked up at Luke.

"Take her back home, I'll catch up shortly..." Stills turned to Tyg as she looked at him with a frown. "Don't worry, just something I thought about needs doing is all, I'll catch up I promise."

"Okay..." Tyg said as Stills stood up and put his arm around her neck and pulled her into him. He kissed her head on top of her hood. Luke grabbed her shoulder and pulled her away.

"Come on..." He muttered and walked off keeping her in front of him.

Stills looked over at the gypsy dancers and smiled to himself, then walked over to talk to them.

As they reached the bottom of the stairs leading up to Barion's house, Stills came running up.

"Thanks guys, I got it from here..." He said panting.

They all looked at him for a moment. Then Bron and Luke both shrugged as Tyg walked up the stairs to the door, knocked on it and leaned on the balustrade.

"So, you're going in?" Luke asked.

"I've been invited for dinner." Stills grinned as he walked up the stairs and stood next to Tyg.

"Dinner?" Bron muttered looking at Tyg.

"Not by me! I don't cook." Tyg spluttered out at seeing the look on Bron's face.

Stills laughed. "No, the lady of the house, Mae, invited me to join them for dinner, as Tyg's boyfriend."

Bron rolled his eyes and turned away and started walking off up the street, giving a wave over his shoulder. "Whatever, don't care..."

Luke laughed. "Okay, well, have fun you two...." He winked as he walked off after Bron.

Stills chuckled at their reactions as Tyg just scowled at all of them. The door opened then and Mae was there smiling at them.

"Oh, you're earlier than expected, good, come on..."

As they walked inside she indicated for them to go into the front reception room. As Tyg walked in there with Stills, Mae stayed at the doorway.

"There's drinks in the cabinet over there..." She pointed to a large wooden cabinet that opened up to reveal decanters of liquor and glasses. "Please, I want you to make yourself at home, Tyg." Mae smiled at her. "I'll just be in the kitchen if you want anything..."

"What's that amazing smell?" Stills asked her. When they had entered they had both smelt the divine smell of baking goods.

"Oh, I'm baking some sweet treats for a birthday coming up soon...I'm catering it."

"You're catering it?" Tyg said surprised.

"Yes, dear, that's what I do...I organise food and other things for people's parties and such."

"Oh, crap..." Tyg said frowning. "You're not seriously wanting me to sing at birthday parties?"

Mae looked surprised. "Oh! Has Palin spoken to you...he said you could sing...but no not quite birthday parties...ah...I'll come back, I have something in the oven..." Mae dashed off down the hall as Tyg collapsed down on the lounge suite.

"Great!" Tyg moaned, rolling her eyes.

"What's all this...I thought Palin didn't want you singing?" Stills said as he sat next to her.

"No, he doesn't...unless it's for the good of the Guild or something...I don't know." Tyg folded her arms grumpily.

"This is what you were talking about earlier?"

"Yeah..."

"Right...well...I got you something that might cheer you up?" Stills said as he turned sideways on the couch to face her.

Tyg glanced at him sideways with an eyebrow raised. He reached into his coat and pulled out a small parcel wrapped in thin white paper and held it out to her. Tyg's eyes went wide as she slowly reached out and took it from him. When she grasped it she felt it was soft and she heard a little musical jingle. She looked up at his smiling face.

"You didn't?" She asked shocked as she held the parcel staring at it.

"Maybe I did." Stills said amused. "Open it."

Tyg delicately tore the paper open and pulled the black crocheted shawl from it, shaking it out causing the little silver bells to jingle musically. Tyg held it out in front of her, smiling widely. She looked at Stills.

"Thank you." She crushed the shawl to her chest and tears formed in her eyes as she squeezed her eyes shut.

"Tyg?" Stills looked at her confused and put a hand on her shoulder.

Tyg shook her head. "It's okay." She smiled. "It's just...I've never been given a gift before..."

Stills stared in shock. "Gods! Really?"

Tyg shook her head and looked up at him. "I'll treasure it."

Stills took her chin in his hand and wiped her tears away gently with the other, then leaned down and kissed her softly. "I'm glad you like it."

"I love it." Tyg breathed as she dropped the shawl and wrapped her arms around Stills' neck and pulled him in to kiss him again, this time she opened her mouth to him and they kissed deeply as she leaned back on the couch with him leaning over her.

Stills pulled back and looked in her eyes. "I'm going to treat you like a pretty girl should be treated Tyg, so get used to it." He breathed then kissed her again, pulling her round so her legs were draped over his as he put his hand round onto her back and pulled her to him. This was the first time they had seriously made out since the bedroom in the little pub and although Stills was aware he had to take things slow he really had to force himself. He hadn't been able to get the image of Tyg kneeling on the bed in just a shirt all day. He remembered his hand on her breast and reached up while they kissed and cupped it. He felt Tyg gasp against his mouth but she didn't pull away. He squeezed it gently and ran his thumb over her nipple, which induced another gasp from Tyg. He pulled away slightly and looked at her with that deep smouldering gaze.

"You okay, baby girl?" He breathed. He smiled when he saw Tyg bite her lip as she nodded her head. Then he dipped his head slightly as he came back to her mouth and started kissing her again as his hand fondled her breast more.

They heard the front door open and close and Barion's voice called out. "I'm home!"

Tyg flinched and pulled her legs up as Stills sat up. He raked his hands through his hair and glanced at Tyg with a grin on his face. Tyg was looking at him with a similar smirk. They both laughed.

"Saved by the landlord, little cat." Stills growled at her as he leaned over and kissed her cheek. He then stood up and went over to the drinks cabinet and searched through the decanters sniffing them then poured two glasses and came back over handing one to her. "Here, I think we can both do with this right now."

Tyg sniffed it then took a sip. "Whisky?"

"Yeah...you know your drinks." Stills noted. "Which is really bad for a girl of your age!" He said in a playful telling off way.

Tyg grinned and shrugged then took another sip just as the door opened and Barion walked in with Mae. He scowled when he saw Stills and Tyg sitting so close.

"So, what's the story here then?" Barion demanded, then he saw the glass in her hand. "And she's too young to drink!"

Tyg scowled at him. "No I'm not...and this is Stills, my boyfriend."

"You're what!" Barion exclaimed.

"Now, Barion, dear, calm down." Mae said as she wrapped her arms around one of his. "Remember, Tyg is a guest and..."

"I know what she is." Barion grumbled making Stills frown.

"Now wait a minute..." Stills said looking at Barion with a frown.

"Leave it, Stills." Tyg said putting a hand on his thigh. "Barion and I go way back, so any fears he may have are probably well justified..." Tyg smiled, then glanced up at Barion. "But don't tell me what to do!"

Barion stared at her a moment then walked to the drinks cabinet poured himself a whisky and left the room.

"Oh, dear." Mae said. "I'm sorry about him..."

"He really doesn't want me here does he?" Tyg said frowning.

Mae smiled wanly at her. "Oh...it's not that exactly..."

"It's exactly that, Mae, don't sugar coat it...he's being forced to keep me here...by Palin though or Kor? Who is pulling the strings?" Tyg folded her arms and crossed her legs. Stills sat back on the couch and scratched his jaw.

Mae's eyes went wide at the mention of Kor's name, confirming it for Tyg. "Tyg..." Mae stepped forward. "Lord Kor is a very important and potentially dangerous man, don't cross him."

"I don't have any intention of crossing him, Mae, don't worry...I just like to be kept informed of what's going on in my own life, is all."

"Okay, dear..." Mae looked at the door. "Well I better go see to Barion, dinner is not far away."

"Okay." Tyg said as Stills smiled at her.

Stills noticed that Mae deliberately left the door open, he smiled to himself.

"So, Lord Kor, eh?" Stills muttered.

"Hmm." Tyg said uncomfortably.

"You ever met him?"

"Once."

22

It was two weeks later, with no sign of Raven and Tyg was surprised by Palin on her doorstep. As she let him into the front room, he sat down heavily.

"Lord Kor will be here soon, prepare yourself."

"What? Why?"

"To talk to us...to you."

"Why, Palin?"

"Mae explained the whole working for her thing?"

"Yes...she wants me to accompany her to some banquets and balls and sing as part of the entertainment...she's branching up in the world, trying to get into the market of rich Lords and needed a special draw card...I'm it." Tyg scowled, she really wasn't happy about this at all.

"Good...well, there's a reason why I want you to do it...and Kor is going to explain it to you."

Just then a knock sounded on the door.

"That will be him...go to the door, Tyg."

"What am I a fucking servant now?" Tyg muttered as she went to the door and opened it.

Kor was standing there in all his finery, holding a posh looking cane. His eyes went wide at the sight of Tyg before him. "Well, goodness my dear, haven't you done some serious growing up since last we met."

Tyg said nothing and just moved aside so he could walk in and she could shut the door. She pointed to the front room. Lord Kor looked at her with an arrogant smile and walked into the room with Tyg behind him.

"Palin, always a pleasure." Lord Kor said, shaking hands with Palin as Palin stood up.

"Is it?" Palin muttered.

"Now, Palin no need to be uncivil."

Palin scowled. "No, forgive me, my Lord." Tyg smirked to hear Palin address a noble man, he made it sound like an insult, she would remember that...Lord Kor seemed to ignore it and sat down, sweeping his short cape back on his shoulders and placing his cane against the side of the chair as he crossed his legs like a proper gentleman. He looked up at Tyg and smiled. "Please sit down, my dear, we have much to discuss."

Tyg frowned and sat down as Lord Kor started to explain why he was so adamant that she join Mae in her new business venture as her new headline entertainment.

"So let me get this straight...you want me to go to these posh banquets and sing under the guise of working for Mae?" Tyg said slowly and quietly as Kor and Palin listened. "But, I'll actually be there to gather information...or whatever, by breaking into offices and safes while there?"

"That's about it..." Lord Kor said smiling.

"Well at least that's better than just being used like some song bird in a cage." Tyg said bitterly.

Lord Kor laughed. "It's always nice to have an ulterior motive to things..."

Tyg looked at him with a suspicious look. This was why he was such a dangerous man, he always had ulterior motives for everything he did. All this was nothing but one big game to him.

"Of course..."Lord Kor continued. "I'm going to have to hear you sing...as is Mae I would say...before we can ascertain your worthiness in this scheme." He grinned widely. "And you're going to have to convince me you can pull off a dress."

"What the fuck!" Tyg said clenching her fists.

"Tyg." Palin growled at her. Lord Kor glanced at Palin amused. "You do seem to keep her on a short leash. That bothers me." Kor pondered as he watched them.

"Why is that?" Palin asked.

"Because you won't be at these banquets..."

"Hmm." Palin grunted looking away. "She can be trusted to do things unsupervised...you seem to forget what she did for you the last time."

"Oh, I have not forgotten, not in the least..." Lord Kor looked back at Tyg. She frowned at him, not liking the way he said that last statement, she could see Palin was frowning also. "So, Tyg I am extending an invitation for you to attend me at my home, with Mae, three nights from now."

"Your home?" Tyg asked shocked.

Lord Kor seemed pleased by her reaction. "You are going to have to get used to more of the finer things in life Tyg, I expect you to be able to fit in with the high class, it is my desire for you to be able to rub shoulders with them, as a rare songbird would."

Tyg scowled and folded her arms as Palin muttered. "You were winning now you're not, my Lord."

Lord Kor laughed. "It matters not, it will be done." Lord Kor faced Palin with a very serious expression.

"Yes, my Lord." Palin muttered causing Tyg to raise her eyebrows.

"Oh and Tyg..." Lord Kor turned back to her. "I expect to see you in a fine elegant dress...I will even finance you to get one."

"What?" Tyg was stunned as Lord Kor took out a small purse full of coins and threw it at her. She caught it wide eyed but then her eyes narrowed and she threw it back. "No way, Kor...I won't take it."

Palin chuckled. "She distrusts you."

"So she should..." Lord Kor said candidly. "Clever girl, but can you afford a fine dress on your own...because I expect it."

Tyg grinned. "I can sort one, don't worry."

"Quite...full of surprises....well I'll be off then. A carriage will come to pick you and Mae up, I will arrange the time and let you both know."

Lord Kor and Palin stood up. "I'll go too." Palin said as Tyg scowled at him. "You want to talk?" Palin said to her.

"Quite a bit, Palin..." Tyg growled, causing Lord Kor to chuckle.

"That's why I'm going too." Palin grinned a rare devilish smile and showed Lord Kor out as he laughed. Tyg didn't even go to the door to see them off. She collapsed down in the chair and sulked.

23

Tyg decided she was going to have to go and see someone about a dress, luckily she knew the perfect person. She grabbed her cloak with the deep cowl on it and made her way over to Rose's establishment.

When Tyg entered and threw back her hood, some of the girls got a fright. Tyg smiled but then scowled when she saw a couple of men sitting in the waiting room. They had both sat up straight and were grinning at her.

"Not a chance in fucking hell." Tyg muttered at them her eyes blazing. She turned to one of the girls. "I'm here to see Tess, but I guess I should see Rose first."

"I'll go tell her you're here." One girl smiled at her.

"Oh, you're Bella aren't you?"

"Yes, you remembered." Bella smiled as she disappeared through the doorway. Tyg stood to one side with her arms folded scowling at the men enjoying making them uncomfortable. When Rose appeared she swept Tyg into her arms in a warm embrace.

"Tyg! What a pleasant surprise, what brings you here?"

Tyg smiled awkwardly at the affection. "I'm actually here to talk to Tess, if that's okay?"

"Of course it is, can I enquire as to what it's about?" Rose took Tyg's arm and walked her through to out the back to the great delight of the men waiting. Tyg heard them whisper to the girls about who she was.

"It's actually about her dress designs." Tyg answered Rose's question.

"Oh, really? Well she will be pleased, it's her favourite subject."

Tyg turned to Rose and looked hard at her. "Tell me, Rose, is Tess a...you know...she doesn't seem..."

Rose laughed. "Actually, dear one, no she is not...she is the cook and cleaner and dress repairer of my establishment...she is far too delicate a flower for this line of work."

Tyg smiled glad to hear that news, just as Bella came back along the hall with Tess in tow. "Tyg!" Tess exclaimed. "Bella said it was you, but I could hardly believe it. You're wanting to talk to me?"

"Use my office if you like, Tyg." Rose offered.

"Thanks, Rose that would be great." Tyg walked down the hall to Rose's office and led Tess in and sat down. "I need your help, Tess."

"You need my help?" Tess looked surprised.

"I need a dress...but not just any dress, it has to rival the dresses worn by ladies of high standing when they attend balls and banquets."

Tess just stared at Tyg, her eyes welling up with tears and she was clenching and unclenching her fists in excitement. She squealed and jumped up and down on her chair.

"Settle down." Tyg laughed. "I haven't told you the bad news."

"How could there possibly be bad news, I get to design an exclusive dress to be worn to a banquet by none other than the most beautiful woman in the whole city."

"Well I wouldn't go that far..." Tyg scowled. "But I need it in two days."

"What!" Tess looked at her blankly. "Are you kidding me?"

"Unfortunately...no."

"Oh, I better get started then, I will show you some of my sketches and you can pick one, what about fabric?"

"I have a few coins here for you to buy what you need." Tyg took out a small purse of coins and handed it to Tess. "Whatever you don't spend you can keep for your troubles."

"Oh, that's not necessary, Tyg."

"I insist." Tyg said firmly, making Tess look at her a little frightened.

"Okay..." She looked down at her hands. "How is your wound, Tyg?"

"It's fine...all healed and gone."

"Oh that's great news, I was so frightened for you..."

"Don't be, Tess, that isn't necessary at all. Can you go and get those sketches?"

"Oh, sure, and I'm going to have to take measurements too."

"Right okay."

Tess ran off to get her things as Tyg waited, she noticed a carafe of amber liquid on a side table. She got up and went to check it out, sniffing at it. Tyg smiled and poured a glass, she noticed the glasses were thick cut crystal. 'Rose is doing well for herself.' Tyg thought. She sat down behind Rose's desk and leaned back in the seat, putting her feet up on the desk, whisky glass in hand.

Tess came back in and saw Tyg behind Rose's desk. "If she sees you she'll have you." Tess said smiling.

"I doubt that." Tyg snorted, causing Tess to look at her with fright. Tyg smiled at her and put her feet down. "Show me the drawings."

Tess grinned and opened her sketch book, flicking through several pages back and forth randomly.

"This one would look nice."

"No."

"How about this one?"

"No."

"Okay...what about...this one?"

"No."

"You're not going to say yes to any of them are you?" Tess accused pouting.

"I'm sorry Tess, it's not that they don't look lovely, but I just don't want to wear one...maybe I should just leave the choice to you."

"How about I get a panel together?"

"A panel?"

"Yes, Rose, me and maybe one other person to pick one for you that we all agree would be perfect."

"Okay, I trust you and Rose, but who else?"

"We can think of that while we go material shopping."

"Oh no, I am not going with you..."

"It's still early, of course you can."

"No."

"But you have to pick a colour and type."

"Black."

Tess laughed. "Oh dear, no, you can't have a black dress, no that will never do."

Tyg sighed. "I'm not going to get out of this am I?"

"We really only have today to make these decisions if you want it in two days, as it is I'm going to have to work all night, probably both nights."

"You don't have to do this, Tess."

"Don't get me wrong, I want to do it." Tess smiled

"Alright then, let's go..." Tyg stood up and downed the whisky and made her way to the door.

They were walking down the street when Tyg heard a whistle from an alley. She glanced in the direction and saw two familiar figures. "Wait here a moment, Tess." Tyg said as she walked over to the alley. "What? Are you following me now?"

"Always..." Luke grinned. "Does Palin know you're out wandering the streets in broad daylight?"

"He should, since he left me to organise a bloody dress to wear for Lord fucking Kor." Tyg spat bitterly. Luke and Bron looked at each other strangely.

"Do we even want to know?"

"Best you don't." Tyg shrugged.

"Does Stills know about this?"

"Not really, I haven't seen him since my meeting with Kor and Palin this morning."

"Geeze you are hob knobbing it, meetings with Lord Kor..."

"Shut up, Bron, I would happily let you take my place if I thought you could fill a dress out better than me." Tyg grinned.

"Oh, I don't think that would be at all possible." Bron grinned back.

"Only in all the wrong places." Luke laughed.

"If you see Stills tell him I'm with Tess from Rose's establishment, she's the maid there."

"Ah, thought I recognised her." Luke said. Tyg gave him a filthy look and he looked away. "Okay, we'll let him know."

Tyg walked back to Tess and continued on to the material shop that according to Tess was the best one in the city. At least it was in a decent neighbourhood so Tyg was less jumpy, but she still kept her hood up until she got inside.

The next two hours was spent in absolute torture for Tyg, as she sat in a chair with her feet up on the shops counter, as Tess kept bringing bolts of fabric over for her to look at. Once Tyg had finally agreed upon a pale lilac satin, Tess then spent an age getting the matching cottons and bias and Tyg didn't know what or cared, that she needed to sew the dress.

Finally they returned to Rose's to find Rose in her office with a familiar young gentleman. They were drinking whisky together and Rose was laughing delightfully at something funny he had said as he charmed the pants off of her.

"Stills?" Tyg said surprised as he turned when the door opened.

"Little cat!" Stills stood up and embraced her. Tyg put her arms around his waist and as she looked up at him he kissed her soundly on the lips with a smacking sound. "I missed you, ran into Luke and Bron who were supposed to be keeping an eye on you and they said I would be able to find you here...but you weren't here." His tone was slightly pissed off.

"They knew I was with Tess, buying material..."

"I explained to him how long Tess can take..." Rose said amused, looking at them.

"I'm sorry." Tess said behind Tyg.

"No, that's alright, everything is fine." Stills said, but his voice sounded troubled.

"You're acting weird, Stefan?" Tyg said to him. He looked down at her and ran a finger down her cheek.

"I worried that's all, that guy is still out there somewhere, and you know you're not supposed to go wandering off on your own...you promised me."

"Oh, so you're mad at me."

"A little yes." Stills frowned.

"I'm sorry." Tyg said as she placed her hands on either side of his face. "I told you I wasn't good at this sort of thing." Tyg kissed him softly.

"You have a boyfriend?" Tess blurted out suddenly.

Stills looked at her amused as Rose laughed. "Not very quick on the uptake this one." Rose said.

"He can be the third person on the panel." Tess announced clapping her hands together.

"Panel?" Both Rose and Stills asked.

"No." Tyg said firmly.

"Why not?"

"What is she going on about?" Stills asked.

"Tyg has to wear a dress and she can't pick a style so I suggested a panel of me and Rose and now you, to pick it for her."

"Oh...yeah...no." Stills said uncomfortably as Rose chuckled.

"Let's see the designs, Tess." Rose asked. Tess walked over and gave her the sketch book. Stills wandered over and looked over her shoulder. He stared at the drawings and then looked at Tyg.

"Why the fuck do you have to wear a dress like this?"

Tyg rolled her eyes. "See I told you he wasn't right for picking a dress..."

Rose looked up at him. "Do you think she would look too sexy in this one?" She teased.

Stills flushed. Tyg sat down amused and folded her arms. "Maybe this could be fun."

Stills glanced at her with a look that could kill. "You still didn't answer my question, baby girl." The sheer dominance in his voice made them all shudder.

Rose and Tess both looked at the two of them smiling at each other. Tyg rolled her eyes.

"I have a dinner to attend at Lord Kor's home."

Rose's eyes went wide and Stills' eyes narrowed. "This about the singing?"

"Yes."

"Damn Palin!" Stills spat and came round the desk and sat on the arm of the chair Tyg was sitting in. "I don't have to pick and I would rather not fucking know to be honest how damn sexy or beautiful you look cause I know it won't matter what dress you wear, you will be amazing and it pisses me off cause I can't be there to protect you." He hung his head as Rose and Tess both smiled at him endearingly.

"Well your speech won their hearts." Tyg muttered.

Stills glanced at her sideways. "But not yours?" He asked with a smirk.

"I didn't say that, but what can I do about it?"

Stills frowned again his eyes darkening, he stood up and grabbed Tyg's hand and stalked to the door. "Excuse us a moment." He pulled her out of the office and closed the door, then pushed Tyg's back against it and grabbed her face with one hand as the other was pressed palm down on the door above her head, and he kissed her deeply. Tyg kissed him back her hands on his chest. Breathless he pressed his forehead against hers. "I just needed to...."

"I know." Tyg said with a smile. "I wanted to as well....but what are you going to do in a room full of nattering people."

Stills chuckled. "Ah, baby girl. What have you done to me?" He kissed her again slower this time savouring the passion, then pulled away again with a reluctant groan. "Well, we better go back in."

"As soon as they pick a style and take measurements I can leave." Tyg said with a cheeky grin.

Stills tucked a stray lock of hair behind her ear as he looked into her eyes. "Well, let's just hurry this up then, shall we."

24

Tyg was on her way home from Rose's after seeing Tess for a dress fitting the following evening when she rounded a corner and walked straight into a patrol of the City Watch. Tyg contemplated bolting back the way she had come but it was too late, they had seen her.

"Hey you!" The Captain called out. "Stop right there!"

Tyg grimaced, she didn't want to have to kill city guards but if they started to ask her hard questions she wasn't going to let herself be hauled off to jail either. There was only one track she could take in this, which made her grimace even further. She hated using the fact she was a girl.

She lowered her hood and smiled at the Captain. He was tall with sandy blond hair and slate grey eyes – the closest to blue anyone in this land ever got, except her. He had a long proud nose that steeped of aristocracy.

"Yes Captain? What can I help you with?" Tyg asked sweetly as she pulled her cloak around herself hiding her weapons.

"My Lady!" He exclaimed. "What on earth are you doing out here at this time of night? And unaccompanied?" He removed his helm and tucked it under his arm. Tyg had to hold herself back from rolling her eyes.

"I am just making my way home now, Captain...thank you."

"Where have you been at this time of night, miss? It is unusual to find a young lady such as yourself out." Tyg scowled at him and her eyes changed colour. The Captain stared at her.

"I rather think it's none of your business, Captain. However I had an emergency situation with my dress maker...if you must know." It was true but Tyg hated how it made her sound like an air head.

"Oh I see...well please excuse my impertinence at asking, but there are criminals out at this hour...it's really not safe."

"You don't say..." Tyg said amused.

"Indeed there are, miss." He informed stiffly. Tyg grit her teeth at the formal way this guy spoke. "Even in this area."

"I must stop you, Captain...I am not a Lady...my name is Tyg, I'm merely a merchant's daughter."

"Forgive me...I assumed...thank you for correcting me."

"No problem...do you think I can go home now, Captain?"

"Of course, allow me to escort you."

"Oh, there's no need for that..."

"Nonsense, I won't hear of it." The Captain turned to his patrol. "Carry on patrol while I escort this young lady home. I will see you back at Precinct."

"Yes Sir." They saluted but were grinning as they looked at Tyg. The Captain turned back to her.

"Come, miss." Tyg did roll her eyes this time and walked off down the street with the Captain in tow. "So where do you live exactly? I haven't seen you around these parts before...I am sure to remember you..."

"I'm staying with the jeweller, Barion and his wife on Merce St."

"Right, that's not too far...good." The Captain seemed pleased.

Tyg glanced sideways at the Captain. He wasn't very old and looked very pompous in his bright red uniform and brass helmet and buttons. She could tell he held his position because he was obviously a Lord's son.

"So what's your name, Captain?"

"Captain Thomas Doven, miss."

"Well, Thomas, it's nice to meet you." She grinned when she saw him baulk at her dropping his title and just calling him by his first name.

"Ah...nice to meet you too, miss." He flustered, his neck going red.

"I told you it was Tyg."

"Ah...right, Tyg." He smiled at her and blushed.

"Well, here we are...thank you, Thomas." Tyg stood on the front step and looked at the Captain. "Goodnight." She prompted for him to leave.

"I'll just see you safely inside, miss...ah...Tyg."

"Really...isn't that going a bit far...nothing's going to happen to me standing on my own porch...unless you don't believe me?" Tyg banged on the door behind her without turning around.

"Oh, of course...I don't doubt you." The Captain said flustered.

Just then the door swung open and Mae stood there in her dressing gown.

"Tyg...you're home." She startled with surprise when she saw the Captain standing there. "Oh dear, what's this? Is there trouble?"

"No trouble, ma'am, just escorting the young lady home. You know she really shouldn't be out walking on her own at night?"

Mae's eyes relaxed and she smiled at Tyg as Tyg rolled her eyes again. "Oh, of course not. She's my cousin's girl...strong headed...Captain..." She paused waiting for a name.

"Doven, ma'am...Captain Doven."

"Yes, Lord Doven's son."

"Ah." He seemed surprised. Tyg grinned and leaned back on the balustrade and folded her arms. Mae knew everyone. "Yes, that's correct, do I know you?"

"No, probably not." Mae smiled.

"Right well, enjoy your evening, ma'am." He turned to Tyg. "Tyg." He bowed his head at her.

"Goodbye, Thomas." Tyg said as she stood up and walked inside. He looked surprised and watched her leave.

"Oh, okay...yes well...goodnight." He looked at Mae who was still smiling at him.

"See you again, Captain Doven." She said making him frown, as she closed the door. He stood there confused a moment then turned and headed off to the Precinct. He looked back once then put his helm on and stalked off.

As Mae walked into the front room she found Tyg pouring herself a whisky and downing half of it immediately.

"Looks like you have an admirer." Mae said with a smile.

Tyg turned to her. "Shut up, Mae, that's not even funny, his patrol caught me coming back from Rose's. If he had seen these..." Tyg pointed to her weapons. "I would be in the jail right now."

"Oh, yes...you need to be careful."

"Hmm." Tyg snorted. "Anyway, I'm going back out..."

"What?" Mae seemed surprised.

"I do have actual work to do, you know." Tyg sneered at her. "And the amount of money I just gave to Tess for this blasted dress for Lord Kor, I'm going to have to work for the next year to get back."

"Ok dear, be careful."

"That's the second time you have said that, Mae." Tyg said amused.

"Because I mean it." Mae smiled at her.

"Don't worry about me." Tyg growled as she changed her cloak for her form fitting, black, long coat, pulled up the hood and left.

The next morning Tyg stepped out her front door and saw Stills wandering down the street on the shady side. She leaned on the balustrade and watched him, smiling. He stopped and looked behind himself then put his hands on his chest, indicating himself, then acted all embarrassed. Tyg laughed and shook her head as he smiled and wandered over, looking up at her.

"You're a dick." Tyg laughed.

"I'm mortally offended by that." Stills said acting hurt. "That's no way to talk to your boyfriend."

Tyg leaned further down and kissed him. "You're in a good mood."

"Because I'm seeing you." Stills smiled as he took her hand and pulled her down the steps and wrapped his arms around her.

"Okay..." Tyg said.

"So why are you out on your stoop?"

"I was heading back to Rose's to get the dress."

"Oh, Tyg..." Stills said wearily as he bopped her on the nose.

"What?"

"How many times do I have to tell you not to go alone?"

"What choice do I have, I can't sit around waiting for people to turn up, I'm careful...besides no one has seen any sign of Raven." Tyg looked behind Stills's shoulder. "Oh shit."

"What?"

"Don't turn around." Tyg put her hand on his cheek to stop him. "It's Captain Doven of the city watch."

"What the fuck? How do you know a captain from the city watch?"

Tyg rolled her eyes. "Don't ask..." Stills frowned at her and turned them both around so he could see the Captain, Tyg turned in his arms putting her back against his chest.

As the Captain and his men patrolled down the street he stopped and smiled when he saw Tyg. He frowned when he took in her attire and then scowled when he took in Stills, who was leaning back on the balustrade with his arms around Tyg's waist.

The fact that he was wearing all black and was clearly armed made the Captain halt his squad with a raised hand. He walked over to them.

"Tyg...are you alright?"

"Yes, Thomas I'm fine...this is Stills...my boyfriend."

Stills gave Thomas a beaming smile and held his hand out, as Thomas almost choked on Tyg's words. "Your boy....ah...right..." Thomas slowly took Stills' hand and shook it.

"Pleased to meet you, Captain." Stills said still grinning.

"Quite..." Thomas said. "Care to explain why you are armed, Sir?"

"Sir?" Stills chuckled. Tyg rolled her eyes again. "Well, Captain...it's a dangerous place and Tyg here needs protecting wouldn't you say?"

"Oh for..." Tyg went to say but Stills cut her off.

"Tut, Tyg...shush now." Tyg pressed her mouth together and stared at Stills as he stood up and stepped closer to the Captain. Thomas baulked slightly at the menacing figure that Stills actually posed. Everyone knew people that dressed all in black were to be avoided. The fact that Tyg was also dressed all in black was a deep concern to the Captain.

"So what are you? A mercenary or something?" Captain Thomas demanded.

"Or something...it's a legitimate job."

"Then you will have papers?"

"Of course..." Stills folded his arms and stood like a stone wall between Thomas and Tyg.

"Well?" Thomas asked annoyed, looking round Stills at Tyg.

"Well what?" Stills asked grinning wider and cocking his head to the side.

"Where are your papers, Sir?"

"Stills..." Tyg muttered, but Stills dropped a hand back for silence from her. She grumbled and sat down on the step. "Fine." She huffed. Stills put his hands in his pockets and leaned back on one leg.

"I hardly carry them around on me, Captain, but rest assured my employer keeps them safe."

"Your employer...and who would that be?"

"Lord Kor." Stills said making Tyg look up at him strangely, Tyg also saw the reaction that name had on Thomas as he backed up a step.

"Lord Kor is your employer?" He asked dubiously.

"Yes, check with him if you like...tell him I'm the one who is also Tyg's boyfriend...he'll know."

Tyg put her elbows on her knees and buried her face in her hands, "Oh geeze..." She muttered.

"I will." Thomas said firmly. He appraised Tyg for a moment. "Good day to you both."

Tyg looked up as Stills stepped back and sat down next to her. "Goodbye, Captain." Stills said.

"Goodbye Thomas." Tyg smiled wearily at him. Thomas clenched his jaw and stuck his face in the air, turned and marched away with his men following.

"Fucking hell, Stills...what was that?"

"Well I had to say something...and you are seeing Lord Kor tonight, you can warn him."

Tyg looked at Stills a moment, then shook her head. "I suppose so..."

"See..." Stills smiled. "So what's the deal with Thomas?" Stills said the name Thomas in a drawl making Tyg frown.

"No deal...he stopped me coming home last night after dark, and insisted on escorting me home."

Stills face went like thunder. "Tyg! Are you fucking serious...you went out last night...I should seriously put you over my knee and fucking spank you!"

Tyg's eyes widened in surprise at Stills anger. "I'm sorry...what?"

"You keep saying that Tyg but you keep doing the wrong fucking thing! Do I have to tell Palin you're being disobedient?"

"Disobedient?" Tyg's eyes changed to ice blue.

"Palin gave you strict instructions, Tyg. Don't make me have to speak to him, I just want to keep you safe. Raven is out there somewhere...no one believes he would have just given up." Stills ran a hand through his hair. "Fuck, why are you so stubborn?"

"I can look after myself."

"Oh yes, you did a fine fucking job of it last time!" Stills said sarcastically.

Tyg stared at him with her eyes blazing, stood up, walked inside and slammed the door.

Stills heaved a deep sigh and rested his elbows on his knees, hanging his head. "Fuck." He muttered to himself. He got up and stepped up to the door and banged on it. "Tyg! I'm sorry! Tyg? Open the damn door!" The door opened and Stills looked at Mae. He grimaced and put his hands in his pockets. "Hello Mae." He said contritely.

Mae frowned at him and grabbed his arm. "Come in, hurry up, you're causing a scene..."

"Sorry about that..." Stills said as she closed the door behind him and manoeuvred him to the front room. "I need to speak to Tyg, where did she go?"

"To her room, and slammed that door too...what happened?"

Stills sat down and rubbed the back of his neck. "I said something I shouldn't have...in the heat of the moment."

"Your first spat..." Mae said smiling at him.

Stills looked at her and grinned. "Yeah, I guess so..."

"Well put it right dear, quickly."

"Your letting me go up to her room?"

"Well, I don't think she's going to come out." Mae smiled at him. "Go on..."

"Thanks." Stills said as he got up and wandered off and up the stairs. He guessed which room was Tyg's by the fact that it was the only door that was actually shut. He tapped lightly on it.

"Tyg, let me in." He said quietly to the door.

"Go away."

"Tyg...don't act like a child...let me in."

"Fuck off." Stills heard the growling menace in her voice.

"No." He said simply. He sat down on the floor with his back leaning on the door. "And don't you dare think to jump out the damn window!"

He heard Tyg mutter to herself, he smiled. "You know this is good, at least you're where I can keep an eye on you."

Even angrier muttering ensued. Stills chuckled to himself. "I can sit out here all day...or we can talk...I can apologise, you can forgive me and we can go together to get that damn dress you need for tonight."

The door suddenly opened causing Stills to fall back, he looked up at Tyg standing over him. "Fine!" Tyg growled and walked back over to her bed and sat down. Stills got up off the floor and closed the door.

"I really am sorry Tyg, I shouldn't have said that, I don't even know why I did...it just came out." Stills said as he wandered over and sat down next to her. "It was a hurtful thing to say."

"I'm sorry too...I won't go out again by myself..."

"Okay..." Stills smiled and put his arms around her. She turned into him and put her head on his chest. "I'll make a deal with you that I will be here every day at noon, okay. If I can't because of work, then someone will always be here at noon for you."

"Alright." Tyg grumbled. "If that's the way things have to be..."

"It is Tyg, Raven really isn't someone you want to come up against alone." Stills felt Tyg shudder against him and he pulled her further into himself and rested his head over hers. "But you know that already."

Tyg raised her head and kissed him. "I don't like fighting with you." She said smiling shyly.

Stills stroked her cheek. "Good, so we don't need to do it anymore, okay?"

Tyg nodded and reached up to Stills and raked his hair back from his face as she got up on her knees and leaned over him. He watched her intently as she held him by his hair and brought her face to his. She kissed him, forcing her tongue into his mouth and pushed him back onto the bed. She straddled him as she continued to kiss him. His hands ran up her back as he kissed her back. He then pulled his arms inside hers and pushed her back.

"Tyg..." He said with dark eyes as he searched her face.

"What?" She breathed.

He sat up brushing her off him, and raked his hands through his hair. "Fuck, baby girl, are you sure about this...?"

"Not really sure about anything, but..."

He looked at her, she was looking at him intently her eyes a pretty mauve blue. He trailed a hand round her neck and leaned over her and kissed her passionately. She lay back pulling him down with her. He lay beside her on one hip, propped up on one hand as he leaned over her. She put her arms around his neck as they continued to kiss. His hand roamed up and undid the buttons on her shirt and slipped his hand inside and cupped her breast. She moaned against his mouth and kissed him harder. He trailed his hand down over her stomach and down her thigh, then he brought his hand back up between her legs. Tyg suddenly pushed him off her panicking and sat up.

"I can't do this...I'm sorry..." She looked at him bewildered. He lay down on his back and smiled, putting his hands behind his head.

"That's okay, little cat." He took a deep breath calming himself. "To be honest, I'm glad."

"What?" She looked back at him, confused.

He sat up and looked in her eyes. "I don't want you to think you have to do this, for my sake, Tyg. You do what you feel comfortable with...then I'll be comfortable too."

"What does that mean?" Tyg said confused.

Stills rubbed the back of his neck. "Tyg, all the girls I've been with...they haven't been...you know...they have all had experience..." Tyg frowned and hugged her arms around herself. "Don't get me wrong, it's not a bad thing that you're a..."

"Don't say it." Tyg squeezed her eyes shut. Stills smiled and grabbed her braid and twirled it round.

"Tyg, this is a major decision for you, I get that...it's a big deal for me too, I've never taken a girls...ah...virtue before...it's kind of freaking me out too...girls never forget the first time...good or bad..."

Tyg looked at him strangely then smiled. "Okay I think I get it now."

Stills put his hand around her head and pulled her into him and kissed her hair. He lay down on his back and pulled her down with him, holding her gently. She put her head on his chest and smiled to herself. "Thank you, Stefan."

"No problem, little cat...I'm here for *you* remember."

25

As the carriage arrived at Lord Kor's Tyg stared at the large Manor before her. She even noticed that he had guards, something that was very rare to see, but given his status in the country it wasn't surprising.

Mae was beside herself grinning in delight as the butler came out to greet them, giving them a bow of his head like they were Ladies.

"Please follow me." He said in a pompous voice. Tyg rolled her eyes as Mae dutifully followed.

He led them down a hall to a double set of doors. "Please wait here while I announce you."

"Oh for fuck's sake..." Tyg said rolling her eyes again.

Mae scowled at her. "Tyg, we spoke about this...this is normal etiquette...stop swearing!"

Tyg sighed and almost rolled her eyes again. "And stop rolling your eyes." Mae said before she could.

"My Lord, Madam Mae and Miss Tyg are here as requested." Tyg heard the butler say.

"Good." Lord Kor's voice boomed out. "Show them in."

The butler opened the doors wide and bowed his head as Mae entered the opulent room followed by Tyg. It had lavish furnishings like Tyg had never seen, with ornate chairs and couches and a large piano to one side. Pianos were a very rare thing to see, since they had only been around for a few of years...that showed Kor's wealth off immediately. Tyg noticed a man sitting at the piano smiling and looking at them.

"Tyg! Wonderful for you to make it." Lord Kor said approaching her first. Tyg scowled but let Kor take her hand and kiss it. He then turned to Mae and greeted her. Turning his attention back on Tyg he indicated for Mae to sit. He looked Tyg up and down.

"Turn for me." Kor ordered.

Tyg scowled deeper and stood still raising an eyebrow in defiance. "You don't own me, Kor."

He laughed. "No, but I own your boss." He turned away. "Remember that." He muttered causing Tyg's eyes to widen in surprise then narrow.

"You are of course quite right, my Lord." Tyg said not in a nice way. Kor turned back with a grin. "However I believe I am here to sing, not twirl."

Kor laughed. "Oh my...you are a treasure...I only wished to study the dress, Tyg, nothing more...as you will recall I asked for something special." He looked at her up and down again. "I see you didn't disappoint." Tyg frowned and saw Mae was biting her lip suddenly very nervous. Kor turned away again and indicated to the butler. "Would you like a drink ladies?"

The butler came round with a tray with filled wine glasses on it offering one to each of them. Kor settled himself in a large ornately furnished and padded chair and inclined his head for Tyg to sit.

"I will have to get the name of your dressmaker, Tyg...that dress is simply stunning." He said as he watched Tyg walk across the room and take a seat in a chair opposite him.

"She works exclusively for me, Kor." Tyg said possessively of Tess.

"Really? Your own dressmaker...well I never...are you sure you don't have some secret title we don't know about?" Kor smirked.

Tyg sipped her wine and said nothing. Mae jumped in instead. "Are you going to introduce us to the man at the piano, my Lord?"

"Oh yes...quite...this is Sebastian, he plays...and will accompany Tyg with her performance tonight." Kor grinned at Tyg.

"So should we get this over with then, Kor?" Tyg said with a huff.

"Ah, not quite, Tyg...the guests haven't arrived yet." Kor said still grinning.

"Guests?" Both Tyg and Mae said at the same time.

"Quite...I'm not sure I really have an ear for music or song so I thought it best to invite some others to cast their votes into the pot on whether Tyg is a good singer or not."

Tyg growled. "You're going to be paying me for this, Kor." Mae's eyes went wide at the menace in Tyg's voice. Kor still just grinned.

"Yes indeed, I shall, Tyg...do not worry about that...and I will pay you any amount I see fit depending on your performance."

Tyg leaned over towards him. "What the fuck does that mean?" Her eyes blazed and Kor lost a little of his confidence.

"Nothing untoward...just that I will determine what your singing is worth...it will establish a standard by which others will know what to pay when hiring you...according to the structure in place with other musicians and singers."

Tyg relaxed back and sipped her drink. "Okay...that sounds fine." She conceded.

"Good." Kor smiled. "Perhaps you would like to converse with Sebastian on a couple of songs that would be appropriate to show off your vocal talent."

'Gods what an ass.' Tyg thought. "So no bawdy tavern songs then?" Tyg grinned as she got up and walked over to Sebastian. She saw Sebastian smile at the comment and heard Kor chuckle.

After a couple of minutes of polite conversation the butler arrived announcing guests. Tyg watched as Lord Irion, Lord Karon, Lord Ranor and Lord Maton entered the room one after the other as Lord Kor greeted them and indicated for them to sit. Tyg's eyes went wide as Lord Maton entered.

"Oh shit..." Tyg muttered under her breath. She caught the grin on Lord Kor's face and wondered what the hell he thought he was doing. As she turned her head to glance at Lord Maton however all she saw was a beaten dog submitting to Lord Kor's power and influence.

'Obviously the aftermath of the Mandos Contract.' Tyg thought. 'But why invite him here knowing he might easily recognise me?' He only had to look at her eyes. Lord Kor seemed to feel her angst and wandered over after they were all seated and getting drinks from the butler.

"Do not worry Tyg...there is no way Lord Maton will recognise you, I'm sure of it...it was well over a year ago."

"You better hope he doesn't."

"Even if he does...who is he going to tell?" Lord Kor said it not really as a question. "Have you agreed on a song or two?"

Tyg looked at Sebastian who was staring at her and Kor wondering what they were talking about. He blinked and nodded. "Yes I believe so." He answered.

"Good, I will get the ball rolling then." Kor turned and clapped his hands. "Welcome gentleman as you know I have found a new talent, and would like to have you all share your worldly wisdoms and critique her singing prowess so that we may between us determine if she has what it takes to become a great singer."

"She's certainly got the right look." Lord Irion muttered causing Tyg to scowl. So this was her life now was it? Being an object of blatant ogling from the Establishment. Great. Well she was going to make them pay dearly for the opportunity. She whispered to Sebastian and changed the song choice.

He looked at her surprised. "Are you sure?"

Tyg grinned her eyes glowing. "Positive."

She was going to sing a simple love ballad followed by a beautiful aria, but not now she knew price was on the line...she started singing the choral song of the angels. She had often heard it sung in the temple when she was a young pickpocket, standing outside below the high stain-glassed windows listening to the solo singer. She had never sung it herself, but she knew she could.

As she started Kor sat down and stared at her with wide eyes. She stood up and stood in front of the piano and let her voice soar. It always amazed her how confident she felt once she started singing...she was always nervous as hell beforehand, but it was like something else took over her body as soon as the first note left her throat.

When she finished the song there was no applause. Everyone was staring at her wide eyed in wonder. Tyg smiled, swished past Kor to the drinks tray grabbed a wine and sat down in the chair that was opposite him. She sipped it then regarded him with an eyebrow raised as she leaned back in the chair and crossed her legs, the split making the fabric fall away and reveal her knee high black boots with the dagger hilt sticking out of one.

Everyone then erupted in applause and gracious compliments as Tyg just sat looking at Kor over the rim of her glass. He was still staring at her with open adoration. He smiled beguiling at her his top lip twitching.

"Tyg, you are simply amazing...better than I could have hoped for going on Palin's description."

"Price, Kor." Tyg said coldly.

He baulked and sat back surprised as the other Lords were all conversing about how they were all going to get her to sing at this and perform at that already planning balls and banquets months down the track. Mae was listening to them wide eyed.

Tyg turned and looked at her with a smirk. "All appearances will need to be booked through Mrs Barion." Tyg said. Mae's eyes lifted to her and Tyg smiled at her...she wasn't letting Mae off the hook as being part of this set up.

"Oh my..." Mae said as she was suddenly rallied by the Lord's with dates and bookings. As she raised her hands and started explaining to them that no bookings could be made yet, and they would have to discuss things with her at a later date once everything was finalised between Kor, Tyg and herself, Tyg turned back to Kor.

"Well?"

Kor had been watching the Lord's and turned back to her. "There was supposed to be two songs."

"I'm only singing one tonight, Kor...you got what you wanted."

"I haven't yet." He mumbled making Tyg frown. "But it seems the Lords are definitely willing to pay any price so it rather looks like you, my dear, have just become the most favourite of all entertainment on offer in Arial City."

"So...price...who was the highest paid?"

"That was an operatic singer by the name of Giselle Barquoe"

"And what was her rate...and don't lie to me Kor."

Kor smiled and stood up walking across the room and sitting in a chair next to her. "I wouldn't dream of lying to you, Tyg, I solemnly believe you deserve the highest rate of pay for a voice like that, so I'm going to suggest a rather ridiculous amount that should see you rich within a year."

Tyg's eyes went wide. "Why would you do that?"

"Because your voice demands it. Giselle would get a gold piece for her singing performance."

Tyg frowned. "Palin paid more than that for a pickpocket." She looked at Kor meaningfully as he stared at her, she saw his jaw clench as he glanced at the Lords who were all chatting happily among themselves and enjoying appetisers that the butler was handing around.

"Quite...I was thinking somewhere in the realm of five for you anyway my dear."

"Five!" Tyg exclaimed and the Lords, Mae and Sebastian all turned to look at her.

Kor grinned and sat back contented with her reaction.

"Five gold coins?" Lord Irion asked.

Kor glanced over at him. "Yes, I think that's more than fair."

"That's extortion!"

"So don't pay it." Tyg said frowning. She didn't like Lord Irion anyway, besides she was guessing Kor would take at least one of those coins for himself. Palin one as well...that left three.

"Five gold..." Mae whispered to herself in amazement. Tyg turned to her.

"Hmm, seems we need to have a talk when we get home."

"Oh?" Mae looked surprised.

"Regarding your percentage..."

"Oh." Mae said quietly.

The rest of the hour went past with polite conversation and Tyg avoiding Lord Irion's touch. Kor had actually aided in blocking Lord Irion's approaches by effectively keeping Tyg by his side and with a light hand on the small of her back he guided her around the room away from Lord Irion at every chance. When the Lords finally left Tyg sat down on a chair and looked up at him to find him smiling down at her.

"Thank you for tonight." Tyg admitted with a smile.

"No problem...but what exactly?" He asked amused.

"Your aid with Lord Irion...if you hadn't have done what you did he would have ended up dead with my dagger in his chest."

Kor chuckled. "Yes, I thought as much." He sat down next to her and took her hand. Tyg looked up at him surprised. "Tyg I would very much like your permission to court you."

Tyg's eyes went wide as Mae's popped out of her head and she choked on her wine. "Oh shit, Kor...I have a boyfriend." Tyg said quickly as she stood up and backed away from him.

"You do?" Kor asked annoyed.

"Yes, actually I needed to talk to you about him."

"What?" Kor seemed confused. "Please, Tyg sit down. I'm not a lech like Irion, and please call me Adrian."

Tyg slowly sank back into the chair, her heart was racing. She never thought to be in this position. "Ah...yeah...you see we were questioned by Captain Doven of the city watch..."

"Thomas?" Kor said, still confused.

"Yes, and he asked Stills for papers cause he was wearing arms in the street and...."

"Stills? Your boyfriend..." Kor rumbled under his breath.

"Yes." Tyg looked at Kor's face. "Do we have a problem?" She asked with a growl.

Kor's face went stony and he leaned back in his chair. "Not at all...continue."

Tyg frowned, she didn't like the way he said that. "Well, Stills said his papers were with his employer...you."

"Me?" Kor looked a little surprised. "What the hell?"

"Well he couldn't give Palin's name now could he?" Tyg said a little sarcastically.

Kor's eyebrows shot up as he realised what she was saying. "Your boyfriend is in the AG?"

"Yes." Tyg smiled as Kor finally understood. "So will you cover him if Thomas comes for credentials?"

"Of course, Tyg nothing will give me more pleasure...on one condition."

Tyg frowned deeper. Damn it she knew it was wrong to owe a man like this favours. "What is it?" She said sighing.

"That you give me a month of courting you versus your boyfriend, if I can't sway you to become my lady after that time, I'll drop it."

Tyg sat staring at him her mouth pressed together, for a long time. He was debonair and handsome, with intense dark green eyes and dark hair. "How old are you?" She finally said.

Kor laughed. "I'm only thirty two."

Tyg knew he was an eligible bachelor, but didn't realise he was that young for being so rich and powerful. "But why me...I'm not a lady...I have no titles...aren't you people supposed to marry for benefit."

"You people?" Kor laughed. "Tyg I can buy you a title."

Oh shit! Tyg didn't know what to say. "I think I need to think about this." She said as she stood up, she knew she couldn't outright refuse him, he was far too important and dangerous. "Mae, we are leaving."

"That's fine, Tyg, but what do I say if Thomas comes calling in the mean time?" Kor was not going to let this go. Tyg grit her teeth.

"A week." She countered to his offer.

"A month." He replied firmly.

"Two weeks."

"Everyday..." He added, his eyebrow raising along with his lips.

"Everyday?" Tyg frowned.

"Every day for two weeks, if I call you come." His voice went low and commanding.

Tyg sucked her teeth in thought for a moment, her eyes intensely focused on him as he calmly met her gaze and blinked. "Fine." She huffed in annoyance.

"Fine?"

"Yes, fine...I agree to your terms. Only if Thomas comes calling...and you have to cover Stills, if he does not, no agreement will be put in place, and I will check."

Kor smiled. "You are a cunning one...that's why I like you...agreed." They shook hands.

Kor stood up and walked Tyg to the front door with Mae leading the way. He walked down to the carriage with them, taking Tyg's hand and curling her arm and his around her stomach and drawing her into him, pressing his chest against her back. He breathed into her ear as she froze.

"Just to let you know...Thomas came straight here this afternoon, my dear...lucky for you I covered for your beau."

Tyg's eyes widened as she realised she had just been out played as Kor placed a kiss on her cheek and let her go. "You fucking bastard." Tyg muttered and Kor chuckled to himself. Tyg stepped up into the carriage and slammed the door shut.

"I'll be sure to call by tomorrow, Tyg." Kor said laughing to himself.

Tyg let all sorts of expletives out on the way home as Mae just sat in the seat across from her staring at her in awe. Tyg finally couldn't take it any longer.

"What!" She yelled at Mae.

"Dearest, I don't think you have really understood what's just happened."

"Oh, and what's that besides a jumped up arrogant egotistical moron has just blindsided me into agreeing to a courtship I don't want because I already have a boyfriend!"

"Tyg...the most powerful man in the whole of Arial has just basically made his intention to marry you known."

Tyg baulked and went silent.

She stormed into Palin's Hide in the middle of the night to find him playing cards with Brax. Tyg halted at the sight of him and grit her teeth. Palin looked up at her surprised.

"What are you doing here? Didn't you have a thing with Lord Kor tonight?" Palin chuckled to himself as Brax looked at her surprised.

That was it. "Did you know what he was going to do?" Tyg demanded with menace.

Palin stopped laughing. "What did he do?" He growled causing Brax to frown.

Tyg sighed and sat down in a chair grabbing the whisky bottle off the table and downing a few gulps of it before continuing. Brax sat up straight and whistled under his breath. Tyg wiped her mouth with the back of her hand and grinned at him.

"Tyg?" Palin asked still waiting.

"He has managed to trick me into agreeing to let him court me every day for two weeks."

Palin and Brax's eyes went wide, but then Palin's went dark and vengeful. "No, he fucking did not!"

"Oh, he fucking did! And after I told him I had a boyfriend too."

"What did he say? What exactly happened...?"

Tyg told Palin everything and by the end of it he grimaced. "Sneaky bastard..."

"What are you going to do about telling Stills?" Brax asked.

"Oh, found your voice have you!" Tyg spat at him, then frowned and looked at the table. "I don't know..." She answered quietly. "But it doesn't matter because it doesn't matter how much Kor courts me I am not interested, and if he thinks throwing money and jewels at me will work he will find out very quickly that it will have the opposite effect."

"That a girl." Brax smiled. Tyg turned to him with a frown. "What? I actually think you and Stills are cute together."

"Cute?" Tyg said incredulously. "I didn't even think you knew that word." Brax shrugged and grinned

Palin stood up. "Just be careful...very careful...Kor never does anything without a long game. I'll have a word with him, but I'm pretty sure he's not going to let you out of this agreement."

"Just promise me one thing, Palin..." Tyg said quietly as she looked at the table top, picking at a loose splinter.

"What's that?" Palin asked curious.

"If he ever offers you money, please don't take it."

"Offers me money?" Palin frowned, then his eyes went wide and he looked up to see Tyg staring at him. "Never, Tyg that I promise you...you will always be mine...okay."

Brax frowned and looked from Tyg to Palin completely confused. Tyg smiled and stood up. "Okay."

26

Next morning Tyg was just getting up, the cat was sitting on the window ledge and Tyg was sitting on the end of the bed looking at him while tying the laces of her boots, as the early morning sun was hitting his fur. Tyg was not looking forward to today. She had no idea what Kor had planned and she hadn't been able to talk to Stills, as Palin said he was on a job. Palin and Brax had said they didn't want anything to do with telling Stills about Kor so she didn't have to worry about them telling him before she had a chance to. Bloody cowards. Palin had promised to tell Stills to go see her as soon as he got back. Now the sun was up and he still hadn't come round. She frowned and fell back onto her back on the bed. Today was not going to be a good day.

Sitting up with a heavy sigh Tyg got up and went to the window. Opening it she scratched the cat's chin as he purred and stood up stretching his back out. She leaned on the sill as the cat jumped off and went to lie on the bed. She saw that familiar swagger coming down the road. She grinned and bolted out the door and down the stairs.

Tyg flew out the front door and down the street and crashed into Stills, wrapping her arms around his waist. "I missed you!" She muttered as Stills stumbled back at the impact stunned. He grabbed her, wrapping both his arms around her, bracing himself.

"Well that's a greeting and a half." He chuckled. "What's up with my little cat?" He stroked his hand down her braid, pulling it slightly, making her lift her head. "Palin said you had something to tell me?"

Tyg grimaced, but then Stills pressed his lips on hers briefly. "Come on, let's get off the street...wait...what the hell?"

Stills was looking up the street towards Tyg's house. He let her braid go and she turned her head. "Oh, shit." Tyg muttered.

At her doorstep was a man dressed as a manservant for someone rich, in a navy blue uniform. In his arms was a massive bouquet of flowers, the most of which were red roses. On the street was a small enclosed two seat carriage with a white pony. Tyg watched horrified as Mae opened the door and spoke to the manservant. She saw Tyg and Stills and pointed at Tyg, the manservant turned and looked at her. Tyg flinched.

"Damn him!"

Stills frowned. "What the fuck is going on, Tyg?" He grumbled as he scratched his chin.

"Lord fucking Kor!" Tyg said fuming as she grabbed Stills by the hand and walked back to the house. She brushed past the manservant and Mae and stalked inside, all the way to her bedroom, with Stills dragging along behind as he mumbled a quick hello and excuse me to Mae. Tyg slammed the bedroom door shut and went to the window.

"Mae!" Tyg shouted down.

Mae looked up a bit startled. "Tyg? What..."

"Deal with those, please...I can't."

"Oh, ok..."

Tyg pulled her head in and closed the window, turning she leaned back on the window ledge and faced Stills, who was standing in the middle of her room with his arms folded. He had a rather nasty looking scowl on his face.

"So why exactly is Lord Kor sending you red roses?"

Tyg gritted her teeth. "You better sit down..."

"No, I'll stand."

Tyg sighed and told him everything that happened the night before. She watched his demeanour change slowly as she told him more and more of the story. He had dropped his arms and stuffed them in his pockets. He had planted his feet and rolled his shoulders, now his head was down. It was a very dangerous looking posture and Tyg had seen it before.

"I'll fucking kill him!" Stills said quiet and menacingly when Tyg finished. "I knew it...I knew something like this would happen...that's why I didn't want to see you in that fucking dress." Stills turned away raking a hand through his hair. "It's going to keep happening...they are all going to come calling...how the fuck am I supposed to compete with the likes of him!"

Tyg frowned. "What are you talking about...compete with who?"

Stills sighed then laughed. "Of course, you have no bloody idea...you naïve little fool." Stills turned back with a lopsided smile. "I suppose I should be thankful of that at least."

Tyg got it...she did...but didn't understand why Stills thought he had to compete with anyone. She stood up and went over to him and wrapped her arms around his waist, laying her head on his chest. "There is no competition, Stefan...it's you I want to be with...no one else."

"But don't you get it...he's the type of man you should be with."

Tyg looked up at him and stepped away shocked, straightening out her arms so as not to break contact. "What! Why the hell would you say that?"

"He's rich, he's good looking...he can give you everything I can't." Stills still had his hands in his pockets standing like a statue.

Tyg pushed away from him, her anger rising. "Oh, and what is that exactly? You really have the audacity to think I want riches and fancy clothes?"

"It's what you deserve, baby girl." Stills said sadly. "And I can't give them to you."

"You're a moron!" Tyg shoved him in the chest. He staggered backward and his back hit the wall, his hands still stayed in his pockets. "Don't you fucking get it...I love you, you fucking jerk!"

Stills head came up and their eyes met. Tyg crashed into him again, grabbing his face with both hands and kissed him, crushing her lips against his. He finally took his hands out of his pockets and placed one hand on the back of her neck the other on the small of her back and pulled her into him powerfully as he kissed her back, pushing his tongue into her mouth as she opened hers to him.

Stills broke off the kiss and leaned his forehead on hers, not letting go of his grip on her. "Baby..." He breathed.

There was a soft tapping at the door.

"Tyg...?" It was Mae.

"What?" Tyg said as she looked into Stills eyes.

"I don't want to intrude on what I'm sure is a rather important conversation, but there was a note with the flowers..."

Tyg grimaced as Stills dropped his hands and returned them to his pockets, the moment lost. Tyg stepped away and opened the door. Mae saw Stills brooding against the wall and gnawed on her lip as she handed Tyg the hand written note. Tyg looked at it and swore again.

"That bloody bastard!" Tyg scrunched the note up in her fist.

"Do I even want to know?" Stills muttered as he looked away at the window.

"Probably not..." Tyg mumbled back. She looked at Mae. "Thanks."

"Are you okay, dear one?" Mae asked. "Want some breakfast?"

"Sure...I'll be down shortly." Mae smiled encouragingly as Tyg closed the door.

"I want to know now." Stills grumbled as Tyg went and sat on the bed.

"What?"

"Because you said, probably not...I want to know now what it says."

"Oh...here..." Tyg held out the crumbled note.

Stills clenched his jaw and stood up off the wall and took the couple of steps to stand in front of her, taking the note delicately from her and uncrumpling it.

To my most Radiant Angel
I will be sending a carriage for you at 12.00 noon
Please be dressed and ready to go.
Dress will be supplied.
Yours, Adrian Kor

Stills crumbled it in his fist, shaking with rage. He threw the note over into a corner of the room.

"Fuck!" Stills yelled and fell on his knees at Tyg's feet. He put his head in her lap as Tyg ran her fingers through his hair.

"It doesn't change anything, Stefan...we can do this...we can get through it."

Stills put his hands on either side of her thighs and held them firmly. "You can do anything, Tyg...anything at all."

"What?"

"The skies the limit for you..."

"Stefan..."

Stills head came up and he looked at her seriously. "I am just saying Tyg...if you do this thing and placate the guy for two weeks, but you decide after that you want to..."

"Shut up, I've already told you...enough already!"

Stills stood up, coming up towards her face like a predator and kissed her, his hands sweeping under her thighs onto her buttocks and shifting her up the bed as he lay her down. Kneeling up slightly to take his own weight, he pushed her knees apart with his and leaned over taking his hands from under her and placing them on either side of her head – all in one fluid fast motion. He pulled his head away and looked down on her. Her hands were on his chest and her eyes were wide with shock, but they were a beautiful mauve blue. Her lips were parted and her heart was racing. Stills smiled. "No one gets to see you like this, but me, baby girl."

"Of course not..." Tyg breathed with a smile. "But don't do that again without warning, I just about hurt you."

Stills kissed her again and she ran her hands into his hair kissing him back. He chuckled against her mouth causing her to pull back with an eyebrow raised. "What's so funny?"

"Exploit him, Tyg."

"What?"

"He thinks he's so smart, lavishing you with gifts, take them...take him for everything you can get. Teach him to not mess with you...a member of the AG."

Tyg smiled. "And a thief and a pick pocket."

"And that..." Stills muttered as he kissed her throat and trailed kisses back up to her mouth. Lying down beside her and pulling her close.

An hour later the manservant arrived back with a woman. Tyg answered the door and the woman handed Tyg another hand written note.

To my beautiful rose
Let me introduce Naomi
She has your dress
Always yours, AK

"Fuck's sake." Stills grumbled as Tyg led the woman, carrying a large bag, into the main lounge room, as she handed Stills the note to read.

Naomi smiled at Tyg. "Goodness, my dear...I didn't realise how lovely you were going to be, even after all of Lord Kors lavish descriptions."

Stills groaned and collapsed into a chair. Naomi looked at him curious. "And you might be?"

"I'm the man she is currently courting." Stills said sarcastically.

"He's the man I love!" Tyg countered with a growl. Stills smiled up at her.

"Oh." Naomi said shocked. "But..."

"Lord Kor can't take no for an answer..." Tyg said.

"Ah, I understand." Naomi said like she understood perfectly.

"So you have a dress?" Tyg said folding her arms.

"Yes, and I have two hours to get it fitted before Lord Kor comes to get you."

Tyg rolled her eyes and looked at Stills. He frowned and stood up, he put his arms around her and kissed her, dipping her, making her grab onto him in surprise. He broke off the kiss and grinned at her.

"I'll take my leave then, little cat, have fun."

"Are you really sure about this?" Tyg asked him as he put her back on her feet.

"No, I hate everything about this and I'm going straight round to Palin's to see what we can do." Stills said, raking a hand through his hair.

"He said he was going to talk to Kor, I don't know if he has yet...but he said it probably won't do any good."

"I'll make him talk to him again...or I swear, I'll kill him...if he lays one filthy paw on you, Tyg."

Tyg reached a hand up and stroked his cheek and kissed him. "I love you, don't do anything stupid."

Stills grinned. "No risks, remember."

He bowed his head to the shocked seamstress and left with a wink.

"My goodness." Naomi breathed. "Why is...oh...never mind...not my business." She muttered as she opened her bag and pulled out a neatly folded heavy velvet dress the same colour as the red roses.

"Crap." Tyg said as she looked at it as Naomi held it up against herself so Tyg could see it. It was strapless with a boned corset bodice with a skirt that went straight down to the floor. It was simple and stunning. Tyg was glad Stills hadn't stayed to see it.

An hour later Tyg was standing on a low table wearing the velvet dress while Naomi was hemming it. Naomi had been a bit shocked when Tyg had told her she was wearing her boots underneath, but had decided it was best to just do her work and get paid. Someone knocked on the door and Tyg heard Mae call out that she would get it.

Moments later Mae was in the room standing in front of Tyg with the manservant. Tyg scowled.

"What the hell now?" Tyg grumbled as the manservant smiled and held out a small box with a note attached. Tyg rolled her eyes. "This is getting ridiculous."

"I think it's very romantic." Mae said, smiling happily at Tyg in the dress. "You do look very lovely, dear."

Tyg's eyes flashed. "You're not helping Mae...this is only day bloody one!"

"And not even midday..." Mae chirped.

Tyg growled. "Mae...go away." Tyg looked at the manservant. "You got a name?"

"My lady?"

"Your name...I'm obviously going to be seeing a lot of you over the next two weeks."

"Oh...yes...my name is Brandon, my Lady."

"Ok Brandon, stop calling me Lady...and call me Tyg."

"Ah...okay...ah...Tyg." The manservant smiled. "I have to stay for you to open the box."

"Why is that?"

"To report your reaction."

Tyg grimaced. "Fuck's sake...he's really getting off on this, isn't he?" Tyg looked at the note.

My dearest Tyg
I thought this would go
Nice with the dress.
See you very soon
Always yours, AK

Tyg frowned and opened the box. "Fuck." Tyg was staring at a beautiful ruby and gold necklace, it had a large drop ruby in the centre with four smaller rubies, two on either side in an intricate filigree setting than narrowed off to a delicate chain that went round the neck. Tyg snapped the box shut and handed it back to Brandon.

"No way...I am not taking that...give it back to him." Tyg held it out to Brandon.

"I can't do that my lady...ah...Tyg."

"Why the hell not?" Tyg was seething with frustration.

"He specifically said you were not to be allowed to refuse anything I bring to you." Brandon reeled back at the sound of Tyg's voice and her blazing eyes.

"Tyg, may I suggest something..." Naomi said taking a moment from her sewing. Tyg's eyes flicked to her with an arched eyebrow. "Wear the necklace, and take it off and hand it back to him at the end of the evening."

Tyg laughed. "Oh my, that's brilliant...thank you."

Naomi smiled and continued her work. Tyg looked at Brandon. "Report nothing of this Brandon or the next time I see you will be your last."

"Tyg, don't threaten the help it's not his fault." Mae admonished her taking the box and opening it and running her fingers over the necklace.

"I thought I told you to go away." Tyg said flatly, folding her arms.

Mae looked at her with wide eyes. "Oh."

"You are enjoying this far too much too...this is fulfilling an agreement, nothing more." Tyg said it through gritted teeth.

When midday rolled around Tyg saw the carriage arrive as she stood at the window. Mae was once again buzzing around living vicariously through Tyg which just annoyed her even more than she already was.

Mae almost ran to the door and opened it before Lord Kor even stepped out of the carriage. Tyg grabbed her shawl that Stills had given her and draped it over her bare shoulders. She was going to take a piece of Stills with her. She smiled to herself.

Kor came in looking absolutely dashing Tyg had to admit, he was wearing a cream coloured suit with a vest the same colour as her dress. He beamed in delight at the sight of her.

"Tyg, my dear, you look absolutely divine, and the necklace suits the dress perfectly, I knew it would." He kissed her hand as she smiled nicely at him.

"Thank you...can I ask where we are going?"

"Of course...Lord Simon Fairweather and Lady Fairweather are hosting a garden party."

Tyg grimaced, she hadn't expected something quite so public. "Oh..."

Kor just smiled. "I thought it would be a good opportunity for you to network."

"Network?" Tyg didn't know what that meant.

"Yes, mingle around mention you're a singer, mention Mae's business, get some work through it."

Tyg heard Mae's happy exclamation. "Why?"

"Why not?" Kor seemed perplexed. "Is it not a nice gesture?"

"It is...that's why I'm suspicious?"

Kor laughed. "Don't be Tyg, I am perfectly happy to just be seen with you on my arm looking like that and telling the world that we are courting."

Tyg rolled her eyes. "Great."

"Now Tyg..." Kor admonished.

Tyg levelled a blazing gaze at Kor that stopped him midsentence. "You do know I don't do well in crowds?"

"It's not crowds, Tyg, calm down..." Kor muttered.

"Fine, but if I kill anyone it's on your head." Tyg swept past him and headed for the door. Kor looked after her startled and glanced at Mae.

"I'm sure she's joking..." Mae said. Kor frowned at the unconvincing comment before following Tyg out.

He stepped in front of Tyg as she walked out on to the stoop and put his hand out to her. Tyg grimaced but put her hand in his as he escorted her to the carriage. Tyg glanced up and down the street to the people watching. This really wasn't a good way to stay unnoticed. She stopped in her tracks. Up the street in a shadowed corner were two figures one was leaning on the wall, his arms folded and his feet crossed, the other was standing with his feet planted solidly his burly arms folded over his massive chest.

Stills had seen the shawl she was wearing and was smiling at her, he gave her a curt wave. She smiled back but she wasn't happy about him seeing her dressed like this. She thought it was cruel that Palin had put him on security detail knowing she was going to be with Kor, but at the same time a plan was already forming in her head about how she might be able to secret some time with Stills behind a bush or tree or something at this garden party. She grinned to herself as she stepped up into the carriage.

27

As Tyg walked, with Lord Kor holding her arm, through the gardens of the Fairweather Estate, she looked around at the opulence and scowled darkly. There was a quartet playing and tables of drink and food. Obviously Lord Fairweather's wife had organised it all. That was the problem with married Lords, if Mae was ever to get into organising this kind of thing she had to aim at the bachelors.

"Smile at least." Lord Kor muttered to her.

"It's not easy to, I hate this…I'm sorry." Tyg muttered back.

Kor glanced sideways at her and sighed. "Perhaps I was wrong to think you would be a good fit for me."

Tyg looked at him solemnly. "I tried to tell you that."

"There is no harm in trying, however. You look exquisite, Tyg, and will be talked about for weeks to come on the gossip grapevine."

"Great." Tyg rolled her eyes. "Just what an assassin needs."

Kor squinted his eyes dangerously. "Mind your tongue."

Tyg's eyes widened at the quick change of tone, then sneered. "Yes, my Lord."

Kor's jaw clenched as he said nothing. Lord and Lady Fairweather approached them with a pleasant welcome.

After being paraded around for the better part of two hours, Tyg finally found herself without Kor by her side. He had disappeared into the house with Lord Fairweather to discuss 'private matters' he had said. That suited her fine, she wandered off into the small maze that was at the end of the garden.

She soon found herself in the centre, where a marble bench seat was surrounded by fragrant flowers and sat under a pergola of climbing clematis. She sat down and closed her eyes, sighing deeply.

"What's the sigh for, baby girl?" A voice called out.

Tyg looked up and saw Stills step out from behind the hedging, smiling at her as he sauntered over, pulling his mask down.

"Stefan." Tyg called delighted as she watched him walk over and sit down next to her. He took her hand and placed it in his lap.

"You look so beautiful, Tyg...you're making my heart hurt."

Tyg's eyes widened and she stared at him bewildered, not knowing what to say. He smiled and reached up and hooked her chin with a finger and leaned in. He kissed her slow and tender, his lips brushing hers reverently, then he trailed his hand to the back of her neck and pulled her into him, as he kissed her more desperately, lashing his tongue into her mouth. Tyg grabbed him by the neck and kissed him back, leaning back slightly as he leaned over her possessively, his other hand on her back.

He pulled back and sat up, raking a hand through his hair, leaving Tyg panting and reaching out for him. He raised his arm and encircled her shoulders, pulling her into his side as Tyg lay her head on his chest.

"Sorry, I couldn't resist." Stills said as he looked up and around the garden.

"I'm not complaining in fact I want more." Tyg said with a grin.

Stills looked at her and smiled. "Is that so..."

"Of course it is...I love you."

Stills turned on the seat, straddling it with his legs and turned Tyg so she was sitting with her back against chest, her legs stretched out along the bench. He wrapped his arms around her waist and rested his head on her shoulder, nuzzling into her neck and planting kisses on it. Tyg closed her eyes and leaned back into him, her hands on his thighs.

"Gods, I wish this could be us every day." Tyg whispered as she reached up and ran her fingers through Stills hair, holding him as he kissed her neck. She turned her head as he raised his and they kissed passionately.

They heard someone cough and looked up to see Luke standing by the hedge. "Someone's coming through the maze." He warned.

Stills stood up and kissed Tyg's forehead. "That's my cue then, I'll see you later, little cat."

"Okay." Tyg said annoyed as Stills and Luke disappeared. Tyg sat on the marble bench and stared at the flowers. Her back was to the entrance where the person would eventually come from, but she didn't care who it was.

"Miss Tyg?" A voice said astonished.

Tyg cringed and turned to face the man behind the voice. Her eyebrows shot up in surprise to see Captain Doven out of uniform. He looked very dashing in a royal blue suit. He walked over and took Tyg's hand, kissing it politely.

"Where is Lord Kor? I saw you arrive with him."

Tyg shrugged. "Business." She said vaguely.

"May I sit down?"

"Sure." Tyg watched him as he awkwardly sat next to her, his cheeks flaming. Tyg smiled to herself and looked away. "What can I do for you, Thomas?"

I just wondered...about Lord Kor...and that man in black, the other day."

Tyg laughed. "I didn't peg you for a gossip?"

Thomas's eyes went wide. "Oh no...nothing like that...I ...well...I mean."

Tyg watched him struggle with his nervousness for a moment amused. "Don't even try to understand it, Thomas...I don't even understand it myself."

"Hmm." He said in thought. "It's just that...the other day you were wearing..."

Tyg grimaced. "Thomas, I'm going to give you a subtle warning to not push this line of questioning."

Thomas stared hard at her for a moment then looked away. "Okay then, but Miss Tyg?"

"It's just Tyg..." Tyg rolled her eyes.

"Are you safe?"

Tyg looked at him strangely, what a weird question. "Yes, of course I'm safe."

Thomas nodded and stood up. "Good then, shall we walk back..." He held his arm out politely to escort her back.

Tyg smiled and stood up. "Alright, but I think it best to not take your arm."

"Ah...right, okay." Thomas flushed again and Tyg laughed.

"You're a strange one, Tom."

"Ah...am I?" Thomas looked startled as Tyg and he started to wind their way back through the maze.

Stills hunched down with Luke, Luke's hand pressed hard down on Stills' shoulder as Stills shook with rage and gnashed his teeth.

"Calm down, man...don't be an idiot." Luke growled at him.

"What the fuck man! Now that stupid Captain of the City Watch! You know he's a Lord's son as well...what the hell am I supposed to do?" Stills grumbled distraught at having watched Thomas walk off with Tyg.

"She loves you...what does it matter who is interested in her...you heard her."

Stills sighed and rubbed his face as Luke let him go. "Go home, Stills...I can watch her on my own."

"No, I'll stay."

"You're in no fit state...go home."

Stills shoved his hands into pockets and stood up. "No."

"It's been over two weeks and nothing from Raven or the Annul Guild...she'll be fine."

"No...I'm staying."

Luke rolled his eyes. "Fine, just watch yourself."

Lord Kor stood on the steps leading from the house to the lawn, a drink in his hand as he watched Tyg walk back across the lawn from the maze with Thomas Doven. His jaw clenched and his eyes darkened as he watched Tyg take her leave of Thomas and walk over to him.

"What the hell, Tyg?" Kor muttered under his breath.

Tyg smiled sweetly at him. "Don't fuss, Adrian, it was nothing. Thomas is a complete gentleman."

"He's also City Watch...remember."

"Oh, is that what you're worried about." Tyg's eyes twinkled.

Kor's eyes narrowed. "I think it's time to leave."

"Good idea."

Kor smiled at Tyg and indicated a servant over. "See to my carriage, please...I'm leaving."

The servant bowed his head. "Certainly, my Lord."

Kor walked Tyg over to Lord Fairweather. "We are going to go now, Simon."

"Certainly, Adrian. It was wonderful of you to attend and bring this lovely young lady with you." Lord Fairweather gushed making Tyg's stomach roll. She looked away with a faint look of disgust.

"Quite." Kor said with a smile.

"I can't wait to hear her sing, it's such a shame you couldn't allow it here today."

Tyg looked at Kor surprised, but he squeezed her arm and laughed at Lord Fairweather. "Well, like I said, Simon, she's a professional, it would be unfair to expect her to perform here for free."

"Indeed...and unfortunately my wife refused to pay the fee." Lord Fairweather actually pouted.

Kor laughed. "Her decision is it?"

Lord Fairweather grimaced. "One must keep one's lady happy."

"Hmm." Kor grunted as he looked at Tyg. Lord Fairweather caught the look and snickered.

"Perhaps you will find that out all too soon, Adrian."

Tyg looked at Lord Fairweather with a flat expression. "I doubt that." Tyg muttered.

Lord Fairweather's eyebrows shot up in surprise and he grinned as Kor frowned at Tyg, but said nothing.

He bowed his head stiffly to Lord Fairweather and turned away. "Come on." He said to Tyg and dragged her off round the front of the house just as his carriage was coming from the other direction. He opened the door and practically pushed Tyg in, then climbed in and sat down as the carriage set off.

He stared at Tyg for a long moment then looked away out the window.

"What?" Tyg asked.

"You."

"Me what?" Tyg asked indignantly.

"You look like a princess, you sing like an angel, but you are a devil...a wild, untamed devil." Kor sighed.

"Don't blame me."

"I don't blame you...how old were you when Palin took you in?"

Tyg frowned, she didn't like talking about herself. "Fourteen, fifteen...maybe."

"And before that?"

Tyg looked away, she was surprised Kor didn't know. "I was a pick pocket."

Kor's eyes widened. "Really? Well you truly are a wild one then..."

"So are you going to give up?"

"Give up?" Kor asked amused.

"On this courting thing...I'm not right for you."

Kor frowned and looked out the window again. "It's been one day and it did go better than I expected."

Tyg sighed and leaned back in the seat dejected, causing Kor to laugh.

"I'm a little bit more tenacious that that, sorry Tyg."

"Yeah, whatever...just stop with the stupid notes every hour...it's annoying."

Kor chuckled. "Annoying for who? You? Or Stills?"

"Leave Stills out of this, you know he's AG, don't purposely try and piss him off."

"You're AG too."

"So don't piss me off either."

Kor rubbed a finger across his forehead. "Don't threaten me, Tyg." His voice was flat. Tyg glanced at him with a surly look but said nothing. "You still have a lot of growing up to do...perhaps I should wait another couple of years."

"Ha! I might be married by then."

"That doesn't concern me." Kor said making Tyg baulk and stare at him. He met her gaze. "Yes, Tyg, I'm that powerful...don't forget it."

"Who's threatening who now?"

"Do I need to?" Kor asked in a deep dangerous tone.

Tyg sighed. "No...my Lord."

"Hmm." Kor snorted, satisfied.

The rest of the journey was silent. As they pulled up to Barion's house Kor stepped out of the carriage and held his hand out to Tyg. As she stepped out he kissed her hand.

"Thank you for a wonderful afternoon."

"My pleasure." Tyg said as she reached up, undid the necklace and put it into Kor's hand. "Thank you for letting me borrow that." Tyg stepped away and up the stairs to the door and banged on it.

"Tyg." Kor said sternly looking up at her. "This necklace was for you to keep."

"I don't want it...I have no use for fine jewellery...I'm an assassin."

Kor jaw clenched as Mae opened the door and stepped out smiling. "Lord Kor, thank you for escorting Tyg today."

Tyg looked disdainfully down on Mae. "You are not my mother, shut up!" Tyg barged past her and inside. Mae looked terrified as she glanced at Kor apologetically.

Kor was gritting his teeth. "Tell Tyg to expect me at lunchtime tomorrow."

"I certainly will, my Lord." Mae said quietly as Kor stepped up into the carriage and closed the door. Throwing the necklace on the seat opposite and folding his arms.

Tyg was back downstairs and grabbing her coat, dressed in her black work gear, in a matter of minutes.

"I'm going out." Tyg called to Mae.

Mae stepped into the hallway from the kitchen. "Oh, okay, when will you be back?"

Tyg fixed her with a baleful stare. "Late." She stepped out and closed the door. She scanned the street, then saw a figure step out of the shadows about fifty yards away. Tyg stepped off the stoop and walked down the street.

"Well, you're looking pissy." Stills said to her as she reached him. "You look like how I feel."

Tyg walked into him and sighed heavily. "Can we just go and get drunk now?"

Stills laughed. "By all means, baby girl...let's go."

28

Tyg was not surprised to see Kor's servant, Brandon on her doorstep. It had been five days straight now. This morning he stood there with a wicker picnic basket and a note. Tyg sighed and took the basket.

"Thank you."

Brandon bowed his head. "It is my pleasure, miss."

"Tyg...how many times..."

"Ah, quite...well..."

"Well what? You're waiting for me to open it, aren't you?"

"No, miss...ah...Tyg, just read the note."

Tyg narrowed her eyes at Brandon when he slipped up but grinned when he corrected himself. She picked up the note and flipped it over. She frowned.

> *This basket is from my*
> *Favourite baker in Arial*
> *Bring it with you*
> *And meet me beside the river*
> *By Lowden Bridge at 1pm*
> *Yours, AK*

"Fine." Tyg sighed. "Anything else?"

"No, the carriage will be back just before 1pm."

"I can walk..."

"Ah, you probably don't want to do that today." Brandon said looking at the sky.

"Why not?" Tyg sounded confused.

"Because it would cause you all sorts of discomfort to walk that distance in this heat, in a dress."

"In a dress?" Tyg grit her teeth. "Damn it...fine then." She huffed, turned and walked back inside, going through to the kitchen and placing the basket down on the table.

"What's that?" Mae asked.

"A basket of stuff from some bakery...looks like I'm going on a picnic..." Tyg said drolly.

"Oh, with Lord Kor?" Mae smiled as she peeked into the basket at the delicious looking food.

"Don't look so happy about it..." Tyg grumbled. "And while we're at it, stop trying to act like you're my family...you're not and you have no say in what I do, got it." Tyg was still surly about Mae's constant interference.

Mae blinked in terror at the dark menace in Tyg's eyes as they flashed. "I'm sorry, Tyg...I didn't mean to...I just..."

"Just don't!" Tyg snarled and stalked out of the room, up the hallway and grabbed her coat. She put it on and noticed Mae come up the hall and stand awkwardly, staring at her. Tyg turned. "What?"

"I really am sorry, Tyg, I just...I never got to have children of my own..."

Tyg frowned and looked at Mae. "You're not that old?"

"We have tried and failed, I'm afraid."

"Oh." Tyg didn't know what to say and scratched her neck awkwardly.

"So you see...it's nice having you here..."

"Well...I suppose it's nice being here..." Tyg wanted to just leave, she hated situations like this, she hoped Mae didn't try and hug her. She shivered at the thought. "Anyway, I have to go...got to get another dress apparently..."

"Okay, Tyg...take care."

Tyg turned with a slight smile at Mae's habitual farewell. As she stepped out she looked up the street and frowned. She was supposed to wait for someone to come from the AG, but she needed to go to Rose's to get a dress. She decided to stop at Palin's hideout before heading over to see Tess.

As she walked in through the door she found Brax and Jared sitting in the kitchen scoffing back chunks of ham on the bone, which they were carving off with their daggers.

"Tyg!" Jared exclaimed with a grin. "What brings you here?"

"I couldn't wait around for an escort so I came here to get one..."

Brax huffed. "Looks like it's us."

Tyg grinned. "I'm heading to Rose's."

Brax sat up his eyes widening with delighted surprise as Jared laughed. "Alright then..." Brax said standing up and tidying himself up.

"Thought that might change your tune." Tyg said darkly.

On the way back from Rose's they stopped when they heard a shrill whistle. Brax casually walked off into a nearby alley, then came back out with Stills. Tyg smiled at him, but then frowned at the look on his face.

Brax grinned and motioned with his head to Jared. "Let's go, Tyg's in trouble..."

Tyg scowled at him and pressed her mouth together as she turned back to Stills. "Why? What did I do this time?"

"You didn't wait." Stills said crossly. "How many times..."

"I had to go...I need to have a damn dress before meeting Kor at 1pm...I don't have time to wait around for you."

Stills eyes went wide and he stepped back a little. Tyg frowned and looked at the ground.

"I'm sorry...I didn't mean it like that..." She grumbled, her confusion apparent in her voice.

"He's really making an impression, huh?" Stills muttered darkly.

"No, he's really not..." Tyg grumbled.

"Seems like he is...running around picking up dresses for your dates...like some infatuated little high society miss."

Tyg stared at him, gritting her teeth, turned and walked off. He followed behind, his arms folded across his chest and his eyes dark. As they reached Barion's house Tyg walked in and slammed the door. Stills made no effort to go inside and kept walking past the house and into the nearest alley to wait, he leaned against the wall and rubbed his face and made frustrated strangled noises then sighed deeply and closed his eyes for a moment to compose himself. This thing with Tyg was really becoming a pain. He didn't know what to do with himself, he thought about her every minute of every day, his gut spinning with worry every time she wasn't where she should be. Couldn't she understand what it did to him, knowing she could be in the clutches of Raven every time he couldn't find her...he had to let her know how deeply he felt about her. Lord Kor be damned, he wasn't going to let him or Captain bloody Doven take her from him either.

Tyg was still in a foul mood when Lord Kor's carriage came to pick her up. She swept past the attendant without a word and stepped into the carriage while Mae handed the basket to the attendant. He bowed his head graciously and glanced at the carriage with a frown.

"Don't worry about it." Mae said cheerfully.

The attendant looked back at her and inclined his head, then sat up next to the driver and the carriage pulled away.

As Tyg stepped out of the carriage at the designated spot, Lord Kor was standing there, his hands in the pockets of his pants, his coat swept back behind his arms. He stared in shock and then scowled as he saw Tyg was dressed in her black leather pants and a soft cotton collared shirt of a pale green colour. His eyes darkened appreciatively over her slim hips and long legs and smiled as she walked up to him.

"Tyg, this is a surprise."

"I'm done playing games, Kor, this is me, not some strumpet wearing bloody fancy dresses...I'm willing to do it for Mae's work, singing and getting inside the mansions of the Lord's but I'm not doing it anymore for you and this stupid agreement." Tyg folded her arms and stared at him her eyes blazing ice blue in challenge.

Kor smiled. "Did something happen?" He asked as he indicated for her to walk with him. As they walked along the part of the river that crossed through the park passing other couples, Tyg glanced at Kor with a look of distaste.

"It doesn't concern you."

"If it means you are not giving this agreement your full attention, I think it does." Kor stated sternly.

Tyg grimaced and sighed looking away to the river. Kor looked at her side profile and sighed too, she was lovely to look at.

"Really, Tyg...I think honestly we may be at a crossroads here." Kor said with a deep sigh.

Tyg stopped walking and looked at him. "You're going to give this charade up?"

Kor chuckled. "Not at all, Tyg...sorry to burst your bubble, but an agreement is an agreement and I as a serious businessman refuse to break any agreement. So, I will continue to meet with you every day for another six days. If you wish, I can supply the dresses for you to wear, but I expect you to look nice and not like a mercenary killer."

Tyg rolled her eyes and folded her arms. "Fine, six more days...supply the dresses if you want, my girl can't keep making them daily."

"Of course she can't, you do realise you can just shop for dresses, don't you?" Kor smiled.

"Why would I know something like that?" Tyg said wearily pinching the bridge of her nose as she felt like she was getting a headache, she had been getting them a lot lately.

"Palin really has kept you sheltered from normal life, hasn't he?" Kor said speculatively.

Tyg grinned viciously at him. "That's how come I'm able to slaughter people in their sleep."

Kor stared at her with a disgusted look. "Tyg, enough of that talk, it doesn't impress me and will not make me change my mind on this."

Tyg rolled her eyes again. "Fine...let's find somewhere to sit and eat then, 'cause I'm starving."

Kor beamed a smile at her and took her arm in his. "Excellent, this way...."

29

It had been a month since the incident with Raven with no sign of Raven or his crew, still Palin and Stills felt it best to make sure Tyg was accompanied wherever she went. She didn't mind so much when it was Stills accompanying her, or even Bron and Luke, but sometimes it was Brax and Jared. Although they were always on their best behaviour now, with her, it was still awkward, especially with Brax. He hardly spoke to her at all now, which was fine by her.

She had finally completed her two weeks of Kor's incessant courting, and after several walks by the river, picnics in the park and attending a couple of boring dinners, she had finally been able to decline his proposal and move on. Kor had promised to try again in a couple of years. She had ended up with several dresses, jewellery and even a beautiful gold watch when she had turned up late one time, and she had had them all packaged up and returned to Kor as soon as the two weeks was up.

After her singing at Lord Kor's she had performed at one banquet and had run into Captain Thomas there. He had been very surprised to find out she was a singer for a living...she thought it best not to rock the boat on that one, he knew very well she was something else, but had – for his own reasons – decided to turn a blind eye to it which suited her, a Captain of the City Watch in her back pocket was always going to be an advantage.

All in all she felt her life was settling into something rather nice.

Tyg, Stills, Bron and Luke were making their way to the warehouse early in the afternoon like they did every day. They were laughing at a joke Bron had just told, a very lurid joke. Stills, with his arm around Tyg's shoulders pulled her in and kissed her on the head as she grumbled.

"I don't get it."

"No matter, baby girl." Stills said to her. "It's good that you don't."

"Oh..." Tyg realised it must have been a rude joke. She scowled at Bron who flinched and looked away.

They turned down a back street, taking their usual short cut. Luke was lagging behind and as he turned down the street a movement caught his eye on the roof. He called out a warning as the archer fired their shot.

Stills instinctually stepped in front of Tyg and the arrow hit him square in the chest.

Tyg yelled as Stills fell against her. She caught him under the arms and lowered him to the ground. Another arrow shot past her as she bent over and hit Bron in the throat, sending him flying backwards and falling heavily, dead.

"Tyg! Take cover!" Luke called out as he dived behind a barrel.

Tyg wasn't listening, she was staring at Stills, his head in her lap as she knelt, bent over him and wiped his hair back from his face.

"No, no, no, no, no, no, no, no." She kept muttering as she looked into his pale hazel eyes, now rife with pain.

He smiled up at her and reached a hand up to touch her face.

"Shoot her!" Tyg heard Raven yell. "For the Guilliano's bitch!"

Tyg turned her face up to look at the rooftop and saw Raven, with his long coat flashing red in the wind standing there, a bowman crouched beside him. Tyg's eyes went black and she screamed at him as she saw the bowmen notch another arrow. Tyg drew her dagger and miraculously cut the arrow in two as it flew towards her face, effectively swiping it out of the air.

Raven baulked. "What the fuck! She's not human, let's get out of here." He clapped the bowman on the shoulder and they retreated over the rooftop and disappeared.

Tyg dropped her dagger and held Stills' face, leaning over him as the tears were flowing down her cheeks.

"You can't leave me!" Tyg wailed as Stills weakly coughed, blood dripping from his mouth. He reached up again and pulled Tyg's face towards him, angling to her ear.

"It's okay Tyg...you'll be okay...know that I love you..." Stills coughed again, more blood gushed from his mouth as he struggled to breathe.

"I love you too, Stefan...hold on, please...hold on...I need you."

"No, Tyg...you are and always were meant for more...I've always known that you were special...and I was always blessed for the time I got to spend with you...your destiny awaits you out there....Tyg...find it..." Stills body wracked with coughing and more blood and foam gushed from his mouth.

"Stefan...no..." Tyg whispered as he suddenly stopped breathing, his hand dropped to his chest.

Tyg screamed a gut wrenching animalistic sound and fell over his body, clutching to it for dear life, as she pulled him into her. She cried and rocked back and forth holding Stills' body as Luke stood and watched for a moment not knowing what to do. The sight of her pure grief brought tears to his eyes and he dashed them away.

"Tyg...we can't stay here." He said finally, approaching her carefully.

"Go away!" Tyg screamed at him.

"Tyg...please listen...we have to go."

"I'm not leaving him here!" Tyg growled fiercely as she lifted her head and looked at Luke. He stepped back when he saw her eyes were completely black.

"Okay, Tyg, calm down..."

"Don't fucking tell me to calm down!" Tyg growled again in that animalistic tone. "Stefan is dead...because of me..." Tyg choked on her words and was again reduced to tears as she hugged his body close and again started rocking back and forth crying uncontrollably.

"Shit." Luke said as he looked around the dirty side street. He needed help, but couldn't leave Tyg there on her own.

He grabbed the shoulders of Bron's coat and pulled his body off the street and behind the barrels. He walked slowly back up to Tyg and stood behind her. He crouched down and wrapped his arms around her and hugged her. Tyg flinched but didn't pull away.

"I'm so sorry, Tyg." Luke whispered as he held her, resting his head on her back.

They sat that way for a long time. Luke was finally able to turn her round and into himself. As she wrapped her arms around his waist still crying, he rubbed her back, until finally her crying started to ease. He pulled her up to standing and she stepped back out of his arms.

"Thank you, Luke." Tyg said in barely a whisper as she wiped her face with her sleeve.

She turned and looked down at Stills, then crouched and closed his eyes, and kissed his lips. "Goodbye my white knight." She took his bow and quiver and grabbed her dagger, then looked at Luke as she stood up. Her eyes were still black and that worried him.

"Please take care of his body...bury him...and Bron...promise me." Tyg said to him.

"Sure Tyg...but what are you going to do?"

"Say it, Luke." Tyg growled.

"I promise, Tyg...but..."

"I'll be seeing you..."

"Wait, Tyg...where are you going?"

Tyg looked at him and smiled a small sad smile. "Tell Palin I'll be back ...someday soon."

"Tyg!" Luke called to her but she pulled up her hood and sprinted away. Luke clenched his jaw then moved Stills body, hiding it and went to find Palin.

"What the hell happened?" Palin asked as he strode into the side street. Luke, Brax and Jared were already there with two others and a cart, getting the bodies. Palin had just received word to get to the street behind the Woolshed Tavern as quickly as possible and it involved Tyg.

"It was an ambush, but I know who did it." Luke explained.

"Who?" Palin demanded, seeing Stills body on the cart. He closed his eyes, wiping a hand over his face. "Fuck" He muttered and threw the cover over.

"It was the guy from the Annul Guild, Raven. I recognised him."

"Fuck." Palin muttered as he wiped his face frustrated.

"I heard him shout something about it being for the Guilliano's."

"Hmm." Palin snorted.

"That must be the Guilliano murders in Annul, right?"

"Yeah." Palin spat bitterly.

"You mean she did the Guilliano murders? Fuck, I can't believe a girl was able to do that..." Jared exclaimed.

"She said she had no choice." Palin muttered.

"Women and children, Palin!" Jared yelled.

"Apparently he used his family as human shields, instead of withdrawing Tyg still got the job done, she didn't kill the kids...I have her word on that."

"Fuck's sake...she has no soul." Brax muttered under his breath.

"I thought her feelings for Stills would help change that, that's why I approved it, give her some empathy."

"Well, she had plenty for *him*..." Luke said remembering her heart-wrenching grieving.

"This is all on you, Palin...you created a killing machine out of a psychopath and now it's gone fucking rogue!" Brax yelled.

Palin flinched "Sociopath...besides...we know where she's heading...we can stop her."

"Annul? Fuck's sake...she's on a rampage of revenge? Gods help them all." Jared shivered.

"We have to find her as soon as possible." Palin growled.

"No shit, but what the hell do we do once we find her? Fight her? Like hell!" Brax said stomping around.

"We have to find her and subdue her before the authorities do. If she goes killing everyone then as far as the authorities will know is that there is a serial killer loose in Annul." Palin explained.

"Fuck Palin, subdue her? How the fuck are we supposed to do that?" Luke asked.

"I guess we'll cross that bridge when we come to it, for now let's just locate her."

"Well, she's a good way ahead of us, if she stole a horse...which is what I would do..." Luke said.

"And how far ahead of her would Raven be?" Palin asked.

"She was here for no more than half an hour grieving over Stills body, took his bow then left."

"His bow?" Brax asked.

"A memento I guess." Luke shrugged.

"See she does have feelings." Palin muttered.

"Not many!" Brax retorted.

"Well, at least we know there is a sliver of humanity in her somewhere." Palin said with a grimace.

"Are you serious right now?" Brax spat back. "Or just trying to convince yourself."

※

Tyg was walking down the main highway road leading towards Annul. The horse she had acquired had gone lame a couple of miles back so she had ditched it and walked the rest of the way. She had no idea how far she had already come or how far she still had to walk but she knew it was going to be at least a couple of days. She didn't even know if she was still behind the bastards or if she had gotten in front of them because they had maybe stopped in a village overnight. She wondered if they even knew or thought she was coming for them.

Tyg heard the sound of approaching horses coming up from behind. She grimaced and ignored the temptation to turn around and look. As they reached her they slowed their horses to a walk. Tyg sighed.

"Well now, what do we have here?" One of the men asked. Tyg glanced sideways and noticed four men on horseback leading several pack mules with skins on them. Trappers, Tyg thought, great. She rolled her eyes and adjusted her bag on her shoulder and kept walking.

"Seems she doesn't want to talk."

"Maybe she's mute...or deaf." One of them turned his horse, blocking her way. She stopped and looked up at the man.

"You know how to use that sword and bow, little lady?" The guy asked as he looked her over grinning.

"You don't really want to find out." Tyg muttered and ducked quickly under his horse going through its legs and then continued on her way.

"Hey!" The man shouted as his horse snorted and stomped.

"What the fuck." One of the others shouted.

"She's quick, I'll give her that." Another laughed as they all cantered their horses, pulling the moaning mules along with them, until they were ahead of her and then dismounted waiting for her to walk up to them.

Tyg stopped a few yards away from where they were blocking the road and stared at them. Her eyes were blazing ice blue.

"Interesting eyes, they change colour...never seen anything like that before." One said as the others muttered and fanned out in front of her.

"And you probably won't ever again." Tyg said calmly.

"Oh, she's talkative now." He said back.

"Pretty mouth speaks threatening words." One laughed.

"That wasn't threatening." Tyg said fixing him with a baleful stare. "But if you don't get out of my way threats will be the least of your worries."

"Fighting words now!" They all laughed.

"This girl is going to be fun..."

Tyg closed her eyes and bowed her head, kicking some gravel with one foot. "Fuck's sake." She muttered then dropped her bag and bow on the ground. She looked up and drew her sword, swinging it round and circling her shoulders.

"Ah..." Said one suddenly nervous. "...she does know how to use it by the looks."

"Pah...there's still four of us."

"So you're not going to get out of my way?" Tyg asked shaking her head and sounding fed up.

"I'm sorry, are we boring you?"

Tyg put her left hand on a dagger on her belt. "Yes, actually you are boring me because, let's face it, picking on a girl all alone in the middle of nowhere...it's not exactly original...but looking at all your ugly faces I guess it's your only chance..." Tyg sneered at them. She swung her sword round in an arc and drove it into the dirt of the road and stepped back a step from it. Her right hand went to the other dagger on her belt. "But if you want to play...let's play." Tyg grinned.

"Oh, she's a tough one." One of the men had said as she drove her sword into the ground.

"Come on now, we don't want to hurt you..." Another said, leeringly.

"Fuck that, times up. Get the fuck out of my way!" Tyg growled, her eyes dilating out to black as the calm settled over her. The two men with swords both drew them from their scabbards.

"What the fuck are you, bitch?" One muttered.

"Let's do this boys." Another said stepping forward.

Tyg flicked both daggers out of their sheaths and straight at two of the men, the one on the far right and the one on the far left. They both collapsed dead with daggers protruding from their eyes.

"Fuck!" One guy called out suddenly fearful.

Tyg stepped forward, grabbed her sword and launched herself into the air doing a twist and came down between the two other men. The first died with a back handed slash to his throat. As Tyg rounded on the last man left he countered and the ring of steel hitting steel rang out.

"What the fuck!" The last man said looking terrified at Tyg's grinning face. He dropped his sword and backed up holding his arms up. "Please don't kill me."

"Too late for that." Tyg advanced on him, but he staggered backwards.

"How far to Annul?" Tyg demanded.

"What? Ah...another couple of days by foot...if the travel is good."

"And how much are those furs worth?"

"No, please...you can't...I have a family."

"Ha! A family that doesn't know you like to rape lone girls you come across on the highway I bet. Sounds like they would be better off without you."

"Please you can't do this, I'm unarmed."

Tyg regarded him a moment, frowning. "But, I can..." She said not understanding.

☬

Palin and the guys came across an elderly couple on the side of the highway, dragging a body into a hole. Palin pulled his horse up.

"What happened here?"

The elderly man looked up. "Don't know, we came upon these men's bodies about half an hour ago. Thought it was the decent thing to do, bury them."

Palin slipped off his horse and inspected the bodies. He clenched his jaw. "These men were murdered."

"Yes." The old man said. "Trappers by the looks, must have been a large group to kill these four and take their horses and mules."

Palin heard Brax snort. "Or just one little psycho."

Luke reached over and whacked Brax round the head. The old man studied the four of them.

"Any chance of getting a hand from you strapping boys?"

Palin chuckled and got back on his horse as the old man looked at him strangely. "We don't bury rapists."

"What?" The old man said. "How do you know that?"

"I know who did this, and they wouldn't have if these men had just left them alone."

Palin put his heels to his horse. "Come on, we are definitely on the right track."

30

Tyg had sold the furs, mules and horses to a trader for half their worth as soon as she had entered Annul, but she didn't care about that, with a bit of money in her pocket she was able to buy a loaf of bread and a bottle of wine and now she sat on a roof top tearing bites off the bread in between gulps of the wine straight from the bottle and kept her eyes on the main streets. Moving every hour to a new position she kept watch, she knew sooner or later she was going to catch a glimpse of that red coat flash.

"There you are..." Tyg breathed on the second day. It was late afternoon and she just caught him coming out the back entrance of a tavern and heading furtively down a back alley. She followed, using the roofs until she saw him disappear inside a back entrance to another building. Was this the Annul Guild's hideout? She crept a bit closer on the roof, lying down flat so she could just peer over the top and keep watch.

Sure enough the comings and goings she saw over the next day were enough to convince her this was the place. It appeared to be a legitimate coffee shop at the front, but obviously the back entrance went up to the second and third floors, they were her target. Everyone inside were going to die. As soon as dawn approached she saw a third floor window was open.

She inched over the roofs and slipped down onto the window ledge and slipped inside when she heard no sounds. She looked around the small bedroom and saw one man snoring, sprawled out on the bed. She drew a dagger and quickly clamped a hand over his mouth and slit his throat. She grinned as she watched his wide eyes go blank then stood up and went to the door, opening it a crack she looked out. The hallway was gloomy, with no lighting or windows. Perfect. She walked up to the next door and opened it, ducking in. She saw a replica of the previous room and did the same to the sleeping man. Tyg grinned this was going to be too easy...her plan to have a barrel of ale sent from an anonymous Lord had worked a wonder, they were all sleeping off the drink. She suddenly thought to herself maybe she should have just poisoned the barrel...nah...where was the fun in that?

As she slipped back into the hallway she heard noise downstairs and froze. Someone was still up...maybe the whores from last night picking their belongings up and leaving before the men woke up. She slipped into another room. This had two beds in it with two men and a woman snuggled up to one of them. Tricky...this one was probably going to wake the house. Oh well, she had wanted a fight.

She stepped over to the man sleeping alone and slit his throat. The muffled gurgling made the woman stir and wake up. She screamed, as Tyg turned with a grimace. Damn it. She pounced on the man as the woman shrunk away from her, grabbing her clothes and planning on escaping out the door. Tyg drove her dagger into his heart as he sat up still bewildered by sleep and drink. The woman had the door open. Damn it. Tyg sprang from the bed and caught the woman by her hair as she fled. The woman sprang back as Tyg pulled her hair and the woman's body slammed into her. Tyg grabbed her neck and snapped it, dropping her body to the floor as two men came out of the last bedroom, rubbing their eyes. They had swords in their hands. When they saw Tyg standing like a hooded demon in the gloomy hallway they both shouted and ran at her. She sidestepped round the woman's dead body and drew her sword changing her dagger to her left hand. These men were more skilled than the usual, they were trained assassins after all, so Tyg took care to not let either of them get behind her. She clashed swords with the first one and managed to injure him with a slash across the arm with her dagger. That caused them both to step back and re-evaluate. Tyg grit her teeth, she didn't have time for this...and she could hear others coming up the stairs.

She feigned a side step and as they both were distracted by the movement Tyg threw her dagger. She got the second man in the chest. He staggered backwards and she clashed swords again with the first as two more men appeared on the landing. They caught the man with the dagger in his chest and were momentarily trapped by his staggering form to be able to get past. That gave Tyg the time to fight the first man, disarm him and run him through as she held him by his throat against the wall, grinning like a demon.

"Who the fuck are you?" One man yelled out as he pushed the dead body of the second man out of his way.

Tyg turned to him and he halted as he saw the black eyes, shining out from the black hood. "Your worst nightmare!" The sound of Tyg's growling voice gave both men pause.

One died as Tyg ran him through, but she lost her sword, unable to pull it from the man's body in time, so she held the body up and rammed it into the other man, making him stagger back against the weight. More men appeared on the landing. Tyg stepped back a few paces and grinned.

Raven had appeared on the landing.

Tyg however had no weapon.

"You!" Raven breathed unbelieving. Then he grinned back and stood up. "I'm so glad you came, little one..."

Tyg frowned, and backed up. She had never retreated from a fight, but she knew now was the exact time to do exactly that. She slowly paced backwards back down the hall as Raven advanced. The timing would be close...was she faster than him? Only one way to find out.

"I'm coming back for you." She muttered as she suddenly turned and ran, back through the door of the first bedroom she had entered, slamming the door closed and dived out the window. Raven was right behind her. He shouted as he saw her dive headlong out the third story window and leaned out. He saw her sail through the air, flip turn and forward roll onto the ground. She stood up and looked back at him. Her hood had fallen and he saw her silver braid. He yelled at her.

"You won't get away with this...I'm going to have you, bitch!"

Tyg bowed mockingly with a frown, did he say 'have you' not 'kill you'? She shivered and took off up the street. Raven turned and pushed past the men behind him. "Get out and find that bitch, now!"

He looked over and saw the dead body and clenched his jaw. "How many?" He growled as he stalked back into the hall. The men quickly inspected the rooms and shouted the numbers of dead as Raven looked down at the dead whore at his feet. She stops at nothing...he thought to himself.

"Seven, Sir...eight if you include her." One man said indicating the whore.

Raven rubbed his jaw. "Fucking hell, she is everything I had hoped she would be." He muttered as his pale brown eyes sparkled, looking red in the light...

"Sir?" The man questioned. But Raven just brushed past him and stalked off.

"I want that bitch brought back to me alive!"

Palin and Luke were looking round the corner of a building towards where Palin knew the Annul Guild's hide to be.

"Fuck we're too late." Luke muttered as they saw a wagon loaded with dead bodies roll past them quickly.

"No, we're not...look." Palin indicated as he ducked his head back and hid from the view of the person. Luke looked back round quickly and ducked back.

"That's him." He said as he had seen Raven, standing at the doorway talking to another man dressed in black.

"So she didn't get him...she will try again." Palin muttered. "Come on, let's go, we don't want to be seen to be here." He pulled his hood further down over his face and moved quickly away.

"Problem is he will be trying to get her now too." Luke said back as they ducked down an alley way.

Palin's jaw clenched. "I know...and problem is he won't want to kill her."

"What...why?" Luke stopped for a moment, frowning deeply. Palin stopped and looked back at Luke with a meaningful gaze.

"Exactly what you're thinking...but ten times worse...that man is a monster!

31

Palin crouched just inside the alleyway staring out at the small cobbled square where four streets met, there was a fountain in the middle and it would seem quite pretty if it weren't for the mad man in the black coat with the red lining that was walking around the edge of it screaming out Tyg's name. Palin was stunned, he really didn't think Raven would have dared call her out for a direct confrontation. Was he really that confident of his own skills...Palin knew better. It had to be a lure, a trap, but Palin's men had scoured the entire area and hadn't been able to find any evidence of one.

"He's definitely up to something...that cocky son of a bitch hasn't got what it takes with a sword to beat her, and she won't fall for his whip action if what you say is true Luke, and she's seen it before."

Luke grimaced. He had told Palin on the ride to Annul the truth of that fateful day she was almost taken by Raven. Palin hadn't been very happy to learn the truth of it at all, but had put it down to the past. They had to concentrate on the now.

Tyg had ventured up onto the roofs of the town early and had watched as Raven had stalked to the fountain in the square and started calling her name. She had laughed at his outrageous behaviour but was glad she had obviously gotten under his skin.

She made her way to his hide and watched to see how many men were left there. She had noticed that there were four with him, hiding in various buildings keeping watch out the windows. Leaving only one to man the hideout. She walked boldly up to the door and kicked it in. The lone man came running and Tyg had killed him with a dagger thrown to his face before he had even got his sword out. She walked through the second floor of the building, looking at the items left on tables with bored disinterest. She picked up a couple of daggers, feeling the weight of them, took one and dug the other blade back into the table. She looked into the rooms. There were a couple more bedrooms on this level, a lounge room and a rudimentary kitchen area. She opened the door to the last room and smiled to herself. His room. She walked slowly in and looked around. It was sparse, as she had expected. Perhaps this is not where he actually lived. Probably not, she knew Palin didn't live at their hide...I want to kill him where he lives, his sanctuary, Tyg decided.

She turned to leave, then saw her sword leaning up against the wall behind the door. She grabbed it and sheathed it then looked around the room for something to write on, she felt she should give Raven a note of thanks. She smiled as she went to some drawers beside his bed and opening the first drawer she saw some paper. She couldn't find any ink or a pen however, so she decided to use her own blood for dramatic effect. She nicked her finger with the blade of her sword and rubbed the blood along the paper as she wrote, it was smeared and messy but she knew Raven would appreciate the effort made. This was a game now, a dangerous game of cat and mouse. But who was the cat and who was the mouse was something only ending the game would reveal.

She went back into the back kitchen where she had left the heavy dagger and pulled it from the table then walked back and left the note pinned to the back of Raven's door.

She smiled to herself. 'I wish I could see his face when he realises I've been here snooping through his hideout while he's been hollering for me at the fountain.' Tyg laughed to herself and returned to the kitchen, she took a loaf of bread and some cheese, wrapping it in a cloth, and tying it to her belt then grabbed a bottle of whisky and walked smugly back out the entrance door, leaving it wide open, the body lying in the hall clearly visible from the stoop. She lingered a second, revelling in the simplicity of it all, drank a draught from the whisky bottle, wiping her mouth on her sleeve before she walked off in the opposite direction to where she knew Raven was.

☬

Palin was still watching Raven from the alleyway when Jared came running up to him. "We saw her, Boss."

"What! Where?" Palin said surprised as Luke sprang up from where he had been sitting with his back to a wall.

"She came out of Raven's hideout, just as we were about to go check it out."

Palin chuckled at her vivaciousness. "I should have known, damn cheeky little so and so..."

"Yeah, she stood on the stoop drinking whisky like she owned the place, then just walked off."

Palin scratched his jaw and he laughed. "Sounds like her...did you follow her?"

"Tried to...but she scaled the side of a building and took off across the roofs."

"Damn..."

"Okay, well, no point staying here watching Raven make an ass out of himself, it's obvious she has no intention of showing to his challenge, I had figured as much, but I wasn't sure if she was still thinking straight."

"She looked pretty pissed to me. Had a slight swagger on as she walked off, but then seemed to sober up and just ran straight up a wall."

Palin regarded Jared for a moment, clenching his jaw. "Damn, so she's drowning her grief in drink..."

"What's our next move then, Boss?" Brax asked. He had been leaning on the wall with his arms folded listening to everything Jared had said, he had been with him and was annoyed she had gotten away.

"Let's go to where you guys last saw her, hopefully if we range our search that way we can find her."

Tyg woke from her nap to the cacophony of evening sounds, men heading home from work, people calling out selling their wares as those men walked by, bars open to the cold but still night air. She stood up and stretched out her tight limbs. Sleeping on roofs was not the most comfortable place she could pick to sleep but it was the most isolated and here, on top of the temple to the God Ra, well it was not a place anyone would ever stumble upon her. She looked out over the view of the city, from this high advantage point at the crest of the temple's large dome roof, she could see for miles. She saw the sun heading towards its own rest far to the west. She wondered if Raven had seen her note yet, or realised she had been in his hideout and taken food and drink. Of course the dead man in the hall was a bit of a give-away. Tyg admonished herself. 'Think...keep focus...perhaps I should stop drinking?' She thought to herself as she surveyed the world from on high. 'No, then the nightmares would return.'

She could handle the hang overs, she was always dealing with a headache of some sort these days anyway, but she couldn't handle the nightmares. As if to affirm her decision she took a long draught from the whisky bottle she had procured from the Annul Guild, then slid down the arch of the dome onto the corner, catching the spire with the other hand and swung out precariously, until she regained her balance. She grimaced to herself and put the bottle down, leaving it behind. She jumped down to the roof proper and walked across it then scaled down the back wall to the ground.

She walked across the gardens and was just about to jump over the wrought iron fence that surrounded the temple gardens, separating them from the streets outside, when a voice called out to her.

"Stop right there!" She grimaced and turned to peer out from under her hood. She saw a man in long flowing robes of a bright yellow. They were fine silken robes and were tied with a sash around his waist with long flowing sleeves. The man was elderly, and had a pleasant demeanour about him. Tyg straightened as he approached and folded her arms, making no indication she intended to lower her hood. He stopped a yard in front of her and seemed surprised at the bright intelligent eyes that regarded him coolly, and the beautiful flawless young face they looked out from, as he peered intently into the darkness of the hood.

"Oh, I see you are not just some miscreant...but what are you doing scaling the temple walls?"

Tyg raised a brow at him at the word miscreant, but said nothing. The old man scratched his jaw and re-evaluated. "I have seen you standing on top of my temple, like some angel sent from the heavens...you are lucky no one else has...or if they have they have not reported it...I am guessing you don't want it reported?"

Tyg frowned and looked away. "No."

"Are you hungry?" The old priest asked, smiling.

Tyg's expression darkened. "No."

"Not one for small talk, are you?"

Tyg sighed. "No, look can I go, or do we have a problem?"

"No problem, except the damage you're doing to my roof."

"Your roof...that's rich."

"I am the High Priest."

"But it's Ra's temple."

"Touché." The priest chuckled. "However that doesn't negate the fact you could be damaging it."

"I'm not damaging it." Tyg said simply as she shifted on her feet and looked around. She had already been standing still for far too long.

"I'm amazed you can even get up there..."

Tyg shrugged and continued to watch the street through the fence.

"You are hiding from someone? Perhaps I can help you?"

"You don't want to help me, priest...just leave me alone." Tyg pulled her hood further down over her face, jumped into the air, turning sideways, with a hand out she grabbed the top of the fence and pulled herself over it, then came down lightly on her feet and disappeared behind a horse drawn wagon.

The priest watched then turned back to the temple. She seemed so angry, he felt compelled to try and help her.

Tyg was sitting with her legs folded on the edge of a roof, leaning her back against the chimney, watching the street. Raven was still at the fountain, she had to give him praise for his tenacity at least, but as it got darker he was obviously giving up and had called his men to him. He was sitting on the edge of the fountain with his four men standing in front of him and was talking to them. Then he stood up and walked off with them all in tow, discreetly. Tyg grinned and crouched up, she hadn't missed the show. She quickly made her way over the roof tops and settled into a place where she could see the entrance to the hide. It was then that she saw Palin. He was following along behind Raven and his men furtively, keeping to the shadows. It was only because he had to cross the street that she even noticed him. She scowled and cursed. What the hell was he doing here? This complicated things. Especially if he had come to stop her. She wondered if he had come alone, no of course not, Luke was there when it happened, there was no way he would have stayed in Arial.

She lay down on the roof so she could just stick her head up to watch. She had a clear view of Raven and saw he had stopped walking and taken out his sword. He was standing just off the steps and was looking into the darkened depths of the hallway beyond. He sent one of his men in...coward, she thought. Tyg heard his expletive from her vantage point when the man declared his mate in the hall dead. Raven stormed inside. Tyg grinned, she wished she could see Raven's face. She also wished she had a bow...that might be the easy option, but she had stashed Stills bow in a safe place. Did she even want easy? She wanted to make him suffer.

She reached for the bottle of whisky or wine that was always beside her, then cursed when she remembered she had left it on the roof of the temple. She chuckled to herself. That had reminded her of the priest, wanting to help her, yes please, help me have my vengeance. Tyg cackled maniacally. Stupid priest. She hoped she wasn't going to have to kill him too.

She looked up as she heard her name. Raven was standing out on the stoop screaming her name and shaking a fist. Tyg laughed, such an idiot...she really wished she did have a bow right at that moment, just to teach him a lesson. Focus Tyg...there is a bigger lesson for him to learn.

She watched as he walked up the street and back onto the main street. Tyg got up and followed along the rooftops, until they ran out. Then she jumped down and hurried scaled the walls to the next row of tenement housing, hoping she hadn't lost track of him. It took her a moment to find him again, he was just turning down another street. Tyg quickly jumped from the roofs and ran down an alleyway then peeked around the corner. Raven was definitely heading somewhere interesting.

She tracked him for several blocks and noticed that the streets had become wider, with trees and the housing had become more separated, instead of ten houses joined together, here there were only up to four. They even had little gardens in front of their doorsteps, rather than open straight to the street. Raven walked up to one such house, a middle one of a four row, two storied townhouse. He rapped on the door and was admitted by a maid. Tyg watched from the roof opposite, these roofs were high angled pitched, so she had to lie down and look over the top of the peak. She really didn't know if this was his house or not...she had to wait and see. She made her way back down to the street and retraced her footsteps, she had to also keep an eye on Palin and find out exactly how many men he had brought with him.

32

Tyg headed back to the temple to rest. Up on that rooftop was the only place she felt safe enough to sleep, not that sleep was easy these days, it was more of a drunken stupor than actually sleep.

As she jumped the fence back into the gardens of the temple Tyg grimaced to find the priest sitting on the marble bench seat, feeding the birds with a loaf of bread. He raised his head and smiled at her as she walked through the bushes towards him and stopped in front of him, causing all the birds to take off in a flurry of hastily beating wings.

"Are you waiting for me, Priest?" Tyg folded her arms and stared at him.

He regarded her calmly, noting the sword and daggers, the black leather pants. "You are not really welcome here...you know that right?" He smiled at her, which was in contradiction to his words.

"But..." Tyg smirked as she got his meaning. He had to say the words, formally, so they were on the same page.

The Priest looked away and stood up. "Follow me, please..."

Tyg watched him walk away for a few steps then turn and look back at her, waiting. "You don't need to do this, Priest, I'm not some pity case to take off the streets...I'm not planning on staying here long."

"You are the murderer that killed all those men over in the south quarter." The Priest said matter-of-factly as he tucked his hands into the sleeves of his robes and watched her intently.

Tyg rolled her eyes. "Don't go saying something that's going to get yourself killed, Priest."

"My name is Mathias...please follow me." He turned and continued to walk around to the side entrance of the temple.

Tyg sighed and dropped her hands and walked slowly behind him.

Once inside he led her to the kitchen, Tyg noticed the strange looks on the faces of the other few priests they past. They stopped and stared and bowed their heads in respect to Mathias, but dropped their mouths open at the sight of the black hooded figure following along behind their High Priest. This was the inner sanctum of the temple, for priests only, very few outsiders got to come through to their cloister, and certainly not a mysterious hooded dangerous individual such as this.

Mathias stopped and turned to her slightly. "It would be much preferred if you would lower your hood, in respect."

Tyg chuckled to herself. "You think I have respect for this place?"

"Clearly not if you think it okay to climb onto the roof." Mathias answered with a smile.

"So why are we doing this, Priest? I told you I'm not interested in being saved."

Mathias sighed and looked around, his gaze settled on a priest that was kneading dough, but had stopped in his action to stare at Tyg and Mathias. He caught the High Priest's look and wiping his hands off on his apron, fled the kitchen.

Tyg smiled as she watched the interaction, then raised an eyebrow at Mathias.

He raised an arm from within his robes and pointed to a stack of loaves that were cooling. "Help yourself."

Tyg stared at him, the smell of baking bread had made her stomach growl, and he must have heard it. She grit her teeth stubbornly and looked away. "No thanks."

Mathias laughed. "No need to be obstinate...it has been offered in good faith...take it, you are clearly hungry."

Tyg scowled at him and reached out and grabbed a loaf, biting a chunk off and chewing it while not taking her eyes off him, she slowly reached a hand up and lowered her hood.

Mathias's eyes went wide at the sight of her. "Oh, my." He stammered.

Tyg's scowl deepened and she went to raise her hood again. "No, don't do that...child...please...I meant no offense...but you are angelic."

"Hardly." Tyg scoffed as she took another bite of the bread. Mathias turned away and grabbed a pitcher full of water and an earthenware cup and poured out some water, holding it out to her.

"Quite, your looks are but perhaps not your personality...hmmm?"

Tyg laughed, causing Mathias's eyes to widen again in surprise at the purely angelic sound. "Perhaps...you know, Priest...you're a funny guy." Tyg took the water and drank it down gratefully. Mathias smiled and bowed his head slightly in acknowledgment.

"I have had a dream regarding you." Mathias said then as he watched her drinking. She froze then lowered the cup slowly.

"Doesn't that go against your vows or something?" Tyg asked bitterly.

Mathias laughed. "Oh, not that sort of dream, goodness...I meant a prophetic dream."

Tyg scowled. "I'm not going to want to hear this, am I?"

Mathias rubbed the back of his neck. "Well, perhaps not, but I feel I should say it anyway."

Tyg sighed and looked around the rudimentary kitchen. It was simple and clean, but she could see that the priests obviously ate well. "For a decent meal...I'll listen to your dream, Priest."

"I can go one better than that and offer you a bed for the night too." Mathias smiled genuinely at her.

"A bed...in a male cloister? That's interesting..." Tyg said with a raised eyebrow and she chuckled a musical laugh.

Mathias stared at her. "Do you sing?"

Tyg flinched. "Did you dream that too?"

"No, but your laughter is quite musical to the ear."

"Huh...yes...I can, want me to sing you something?"

"Perhaps...how about after supper..."

"I tell you what, Priest...if you give me the most amazing meal and soft bed to sleep in tonight I will go through to your temple and sing the Setting of the Sun to Ra for you, I think I know the whole hymn..."

Mathias's eyes went wide and his mouth dropped open. "I can't wait..." He said breathlessly.

So it was that Tyg found herself in the temple of Ra looking up at the vast dome from the inside, she smiled at the way the setting sun hit the glass panels in the dome and sent the rays of sunlight cascading out around the inside of the temple in an amazing array. She knelt piously in front of the large statue of Ra and lifted her chin as she started to sing. The temple was full of priests all curious about the strange silver haired girl that the High Priest had broken the rules for and admitted into the cloister. As she started to sing, her pure angelic voice soaring and echoing around the domed temple, all the priests fell to their knees behind her. Mathias stared at her back in awe and trembled slightly as he thought about his dream.

When Tyg finished the short melodic hymn, she stood up and turned around, her eyes going wide at the sight of the priests all genuflecting at her feet. Tyg staggered back in shock as Mathias stood up and took her hand, then sunk to one knee.

"Child, please don't startle...they wish to worship you."

"Worship?" Tyg baulked and snatched her hand back from his grasp.

"You are truly an angel."

"No I'm not...I'm a murderer, remember..." Tyg said with contempt, turning and walking out of the temple room, Mathias flowing along behind.

"Please, I haven't yet told you my dream."

"I don't think I want to hear it."

Mathias caught up to her and grabbed her arm to stop her walking away. Tyg spun fast and slammed Mathias up against the wall a dagger at his throat. "Don't touch me." Tyg said flatly as she stepped back, putting her dagger away. "That's a quick easy way to get yourself killed, Priest."

"I'm sorry...I meant no offense...but please, stay."

Tyg sighed and leaned on the wall opposite and folded her arms. "It would be nice to get a decent night's sleep, especially before tomorrow."

"Tomorrow?"

"Tomorrow I get my vengeance." Tyg stared at Mathias coldly, her eyes ice blue. He swallowed hard and bowed his head.

"Yes...a vengeful angel...exactly what you are."

Tyg rolled her eyes. "Knock it off!"

"I apologise." Mathias said with a coy smile as he looked up at her with his head still bowed. "Please come through to my private study."

Mathias walked off, tucking his hands into his robes. Tyg watched him walk a few paces then sighed again and lurched up off the wall like a sulky teenager and followed the High Priest down the hallway.

His study was a contrast to the rest of what she had seen, so far everything seemed rudimentary and basic, but here the desk was a rich dark wood and the chairs were expensive textured fabrics, the books that lined the walls looked old and well read. The whole room smelt of aged paper and candle wick burning.

"Please sit." Mathias said, "Would you like a drink perhaps?" He indicated the carafe of dark red wine on the corner of his desk.

"Well, this is a little different to the rest of the temple, huh...perks of the position?" Tyg said with a grin as Mathias poured them both a glass of the fine red.

"Quite." Mathias smiled as he pushed the glass of red wine across the desk towards her, then settled down in his chair and sipped his wine.

Tyg took the wine gratefully, not having had any alcohol all day. She gulped back half the glass and put it on the desk. Leaning back in the chair and crossing her legs.

"So Priest, tell me about your dream before I change my mind."

"Certainly...but I haven't even asked you for your name yet."

"Don't, that way you won't be disappointed when I refuse to give it to you."

Mathias chuckled. "You have a way about you that says you have had a very hard life so far, you appear only young but your words say you are old and learned."

Tyg shrugged. "It's not a life I would wish on anyone."

"Hmm, well I fear it may not be going to get any easier in the future..."

Tyg grimaced. "I always thought that way..."

Mathias stared at her as she looked down with a touch of sadness on her face. "You will have many trials and cross roads to decide upon in your journey through life...but ultimately you will be given a most worldly involved choice to sacrifice one you love deeply for the fate of the world."

Tyg looked up and met his gaze. "What do I care about the fate of the world?"

"Perhaps you do not, yet...but your journeys will be vast and many lessons will be taught to you along the way...you will love two, and have to choose one. Which path you choose will determine how everyone's life proceeds."

Tyg flinched. "I don't want that sort of responsibility."

Mathias smiled knowingly. "Fate and destiny are seldom something anyone wishes for."

33

Tyg went back to the house she followed Raven to the night before. She hadn't bothered to notify the priest, why should she? After today she had no intention of going back. Besides, he had freaked her out with his strange predictions and she really didn't want to have any more conversations with him.

As she perched over the roof of the house opposite she wondered whose house this actually was she was looking at. She hoped it was Raven's. She remembered the maid and decided to be adventurous. She made her way down to street level and walked up to the house. It was about an hour after dawn, servants would be awake.

She strolled up to the door and knocked soundly on it, then stood back and waited. Sure enough a maid opened the door and looked nervously out. Seeing a young woman standing on the doorstep the maid opened the door wider.

"Hello, miss, how can I help you?"

"Is the man of the house in?" Tyg asked with a smile.

"Yes, but he is still indisposed, I'm afraid."

Tyg grinned and pushed the maid in the chest, pushing her backwards out of the doorway. Tyg stepped in and placed a dagger at the maid's throat as she placed a finger to her own lips and flicked her foot, catching the door and shutting it behind her.

"Kitchen...go..."

Tyg knew the one place a person with a maid seldom went was the kitchen. The maid was near to tears with fright as Tyg walked down the hall beside her. When they reached the kitchen Tyg indicated for the maid to sit. As she sat down in the ordinary wooden chair at the rudimentary small table Tyg took off her cloak, draping it over the back of a chair and sat opposite her, placing the dagger on the table.

"How many people are here?" Tyg asked, her eyes blazing ice blue.

The terrified maid was wringing her hands together, tears falling down her cheeks. "Just my master and myself."

Tyg smiled and leaned back in her chair, placing her feet up on the table. "Excellent."

"Wh-what are you going to do?" The maid asked timidly.

Tyg glared at her with a frightening expression. "I intend to kill him."

The maid's eyes went wide and she gasped. "Can you?"

Tyg frowned. "Not the reaction I expected, does he hurt you?" Tyg remembered the strange things Raven had always said to her. "Don't answer that...I know he does."

The maid looked at her lap and said nothing but her cheeks burned with a deep red blush.

"Don't be embarrassed...make me some tea." Tyg said thinking to keep the maid busy and not thinking too much.

"Oh...okay..." The maid got up timidly and set about putting the kettle on the coal range.

"What time does Raven usually get up?"

The maid looked at her a moment in thought at the strange name, then realised Tyg meant her master. "Soon, he eats breakfast in the front reception area."

"Perfect, I'll be in there waiting for my tea then."

As Tyg stood up the maid turned and watched her leave. Tyg stopped in the doorway, the dagger back in her hand. "Don't try anything stupid."

The maid slowly shook her head as Tyg grinned and left the kitchen. Instead of going to the front room however, Tyg swung a right and went up the stairs.

As silent as a cat Tyg made her way to the master suite. Why was every town house almost the exact same layout? She thought to herself as she silently opened the door, she entered and saw Raven asleep in his bed. She grinned viciously and thought about just running him through right there, but no...she intended to make a lesson of him. She sat down in the upholstered chair that was in the corner of the room, where the two large windows met, reached out and dramatically threw the drapes open, then sat back to watch the show, placing her sword across in front of her so it rested on both arms of the chair and crossed her legs.

Raven stirred at the sudden intrusion of light. Sitting up and rubbing his eyes. He was shirtless and his long raven black hair was down and flowed around his shoulders. Tyg had to blink and shake herself to her senses. He was actually quite a handsome, well-muscled individual and as he woke the evil hardness to his face wasn't evident.

"What the hell are you playing at, Tanzi!" Raven grumbled as his eyes slowly came into focus. "I'm going to punish you for that!"

His eyes stopped on the figure in black sitting in the chair in the corner, her silver blond hair iridescent in the early morning light streaming in behind her.

"You!" Raven spat out surprised as his brain finally freed of the fog of slumber and caught up to the situation he now found himself in. He grinned as he became fully awake and got his senses back.

"Well, well...I never figured you would be so forward as to actually come to my bedroom so willingly." He smirked.

Tyg scowled at him, but didn't move...she was not going to be baited.

"I got your message...it was delightful to be able to smell your blood...exquisite...I never thought you to be so polite though." He chuckled as he raked his hands through his hair, sweeping it off his face and regarded Tyg with a steely gaze. "What do you want from me, princess?"

Tyg frowned at the endearment. "I want the opportunity to kill you."

Raven scratched his jaw and chuckled again. "It seems to me you have had several chances at that already but you haven't acted on them...curious." His eyes sparkled at her with that reddish hue.

"It's not curious...I want to fight you not slay you, that would be too easy."

Raven's eyes widened slightly. "Why on Gods' earth would you want to do that, you hardly respect me...do you?"

"No." Tyg said simply. "I wish to make a lesson of you."

Raven burst into laughter and swept his legs out of the bed and placed his feet on the floor. "Oh, little one...you do beat all my expectations, it really is a shame we have ended up on the wrong side of friendship."

"Friendship?" Tyg snorted. "Are you fucking serious?"

Raven stood up and turned to face her, he was completely naked and stood proudly showing off his tall lithe frame and his more than mediocre package. Tyg didn't even blink and just kept her eyes on his face. He grinned evilly and grabbed his pants from off the chest at the end of his bed and proceeded to put them on.

"Are you sure you're not here to become friends?" He teased, buckling up his pants.

"No."

"Then why are you here?" Raven asked sitting down on the chest, which brought him only a yard away from Tyg. She tightened the grip on her sword. He noticed and his eyes sparkled with delight. "Come on now, little one...you obviously like what you see...I can see it in your eyes...did you really just come here to offer me a challenge...you could have just met me in the street yesterday."

"That was a trap."

Raven chuckled, he was enjoying himself immensely. He didn't think he would ever get the chance to converse so candidly with this strange girl. He found her absolutely fascinating and really wanted to know how much she bled and how much pain she could endure before screaming. His top lip twitched at the thought.

"Stop." Tyg growled.

Raven looked up at her with an arched brow. "Stop what?"

"Whatever it is you are thinking...it's never going to happen." Tyg said sourly.

Raven laughed and leaned back. "Oh, you really are quite something, I have to admit, little one...you really do have me in complete enthrallment."

Tyg's frown deepened as she suddenly had the feeling she shouldn't have come here. She stood up to leave but at the same moment Raven suddenly lurched forward and grabbed her wrists, twisting them up over her head as he turned with her and fell onto the bed on top of her, her arms held above her head, her sword still in her hand.

Tyg grit her teeth as Raven brought his face down over hers, pressing his body hard against her.

"Now, isn't this better, little one?" He breathed against her lips as he wrenched her sword from her grasp.

Tyg glared at him, keeping herself calm, not letting the panic rise...if it did she lost.

He crushed his lips against hers, forcing his tongue into her mouth briefly and then looked down at her with a satisfied smirk.

"Thank you for coming to me, princess...we are going to have so much fun together."

He sat up so he straddled her hips, her sword in his hand now. She raised up on her elbows but Raven rested her sword across her throat.

"Tut tut...don't move." Raven warned in a deep bark.

Tyg clenched her jaw and her eyes blazed ice blue fire in fury.

"Oh, princess, you are so delectable...I can't wait to taste you." Raven said as he licked his lips in anticipation.

"You really think you're going to get that chance?" Tyg said scornfully, she couldn't believe how full of himself Raven actually was. It would only take for him to go to move off her, the slightest little distraction as he looked away, and she was back in control.

Raven frowned at her words, re-evaluating, then grinned. "I do love your incessant challenging of my abilities...but once I have you tied down at my mercy...you will come to understand just what an experienced attentive lover I can be."

Tyg shuddered involuntarily at the snake oil in his voice. He felt it and chuckled.

"Oh, you shudder in anticipation."

"Not really..." Tyg said in revulsion.

Raven suddenly nicked her neck with her sword, causing a fine ribbon of blood to emerge on one side of her windpipe. Raven rubbed the blood with his thumb and sucked it into his mouth. Tyg's eyes widened in shock as Raven's darkened in barely suppressed evil intent. Was that what he meant by taste her? Tyg thought fearfully...then just as the panic was nearing winning the fight in Tyg's mind, she saw Raven close his eyes in a slow blink of pure delectable pleasure at the taste of her blood.

Raven wasn't even sure what just happened...it was so quick, so fluid, so strong, but he suddenly found himself on his back, with Tyg standing over him, her sword back in her hand and pointed at his throat. He stared at her with fright as he saw her eyes were completely black.

"Now, now, Princess...what happened to wanting to kill me in a fair fight?"

"I changed my mind, you're a monster!"

"Ha! I'm the monster? Look at you!"

"I will meet you soon...be ready to fight." Tyg said as she jumped off the bed and stepped to the door. Raven surged up off the bed and ran after her.

He reached out and managed to grab her by the back of her shirt, as he stepped out onto the landing just before the stairs. He pulled her back as he was still surging forward. They crashed together and tumbled in a tangle of arms and legs to the floor. Tyg let go of her sword and grabbed a dagger, bringing it round as she got on her knees, slashing it back to make Raven dodge backwards, and fall back again.

Tyg grabbed her sword in her left hand, gained her feet and leaped down the staircase, missing all the stairs and landing lightly on her feet at the bottom.

"Tea is ready in the front room." Tyg grinned at him as she saw the maid standing in the doorway frozen in fear. Tyg turned and fled out the front door.

Raven gained his feet and ran down the stairs and ran out the front door to find Tyg standing in the middle of the street, hands on her hips, her sword sheathed.

The other people on the street couldn't help but stop and stare at Raven in his half naked state. He straightened and composed himself, running his hands through his hair, a large smirk on his face.

"When and where, little one?" He asked confidently as he smirked, his eyes dancing with delight.

"As soon as you're ready, I'll find you." Tyg grinned. "Oh and bring my cloak with you, if you please?"

Raven chuckled. "You left me a memento...how sweet."

Tyg pretended to doff a cap and turned and walked off down the street. Raven watched her, licking his lips in nervous anticipation.

34

Raven had been on edge all day, the slightest noise behind him had him flinching back and whirling round expecting to see Tyg standing behind him. He cursed her for what she had managed to do to his resolve.

"Clever little bitch." He muttered as he stepped out of the hideout just as the sun was disappearing. He paused on the stoop as a figure stepped out of the deepening gloom, he saw the flash of steel and grinned.

"Are you ready, Raven?" Tyg asked him as she walked up the alleyway. He shuddered due to the husky way she said it.

"I've been ready all day...just how you wanted me."

Tyg smiled at him and he couldn't help but recognise how beautiful she was. He drew his sword.

"Did you bring my cloak?" Tyg asked as she circled her sword around in an arc and took a couple of steps closer.

"Forgot it, sorry, princess." Raven said sounding genuinely apologetic.

Tyg shrugged. "Just you and me, Raven..." Tyg said looking at the two men that were standing behind him.

Raven raised a hand and waved them back as he stepped off the stoop. "Of course, princess...it was always going to be just you and me."

"I'll make sure of it." A voice suddenly boomed out from behind Tyg at the entrance to the alley way. Tyg flinched but didn't turn around. Raven stared contemptuously at the tall burly figure outlined in the gloom.

"Palin! What the fuck are you doing here? Can't you see your little cat obviously prefers my company?" Raven chuckled.

Palin scoffed and stuck his hands in his pockets. "I am here merely to observe."

"Fine, whatever." Raven said "Do you know she was in my bedroom this morning, lying on my bed, underneath me?" Raven grinned wickedly at Tyg. "She won't deny it...it's the truth after all..."

Tyg growled. "Enough Raven, fight me." Tyg lunged forward, bringing her sword up and grabbing her dagger in her left hand. Raven easily met her blade with his own in a flash of sparks and the ring of steel echoed through the alleyway. Raven quickly jumped back as Tyg's dagger slashed past his chest. Tyg was holding the dagger in a reverse hold, the blade lying against her forearm, ready to slash out.

Raven dodged and weaved and used his sword defensively against Tyg's onslaught for several minutes as she came at him in a blur of unbridled skill. She jumped back for a moment to catch her breath and Raven wiped the sweat from his brow. He saw Palin standing with his feet planted, blocking the alleyway, watching calmly.

"You have taught her well, Palin." Raven saluted him cheerfully. He couldn't see Palin's expression in the deepening darkness.

"Don't you dare look away from me!" Tyg snarled vehemently as she lunged forward to strike again. Raven dodged too slow and got a slashing cut to his left bicep. He staggered back.

"My apologies, princess." Raven breathed raggedly. He looked into her eyes and noticed how they glowed in the darkness. "First blood, I'm impressed."

"You'll be more than impressed soon, Raven." Tyg purred at him as her eyes went black as he watched. He swallowed hard and took an involuntary step backwards, just as she swung again, then disappeared. Appearing suddenly behind him and slashing at his back with her dagger in a crisscross pattern, cutting deep. He staggered forward and turned around bringing his sword up to defend against another series of sword thrusts and slashes from Tyg as she chuckled. Raven's blood went cold at the sound and he suddenly feared for his life. In the darkness she was everywhere, the true monster. He hadn't even seen her leap over his head the first time, but he saw it now and just managed to turn enough to fend off her dagger with his forearm.

Raven was now bleeding from his bicep and forearm of his left side and from the two slashes on his back. Tyg was relentless, never giving Raven a moment to even think, all he could do was constantly defend. He knew there was no way to win a fight that way.

Tyg jumped back again and stalked around him.

"Get your breath back, Raven...I have no intention of ending your life just yet..." Tyg said coldly. Raven watched her intently, she looked like a black panther stalking its prey.

"Tyg!" Palin growled disapprovingly at her statement.

Tyg ignored him, like she hadn't even heard him, just as she came at Raven again. Raven heard Palin curse.

"She's lost...no stopping anything now, stay alert!"

Raven realised Palin had more men standing behind him. He grit his teeth and called out to the two men still standing up on the stoop.

"Watch those men don't interfere!"

Tyg suddenly jumped away from Raven and ran up the wall, twisting and somersaulting over towards the two men, slashing down with both her sword and her dagger and she landed between them. She drove her dagger down into the fleshy part between the neck and shoulder of one and with her sword she slashed the throat open of the other man.

Raven stared at her bewildered as she stared back at him with a hideous grin, her face now splattered with blood. She stalked up, the bodies falling to the ground behind her.

"You are the true monster!" Raven yelled, taking his sword in both hands and running at her.

"Yes, I am." Tyg said bone chillingly calm as she met Raven's attack. "But you created me."

He was tiring and knew he didn't have much left. He felt Tyg's dagger bite into his stomach and looked down to see the hilt and Tyg's hand around it, then she pulled it out with a cruel twist. A gush of blood erupted out of the wound as he staggered back. His face coming up to look at Tyg.

The face looking at him was no longer a person, he could see what Palin meant when he said she was lost. The black eyes stared at him soullessly in the darkness and he could see her white teeth clearly as she sneered at him as she advanced mercilessly. She slashed her sword out and Raven raised his sword to meet her swing but she suddenly changed its trajectory and slammed it broadside into his hand, smashing his sword out of his grasp and breaking the bones in the back of his hand. He staggered back further as she swung her sword round playfully, grinning at him as he was now at her complete mercy.

Of which she had none to give.

Tyg as the tormenter stalked her prey slashing and hacking at him at every step as he slowly kept staggering away from her, until he was nearly dead on his feet through loss of blood. She ran him through with her sword, pushing him backwards, with her dagger in his shoulder as well, until he hit the wall. She leaned in and breathed heavily as he raggedly drew in breaths, their faces only inches apart.

"I'll see you in the Underworld, Raven!" She whispered hoarsely to him as he clutched at her shirt and pulled her closer like he wanted to say something.

He grabbed her round the neck and pulled her lips to his. He heard her growl a deep menacing growl in her throat as she twisted the sword in his stomach, changing the angle and ripping it up through his flesh. Blood gushed out of his mouth as Tyg pulled away in disgust. He slumped to the ground, her sword still stuck in him as Tyg turned suddenly and stared at the figures standing in the darkness around her, unseeing...she raised her dagger.

Luke suddenly ran up to Tyg and threw his arms around her. "It's okay Tyg, you got him, it's finished, now come home. I buried Stills, just like I promised...you'll like the spot I chose...by a river, under a great weeping willow...come on now, little cat... let's go home...so I can show you..." Luke never stopped talking quietly to her, just like he had seen Stills do several times when she was lost and out of control. Just like he had himself as she grieved next to Stills body. He didn't stop talking until he felt her body relax into him, and her arms go around his waist.

Palin watched amazed, as did the others.

"What the fuck just happened?" Brax asked. "Is he sleeping with her?"

Palin growled and whacked Brax around the head. "No! Of course not you dolt!"

Jared chuckled. "Idiot, is that all you ever think about..."

"I don't get it then...how was he able to do that?"

"Respect and love, Brax...something you'll never truly get." Palin muttered and walked off shouting. "Come on, we have to get out of here!"

Tyg was sitting under the great weeping willow, looking at the river. It was a perfectly lovely sunny day and she watched as Luke waded around in the water trying to catch a large trout he had seen. She laughed as he tried to grab it and almost fell on his ass. He looked up at the sound. He smiled at her and walked out, glad she had finally stopped crying over the grave of Stills that was beside her. With the grave of Bron beyond that one. He walked up and lay down on the grass nearby, taking a blade of grass and sticking it in his mouth.

"Thank you, Luke." Tyg said with a smile.

"No problem, Tyg, you know that...I promised."

"And it's perfect...he would have loved it here."

"Yeah, almost makes one not want to go back, huh?' Luke said looking at the sun sparkling off the flowing water.

"Yeah...back to our stupid lives..."

Luke looked up at her. "So, you really going to do this singing thing?"

Tyg nodded. "Stills said I was meant for more...maybe this is it."

"Nah..."

Tyg looked at him funny. "What do you mean...nah?"

"Stills is right...you are meant for more...but singing isn't it."

Tyg frowned at the way Luke said it, giving her thoughts of the High Priest of Ra. "Well, whatever...it seems like it's going to be quite a lucrative job...plus Mae seems to want me to help with the rest of her business too."

"So not much time left for us then?" Luke said meaning the Guild.

"Always Luke...Palin still has work for me, don't worry about that...I'm not going anywhere, that's the whole reason behind this singing lark." Tyg smiled.

Luke glanced up and grinned. "Good, glad to hear it. Although I get the feeling you may be going to see a lot more of Jared and Brax."

"Why?" Tyg scowled.

"They're my new squad partners...that means they are your new squad partners too."

Tyg rolled her eyes. "Fucking great!"

35

It was four months later and Tyg was sitting in the small dining room slowly pulling apart a muffin and putting the pieces into her mouth while she stared unblinking at the cost sheet in front of her.

Suddenly a crash came from the kitchen and Mae yelled out. Tyg was on her feet and standing in the kitchen doorway in no time to find Mae slamming the coal range door closed. Tyg had never seen Mae upset like this before.

"Mae? What's the problem?" Tyg said in a dead pan voice, she rarely spoke with any emotion anymore.

She turned and looked at Tyg with a hefty sigh and wiped her brow. "I'm going to need some help. I'm starting to get behind in all this work."

"Too successful?" Tyg smiled coyly.

Mae regarded her solemnly. "It appears so...thanks to you."

"Don't blame me."

"Why not, it's your fault...ever since you've been helping me with the organisation of the catering and entertainment suddenly everyone wants to hold a ball or banquet, just to see you, their national treasure."

Tyg scowled. "I can stop helping then." She said simply, folding her arms.

Mae's eyes went wide. "Oh no, dear...please don't do that."

Tyg shrugged. "I couldn't even if I wanted to...you know that...I wouldn't be allowed too." Tyg rolled her eyes. Even though Palin had taken her back without any question, she had still not been able to free herself of the espionage work that Lord Kor expected of her, although after hearing what she did he no longer pursued her on a personal level deciding she was far too wild and dangerous for a man of his standing to get involved with, which suited her just fine. Coping with Stills death was still too raw and she doubted if she would ever love again, but thoughts went to what the priest had said...she would love two...did that mean two more or was their only one more love left in her life?

"So what is the problem exactly?" Tyg leaned on the doorframe, her arms still folded.

Mae sighed again. "Barion has been giving me a hard time about not being able to do my wifely duties properly because this business is taking all my time."

"Your wifely duties?" Tyg raised an eyebrow.

Mae's eyes went wide. "Oh no...not those duties...no..." She chuckled. "I mean keeping this house in order. You know, cleaning and stuff."

"Well don't look at me...I don't clean." Tyg said indignantly.

"No, I didn't mean you." Mae said flatly. She knew Tyg too well to suggest that, especially now she was back after her disappearance that no one wanted to talk about. She had become cold and distant, rarely speaking, and quick to rage. Mae had also noticed that the good looking young man never came around anymore, but for some reason she felt it best not to ask why. "I was actually thinking now the money is starting to come in quite well that perhaps I should hire a maid."

"A maid?" Tyg's eyes narrowed. "Don't hire one yet...I may have a solution for you..." Tyg turned and walked away while Mae blinked and wondered what Tyg was up to now.

Tyg had headed to Rose's establishment and after asking to speak to Rose she was now in Rose's office sharing a drink with her.

"So what brings you back here again, Tyg? Needing another dress from Tess?"

"No actually I'm needing Tess."

"I don't think I understand..."

"I'm here to give Tess a job offer, one she won't be able to refuse...I'm just giving you the courtesy of letting you know so you can find yourself a new maid."

"Oh." Rose breathed. "Well...I..."

Tyg looked at her over the rim of her glass and grinned. She knew Rose wouldn't try and argue with her, after getting back from Annul everyone who was anyone in the right grapevine knew what she had done. Rose was cautious and friendly around her now but Tyg knew fear ran closely behind.

"Very well." Rose said with a faint smile. "Actually I'm glad...Tess was never meant for this place...I wish her all the best."

"Thank you, Rose." Tyg said genuinely.

"I'll go and get her, shall I?"

"Sure thing."

End of Part One

PART II

SOMETHING MORE...

ANTYN'S
PROPHECY COLLECTION

In order to control the world seek the
One born of Three
but Beware!
To usurp the power
be prepared to kill God's born
and you shall yourself become a God!
– excerpt from Seer Gwenth's Reading 1620

The blood of three
Flows in One's veins
Conflict rules
And pain reigns
To harness the power
One must control the spirit
Harness the pain
And you shall cloak Her in it
- Prophetic Poet 1560

36

Mae arrived back one day, bubbling over with excitement. She searched for Tyg and found her in the study, pouring over the accounts.

"Tyg! I have great news." Mae exclaimed as she entered the room.

"What is it, Mae?" Tyg asked a small smile coming to her lips, Mae's enthusiasm infectious.

"I have been told by Lord Karon that there will be two special guests at his party tonight...from across the sea!" Mae almost jumped up and down with excitement.

"From across the sea? I wonder why they're here. Better yet, I wonder why they're dealing with an idiot like Lord Karon." Tyg mused.

"Oh, bother that, Tyg. Don't you see...foreigners, with lots of money, straight from a long voyage. Every nobleman in the kingdom is going to want to have some sort of grand dinner or ball with them as the guests of honour. There will be a competition to outdo each other. And, guess who is going to be at the forefront of organising these banquets?" Mae stated confidently with a gleam in her eye. "There is much money to be made, dear one, which means a new house quicker."

"Yes, I see your point. Well, does anything extra need to be done before tonight then because of these special guests?"

"Well, I have already changed the menu. A couple of the better looking girls who I was going to let off tonight now have to work, but apart from that the only thing yet to be done is to find out where they're from and possibly get the musicians to play a couple of tunes from their country...what do you think?" Mae replied almost tumbling over her words as she thought too fast for her mouth.

"I think that would be a good idea. I'll do it, you take a rest. You'll need it for tonight." Tyg took Mae's hand and led her back to the door. Once in the hallway Tyg gently pushed Mae towards the stairs leading to the upstairs bedrooms and grabbed her own coat from the stand by the front door.

"Where are you going?" Mae asked as she stepped up onto the first step.

"To talk to Lord Karon, about where these gentlemen are from. I won't be long, now go have a rest." Tyg pointed up the stairs as Mae turned with a smile and scurried up them.

Tyg turned and opened the door, stepping out into the chill of autumn's afternoon.

Tyg waved down a carriage, giving the porter her directions and stepped inside. It was a relatively quick journey through the city to Lord Karon's estates just on the outskirts (as all the Lords' city estates inevitably were) as she arrived she looked out at the sweeping lawns and sculptured hedgerows. She stepped out and told the porter to wait, then proceeded to the door, which was just being opened by the maid.

"My Lady, please come in out of the cold. Let me take your coat." The maid said as she did a small curtsey to Tyg.

"How many times must I tell you not to do that, I'm not a Lady." Tyg reprimanded the maid in good humour. "And, I won't be here long enough to warrant taking my coat."

"Sorry, my Lady...I mean, Tyg. I just don't feel right about it." The maid stammered as Tyg smiled.

"Is Lord Karon in? I need to speak with him about his special guests at tonight's festivities."

"Yes, please come this way." The maid replied as she walked briskly down the long hallway to where Lord Karon's study was near the back of the large manor house. Tyg often wondered why he didn't use the large comfortable drawing room off the main living area. Passing the doors to the huge ballroom in which the festivities were to be held, Tyg took a quick peek at the work going on inside and then continued on after the maid. They arrived in front of a large oak door and the maid knocked on it softly and entered upon her Lord's command. Tyg waited in the hall and the maid soon returned.

"Lord Karon will see you now, Tyg." She said with a smile as she held the door open for her, then closed it behind Tyg and quietly left.

Inside the study Lord Karon was on his feet, wringing his hands.

"Ah! Tyg, so nice to see you again." He took Tyg's hand and kissed it soundly. "You're looking as lovely as ever, I do hope you will be attending tonight?" He looked nervous when he said it, which made Tyg frown.

As Tyg wiped the back of her hand on the side of her coat she smiled wanly at Lord Karon. "Yes, Karon, I do intend to be there tonight. About that is why I've come to see you...Mae says there are going to be special guests tonight? Foreigners?"

"Yes, indeed there is." Lord Karon puffed himself with pride. "I have been dealing with them for these past months through their underlings and they have finally decided to come here and meet with me themselves."

"Really?" Tyg said with disinterest. "What I need to know, Karon, is where they come from. Mae hopes to be able to have some tunes played for them from their homeland."

"Splendid idea!" Lord Karon clapped his hands together. "They are from a kingdom called Tylandria. But, alas it is extremely far away, I doubt the musicians have even heard of it."

At the mention of the kingdom's name Tyg's head went into a spin, feeling like she had heard of this place before. A feeling of dread washed over her and she staggered slightly.

"Are you alright?" Lord Karon asked as he motioned ready to catch her if she fainted. Tyg quickly recovered and pushed Lord Karon's hands away.

"I'm fine, Karon. Well, I must be off to see the musicians. I'll see you later this evening." Tyg turned to leave then suddenly thought of something else, she turned back. "Tell me Karon, when do your guests arrive? You speak like they're not here yet."

"No, indeed they're not. The ships are just coming into view now at the harbour, so they will be here in plenty of time. Don't worry about the guests of honour being late." Lord Karon answers with a smile.

"Ships? Plural?"

"Ah, yes...They are very important Lords where they come from so they are bringing an entourage."

"What sort of entourage needs more than one ship?" Tyg asked half to herself.

"Quite a large one?" Lord Karon laughed nervously.

"Indeed." Tyg replied looking at Lord Karon strangely as she turned and left the study. As she walked down the hall towards the main doors the maid appeared again.

"Leaving already, Tyg?"

"Yes, I have many things to do before tonight, good bye." Tyg answered as she made her way out the massive entrance doors and into the still waiting carriage.

Upon her arrival home Tyg sensed someone inside. She opened the door to find Tess waiting for her, she took Tyg's coat and whispered to her.

"Lord Kor is here, he's waiting for you in the sitting room with Master Barion and Mae."

"Really? I wonder what he wants." Tyg said with some apprehension. Things were still awkward between them and Kor usually didn't speak to her directly anymore, especially after Palin had put his foot down and insisted everything went through him.

She crossed to the sitting room door and opened it suddenly. She entered and found Lord Kor, Barion and Mae sitting on the couches by the fire chatting idly. Barion, Tyg noticed, looked particularly nervous. They all stood as Tyg entered the room.

"Tyg dear, please come in, you know his Lordship of course, Baron Kor?" Mae said as Barion shuffled on nervous feet.

"Adrian." Tyg nodded her head to him in greeting as Lord Kor scowled at her impertinence at using his first name when addressing him.

"You're still refusing to speak peoples' titles, Tyg. It really is a bad habit to get in to." Lord Kor grumbled in response.

Tyg just smiled in answer, everyone knew the real reason he was annoyed. She sat down on a divan opposite him.

"What do you want from me, Kor?"

"You are going to this party held by Lord Karon tonight, are you not?"

"You know that I am, Kor. What's this all about? Spit it out." Tyg replied bitterly, causing Barion to spill his drink and Mae to cough delicately.

"Your insolence will get the better of you one day, girl." Lord Kor replied angrily. "What I want from you is to get something for me from Karon's house...while you're there."

"Oh, I see, and what would that be?" Tyg asked getting interested.

"A few documents, nothing more." Lord Kor said suddenly becoming vague.

"What few documents, Kor, there must be several...I need to know which ones?" Tyg replied becoming amused as she started to guess where this was headed.

"Just a few business documents that Karon has...that I want to know about...is all."

"To do with his dealings with the foreigners?" Tyg stated.

"You're much too clever for your own good, girl, you know that?" Lord Kor replied agitated.

"Yes, that's why you like me, isn't it? And why I'm still alive." Tyg stated simply which made Lord Kor scowl slightly. "But, that's it, isn't it? You want me to find out what Karon is up to with these foreigners and let you in on it...correct?"

"Correct. Can you do it?"

"Shouldn't be a problem, I was in Karon's study today, so I know where it is." Tyg levelled a serious look at Kor. "How much?"

Kor started spluttering and choking at the mention of payment. "Haven't I given you enough?" He sneered. Tyg smiled.

"Come on, Kor, such a high profile theft can't be done for free...look at the risks." Tyg said business like. "Or, is that why you seem to have left out the middle man and come straight to me? You know Palin will be quite upset." Tyg said with a vicious grin.

"Nothing like that at all." Lord Kor said chagrined. "Actually I came straight to you because I can't find Palin anywhere. I put a call out for him a day ago and nothing..." He replied earnestly.

Tyg frowned at the news.

Kor sighed deeply. "So, my dearest Tyg, how much do you want?"

"Well, that depends on the information I find out and how much I think you really need to know it...now, doesn't it? How about we negotiate price once I have the merchandise in my hand and I can truly value it? Hmm?"

Kor groaned again. "You're just as bad as he is! You're going to rob me blind. Again! You're vicious, Tyg!" Kor exclaimed.

"Not really, Kor, besides I offered all that back to you...just think of it like this...no merchandise...no payment. I think that's fair isn't it?" Tyg appraised him with his neatly groomed and clipped goatee and moustache, his short black hair also well maintained, not to mention the wealth of his clothing. He was a handsome man and powerful, and with their history she didn't want to piss him off anymore.

"Alright, I agree to negotiate price when...and if...you return with the documents." Kor replied still feeling swindled.

"Done then." Tyg agreed with a self-satisfied smirk as Kor stood up and they shook hands. Kor swept her hand up to his lips and looked at her with a smile.

"I'm still here, waiting, Tyg."

Tyg pulled her hands back and growled at him. "Wait." She said nonchalantly with a shrug.

Kor frowned and turned to leave and Barion and Mae also stood to show him out. Tyg leaned back deeper on the divan with no intention of seeing Kor to the door.

"Will you be at the party tonight, Adrian?" Tyg asked grinning.

"Yes." Kor replied.

"See you there then." Tyg grinned as Kor raised an eyebrow at her.

"You most certainly will, my dear." He smirked as he stalked from the room.

Tyg laughed to herself, then mused as to why these foreigners were here and where the hell was Palin.

Palin it seemed, had gone undercover at the docks, helping to unload the foreigners' ship. Trying to find out all he could himself about them and why they were here. He had heard ripples about them being royalty and that they were interested in setting up a trading agreement with Arial. He was aware of several envoys going back and forth for the last few months, but now the Lords themselves had decided to make the arduous journey and that had sparked his interest.

37

The party was going smoothly. The guests had started to trickle in and the food had started to arrive. Tyg and Mae stood in one corner as Lord Karon was greeting his guests.

All eyes kept going to Tyg as the guests entered the room, men and women alike. The men with lustful adjure and the women with enviable hate. Tyg was dressed in a simple pale blue, off the shoulder gown with a figure hugging skirt, made by Tess – and not of the current fashion already set by Tyg and Tess. Her hair was piled atop her head in amass of curls that tumbled down over one shoulder and entwined with a string of pale blue gems to match her eyes and dress. She was oblivious of the stares. Mae, however wasn't.

"You're causing quite the stir tonight, Tyg my dear. How do you expect to sneak out of here later when every eye in the room is on you?" Mae whispered under her breath.

"Don't you worry about that? When the foreigners arrive I'm sure all eyes will be on them for the rest of the night. I'm sure I won't get a second glance after that."

"Hmm, perhaps you're right?" Mae replied. "Look out, here comes Lord Karon."

"Absolutely smashing, my dear, you have excelled yourself." Lord Karon said as he approached Mae and kissed her hand. He then turned to kiss Tyg's hand. "You look most ravishing tonight, my dear, the ladies of high standing are all jealous." Tyg folded her arms to avoid the kiss, she looked at him distastefully.

"You're too kind, Karon." Tyg replied with little interest as she watched Lord Kor arrive through the doors. She smiled at him as he inclined his head towards her with a dashing smirk, looking handsome as always.

"Did you manage to get the musicians to find a tune from Tylandria?" Lord Karon inquired.

"What? Oh, no sorry. You were right, they have never heard of the place." Tyg replied, as that same wave of dread washed over her.

"Are you alright, my dear? You look a bit peaky?" Mae asked concerned.

"I think I just need a drink. I'll be back in a moment."

As Tyg headed for the punch bowl a group of young men started to crowd round her asking her several questions at once. How she was? What she had been doing? Would she like to dance? She held a hand up and they quieted down.

"Can someone just get me a drink, please?" Tyg asked, knowing she wouldn't reach the table herself through the throng now. She felt the start of a headache coming on.

Several young men scrambled to reach the drinks first as another young man stepped through them all and handed her a drink, several sighs of dismay could be heard. Tyg looked up to see her friend Thomas, she sighed with relief as he offered her his arm. As she took it he led her away from the group of disappointed young men.

"You really need to do something to make yourself uglier, Tyg. Me saving you from those airheads is beginning to weigh me down." Thomas said laughing.

"Don't tease me, Tom, please, I don't feel very well." Tyg replied taking a sip of her drink.

"What's wrong?" Thomas asked full of concern.

"I don't know, I just feel like something bad is going to happen."

"Ah, you worry too much, you're always so serious. Look. Lord Karon looks like he's about to introduce his guests of honour." Thomas said pointing to where Lord Karon was standing on a dais calling for attention. The room went quiet and all attention fell on Lord Karon as he started his announcement.

"Ladies and Gentlemen, Lords and Ladies I would like to welcome you all warmly to my home and in helping me welcome some special guests who have travelled a month by sea to be with us tonight. But, just before I introduce them I would like everyone to thank Madam Mae and Miss Tyg for the wonderful organisation of my little get together. Without them nothing would have been possible."

Polite applause followed as Lord Karon indicated to Mae and Tyg, Mae did a small curtsey while Tyg just faked a smile and inclined her head.

"Now, without any further ado, I give you my guests of honour to tonight's festivities. Please welcome Lord Leviathan Adramelech and Lord Antyn Adramelech. Brothers from the distant land of Tylandria."

At the mention of the brothers' name Adramelech Tyg's blood ran cold and she started to shake. Then, as the large doors opened the two brothers entered, as everyone turned to look.

One brother entered wearing black leather trousers, black shirt and leather jerkin trimmed in silver. His shoulder length black hair was half tied back with a silver clasp. He still wore his weapons which were all plainly in sight. A sword strapped at his waist, a dagger on his belt on the opposite side and, Tyg noticed, a dagger in his boot. Black steel vambraces on his wrists and padded leather shoulder guards made him look like he was ready for battle rather than a banquet. He was drop dead handsome with a chiselled jaw and with that twist of something dangerous all the women in the room swooned. He was extremely tall, nearing seven feet and towered above everyone in the room making an impressive sight as he exuded male dominance. He surveyed the room like a vulture surveyed its lunch, waiting for it to die, with piercing blue eyes – a match to Tyg's own not seen here – but of a darker sapphire blue.

The other brother was dressed more subdued in a plain dark grey tunic and black leather pants. His sandy blonde hair was short underneath but long on top and floppy like a furious breeze had attacked it. He was also very tall but still a good few inches shorter than his brother. He had a certain boyish charm, with a roguish smile, about him and the young women in the room giggled at the prospect of two handsome young men to fight over. His eyes, however, had the exact same glint in them. Tyg recognised it as the glint of power and authority. He also had a sword belted around his waist.

Tyg's eyes blazed just at the sight of them as she recoiled in dread. Something deep inside her was telling her to run, but she didn't know why, because she never ran from anything. All she knew was that these two men would bring nothing but trouble for these people, and only she could sense it. However, she felt drawn to them at the same time, like a moth to a flame – knowing it meant possible death but unable to resist. Her trembling became more violent as she felt torn as to what to do…she grit her teeth and a growl emitted from her throat.

"Tyg, what's wrong? You're shaking like a leaf, are you cold?" Thomas asked, his concern turning to full worry.

"What? No, Tom. I'm alright, really, I just need to…" Tyg never finished her sentence as the eyes of Leviathan, the brother in black, fell upon her. It completely took her breath away, he was the most gorgeous man she had ever seen and he seemed to look straight into her soul. She shook her head and backed away as she tore her eyes away from his. She grabbed Thomas's hand and retreated to the far end of the ballroom.

"What are you doing, Tyg? This isn't like you?" Thomas asked as she finally stopped when she ran up against the wall. She turned back and saw through the throng surrounding the brothers that they were talking to Mae. Probably thanking her for a wonderful welcome. Tyg relaxed slightly and turned to Thomas.

"I'm really sorry, Tom, I don't know what my problem is really...I just can't shake this feeling."

"Look, nothing bad is going to happen, so just try to relax ok?" Thomas gave her shoulder a reassuring squeeze. "I'm just going to get something to eat, are you going to be okay?"

"Yeah, sure, go on...I'll be fine." Tyg said more to reassure herself than Thomas as he turned and disappeared into the crowd.

Tyg leaned against the wall and closed her eyes, slowing her breathing and her thumping heart, enjoying the coolness of the stone wall against the back of her neck.

"You must be Tyg? I have heard so much about you in such a short time." A deep, smooth, commanding voice said directly in front of her.

Tyg opened her eyes startled and came directly face to face with the brother in black.

'How did I not hear him approach?'

He smiled at her, with that same vulture like gaze, studying everything and missing nothing, and took her hand – which was again shaking. He kissed it causing her heart to hammer in her chest again.

"I hear you are in part to thank for the festivities? I thank you for going to so much trouble." Leviathan said, his height crowded in on her as he placed a palm on the wall beside her head and leaned in.

"Ah, well...thank you. Which brother are you then?" Tyg stammered trying to think of something intelligent to say and not succeeding.

"Forgive my rudeness at not introducing myself. I am Leviathan...he is Antyn." Leviathan indicated with a curt flick of his head to where his brother was conversing with another young lady, but his eyes were looking straight at her. She thought her heart was going to burst out of her chest.

"Crap, how tall are you?" Tyg asked feeling claustrophobic. At 5'10" now she was still looking up at him by a lot, he must be nearly seven foot tall.

Leviathan laughed and shrugged. "Conveniently taller than everyone else, but I can't recall seeing many women your height here either. Or with hair this colour..." Leviathan grabbed a curl and played it through his fingers. Tyg was speechless.

"Ah, Lord Adramelech. I see you have found our Tyg." Mae interrupted. Right at that moment Tyg could have kissed Mae, as she worked her way around so she was standing behind Mae, putting the woman between herself and Leviathan. With an annoying flick of his head Leviathan turned to Mae.

"Our Tyg?" He muttered in annoyance.

Did his eyes just glow...like mine do?

"Yes, indeed. I have heard much of her beauty, which I see was not boasted upon." Leviathan stated coolly. "And, I had to give her my thanks for her part in all this." He indicated the ballroom. To Tyg he seemed more annoyed by it all than grateful.

"Yes, she's my niece you know, from Annul. Have you heard of Annul, my Lord?"

"No, can't say I have. I know little of these parts. Your niece you say? Funny, she looks nothing like you...I would have expected some sort of family resemblance." Leviathan looked behind Mae, like she was invisible, directly at Tyg.

'Oh the gods, he knows!' Tyg thought. 'He knows we're not related...I have to get out of here. It's like he knows exactly who and what I am.' Tyg looked around and spied Thomas as he made his way back with a plate of food.

"Excuse me." Tyg said to Leviathan and Mae, and before they could object she quickly manoeuvred her way over to Thomas, grabbed his arm and swung him round and started heading him in the other direction. She could feel two pairs of eyes boring into her back as she headed for the side doors.

"What are you doing?" Thomas asked as he was pulled along.

"I just decided that I need some fresh air, that's all, and I thought you might like to accompany me...please?"

Once outside Thomas put his plate down and grabbed Tyg by the shoulders making her look at him.

"Tyg, what's wrong? You never say please...what's got you so spooked?"

"It's the foreigners, for some reason they seem familiar to me...and not in a good way." Tyg tried to explain. "Oh, I know that it's impossible, as I have never left Arial and they have never been to Arial before, but I just can't help feeling that they are serious trouble."

"Look, Tyg. The other Lords feel much the same way I assure you. They are intending to keep a very close eye on them. They won't be able to move without someone knowing about it – let alone cause any trouble. Besides, they would be foolish to try and cause trouble so far away from their homeland." Thomas explained to Tyg while smoothing a lock of her hair that had blown across her face in the gentle breeze. "But opening trade up with this country could be very beneficial."

"Yeah, you're right, Tom. I know you're right, and I promise to try and relax." Tyg took a deep breath of the cool night air and turned to face the ballroom again. "Come on then..." she smiled at Thomas. "...I'll let you have the first dance."

"How could I refuse?" Thomas replied as he hurriedly scoffed down a couple of pastries, then took her arm and led her back into the ballroom.

Once on the dance floor everything seemed to come right, as Thomas whirled her around the room to a quick tempo waltz. She started to come right with herself again, forgetting the drama of a few short minutes ago.

"You've been practising haven't you?" Tyg accused Thomas, laughing.

"Well, I can't be stepping on the prettiest girl's prettiest toes now, can I? Even in those bloody boots of yours." Thomas replied also laughing. "Miss Belmont helped me."

"Oh, did she now?" Tyg raised an eyebrow in question. "And, it's got nothing to do with the fact that Miss Belmont is herself very beautiful and available?"

"Well, I guess, maybe a little." Thomas admitted going red in the cheeks. "But, she offered."

"That's probably because she was hoping you would dance with her, and she didn't want you stepping on her toes." Tyg pointed out.

"Oh." Thomas replied as the full meaning dawned on his face.

"Oh, you can be so dense sometimes. Go on, go and ask her to dance...quickly...before someone else snaps her up." Tyg smiled as she let him go.

As Thomas made his way over to where the young lady Belmont was standing, with a group of other young aristocrat women, they all began to giggle. Miss Belmont lowered her head feigning shyness.

"Would you do me the honour of this dance, my Lady?" Thomas asked as he bowed towards the girl causing the other girls to giggle even more. Then without a word the Belmont girl extended her hand to Thomas, he took it in his, kissed it softly and led her to the dance floor, just as the tune changed to a very slow waltz.

Tyg smiled to herself as she watched the little performance, and shook her head. She didn't understand why people had to play these silly games – if they liked each other, why not just say so?

"Would you care for this dance, my Lady?" A voice behind her asked, making her jump slightly, and she had to hold herself back from reacting with force.

"Sorry, I didn't mean to scare you. You were watching that couple, are they friends of yours?"

Tyg spun around and found herself now face to face with the other brother, Antyn, she found her heart hammering inside her chest again. How was it she couldn't hear these guys approaching her? Warnings went off in her head that the weapons they wore were not for show, they were trained.

"One is, Thomas." She answered him. Her eyes changing colour slightly.

"Ah, and perhaps you like him more than friends?" Antyn asked smiling.

"No, actually. He is like a brother to me. He has helped me out several times when I have needed it. I owe him a lot." Tyg replied heatedly, her eyes suddenly blazing, she did not like the insinuation in the question and completely forgot her foreboding.

"Good then, you can dance with me." Antyn replied smoothly as he took her arm and led her back to the dance floor. "I have heard that you are very good at dancing, I hope I'm not disappointed."

"Just what do you mean by that, Antyn?" Tyg barked back, trying to free herself from his vice like grip. How the hell was he as strong as her? Antyn's eyebrows raised in surprise at her lack of title and the venom in her voice as she said his name.

"Just Antyn?" He asked amused.

"If you knew anything about me, like your brother says he does, you would know that I don't call anyone by titles, without them earning the respect of one. Titles are meaningless to me, people deserve titles when they deserve respect, not because of what family they were born into." Tyg replied angrily. Suddenly she realised that she was actually dancing with him. She tried to stop but with his hand securely around her waist he led her on.

Tyg did not like this at all, his strength made her feel weak.

"Quite, I had heard, but didn't believe that someone would be as forward in their independence as to throw protocol out the window in such a reckless manner." Antyn replied with an amused grin as he looked down at her, he was at least five inches taller than her, maybe more.

"Well, now you do." Tyg replied curtly, finally wrenching free of his grip and stopping in the middle of the dance floor. She looked at him, her eyes blazing pale ice blue.

Antyn laughed. "You are the hellcat, aren't you?" He said raising his arms in front of him in mock surrender.

"More than you would care to know." Tyg spat in a very threatening manner as she turned her back and stormed off the dance floor, a soft chuckling echoed behind her. As she turned she saw both brothers standing close to each other, both watching her. Tyg shivered.

Something was not right with those two.

Fuming she stormed over to the drinks table and grabbed a crystal goblet of red wine. She downed it in a few short gulps and as it started to warm her belly she started to relax again, thinking to herself how foolish she was to be so easily goaded into losing her temper. Just then, she noticed Mae approaching her with a very surly look on her face. Tyg took a deep breath and walked straight up to Mae, placing her hands on Mae's shoulders and looked directly into her face as in her peripheral vision she saw Leviathan walking towards her.

"I know what you're going to say, but not now, Mae, okay? I'll apologise for my rudeness tomorrow, I promise. Just not now. I'm not feeling well, remember you said so yourself earlier. So, I might actually retire for the night and head home." Tyg talked very quickly so as to head off any argument, then promptly walked off again, heading for the exit, leaving Mae opening and closing her mouth, swallowing air, not knowing what to say. Not far away two other pairs of eyes watched her leave, one with a very annoyed scowl.

38

Grabbing her cloak on the way out, Tyg stepped into the night, putting her cloak around her shoulders she melted into the darkness. She turned across the front lawn and headed around the side of the manor house on the opposite side from the ballroom. Walking down the length of the building she came across the door leading to the kitchen, she tried it. Locked, should have guessed. Taking two long hairpins out of her hair she started to pick the lock. After several seconds of jiggling the lock she heard the almost inaudible click and the door swung open for her.

Poking her head in, she took a quick look, darkness. She slipped inside and quietly closed the door.

'Excellent.' She thought. With the food all brought in from outside, the cook has obviously been given the night off, she hoped they had been told to not come out of the servant's quarters. She made her way through to the hallway and trod quietly down in the darkness, heading for Lord Karon's study. She reached the door with no problems and finding the door carelessly unlocked she slipped inside. Placing her back against the door she scanned the room...empty. She sighed with relief and locked the door behind her then walked over to the desk. She took a small matchbox from off the desk and used the contents to light the wall sconce and a small candle on the desk. She then started hunting for anything with the words Adramelech or Tylandria on it.

After searching for several minutes she stopped. 'Where?' She thought to herself. '...where?'

Holding up the candle she started searching around the walls, looking for a secret safe, knowing that the rest of the papers were nothing but household accounts. The flame past over a curious little painting of a hunting dog holding a rabbit. She stopped and studied it.

'Funny.' She thought. 'I didn't think Karon liked dogs?' She smiled to herself as she grabbed the side of the frame and pulled it back revealing a hole in the wall behind it. Inside were several rolled documents.

'Got ya!' She yelled in triumph in the silence of her mind, as she grabbed some of the papers and turned to the desk. Opening the documents one by one and returning them safely when they were not what she was looking for, she started to scan them all. Finally, she found the ones she was looking for. The top document naming the Adramelech brothers as the new owners of Lord Karon's estate in Landau. It also mentioned several other items of extreme value to Lord Karon that Tyg would have imagined he would never give up. She also noticed no mention of money being paid for these items and wondered if Lord Karon had perhaps owed money to the foreigners and they had taken its worth. Funny that he would be so happy to see them here, if that were the case.

"Perhaps I can help?"

Tyg just about jumped out of her skin as a deep voice sounded directly in front of her. She looked up directly into the face of Leviathan, smiling amused.

"How did you...?" She asked looking at the door she knew she locked.

"I should ask you the same question. I have in fact been looking for you. Mae said you had returned home, not feeling well, but surprise...I find you here...and looking at what?" Leviathan said as he placed a hand on the desk and leaned towards her. He then hovered a finger over the document she was reading and turned it round on the desk towards him. Tyg looked stunned as the paper turned on the desk without him touching it. He looked down to see what the document was, then with an amused expression he looked back up at Tyg. Tyg, was standing frozen to the spot unable to move. Leviathan straightened up and walked around the desk towards her. At the same time the documents curled themselves up again at being released from his magic, rolled and stopped precariously on the edge of the desk next to Tyg.

Stopping so he was beside Tyg's shoulder, as she was still facing the desk, Leviathan placed his hands on her shoulders and turned her towards him. She looked up directly into his eyes. They took her breath away for the second time that night, but this time they were definitely glowing. The powerful dominant presence of the man making her strangely docile. He placed a hooked finger under her chin and held her gaze as if trying to see into her soul and find something.

"I was very disappointed when you left midway through our conversation. Now that we are alone, perhaps we may continue it?" Leviathan leaned forward and kissed Tyg soundly on the lips, sweeping his hand round to the back of her neck holding her firmly. Tyg struggled against him, her hands pushing at his chest but he was like an unmovable rock. He held her strongly around her waist, his hand on the small of her back as he pressed her against himself. She couldn't understand how this giant of a man was stronger than her.

No one was stronger than her.

What was happening?

"It's just in here, my Lord, please come in and I'll fetch it for you." Lord Karon said as he stepped into the study, startling himself as he found the room occupied by Leviathan and Tyg. He was followed in by Lord Irion. Leviathan looked up, an amused expression still on his face as he looked from the Lords to Tyg's mortified scowl. He still held her firmly against him, leaning over her like a predator holding its prey.

"Ah...well...it seems the study is somewhat occupied at the moment, Lord Irion. Should we perhaps return later?" Lord Karon's face changed from his initial shock to amusement. "You know, Lord Adramelech, you should really have locked the door."

Leviathan smiled back, as Tyg pushed away from him, releasing his vice like grip on her finally. She took a couple of steps backwards, quickly grabbed the rolled documents off the desk and hid them behind her back. As he straightened up to his full height he took a moment to tidy himself with a cocky grin. Tyg grit her teeth and snarled at his smugness.

"Quite." Leviathan said simply as he looked at Tyg with a questioning yet smouldering look, his eyes still glowing. Tyg returned his look with ice blue fire making his top lip twitch slightly in one corner.

"It really is not on, my Lord, coming from so far away and stealing our one true angel's heart from us, you know." Lord Karon continues.

"Our?" Leviathan muttered again, causing Tyg to frown at him as he glanced darkly at her. "Well, what can I say, my Lord. I have always been a sucker for beautiful women." Leviathan replied holding his hands out and chuckling.

This banter infuriated Tyg and she turned, barged past the two Lords still standing in the doorway, took one last smug look back at Leviathan and stormed from the room. Leviathan caught the look and his brows furrowed, he looked down at the desk to realise the documents were gone. When he looked back up, Tyg had gone too. He scowled with frustration, his jaw clenching.

Outside the door Tyg heard the Lords laughing and with the documents firmly in her grasp she smiled to herself. 'Fools.' She thought. 'They think they're so smart.' She walked off down the hall, not worrying about subterfuge now as she knew tomorrow everyone was going to know about what happened in the study, thanks to Lord Irion bearing witness. She wiped her mouth with the back of her hand, her lips seemed to burn from that man's touch. She stopped a servant with a tray of glasses full of wine and took two. She gulped them down trying to wash the taste and feel of Leviathan's lips on hers away, but the thought of them left a heavy strange feeling deep in her core. The servant gave her a startled look as she deposited the empties back on the tray and walked off towards the front door, completely unaware of the figure following her.

Once outside in the cool air Tyg stopped to take a couple of deep breaths to try and still her heart which was still beating hard enough to leap out of her chest. "What the fuck was that, Tyg?" She asked herself in a mutter. A hundred questions ran through her mind about what just happened, so she decided to take the long walk home to ponder them all.

She wandered along the deserted roads of the large manor houses until she reached the denser housing of the city proper, she avoided the city watch on patrol and as she rounded a corner she noticed a movement in the dark ahead by the entrance to an alleyway. She stopped.

Contemplating what to do she bent down slightly and hitched up her skirt slowly, and removed the dagger that was always in the top of her boot – she always wore her knee high boots even under evening gowns, much to the horror of Tess and Mae. 'Wish I had the opportunity to grab this before...why didn't I?' Tyg thought to herself as she grasped it firmly behind her back.

That man...she scowled, he left her...defenceless.

She walked slowly towards the alley, stopping cautiously a couple of yards before it.

"I know you're there, so you might as well come out." Tyg called out in a hoarse whisper, she didn't want to alert the city watch.

There was no answer. "Come on, I work for the AG...I know you're there." Tyg said more firmly.

Muttering could be heard in the alleyway then and two men showed themselves. Hard looking men, one was rather thick set and short, the other lean, tall and muscular.

"Are you cut throats or just burglars?" Tyg asked indignantly, wishing she had her sword.

"A bit of both actually, you said you work for the Assassin's Guild?"

"I did."

"You don't look like you work for the AG?" He said with a vicious grin.

"If you want proof, step closer." Tyg sneered at him.

"Tyg? Is that you?" The leaner man suddenly pushed forward and asked.

Shocked by that Tyg looked closer at the young taller man. She looked into his dark hazel eyes. 'It can't be?' She thought. His nose had been broken at some stage, but she was sure it was him.

"Dane? Is that you?" Tyg replied.

Dane laughed as he stepped forward. "Tyg!" He exclaimed as he went to hug his long lost friend, then faltered and stepped back again looking at her finery. "Ah...yeah...it is me. How have you been?" Dane asked awkwardly.

"Dane, get real, it's me. Do you think all this finery would have changed me really?" Tyg smiled amused as she held out her hand revealing the dagger. "See, still the same old Tyg."

They both laughed and finally hugged. A heart felt warmth filled Tyg as she embraced her old friend, but the events of the evening soon crowded back into her thoughts and she shivered.

"Are you okay?" Dane asked. "You know you really shouldn't be out here at this time of night."

"Spare me, Dane" Tyg scoffed. "You were the ones in danger, not me."

Dane laughed embarrassed. "Yeah, you're probably right."

Tyg gave him a look at the word 'probably', then turned to the other guy who was standing to the side awkwardly watching.

"Tell anyone who cares that Dane has gone with little Cat, got it?" The other man baulked when Tyg said her alias, realising exactly who was standing in front of him.

"Yeah sure, whatever." He said uncomfortably as he shrugged and moved off back down the alleyway, wanting to quickly put space between himself and her.

Tyg watched his reactions intently and smiled smugly. "Escort me home, Dane?" Tyg said turning to him. He was looking at her strangely, but smiled back.

"Most certainly." Dane took Tyg's arm and they continued down the street, whispering quietly together.

A shadow moved in the street not far away. A figure of a tall man stepped out and watched the pair walk off down the street. The figure returned to the shadows.

"So, you're obviously not sold off into slavery then?" Dane said. "I always wondered if you got your wish, I heard rumours, but really...you're little Cat? Wow. You look beautiful, if it wasn't for the bossy voice and the hair, I wouldn't have recognised you."

"Bossy voice?" Tyg replied turning on him. "I'll give you 'Bossy voice.'" Tyg laughed as she jumped on his shoulder and cuffed him around the head. He feigned fighting back and they both laughed as they continued down the street. Tyg told Dane everything that had happened to her since the day Palin took her from Barion's warehouse.

39

Back at the house Tyg poured Dane a volka and handed it to him. She then sat beside him on a couch in the reception room. Tyg noticed Dane sat awkwardly on the edge not wanting to dirty anything. She laughed, a light hearted little chuckle.

"Oh, Dane, don't worry about getting things dirty, just relax. Tell me what you've been doing? You know I would have stayed in contact but it was a condition that Barion put me on for working for Palin. I wasn't to mingle with anyone from the warehouse, plus, you know I'm sure, there's a certain amount of secrecy involved working for him."

"Not much, just doing pretty much the same thing I was before, just moving into bigger and better things than pickpocketing...not as serious as what you've obviously got yourself involved in."

"You could always come work for me?" Tyg said as the idea suddenly hit her and she thought about how Leviathan and Antyn seemed to be affecting her.

"Me? Work for you?" Dane asked. "Doing what?"

"You could be extra protection." Tyg said, causing Dane to laugh.

"You don't need protection." Dane said. "Of anyone, you're the one who could most look after themselves always, and now...well...if you work for Palin, you must have...well...you know."

"Yeah, well, I have my reasons..." Tyg said vaguely. Dane regarded her a moment.

"Tyg, what's wrong?" He asked her after a brief silence.

Tyg shrugged. "I don't know, Dane. That's the problem."

"Try and explain it to me."

"I really don't know. It's just there are these two brothers that have arrived from over the sea, from a place called Tylandria...no one has ever traded with that country before..."

"Yeah, I saw their ships arriving."

"Ships?" Tyg asked suddenly, so it was true.

"Yeah, one ship had them on it the other was full of soldiers and horses."

"Soldiers?" Tyg says softly. "I met them tonight. I didn't like what I saw. Something tells me they're trouble, and now you tell me they have brought soldiers with them? Shit. I don't think I want to ever be alone with them. There is something distinctly sinister going on with them."

Dane looked at Tyg a moment, he saw something in her he had only ever seen once before. Fear. This caused him to believe her...her instincts were always right growing up.

"You think them being here is somehow connected to you?" Dane asked with doubt.

"Oh, I know it sounds stupid, Dane." Tyg said as she stood up and walked over to the fire.

"It's not stupid actually, when you think about it. Tylandria sounds a lot like Tyg, don't you think?" Dane said half talking to himself. Tyg turned to face him.

"What?" She exclaimed in shock. "I hadn't even made that connection...you think it's possible?" She thought of the fact that Leviathan's eyes were blue and glowed. That made that deep pitted feeling in her stomach again, and what he had done to those papers on the desk...?

Dane shrugged. "Maybe, I don't know. You never were sure where you were from, and frankly we all knew you weren't from here. Maybe you're from there?"

"Maybe...it would answer why I felt the name was so familiar to me. It was like something deep inside me recognised it."

"If you say so, Tyg." He gave her a weird little frown.

"Well, I do know they are here to do some deal with property, but I can't help but feel that it's all subterfuge. That they are actually up to something else." Tyg started pacing. "And, when they spoke to me it was like they knew me." Tyg walked back to the couch and stood in front of Dane. "Come on, Dane. What do you say?" Dane shrugged. "If nothing else it would get you out of the warehouse. Unless, you would rather stay there of course."

"No way, if you're offering a way out of that hell hole, I'll take it." Dane said with a laugh. "Besides, how could I refuse the chance to work with you again?"

"Oh, Dane. I have missed you." Tyg laughed back, collapsing onto the couch beside him and hugging his arm.

As they sat and talked a couple of hours went by when Barion and Mae arrived home. Tyg hushed Dane to silence and hid him behind the couch. She then poked at the fire dying it down and pretended to be asleep on the couch. Mae poked her head in and seeing Tyg asleep she tip toed over and placed a blanket over her, placed a log on the fire and then made her way to bed. Once Mae had left Dane peeked over the couch to look at the grinning Tyg.

"Care to explain that?" He said resting his head on his arms as he knelt behind the couch.

"Having to explain is what I just avoided, I'll talk to Barion tomorrow."

"Today, Tyg. The sun is going to be up in a few hours."

"Yes, but Barion won't be up to talking today, it will have to wait for tomorrow." Tyg looked at him with an eyebrow raised. They both laughed and Dane got up and walked around to the other couch where he sat down facing Tyg, who was still wrapped in the blanket.

"We really should get some sleep too." Dane said to her.

"Yeah I suppose. I am tired." Tyg admitted as she started taking all the pins out of her hair. Dane grabbed another blanket from the back of the couch and lay down. He looked over to her.

"Thanks Tyg."

She smiled at her friend. "Don't mention it."

Tess opened the door to the reception room in the morning and stared shocked at seeing Tyg and Dane asleep on the couches. She padded silently across to the fire and started to relight it. Tyg and Dane both stirred and woke.

"Good Morning, Tess." Tyg said with a smile. Tess turned round with a jump.

"Oh, good morning, Tyg. I'm sorry I didn't mean to wake you."

"That's okay. Actually while you're here, perhaps you could help my friend, Dane, here find some clean clothes."

Tess blushed as she looked over to Dane, who smiled at her in greeting.

"Sure Tyg. Nice to meet you, Dane."

"Nice to meet you too, Tess. Perhaps I could get you to show me where the bath is too...before Tyg gets the chance to suggest it." Dane said with a cheeky grin.

Tess smiled back shyly looking at him beneath her eyelashes. Tyg laughed.

"Yeah, I was just about to suggest it actually, and once you're finished, we'll have some breakfast."

As Tess indicated for Dane to follow her, Dane bowed to Tyg. "Whatever you say, Boss."

He then ducked out the door, just missing being hit by a pillow that Tyg threw at him.

Alone, Tyg went upstairs and changed into a pair of leather pants, a leather jerkin over a tailored shirt and put her dagger belt around her waist. She brushed out her hair and put it up in her usual braid then finally pulled the documents out of her cloak and read them. Nothing but real estate transactions, but Tyg knew there had to be more to it. She got up and went into the study, grabbed a piece of paper, wrote a quick note on it, sealed it up and went to the front door. She waved down a kid that was hanging around the street. He came over and she handed him the message with a coin. "See this gets to the AG." The kid looked up and down the street, put the note into his pocket, nodded and scurried off.

40

Later that morning, as Tyg and Dane were enjoying breakfast in the Day room, there was a knock at the door. Tess answered it to find a tall stranger standing there, the tallest man she had ever seen in her entire life. Dressed in an ankle length black military styled trench coat with the collar up, he appeared quite foreboding.

"Can I help you, Sir?" Tess asked timidly.

"I have come to speak with Tyg." He said barely hiding his contempt.

"Please, come in and wait here. I'll let her know you're here." Tess replied, used to mysterious figures in black coming and going from this house. She opened the door wider for him to enter. "Can I give her a name, my Lord?" As Tess looked up into the piercing blue eyes of Leviathan, as he ducked his head through the doorway.

"Tell her Lord Leviathan Adramelech is here to see how she is, as she left the party last night early, not feeling well." The smirk on his face gave Tess chills.

Tess left Leviathan in the foyer, as he unbuttoned his coat, and made her way to the sitting room, where Tyg and Dane were having breakfast.

"Sorry to interrupt, Tyg, but there is a Lord Adramelech wanting a word with you."

Tyg grimaced at the name. "What? How the hell did he find out where I live? Which one?"

"He said his name was Leviathan."

"Fuck." Tyg muttered and looked at Dane, then back to Tess. "Okay, show him in."

As Leviathan entered the room he scowled noticeably at seeing Dane sitting there close beside Tyg.

"Ah, I see you have another early visitor." Leviathan said as he entered.

"No." Tyg replied coolly. "Actually, Dane here walked me home last night and decided to stay." Tyg smiled to herself as she saw Leviathan's expression turn flat.

"I see." He replied. "Well, I came to enquire to your health. Lady Mae said you left early due to not feeling well." Leviathan lowered his gaze at her, knowing the real reason she left early.

"Quite, well as you can see I'm fine now, thank you."

"Excellent, I was hoping you could join us for lunch."

"Us?" Tyg asked a little taken aback.

"My brother and I, and Lord Karon of course, as it is his house we are intruding upon."

"Not for much longer." Tyg muttered to herself, causing Leviathan to scowl even darker and his eyes to start glowing. "I will unfortunately have to decline your invitation I'm afraid, Leviathan, as I am already meeting a friend for lunch today."

"Oh?" Leviathan drew himself up to his full height, which almost touched the ceiling, and folded his arms. "May I enquire as to whom?"

Tyg regarded him a long moment. 'The unbelievable, arrogant...!' She put a piece of raisin toast into her mouth and slowly chewed it, obnoxiously taking her time. Leviathan's brow furrowed as he scowled even further and raised an eyebrow at her.

The tension in the room was palpable.

Dane was looking on with interest at the verbal parrying going on. He smiled as Leviathan looked at him a moment. This seemed to annoy Leviathan, so Dane smiled even broader. Leviathan slid his gaze unblinking back to Tyg as she spoke.

"Well, I don't see that it's any of your business, but if you really must know...I am meeting a friend called Thomas. He is a Captain of the City Watch. I believe you may have met him last night?"

"I believe so, he is also a baron's son, is he not? The one you danced with." The way he said the last bit sent chills down Tyg's spine it held so much unspoken malice.

"Yes, he is." Tyg frowned slightly as she looked down at her plate.

"Is he courting you?"

Tyg's eyes went wide in surprise. "What? No!"

"Hmm." Leviathan thrummed in a sexy rumble, his gaze went back to Dane.

"And neither is he." Tyg said with a sneer, causing Leviathan to look back at her with a smirk.

"Perhaps dinner then?" Leviathan was starting to sound annoyed.

Tyg laughed a musically sounding little chuckle which actually made Leviathan close his eyes and bite his lip slightly. Tyg didn't see it but Dane did. Tyg looked up as Leviathan recovered his stone faced demeanour.

"I don't think you realise the importance of your being here. You will be so busy with banquets and balls with every Baron, Duke and Marquis, you're the one who won't have time to have dinner with me, probably for the next six months." Tyg took joy from Leviathan's reaction at realising she was probably telling the truth, then she swallowed hard ready for the next bit. "However, I realise we probably have things that need discussing."

"Indeed." Leviathan said with a smirk.

"So, I will agree to have lunch with you the day after tomorrow, as I am having lunch with Lord Kor tomorrow."

"Busy girl." Leviathan said in a manner that made Tyg shiver again, she really didn't like the effect this man had on her. She was strangely weak to his cold manner. "I will have a carriage here to pick you up at 12 noon then." Leviathan smiled, Tyg wondered why he looked like he just won something. "I'm glad we could come to an arrangement and I look forward to our next meeting with bated breath." Leviathan took Tyg's hand, causing her to stand, and kissed it. Dane also stood, causing Leviathan to level a baleful stare at him, which made Dane take an involuntary step backwards. This strange man's aura really was ridiculously dangerous. Leviathan smiled and turned back to Tyg and inclined his head to her.

"Well, I shan't intrude upon your breakfast any longer. Until we meet again, Tyg."

Leviathan then inclined his head to Dane and left the room, closing the door behind him.

Both Tyg and Dane let out explosive breaths as they both sat down.

"Wow, so that's him then, huh?" Dane said in awe. "Big bastard, isn't he?"

"That's one of them, yes." Tyg replied, pushing her plate away, her appetite gone.

"One of them, right." Dane said apprehensively. He turned to regard Tyg. "Is it too late to turn down your offer?" Tyg looked up at him startled, but she saw the cheeky grin slowly spread across Dane's face. Tyg smiled at him.

"Well?" She asked him.

"Well what?"

"What did you get from our little chat, anything interesting?"

"He's a warrior." Dane said simply.

"A what? A warrior, what do you mean?"

"Did you see the size of his arms? Even through his jacket, you could see the muscles rippling underneath. That man is used to wielding a sword, and his sword is not for show like most Lord's around here, it's worn, used well."

"I told you it was bad he is here."

"Yeah, and that's not all?"

"No? What else?" Tyg asked apprehensively.

"He has definitely got an invested interest in you." Dane said remembering Leviathan's reaction to Tyg's laugh.

Tyg shivered slightly again. "Right..."

Tyg got up and left the room. She walked to the front door and opened it walking out on to the stoop and looking up the road. She saw three horsemen, one was Leviathan with two soldiers, one either side of him like bodyguards, she noticed the back of their uniforms had a large gold dragon's head.

'Who the hell are these guys?' Tyg thought to herself.

Just then they stopped and Leviathan turned in the saddle to look back straight at her as if sensing her presence. Tyg flinched inwardly. Damn it, she hadn't wanted him to know she was watching him leave. He turned his horse and cantered back down the street towards her.

"Fuck." Tyg muttered as her heart started hammering in her chest again.

As he reached her he gave her that vulture gaze, looking down his nose. "Was there something you forgot to say?" He asked smirking, clearly amused now. It was obvious to Tyg that he was used to women fawning over his good looks. Tyg grit her teeth, folded her arms and leaned on the wrought iron balustrade.

"No, actually I'm just waiting for someone..."

"Really?" Leviathan scoffed. He looked at her up and down causing Tyg to scowl at him as she felt a heat in that appraising gaze. "You don't dress like a girl." He said, frowning.

Tyg laughed, causing Leviathan to shudder, this time Tyg saw it and frowned. "I'm not like any girl you've met before."

Leviathan grinned, locking eyes with her. "Oh, I can see that." He drawled with a velvety voice.

That caused Tyg to re-evaluate him, he wasn't just some Lord. The confident swagger gave off the vibes of a proper leader...military, powerful. Something told her to be very careful with her words. Just then she spotted the young kid she had given the message to Palin to, he was standing across the street obviously waiting for her chat with Leviathan to end before coming across.

Tyg grinned at Leviathan and beaconed the young boy to come across. Leviathan turned and looked at him. He watched as the boy ran across the road handed Tyg an envelope and scurried off. Tyg folded her arms again, holding the envelope in her hand.

"Well, that's what I was waiting for..." Tyg said pleased with herself.

"Hmm..." Leviathan chuckled. "Nicely done."

"Whatever do you mean?" Tyg asked.

Leviathan levelled that vulture gaze at her again. "I can't wait to spend some real time with you, Tyg, this has been a pleasure and an insight, until our lunch date then." He inclined his head to her, turning his horse and it walked off up the street.

Tyg grit her teeth. "It's not a date." She muttered to herself.

"It kinda is..." Leviathan shouted back laughing.

Tyg stood up shocked. 'He can hear me? What the hell!' She snarled in frustration and walked inside slamming the door behind her as Leviathan pushed his horse into a canter and disappeared up the street with his soldiers, laughing merrily.

Tyg put her back to the door and growled. "Fuck!"

Dane looked at her startled as he came out of the front reception room. "Fucking hell, Tyg, I watched that whole thing from the window."

"Damn him!" Tyg muttered. "He's so bloody egotistical!"

"Well, look at him, if I looked like that I would be too." Dane said. Tyg looked at him her eyes blazing.

"Not helping, Dane."

"I'm just saying, he's one hell of a good looking man, perfect...if I was a girl..."

"Shut the hell up!" Tyg yelled over him and stormed off up the hall.

41

Tyg was galloping to Kor's estate to meet him as agreed regarding the papers she had acquired from Karon's study when she rounded a corner and reined her horse in to a sudden halt. She stared stunned.

Leviathan and Antyn were leading a troop of ten soldiers up the road towards her. Tyg saw both Leviathan and Antyn raise their heads in surprise and Tyg could feel Leviathan's smirk burn into her as he raised his fist to halt the procession. He rested his hands loosely on the pommel of his saddle and waited with a raised eyebrow, amused.

"Tyg...what a pleasant surprise." Leviathan said in a low calm tone.

"Is it?" Tyg said bitterly causing Leviathan to frown and Antyn to stare wide eyed at her. Tyg nudged her horse forward. She knew she had to pass them regardless. She grit her teeth as Leviathan watched her intently. He had purposely halted to make Tyg have to go to him.

As Tyg approached she smiled. "Nice horse." She said truthfully.

It was a massive black stallion battle horse, wearing armour down its neck and it gnashed its teeth at her mount as Tyg steered her horse away from it. Leviathan placed a hand on the horse's shoulder and it relaxed instantly under his touch.

"It's okay now, Tyg, you can approach. What brings you out here...looking for me?" He said arrogantly, his eyes dark and intense.

Tyg glared at him. "Actually...no. If you remember from yesterday when you disturbed my breakfast, I have a lunch meeting with Lord Kor today."

"Quite...a meeting you say..." Leviathan said frowning.

Tyg rolled her eyes, which caused Leviathan's eyes to darken in displeasure. "No, I'm not courting him either...its business." What was he, jealous?

"Business?" Antyn blurted out as he stared at her and the way she was dressed.

Leviathan glared at his brother a moment then turned back to Tyg. "Yes, I remember...Lord Kor is someone fairly important here..."

Tyg grinned. "Fairly."

"Well, you had better not be late then."

Tyg grinned wider. "Indeed."

"I look forward to tomorrow, Tyg." Leviathan's voice dropped to a deep resonating drawl. Tyg blinked and bit her lip as her heart thumped. Leviathan smirked at her reaction.

"Yeah...right...okay...bye." Tyg stammered thrown off balance by Leviathan's strong dominantly sexual tone.

"Tyg..." Leviathan said calling out to her as she put her heels to her horse and it broke into a canter. Tyg ignored him and past his soldiers without a backward glance forcing her horse into a gallop.

"Tyg!" Leviathan yelled as he watched her flee.

"Leave it, Lev, you will see her tomorrow." Antyn said as he watched Tyg take-off up the road.

"I can't wait..." Leviathan said as he licked his lips.

"I can't believe we found her, here of all places." Antyn said incredulously.

Leviathan stared at the retreating back of Tyg, thoughtful. Antyn regarded him and smiled.

"She's beautiful, Lev. What are you going to do?"

Leviathan swung his head and gave his brother a dark dangerous look.

Antyn grinned and shrugged. "Just calling it as I see it."

"Hmm. Did you notice the weapons she was wearing or just the size of her chest?" Leviathan growled.

Antyn laughed. "Oh yes, I noticed. If she comes with weapons tomorrow I'll be sure to take them off her."

Leviathan ran a thumb over his bottom lip as he looked back up the road again. Tyg was gone from view but he felt like he could still feel her presence.

"Lev?" Antyn prompted. "Shall we keep moving?"

"No..." Leviathan said turning his horse around. "I've changed my mind...I'm returning to the manor."

Antyn frowned. "Something wrong?"

"No...but I feel I need to get to the bottom of Tyg's appearance here..."

"Okay..." Antyn said dubious.

"I need proof, Antyn...otherwise she strikes me as the type to try and walk away."

"But she won't...you won't let her."

"We would rather she came willingly, yes?"

"Yes." Antyn agreed.

"So we need to convince her well." Leviathan grumbled, hauling back on the reins as his horse stomped and turned. "I'm going to need to find whatever orphanage took that child in!"

42

As the carriage arrived at Lord Karon's manor Tyg was very surprised to see soldiers at the gates, and once they were let through, she saw more soldiers at the front doors and wandering around the lawns. These soldiers weren't Lord Karon's though, he didn't have soldiers on his payroll. These were obviously the Adramelech brothers' soldiers, the ones Dane mentioned he saw on the ship and Tyg saw with Leviathan when he had come calling and out on the road yesterday. They were dressed in black and silver just like Leviathan wore, with the crest of a fearsome dragon's head on their chests over their hearts in gold and it was also on their backs. Tyg felt quite uneasy seeing them, this was a definite first for Arial, they had never been at war – that she knew of – so had no need for a standing army. The city watch was as military as they got. Now she worried that perhaps with the arrival of these brothers and their soldiers, it would have been prudent to have one.

Tyg saw, as the carriage pulled up to the steps, that Lord Antyn was waiting for her. She was relieved to not see the older brother anywhere. As she stepped out of the carriage she saw Antyn's look of surprise. She smiled smugly to herself. She had deliberately decided to go dressed in her black leather pants, high boots and a very flattering pale blue silk shirt, that clung to her figure and matched her eyes. She was also wearing leather grieves on her wrists and a dagger on her belt. She had gotten Tess to braid her hair up warrior style, with the back tumbling over her left shoulder. Tyg was very satisfied with Antyn's reaction as she walked up the steps and stopped in front of him. Their eyes met and Antyn recovered himself enough to speak first.

"Tyg, I'm so glad you made it. You look stunning, but I'm afraid, no weapons." He indicated the dagger. Tyg grinned and handed it to him, spinning it round on her hand with expertise to hold it out to him handle first. His eyes went wide for a moment as he took the dagger. He then held his hand out and a soldier behind him took the dagger from him.

"You'll get it back when you leave...please follow me..." Antyn walked around the side of the manor heading out to the expansive lawns that were in front of the ballroom. "I thought it would be nice to eat outside, since it's such a lovely day."

Tyg said nothing and had said nothing as yet, which caused Antyn to stop walking and turn to face her.

"Is there a problem, Tyg? You're awfully quiet?"

Tyg gave him a strange look. "I'm reserving judgement is all?"

Antyn raised an eyebrow and smiled amused. "Okay, fair enough." He answered and continued walking. "Leviathan will be joining us a bit later, he's busy with other matters."

"It was him that invited me here." Tyg frowned. She was surprised to feel a pang of disappointment.

"Yes, and he will get here." Antyn said with a smirk.

"And, Lord Karon?" Tyg asked.

"No, Lord Karon, I'm afraid...ah...is also busy."

"Convenient." She muttered, as Antyn looked at her sideways but continued walking.

Tyg shook her head and looked around the gardens as they approached a small table and chairs that had been put out on the lawn. Tyg noticed there were soldiers everywhere, but there seemed to be an exclusion zone around the table. Antyn indicated for Tyg to sit, but she looked around and hesitated.

"Are we out here because it's such a lovely day or because you don't want our conversation overheard?"

Antyn smiled looking amused again. "You're a surprise a minute." He said "You're very perceptive, Tyg."

"Hmm." Tyg mumbled in satisfaction at her thoughts being confirmed as she sat down. "This isn't my first tête-à-tête."

"Indeed?" Antyn said curiously.

Tyg gave him a look to say she wasn't going to expand on her comment.

"Okay." Antyn said understanding the look. "What would you like to drink?" He asked then as they both saw Lord Karon's butler come out onto the lawn and stand nervously a few meters away waiting. Antyn motioned him over.

"Red wine, I think." Tyg said. She noticed how nervous the butler seemed. She made a mental note to pay him a visit later. Turning her head she cocked it forward as she watched him intently. The butler bowed and fled back to the manor. Tyg watched him go until he disappeared from sight. It was strange because he was usually friendly.

"Something interesting?" Antyn asked her as he leaned his elbows on the table and rested his chin on his hands. Tyg turned back to the table and started picking at the cloth.

"I wonder what has got him so terrified." She glanced sideways at Antyn.

"Hmm." Antyn muttered as he leaned back in his chair looking at the doorway across the lawn. The butler appeared again carrying a tray with a bottle and two crystal glasses on it. "Ask him yourself." Antyn offered with an outstretched hand.

Tyg turned to face Antyn, her top lip lifting in a snarl. "Anyone can see he's too terrified to say anything, leave him alone."

Antyn laughed and raked a hand through his hair as the butler reached the table and placed the tray down. As he picked up the bottle to pour it, Antyn waved at him.

"Leave it, go and see how your dear wife is getting on in the kitchen."

The butler bowed and fled back to the manor again.

Antyn grabbed the bottle and glasses off the tray and poured, handing one glass to Tyg.

"I don't know why he is terrified." Antyn said at last. "I guess these people are just not used to having soldiers everywhere."

Tyg took the glass and sipped the wine. "Well, that's a fair assumption." She said indignantly. "Why the need?"

"For the soldiers? It's just what we are used to..." Antyn leaned onto the table conspiratorially. "You see, we're not just Lords. Leviathan is Emperor of our fair land, so security is an essential part of life."

Tyg put her glass down, shocked. "Emperor? Well that explains the narcissism. Why on earth is an Emperor travelling as his own envoy for trade?"

Antyn looked shocked at her words then leaned back again, arching his fingers in front of him, his elbows on the chair arms. He crossed one ankle over the thigh of his other leg as he appraised her question, reassessing her.

"Because, Tyg, he's been searching for you."

Tyg fixed him with a baleful stare, Antyn noticed how her eyes changed colour going from sky blue to an intense ice blue.

"What the hell would he be searching for me for? I think you've got the wrong person...I'm nobody."

Antyn looked at Tyg with an eyebrow raised. "You can't seriously believe that of yourself?" He scoffed. "Look at you!"

Tyg scowled darkly and surprising Antyn, she suddenly drained the whole glass of wine in one gulp, banging it back on the table. He was watching her intently, like a bug under a microscope.

"You don't like people pointing out your looks to you, do you?" He asked still smiling.

Tyg was forcing herself to stay seated and not make a run for it. She suddenly envied the butler as she looked at Antyn and shook her head. "It's inconvenient."

Antyn was taken back by that answer. She grabbed the bottle and poured more wine and took another big swig of it.

"You don't have to be nervous, Tyg. No one here is going to hurt you." Antyn said, but his eyes were looking behind her.

Tyg suddenly felt his presence wash over her and she stood up suddenly. Pushing the chair back and turning around. Both brothers noticed the slight defensive fight posture.

Leviathan was striding across the lawn.

He stopped momentarily as they stared at each other. He was midway through putting a clean shirt on, showing his very muscular physique as the shirt billowed out behind him. He grinned and continued walking towards Tyg as he buttoned it up and tucked it in. Tyg was awe struck at the perfection of the man for a moment and again by the immense dominant aura he possessed, then wondered why the need to change his shirt. Had he been working out? He looked a little sweaty, she could see it glistening on his skin. She down cast her eyes as he approached not knowing where to look, when she realised she was staring.

"Tyg, you look amazing." Leviathan said as he reached her and grabbed her hand to kiss it. As he did Tyg looked back up at him and their eyes locked. He dropped her hand and reached out to touch her hair as he straightened to his full height, towering over her.

"I like the hair...there are women where we come from that wear their hair similar to this."

Leviathan looked at his brother who hadn't moved, except to lower his arms to the chair.

"So what have the two of you been talking about?" He asked as he walked round the table and sat down in the third chair, pulling it out away from the table to allow his legs room to stretch out straight as he crossed his ankles. Tyg sat back down slowly, forcing herself to breathe.

"I was telling Tyg how you are really here because you've been searching the world looking for her." Antyn said. The brothers' eyes now locked on each other. Something else seemed to pass between them which made Tyg all the more nervous. She wished now that Dane had been able to come with her.

"And, I told him you have the wrong person." Tyg answered playing with her glass of wine.

"No, Tyg. I have the right person." Leviathan said in a low voice making her look up at him.

"How do you know?" Tyg spat at him, making him smile.

"Because, I can tell, that's how."

"Tell what exactly?"

"Tyg..." Leviathan sat up in his chair leaning over towards her. "Anyone with eyes can plainly see you don't belong here." He waved his arm around indicating the land.

"How so?" Tyg pushed.

"Your height, your hair, your eyes – especially those eyes. You stand out among boring people. Why do you think they parade you out at parties, like some novelty?" He growled. "Because here, you are a novelty, but in my land...you would be nobility...nah...royalty!"

"Royalty? Now I know you're kidding me." Tyg scoffed as she looked from Leviathan to Antyn and back. Leviathan looked at her with that vulture gaze of his.

"No one here is kidding about anything." He said flatly in a low tone of authority that gave her chills.

Tyg looked at Antyn, he gave her a small smile. "No one!" Leviathan said again more forcefully. Tyg's eyes snapped back to Leviathan shocked.

A soldier came up then and stood a couple of meters away and gave a salute. Tyg looked at him, he didn't quite look the same as the others. His uniform was different – obviously some sort of officer, Tyg surmised. Leviathan stood up.

"Excuse me a moment, Tyg." He said to her, inclining his head. He walked off with the officer a ways in deep conversation.

At that same moment the butler arrived, walking across the lawn with a tray of tasty morsels that he placed down on the table, bowed and turned back to the manor.

"You better grab an extra glass for my brother too while you're here." Antyn suggested.

The butler stammered a sorry and scampered off with a frightful glance over to where Leviathan was.

"No worries." Antyn said casually as he popped a tiny pastry into his mouth. "Hmm, try one Tyg, they're delicious."

"I've kinda lost my appetite." Tyg muttered as she mulled over what Leviathan had said. She sipped her wine and stared over the lawn at the back of Leviathan. Antyn watched her with interest as he grabbed another pastry and popped it into his mouth.

The butler came back with another tray of a different array of delicacies and another glass.

"Sorry, good sir." Antyn said to him. "But, you better grab another bottle of wine too...the lady here seems to quite like it."

Tyg looked over at Antyn with a wide eyed look. Antyn just grinned at her, as the butler bowed and left.

"I'm not a drunk, if that's what you're implying." Tyg said snarly.

"Don't worry Tyg, I know alcohol doesn't affect you the same as these people." Antyn said then appearing amused by her again.

"Because I'm not from here?" Tyg said sarcastically.

"Exactly!" Antyn said as he grabbed his glass and drank from it, looking over the rim at her.

"Am I amusing to you?" Tyg asked indignantly getting a bit annoyed at his constant smirking.

"You're refreshingly naïve to yourself, Tyg."

Tyg shook her head. "I don't even know what that means?"

"Exactly." Antyn said again laughing.

Tyg scowled then, her eyes blazing, as she stood up.

"I think I should go now." She said flatly.

"Shit!" Antyn said, looking down submissively as Leviathan was suddenly right next to her, levelling a baleful stare at his brother.

"What the fuck is going on here?" Leviathan ordered of his brother, the menace in his voice clear.

Antyn raked his fingers through his hair avoiding Leviathan's stare.

"Nothing, really...sorry...I just..." He sounded like a beaten cur.

Tyg suddenly felt sorry for Antyn and interrupted.

"It was nothing, Your Imperial Majesty." Tyg said to appease Leviathan. He turned his vulture gaze on her at the address of his title and his eyes darkened into a deep smoulder. Tyg's breath hitched, she hadn't seen a smoulder like that since Stills.

"Then why, pray tell, are you saying you're leaving?" Leviathan asked in that low authoritative voice that was not to be ignored.

Tyg took a deep breath, regained her composure and sat down again.

"I'm not...I just over reacted..." Tyg turned to Antyn who was looking shocked. "I'm not naïve."

"No, sorry." Antyn said, still avoiding Leviathan's gaze.

Leviathan loomed over the two of them a moment, then reached out for the bottle of wine and poured himself a glass. He downed it in one gulp and placed the glass back on the table.

"A word with you, brother." He commanded, the word brother rolling off his tongue like ice. "Excuse us for a second, Tyg."

Antyn looked pale, which got Tyg riled up. She stood up to face Leviathan, her eyes were blazing pale ice blue again.

"No! Don't go reprimanding your brother for your own indiscretions."

"What!?" Leviathan said actually taken aback as he glared down at the fiery girl, her eyes blazing at him in a challenge he knew she couldn't possibly win. Antyn baulked.

"You invited me here and so far I've spent all my time in Antyn's company, not yours. While you are busy doing fuck knows what else!" Tyg was angry. "You leave us alone, to get to know each other. Antyn is telling me things I, frankly, am not ready to listen to at all. So, it's me who is reacting wrongly and rudely. Not him!"

Leviathan turned his gaze to Antyn who was sitting in stunned silence staring open-mouthed at Tyg. He glanced up at Leviathan and gave him an incredulous look. Leviathan slid his gaze back to Tyg.

"No one has ever spoken to me that way." Leviathan said with unveiled ire.

Tyg glanced down at the table and saw a butter knife. She went to grab it, but suddenly found her hand slammed and pinned down onto the table, over the knife, by Leviathan's hand. She looked up at him, her eyes flashing, but saw Leviathan was grinning, his eyes glowing softly.

"No need to defend my brother's honour, Tyg." Leviathan chuckled. "I surrender to your argument and you're right."

"I am?" Tyg was suddenly confused, as he released her hand.

"Yes, I have been rude and not given you my full attention. You have it now." Leviathan said as he fixed her with that stare sending her heart racing.

"Oh." Tyg said deflated. She hadn't actually wanted his full attention so now she felt like her whole argument had just backfired on her. Especially as Leviathan then grabbed her arm, spinning her round to face away from the table, and hooked her arm over his.

"Walk with me." He said as an order not to be disobeyed.

"Ah...okay...do I have a choice?" Tyg asked as he walked her away from the table across the lawn.

"Frankly? No." Leviathan answered. "You wanted my full attention, now you have it." He reiterated.

"I never actually said that..." Tyg said as she tried to free her arm from his vice like grip.

They were soon walking through a small square garden of roses, surrounded by trellis with flowering creepers on them. There was a small marble bench seat in the middle, to which Leviathan steered her before letting go of her arm and grabbing hold of her shoulders, turning her towards him.

He kissed her, pressing his lips against hers, just like he had done in Lord Karon's study.

Tyg pushed away and stepped back a few steps, staring at Leviathan with those cold ice blue eyes raging.

"You really need to stop doing that!" Tyg said to him through gritted teeth.

Leviathan laughed and sat down, leaning forward, his forearms on his thighs. "Sit." He ordered.

Tyg folded her arms. "Do I look like a dog to you?" She spat.

Leviathan look bewildered and taken aback, then gave Tyg a smile. "Please?"

Tyg sat down next to him, as he looked at the ground between his feet. He turned his head to look at her with a rather perplexed frown.

"You know, I have never had to say that word in my life."

"Well, there's a first for everything, so they say." Tyg said, making Leviathan chuckle.

"You are a breath of fresh air, Tyg, seriously." Leviathan said sitting up and turning to face her, moving his leg so he straddled the bench. "No one back home would dare talk to me like you do, not even my own brother."

"Because, they are all scared of you?"

Leviathan cocked his head like he was thinking about it. "Probably." He admitted, amused. "Are you?" His gaze suddenly intense as he looked across at her.

"Should I be?" Tyg said shrugging, trying to seem calm. "I mean, yes...you can obviously handle a sword by the looks..." She looked him full in the eyes then, hers now calmed to a deep sky blue. "...but, so can I."

Leviathan looked surprised and raised an eyebrow. "Now, that's something I would very much like to see?"

"Kiss me again uninvited, and you may." Tyg growled.

Much to Tyg's chagrin Leviathan burst out laughing. "Oh, Tyg, what sort of life have you had to get so good at banter?"

It was Tyg's turn to look shocked and she turned her head away to look over the roses. Leviathan quietened and regarded her calmly.

"What are you exactly?"

"What a strange question?" Tyg remarked, looking sideways at him.

"I mean. You dress like a man...and not just any man, like a warrior...with weapons. People skirt around you with caution in the street. You seem to know some very dangerous individuals that you meet in the shadows..."

"Have you been following me?" Tyg turned to face him.

Leviathan ignored the question and just looked at Tyg waiting for an answer.

Tyg shrugged. "I grew up on the streets, so I did what I needed to...to survive." She folded her arms and looked down.

They were both silent a moment then Leviathan spoke.

"What I have to tell you next will change your life forever."

Tyg pinched her nose with her fingers. "Not this again?" She muttered.

"Look, Tyg. The reason I was late was because I was getting proof, I knew you would need to see it to believe it."

Tyg looked at him, his intense gaze was unwavering. "Proof?"

He reached into a pocket of his pants and drew out a piece of paper, he unfolded it and handed it to her.

"What is it?" Tyg asked suspiciously, taking it but not looking at it.

"It's yours...your form from when you were given to the orphanage."

"What!?" Tyg was shocked. "I didn't know they kept papers on us?"

"Well, I had to ask rather forcefully to get it." Leviathan shrugged. "So your full name...its Tygarya Vanarya Essyndyl."

Tyg was reading the paper. It didn't have much information on it, but it did have a full name and a place of origin. Tylandria. Tyg looked up at Leviathan stunned. It also had a birth date, but no parents' names listed.

"Why aren't my parent's named?" Tyg asked sullenly.

Leviathan shrugged. "My guess, is because they wanted you to be hidden, or maybe themselves."

"Hidden from who?" Tyg asked intently. "You?"

"Hard to say really?" Leviathan shrugged, not denying it.

Tyg stood up wary now. "Why are you looking for me then? How did you know who I was? Where to look?"

Leviathan stayed seated and calm. "I know it's a shock, Tygarya, but don't fear me."

Tyg shivered when she heard her proper name used. "It's not you I fear, it's your intentions...I know nothing about you...where you're from, but I know you came here under false pretences...with soldiers."

"No, I didn't come under false pretences. The trade agreement stands and is beneficial for both parties concerned. Mine and the Arial Council, and it will go ahead as planned. I am merely completing two quite different agendas at the same time."

"But, why me?"

Leviathan past a hand over his face. He was getting annoyed and had to remain calm. It was essential that he get Tyg to return with him to Tylandria without knowing the true reason.

"Because you're important to my Empire, Tygarya. I can't explain how or why, just know that you are." Leviathan said cryptically. "You already know it, deep inside, don't you? You knew it the first moment our eyes met the other night across the ballroom."

Tyg was standing staring at the ground. She was unsure what to do, this was all too confusing. How did he know what she felt? It annoyed her that he was right.

"It was the same for me..." Leviathan continued. "...call it destiny, if you like. But, like you, I just knew. I can't explain it, I just knew." Leviathan had stood up and stepped over to her, taking her by the shoulders again and making her look up at him. "We're connected...you and I."

Tyg stared at him, stepping out of his grasp again and retreating back a few steps.

"This is more than I can deal with all in one go." She said to him as he looked annoyed. "I thought you were wanting to talk to me about the document I took...not all this."

Leviathan grinned. "I care naught about some document giving me Lord Karon's estates...or who knows about them."

"You don't?"

"No, I care naught about the espionage that goes on behind closed doors here." Leviathan shrugged and turned to the roses. He picked a pale lilac coloured one that was still a tight bud and held it to his nose.

"Why don't you care about it?" Tyg was very interested to know why it didn't bother him, something about it wasn't right.

Leviathan turned and walked up to her, holding the rose out to her, smiling. "It really doesn't matter, Tygarya, what matters right now, is you."

"Enough!" Tyg growled, then hesitated, lowering her eyes. "Please, I've heard enough for now."

Tyg took the rose as Leviathan held it out again more insistently.

"Of course, Tygarya." Leviathan slightly bowed. "Can we sit back down for a moment?" He indicated the bench and Tyg placated him by moving back and sitting down. She looked down at her lap and the rose she was holding, as Leviathan sat next to her.

"Thank you." Tyg said then, indicating the rose, with a small smile.

"My pleasure." Leviathan smiled back. "You are aware Lord Ranor is having a dinner tonight?"

"Yes, of course."

"Ah, you are involved in organising it?"

"Actually, I've been hired to sing." Tyg said looking at Leviathan sideways with a sly expression.

"To sing?" Leviathan said surprised, then he scowled. "More parading you around?" He said with a strange possessiveness.

Tyg shrugged. "It pays well."

Leviathan looked hard at her then. "You have had a hard upbringing, Tygarya, I apologise for that."

"It's hardly your fault." Tyg scoffed.

"I should have found you sooner." Leviathan muttered, almost to himself, then looked up at her. "Accompany me to the dinner tonight?"

"What?" Tyg looked at him shocked.

"You heard." Leviathan said annoyed again, he wasn't used to this constant questioning.

"I can't. I'm not aristocracy. I'm not invited to attend the banquet. I'm being paid to perform."

"Nonsense. If I say you're accompanying me as my guest, that's what will happen."

Tyg stared at him, she could hear the authority and finality in his voice. He was a dangerous person to cross, she could sense, so again she found herself placating the situation.

"Very well, you're Imperial Majesty." Tyg said locking eyes with him. "I accept."

Tyg saw Leviathan's eyes dilate and darken as she said his title again and his brow furrowed slightly.

"You're the only person I've ever met who can say that to my face and make it sound like an insult."

Tyg's eyes widened. "I'm sorry...I didn't..."

Leviathan shook his head. "No, it's perfectly fine, Tygarya." He grinned. "I'm happy that you accepted my invitation." He gave her that same smoulder and smirked like he was looking at prey again, which always made her heart start thumping in her chest. Tyg stood up, nervous under that gaze, before he tried to kiss her again.

"I think, perhaps, we should go back now."

"Very well." Leviathan stood up and followed as Tyg made her way back through the rose garden. She stopped at the edge of the rose garden where the lawn began. She could see Antyn sitting at the table, leaning back in his chair. He looked like he was enjoying the autumn sun.

Leviathan came up beside her. "Something wrong?"

Tyg looked at him curiously. "When do you plan to sail back?"

Leviathan's eyes went wide a moment, he was surprised at the question.

"I have to travel up to Landau first, take possession of Lord Karon's estate and lands, but I can't be gone from my own Empire for too long...so I will probably want to be heading back within the month."

"So quickly?" Tyg muttered sullenly.

"Why?" Leviathan asked in that authoritative voice, his tone dropping.

"Well, it means I have a month to decide."

"Decide what exactly?" Leviathan asked looking down at her amused as he folded his arms. Tyg looked at him like he was a simpleton.

"Whether I go back with you or not, of course."

Leviathan gave Tyg the look a parent gives a child when they are explaining the way things are going to be.

"There is no decision to make." He said simply. "You're going."

Tyg stared at Leviathan not sure if he was serious, then assumed, by his expression, that he was. Tyg suddenly found her backbone at last. She let him have all her pent up frustrations at the top of her voice as her eyes blazed into ice blue fire.

"I don't know who the hell you are in your own Empire, or who the hell you think you are here, but don't ever...ever...think to make any life changing decisions for me! I am not one of your subjects, nor am I a servant that shakes in fear at the mere sight of you like Lord Karon's butler does. I have killed people! I am not some little girl raised to like fancy dresses and find a rich husband. You may know OF me, but you certainly do NOT know ME...or anything about me! Understand!" Tyg's eyes had dilated to black.

With that Tyg stormed off across the lawn. She saw that Antyn had stood up and was running across the lawn in their direction.

She was surprised to not feel the strong hand of Leviathan grab her shoulder or arm, but she was certainly not going to turn around to see how he was reacting. She glanced at Antyn as he suddenly stopped running and just shouted at his brother.

"Leviathan! No!"

This caused the hairs on the back of Tyg's neck to stand up. She turned around, following Antyn's gaze. Tyg held her breath, and her eyes went back to blue, as she saw Leviathan holding a glowing ball of fire in his bare hand. Tyg was confused at what she was seeing. All sorts of questions suddenly flooded her mind as she saw Leviathan heave a deep breath, as Antyn continued to yell, and the ball of fire disappeared as he flicked his head in annoyance. He stuffed his hands in his pockets and posed a very menacing figure staring at her.

Antyn was suddenly by Tyg's side and grabbed her arm, pulling her away.

"Tyg, I think it's time you were going." He said as Tyg let him turn her back around and lead her away.

Antyn quickly walked her past the table and chairs and back around the side of the house to the front entrance. Tyg also noticed that all the soldiers had drawn their weapons and some with bows had them notched and pointed at her.

As they turned the corner of the building Tyg looked back over her shoulder once and saw that Leviathan had not moved from the spot and she could still feel his anger burning into her.

Antyn let her go once they were out of Leviathan's sight and stopped to stare at her.

"What possessed you to do that?" Antyn said incredulously.

Tyg folded her arms. She was pissed off at Leviathan's assumption and she wasn't going to apologise for it.

"Do what?" Tyg said coolly. "Stick up for myself? I've been sticking up for myself my whole life and I'm not apologising for it."

Antyn raked a hand through his hair exasperated.

"You don't realise the danger you were in."

Tyg suddenly recalled the ball of fire she saw in Leviathan's hand and her anger faltered. She unfolded her arms.

"What was that?" She asked, her eyes wide.

Antyn looked over his shoulder like he expected Leviathan to appear any moment. He snapped his fingers at the guard by the entrance doors.

"Get Lord Karon's carriage round here now!"

"Antyn? What was that fire in Leviathan's hand?" Tyg asked again. This time Antyn looked at her.

"Not right now, Tyg. I need to get you away from here quickly."

"What?"

"Tyg, Leviathan is an Emperor...you can't speak to him like that."

Tyg folded her arms again, indignantly.

"I'll speak to him however I damn well please." She said it calmly and quietly which made it all the more horrifying to Antyn who gaped at her. "I'll have my dagger back now."

Antyn composed himself and drew himself up straight. "I don't think that would be a good idea right now." He could see the same vicious streak in Tyg that was in Leviathan and it worried him. "What happened exactly? I thought things seemed to be going well?" He asked as he watched the carriage that had brought Tyg here, come round the corner from the stable and start heading towards them. He looked at Tyg who was levelling a gaze of pure ice blue fire at him.

"I asked him when he intended to sail back home and when he said a month...why?" Tyg imitated Leviathan's voice making Antyn's eyes go wide. "I said it meant I have a month to think about whether I go with you...to which he had the audacity to tell me I WAS going, no decision needed."

Antyn looked resigned and sighed as he raked a hand through his hair.

"Tyg, you have to understand..."

"I don't have to understand anything! It will be my choice and no one else's...got it!?" Tyg's intense gaze was as terrifying as Leviathan's and Antyn swallowed hard. He nodded.

"Of course it is, Tyg...calm down"

"Tell Mister Fireball to calm down!" Tyg said sarcastically as the carriage pulled up and she grabbed the door handle swinging the carriage door open. She turned and locked eyes with him again. "And, next we meet I expect a full explanation to what the fuck I just witnessed." Antyn, looking closer could see she was shaking. Her rage was covering her fear. "And, you can give me my dagger back now." She held her hand out as she stood half in and half out of the carriage.

Antyn clicked his fingers again and the guard retrieved Tyg's dagger from his belt and held it out to her. Tyg grasped it tightly and disappeared into the carriage, slamming the door without another word.

Antyn indicated to the driver and the carriage pulled out and down the pathway to the gates.

Antyn stood with his hands on his hips watching until the carriage was out of sight, then let out an explosive breath, bending over. His hands on his knees. He suddenly felt exhausted.

A shadow fell on the ground at his feet and he quickly straightened up again to face his brother.

"Why did you make her leave?" Leviathan asked calmly.

Antyn stared at his brother. "Are you kidding me? By the gods, Lev, what the hell do you think you were doing? A fire ball? How the fuck are we going to explain that?"

"Calm down, little brother. What's done is done. The raw power that was emanating from her, I felt I had to prepare is all, I wasn't going to attack her."

Antyn raked his hand through his hair. "I know, how the hell does she not know? How can it still be dormant when it's literally leaking out of her? It's incredible."

"She's incredible...and nothing like what we prepared for. We're going to have to re-evaluate our entire strategy in how to deal with her."

"You don't say?" Antyn said sarcastically. Leviathan levelled a cool gaze at him. "Sorry, Lev."

Leviathan looked up across the gravel pathway. "Understandable in the circumstances."

Antyn chuckled. "And we thought this was going to be so easy."

Leviathan looked back at Antyn with an eyebrow arched. "Indeed, but nothing worthwhile is ever easy." Leviathan suddenly lifted the rose bud that Tyg had dropped in her anger, to his nose and sniffed it. "Do you know she has killed people?"

"What?"

"She told me as much, did you not hear her? She said it loud enough." Leviathan asked amused.

"When I heard her raised voice and looked over all I could focus on was the power field going off between the two of you."

Leviathan smiled as he crushed the rose bud in his hand, turning it to dust. He opened his hand and blew the dust away. "She is so fascinating."

43

Tyg was getting ready to attend Lord Ranor's banquet when Tess knocked on her bedroom door.

"Ah...Tyg...that Lord Adramelech is here for you, he says."

"What?" Tyg said surprised, she had not expected him to still want her to accompany him after what happened that afternoon at Lord Karon's. Or, rather she had hoped he wouldn't. "Fuck! What is it with this guy?" She asked herself and started pacing the room thinking about what to do.

She contemplated escaping out the back door, but after what Leviathan had said to her she knew he was obviously having her followed.

"Um...Tyg?" Tess coughed politely, reminding Tyg of her presence.

Tyg turned to her and took a deep breath. "Okay, show him into the reception lounge, please. I need to talk to him. Tyg didn't want to talk to him, he made her nervous and scatty, like a silly teenage girl – which is what she was – but not silly...was she? She argued to herself, this man was on a complete new level to any she had ever met before.

Tess nodded her head and left the room. Tyg took a moment to regard her reflection, as she smoothed down her dress where it clung to her hips. It was of a deep regal blue, with silver clasps and brocade detailing on the bodice, which did up the front instead of the back. Again, Tess's designs were bucking the trend. Tyg had left her wealth of silver blond hair free and had woven a silver chain with a teardrop sapphire surrounded by small diamonds sitting on her forehead, through it like a coronet. Tyg took a deep breath and went to face Leviathan.

As she entered the room, Leviathan was standing by the fireplace, staring into the fire. His hands clasped behind his back. He was wearing a military style coat with buckles down the front, open with his usual black shirt, leather pants and sword. He definitely cut a formidable figure given his height and stature. He had his hair all tied back in a knot at the back of his head but a few shorter bits still framed his handsome face.

He turned as she entered and as his intense eyes fell on her, Tyg's stomach dropped through the floor. His gaze looked hungry and as he took in the sight of her, she felt naked, but she then saw him close his eyes and shake his head briefly, as if a bad scent had reached his nostrils. Tyg remembered what Dane had said he saw when Tyg laughed, so she knew her look had an effect on him as much as his did on her.

As he recovered Leviathan closed the gap between them in only two strides.

"Tygarya, bloody hell...you look like an angel." He touched her hair, trailing it through his fingers.

"Thank you." Tyg said apprehensively. "So, you got over this afternoon?"

"Meaning?" He asked in a flat tone. He watched Tyg as she turned to the door and closed it. She moved away from the door then and walked past him over to where he had been standing – in front of the fireplace. As she turned she saw he had pivoted round to keep her in his sight and seemed to be enjoying the view of her from behind. Tyg scowled at him but he just shrugged his shoulders and raised an eyebrow, folding his arms.

"You need to explain to me what I saw." Tyg stated coolly.

"What did you see?" Leviathan asked in the kind of way that made Tyg think it was a veiled threat to say nothing.

"So, it's like that then?" Tyg exclaimed. "You can conjure fire balls into the palm of your hand, but I'm supposed to just forget I saw it and yet still trust you? Not that I have ever trusted you. But, you turn up on my doorstep like nothing out of the ordinary happened after you were contemplating throwing that fucking fire ball at my back only hours ago."

Leviathan was rubbing a thumb along his jaw, his eyes intently watching Tyg as she spoke. He noticed how she stayed calm not raising her voice – she doesn't want anyone else to hear. Good, he thought to himself, which means she hasn't told anyone.

Leviathan down cast his eyes and stepped closer to Tyg, like he was approaching a fawn ready to spring away.

"Do you think it wise to discuss these matters here?"

"I believe 'these matters' as you call them, need to be sorted before I go anywhere with you." It was Tyg's turn to fold her arms, but then she unfolded them when she realised – in this dress – it just accentuated her cleavage.

Leviathan smiled as he caught the awkward motion. He decided to tell her what he was. He reached a hand over to a vase of flowers that were on the mantelpiece behind her and grabbed the flowers out of it. Tyg stopped breathing as he brushed past her as he reached out, his chest brushing her upper arm, his face inches from her. The smell of him was divine. He smirked as he brought the flowers round to present them to Tyg, like he felt her reaction to the closeness. The flowers had changed from chrysanthemums and daisies to blue roses the exact colour of her dress. Tyg looked at them shocked then looked up at his waiting face.

"I'm a sorcerer, Tygarya." He said as he put the roses into her numb hands.

Tyg staggered back a step. "A what?"

"I know it sounds impossible, as there is no magic in this land, but in my land magic is alive and well. It is truly a magical place, Tygarya and I want you to see it. I want to show you it."

"Magic?" Tyg breathed as she stared at the roses in her hands. "But..."

"No, Tygarya, don't try to analyse it. It is what it is. Magic exists...just not here."

"So, how does a person become a Sorcerer?"

"You're born that way." Leviathan was watching her reactions very carefully, he knew this could go either way.

Tyg looked up at him again, her brows were furrowed as she was thinking about what he had said. "So, Antyn?"

Leviathan smiled and nodded.

"Shit." Tyg muttered, then her face went devilish. "You do know they burnt witches at the stake here...years ago...like a couple of hundred years, I suppose."

Leviathan snorted and leaned an elbow on the mantle. "Apparently so."

"You're not worried about that?"

"No."

"But, you obviously want me to keep this quiet...yes?" Tyg's eyes were sparkling and slowly changing colour. Leviathan was watching her eyes intently, amused.

"Yes." He smirked on only one side of his mouth.

Tyg turned and put the roses back into the vase of water. "So, how much?" She asked as she fluffed the flowers, not looking at Leviathan.

"How much?" He asked her back, confused.

"Money." Tyg said, turning back to face him. "How much is your secret worth?"

Tyg saw Leviathan's eyes flash with anger suddenly as he stepped forward pushing Tyg past the fireplace and up against the wall, without even touching her. He stood in front of her only inches apart, grabbed her chin and forced her head up to look at him. He was actually still smirking. Tyg had underestimated him, but he had underestimated her. As his eyes suddenly went wide and he looked down to see Tyg was holding a small slender needle, with a strange shaped handle, like a cork screw, right at his groin. He turned his face back to hers. Their faces were now only an inch apart. Tyg held her breath. Leviathan, on the other hand, breathed in deeply closing his eyes.

"I'm sorry, are you smelling me?" Tyg asked bewildered. Everything about this man always put her on the back foot, he was so different...was she this different? Is this how everyone else saw her?

"Yes, actually...what is that scent?"

Tyg shrugged. "What Tess puts in my bath...a mixture? Are you going to let me go?"

Leviathan still had hold of Tyg's chin. "I'm not sure? Do you reckon you could use that needle of yours before I could use my power?" He asked smirking again as he saw the doubt cloud Tyg's eyes.

"I was kidding...about the money. I won't say anything. No one would believe me anyway." Tyg suddenly backtracked.

"Kidding? Really?"

"Yes." Tyg lowered the hand with the weapon, then lifted it up between them and – as Leviathan watched intently – she placed it back into her bodice, where it sat in her cleavage. The strange handle following the line of the bodice as decoration. Leviathan raised an eyebrow as he let her chin go and stood up, stepping away slightly.

"Don't do that, Tygarya. I'm not one to take humour like that well." He was curt, his tone deep and admonishing.

"I can see that." Tyg said as she smoothed her dress down again.

"Interesting weapon." He commented.

"Thank you, I had it especially made after our encounter in Lord Karon's study."

Leviathan laughed then. "You had it made especially for me?"

Tyg adjusted the way she was leaning against the wall, to get comfortable. "Well, I guess you could see it that way...depends on your ego I suppose?"

Leviathan laughed again and grabbed her hand, dragging her away from the wall and over to the couches. He indicated for her to sit, which she did.

He sat down next to her, his body twisted to face her, his arm on the top of the couch back.

"Must we keep dancing around each other, Tygarya, it's getting tiresome."

"To you maybe, but you're the one who wants something."

Leviathan clenched his jaw and looked at his other hand a moment. "Enough, Tygarya."

"You're used to getting what you want, Your Imperial Majesty." Tyg said in a gentle tone, causing Leviathan to lift his eyes to her, his mouth twitching as she called him by his title again. "I can understand your frustration, but understand mine also...you're asking me to take in a lot, and for what?" Leviathan remained silent, watching, always watching. "You're making me re-evaluate my entire life. A life, in which, I have NOT gotten everything I wanted. A life I have had to fight tooth and nail for. Do you even grasp what I'm trying to say?"

"Yes, Tygarya...I do." Leviathan reached out and lifted a lock of her hair and twined it around his finger. "Thank you for talking so candid with me. Yes, I am used to people just obeying my every order, so this is all new to me as well, but I do believe if you trust me enough to spend more time with me...get to talk about all this more...you will come to realise that you don't belong here."

"So, you're asking only for time now?" Tyg muttered.

"Time? Yes, Tygarya...time with you."

"Time with me...what?" Tyg asked as she suddenly placed a hand over his one that was still playing with the lock of hair. Leviathan froze at the touch, his face searching hers for meaning, then he smiled.

"Time with you, please, Tygarya." He let go of her hair and lifted her hand to his lips and kissed it softly. Tyg smiled triumphant, her eyes were shining.

"Okay then, I can accommodate that request." She breathed.

Leviathan dropped her hand and reached out and touched her face, tracing the back of a finger down her cheek and across her jaw line.

"You are something rather special, Tygarya. To get me to say please to you twice now." Leviathan contemplated trying to kiss her, but remembered what she had said earlier that afternoon. Instead, he stood up and held his hand out to her.

"So, shall we go?"

Tyg stood up taking his hand. "I suppose so?"

In the hall Tyg grabbed her cloak, which Leviathan took from her and draped it over her shoulders.

"Thank you." She said quietly.

"Don't get shy on me now, Tygarya." Leviathan laughed and opened the door for her, then escorted her down the stairs to the waiting carriage. As he opened the carriage door for her, Tyg looked at some passers-by walking along the street. They had stopped and were looking at the two of them, their eyes wide with awe. Leviathan noticing her hesitate followed her gaze. He chuckled to himself and whispered to her.

"I told you, you look like an angel...sent from the Gods."

Tyg scowled at him, screwing her nose up as she turned and stepped up into the carriage. Leviathan followed and sat across from her, closing the door. He rapped on the roof. The carriage moved out into the street as dusk started to settle.

Leviathan watched Tyg as she looked out the small window at the street passing by.

"Ask me something?" Leviathan said, leaning back and stretching out his legs.

Tyg turned to him. "Like what?"

"Anything...something you would like to know about me."

"Okay...what was it like growing up...being you?"

This question surprised Leviathan. He had expected something about his magic. He was slowly learning to not expect the normal from Tyg, her mind seemed to work differently.

"My upbringing was nothing like what you probably assume. My father was hard and unforgiving of mistakes. He led in a time of war and expected me to become a great warrior and a great sorcerer, by the cruellest means. I had to grow up too fast."

"Hmm, explains a lot." Tyg muttered as she fiddled with the hem of her cloak.

"Perhaps." Leviathan agreed. "I have a lot to hate my father for...but also a lot to thank him for as well."

"At least you had a father...what about your mother?"

Leviathan shrugged. "I don't remember her, she died when I was young."

"Really? I'm sorry."

"Don't be, like I said, I don't remember her."

"So, how much older than Antyn are you?"

"Four years, but he has a different mother."

"Oh, okay. So, your eyes are those of your father's?"

Leviathan chuckled. "Yes, can I ask a question of you?"

Tyg regarded him a long moment trying to read his stony face, then gave up and shrugged.

"Sure, what is it?"

"You said earlier today, you had killed people. Were you serious?"

"Yes."

"I want to know about it."

Again Tyg sat silent as she thought about it. This was treading dangerous ground. "What do you want to know exactly?"

"Why? What caused you to have to kill a man?"

"A man?" Tyg laughed, causing Leviathan to frown.

"How many?"

"So many questions. What does it matter? Only a vain person keeps count, killing is not something a person should keep score on."

"So true." Leviathan agreed surprised. He knew that answer meant a lot. It also surprised him how old and wise she sounded, like she was quoting someone else. It was hard to keep in his mind how young she actually was sometimes. Her brain was far cleverer than an eighteen year old girls should be.

"Okay, I can tell you of one time... I got lured into a warehouse by four guys to try and...ah...kill me." Tyg swallowed hard and looked out the window at the actual memory, so she didn't see Leviathan's eyes blazing.

"And, you killed them?" Leviathan prompted.

"No, not all. My boss turned up with aide, luckily and helped me finish off the last two."

"Were you injured?" Leviathan's voice had gone cold and flat. Tyg looked over at him and saw his anger. She laughed that same musical laugh and then she saw the effect it had on him as he closed his eyes and shuddered.

"No point getting worked up about it...its history."

Leviathan opened his eyes and fixed her with a fearsome stare. "Were you injured?"

"Yes, I was okay? I slipped up...got smacked in the head with a piece of wood and got a knife in the side."

"Slipped up? Sounds like your 'boss' was like my father, a cruel task master."

"Still is." Tyg muttered as she looked back out of the window.

"What the fuck?" Leviathan exclaimed. "Who is he?" He demanded his eyes darkening to a deep scowl.

"Oh no...that crosses a line I'm not stepping over, that would cost me my life."

"No, it wouldn't." His tone lowered as his gaze narrowed.

Tyg looked at Leviathan surprised at his temper.

"Leviathan, please calm down." Leviathan shivered slightly and took a deep breath. "We're here." Tyg said then as the carriage drew up to the front of Lord Ranor's Manor.

A servant opened the carriage door for them and Tyg went to get out, but Leviathan grabbed her arm and pulled her over to him.

"This conversation is not over." He said in a low tone.

Tyg just looked at him with wide eyes as he released her arm. She stepped from the carriage and waited as Leviathan stepped out behind her. He took her arm and escorted her up the stairs.

44

As they entered the entrance hall an official looking man baulked at seeing the two of them and scurried over.

"My Lord, you must be Lord Leviathan Adramelech?"

"Indeed." Leviathan answered, then the official turned to Tyg.

"And this beautiful woman, my Lord, must be Tyg?"

"Her name is Lady Tygarya Essyndyl, present her as such." Leviathan announced as he removed Tyg's cloak revealing that her dress was now pure white with the brocade detailing now gold. Tyg looked down at herself in shock then looked up at Leviathan with awe, as the official was staring open-mouthed at her.

"Did you do this?" Tyg whispered as Leviathan just winked and carried on towards the banquet room. The official raced ahead of them and entered the hall.

"I present his Lordship, Leviathan Adramelech of Tylandria and Lady Tygarya Essyndyl."

The official boomed out across the hall, making everyone pause and watch as they entered. The looks on everyone's faces as their eyes fell upon Tyg made her very uncomfortable.

"Ah, Lord Adramelech, so glad you could make it. And, Tyg, wonderful to see you. You look absolutely beautiful. I had heard you were being courted by our overseas guest here...you make quite the striking couple." Lord Ranor said coming up and shaking hands with Leviathan and kissing Tyg's hand.

"Tygarya." Leviathan said coldly.

"Pardon me?" Lord Ranor asked perplexed.

"Her name is Tygarya." Leviathan said in that low authoritative voice. Lord Ranor coughed startled.

"Yes, of course, I meant no offence, I had no idea."

"None taken, Ranor, thank you." Tyg said, staring at Leviathan, her eyes blazing.

"Good, good." Lord Ranor stumbled, glancing at Leviathan, who was looking over the room. "Will you be blessing us with a song later?"

"Of course."

"I'm so pleased." Lord Ranor looked at Leviathan again. "Your brother is over this way, at the main table. He gave me your request for the extra seat, I see why now. Please follow me." Lord Ranor walked through the throng of people with Leviathan and Tyg making everyone clear a path for them, looking like royalty had arrived. Which in Leviathan's case it actually had.

Antyn was standing, with a strange look on his face as he watched Leviathan and Tyg enter the hall and make their way towards him. As they came around the main table to take their seats Antyn took Tyg's hand and kissed it.

"Tygarya, you are breath-taking tonight."

"Blame Leviathan." She stated making Antyn look at his brother.

Leviathan just shrugged as he took his seat next to Lord Ranor, after first greeting the man's wife. Tyg was dismayed to see she was to sit between the brothers. 'Great.' She thought. 'No way I'll have an appetite now.'

"Let the banquet begin!" Lord Ranor announced then, making everyone applaud and take their seats.

As the food started coming out there was also entertainment of different styles. Musicians, jugglers, jokers. Each course of food had a different entertainment with it.

Tyg somewhat enjoyed herself. Leviathan and Antyn were kept busy chatting with the steady stream of people coming up to the main table to talk to them. So, when Tyg spotted Thomas she made quick her escape from the table with a quick 'excuse me' and swept through the room.

"Tyg!" Thomas exclaimed as she approached.

"Tom!" Tyg greeted in return as they hugged briefly. "How have you been?"

"Yeah, good. By the Gods, Tyg, you've been busy though, it was only three days ago you were saying to watch out for those two and now you're coming in on the arm of one of them...the worse one at that."

"I know, but it's not what it seems, Tom."

"Really, what is it then?"

Tyg looked at him with an eyebrow raised.

"What's with all the questions, Captain?"

"I'm worried for you, Tyg?"

"Don't!" Tyg said it harsher than she meant too. Suddenly, Lord Kor was at her side and took her elbow.

"We need to talk." He said to her and walked off.

Thomas looked at Tyg serious.

"I have to go, Tom, I'll be back in a bit." Tyg said back to him as she was dragged away.

Thomas folded his arms. "Okay?"

As Kor got her out a side door into the cool night air he dropped her arm and spun on her.

"What the fuck are you doing?"

"What do you mean exactly, Adrian?" Tyg asked with a sneer, not liking Lord Kor's tone.

"Coming in with Lord Adramelech like you're his bloody consort?"

"Watch your mouth, Kor." Tyg said in a lowered threatening voice.

"Watch your step, missy." He spat back, then calmed and traced a finger across the side of her face as he swept a stray hair back. "You know I care for you and seeing you with him made me jealous."

"Adrian, for Pete's sake, let it go…"

Lord Kor looked at her harshly, his jaw clenching. "You're supposed to be finding out information not bedding them like a common whore."

Tyg slapped Lord Kor hard across the face, with great strength, causing him to stagger sideways, spitting out blood as the inside of his mouth was cut by his teeth.

Suddenly a large ominous figure lifted Lord Kor off his feet and sent him hurtling back several feet, taking the wind out of him.

The figure turned to Tyg, it was Leviathan. His eyes were glowing in the darkness.

"What the fuck is going on here?" Leviathan demanded as Tyg put a staying hand on his chest, so he didn't go charging at Lord Kor, who was staggering to his feet.

"Just a misunderstanding is all…calm down, Leviathan." Tyg said shocked at his reaction.

"He had his hands on you."

"He was concerned…we have…history…it's nothing…never was." Tyg growled frustrated that now things were going to be misunderstood.

Tyg's hand on his chest seemed to give him pause and he glared at Lord Kor over the top of Tyg's head.

"I don't want an international incident over this, but if I ever see you near Tygarya again I will kill you."

Lord Kor, baulked, he was standing dumbfounded, and staring at Leviathan, as Tyg pulled him away. "I hope you know what the fuck you are doing, Tyg." Lord Kor muttered as he stumbled back inside.

"Fuck sake, Leviathan, what the hell have you done?" Tyg whisper yelled at him.

"I don't know Tyg, explain it to me? Is he your Boss?" He asked as he grabbed her chin and held her gaze.

"My bo...No! He's not, he's..." Tyg sighed. "I can't say anymore, sorry."

Leviathan stared at her. "When I said I didn't care about the espionage that goes on in this fucking country that was before I knew you were neck deep in it!"

Tyg looked down at the ground uncomfortable, but Leviathan squeezed her chin and pulled her face back up to his. Their eyes locked and Leviathan stared at her a long moment, then let her go. He paced off into the darkness a few steps, his hands behind his neck as he stared at the night sky. Tyg stood rooted to the spot not sure whether she should go or not.

"Tyg?" Antyn suddenly said behind her, then he saw Leviathan approach again out of the darkness. "Lev? What's going on?"

"Nothing." Leviathan spat in a guttural snarl. "At least, that's what Tygarya wants us to think!"

"I just can't talk about it!"

"Why is that, Tyg?" Antyn asked.

"Because I took an oath, that's why...on death."

Leviathan's face suddenly changed. "An oath?" Tyg nodded. "What the fuck?" Leviathan exclaimed through gritted teeth. "What sort of oath? For fuck's sake, don't you dare say a blood oath?" Leviathan was shaking.

"What? No? Ewww." Tyg screwed her face up.

"And what about him...touching you?" Leviathan growled.

Antyn baulked and suddenly looked very nervous. "Someone touched you?"

Tyg looked confused. "He escorted me outside and stroked some hair away from my face...so what...he tried to court me once."

"I'll fucking kill him." Leviathan growled again, pacing, raking a hand through his hair. Tyg frowned and looked at Antyn.

"What's the big deal?"

Antyn stared nervously at Leviathan. "He's possessive Tyg...haven't you got that yet, just stay away from other men."

"Are you fucking serious right now? What the hell do you think this is?"

Leviathan stalked up and stood directly in front of her. "Deadly serious, Tygarya." He reached out and placed a hand around her throat, resting it on her collar bone. It was a strange action, not threatening, more sensual. Tyg's eyes went wide at the heat in the touch, he looked into her eyes, a wall of pure dominate power of will in front of her. "You are now mine."

"Look, can we seriously drop this right now? People are starting to look." Antyn interrupted before Tyg had a chance to answer that statement. "Besides, I think Tyg is wanted back inside...and so are we."

"I don't give a fuck who's wanted where." Leviathan stated his voice full of authority as he dropped his hand. Tyg was just staring at him.

"Lev, listen to me...calm the fuck down...we don't need bad attention here."

Leviathan fixed his brother with a baleful stare. "I don't care, Antyn. I could destroy them all with a glance, I don't need their favours or their accords. I'm through with this pussy footing around bullshit!"

Tyg's eyes had gone fearful at the thought of Leviathan being able to destroy everyone by just looking at them. She took a couple of steps backwards.

"Right, well, be that as it may...I have a song to sing...so, I'll be going now."

Tyg turned quickly and fled back inside.

Right into Thomas, colliding with him as he grabbed her shoulders.

"Fuck, Tyg, what the hell is going on?"

"Why do you ask?" Tyg asked trying to look calm.

"I just saw Lord Kor storm through here like a tornado."

"Don't worry yourself about it, Tom." Tyg said as they both looked at Leviathan and Antyn as they came back inside after her. Tyg stepped very quickly away from Thomas remembering Antyn's words and seeing the look on Leviathan's face. Thomas gave her a questioning look.

"Are you alright?" He asked, reaching out for her again, Tyg stepped back.

"Yes, I'm fine." Tyg said exasperated. "I just need to go do my job now...okay everyone?" She sneered as she flicked a glance at Leviathan and Antyn. Her mind was still reeling from what he had said to her.

Tyg stormed off to go find the musicians, as Thomas took another look at Leviathan and Antyn.

"Don't hurt her." Thomas said to them making Leviathan take a step towards him wanting to pounce on him but Antyn slammed a hand onto his brother's chest holding him back with force.

"We have no intention of hurting her." Antyn said, diplomatically.

"Good then." Thomas said, his jaw clenching. He turned slowly and walked away.

Antyn turned to Leviathan. "What the hell has gotten into you?"

Leviathan shook his head, a dark perplexed look upon his face. "I don't know. I just can't stand all these people touching her. She belongs to me."

Antyn swallowed hard. "Well, for both our sakes, calm down."

"Hmm." Leviathan grunted as they made their way back to the table, just as the first notes from the musicians started signally Tyg's song was starting.

As Tyg started to sing and walk into the centre of the room the whole place went quiet. Leviathan and Antyn were staring wide eyed at her.

"By the fucking Gods! Look at that!" Antyn exclaimed. "Her power is worse than we feared."

"It's exactly as we feared, it's reactionary." Leviathan said breathlessly, watching Tyg intently.

"How does no one see it? Feel it?" Antyn said. "It's hypnotic."

"They feel it, they just don't understand what it is." Leviathan shuddered as Tyg's voice soared high above the music. "Like a fucking angel." Leviathan snarled, shaking his head clear. "Imagine that power once it fully awakens..."

"What possessed you to put her in white?" Antyn asked, mesmerised by Tyg's singing, just as the whole room was.

"She looked like an angel. How the fuck was I supposed to know that she sang like one too, pouring out innate power like that...it's your job to know this stuff."

"How are you enjoying Tyg's....ah...Tygarya's singing, my Lord?" Lord Ranor asked leaning over to Leviathan.

"Simply amazing." Leviathan answered him curtly.

"Isn't she though...a real national treasure."

Leviathan turned to look at Lord Ranor, his eyes blazing, but Antyn put a calming hand on his arm.

"I can't stand much more of this, Antyn." Leviathan said standing up. "She's mine."

Antyn stared at his brother in awe of that statement. Standing up caught Tyg's attention and she locked her eyes onto him, walking up towards the table as she sang her haunting melody. She extended her hand out to him. He frowned a moment, then nonchalantly stepped up onto the table and jumped down in front of her, taking her hand, to the raucous applause of the crowd. Two people were not applauding however, Thomas and Lord Kor. Tyg smiled a radiate smile at Leviathan as she continued to sing. Leviathan took her by the waist and started to dance around the room with her. Tyg moved away and twirled back to him several times, swaying with the music. He was completely intoxicated by her, watching the way she moved and listening to her voice. Her power emanating out of her. Every time Leviathan touched her he could feel her power course through him. It was like a drug and he definitely wanted more. Antyn watched in absolute fascination, this could definitely work in their favour, as long as Leviathan could control his possessive tendencies for the girl.

When she finally finished singing she collapsed into his arms as he dipped her. When he pulled her up, he drew her in and kissed her, to thunderous applause. He would show everyone just who this girl belonged to.

To his surprise, Tyg put a hand round his neck and kissed him back, opening her mouth to him. He stood up, his hands going to her neck and the small of her back as Tyg was on tip toes, her body pressed firmly against his. Their kiss lasted a long time until someone coughed, reminding them they weren't alone. Tyg looked like she was coming out of a dream. She looked at Leviathan and blushed. He looked down at her and his look was a mix of emotions. Their eyes were both glowing.

"Time to leave." He announced, taking her hand as he indicated to Antyn who was standing gobsmacked at the table.

45

In the carriage Tyg was silent, she couldn't even look at either brother, and just wanted to disappear into the seat. Leviathan was still at boiling level and Antyn was doing what he could to keep Leviathan somewhat calm. All Tyg could focus on was why the hell had she kissed him? It upset her that it was possible, with Leviathan being a sorcerer, that he was using his power on her. Would he do that, of course he would. He was egotistical, narcissistic, savage and a sorcerer. Tyg couldn't even think straight anymore. She wrapped her cloak around herself, pulling her legs up underneath her as she leaned her head on the side of the carriage, trying to hide in a ball in the corner as Leviathan and Antyn were still conversing.

"No, Antyn, I told you I've had enough. I am not pandering to these pompous ass fools any longer."

"Lev, you have to..."

"No, Antyn, that's just it...I don't have to."

Antyn raked a hand through his hair frustrated. "So, that's it then."

"Yes"

"No more..."

"No."

"So, just cancel all our other appearances?"

Leviathan grit his teeth annoyed. "Yes, Antyn. That's right, because if I hear one more fucking person here call Tygarya 'our' or 'their national treasure' I am going to kill someone. So, you go if you want and kiss their combined arses to your heart's content, but I have had enough. I just want to lay waste to this capitalist fucking country and be done with it."

"Lev!" Antyn said with caution, looking at Tyg.

Leviathan turned to look at Tyg next to him, noticing how she had curled up.

"Don't mind me..." Tyg muttered not even looking at them.

"What's wrong, Tygarya?" Leviathan asked her, turning in his seat to face her, placing a hand on her knees. Tyg flinched violently.

"Don't touch me!" She spat as she swiped Leviathan's hand off her knee.

Leviathan grit his teeth as his eyes blazed. "What the fuck is your problem now?"

"You!"

"Me?" He looked a bit startled.

"Did you make me kiss you like that?"

Leviathan's eyes became dark and hooded and Antyn tried to speak but Leviathan held a hand up to silence him. Antyn leaned back on his seat with a resigned sigh.

"No." Leviathan said simply.

"Easy to say. But you're a sorcerer by your own admission, so does that mean you can influence other people?"

"You're regretting kissing me, is that it?" Leviathan asked slightly amused.

Tyg looked at him, searching his face for an answer, then looked out the window into the darkness.

"I don't know what to think anymore." Tyg suddenly saw lights on at a large manor house. "Wait, why are we here? Why aren't you taking me home?" Tyg was suddenly on the verge of panic.

"Calm down, Tyg." Antyn says. "It's just that it's late, easier to stay here and leave in the morning."

Leviathan went to say something but Antyn shook his head almost imperceptibly. Leviathan's jaw clenched as he restrained himself from talking.

"Don't worry, Tyg. There's plenty of rooms, as you know and no one will disturb you."

Tyg looked at Leviathan, who was still looking at her with dark hooded eyes.

"Really?" She scoffed.

Leviathan leaned back away from her. "Really." He muttered then got up and left the carriage before it had even come to a full stop and strode off inside.

"Tyg, I understand your confusion with everything that's going on, we feel much the same way. We really didn't expect to find you here."

"What is it, Antyn?" Antyn looked at her directly in the face. "What is this intense force that keeps pushing me towards him?" Tyg asked. Antyn's eyes went dark for a moment.

"Destiny." He shrugged his shoulders.

The carriage door opened. A soldier stood there, waiting, holding the door.

Antyn waited for Tyg to get up and step out of the carriage then followed her, as they walked up the steps Tyg continued.

"You don't really believe in that nonsense do you?"

"How would you explain it then?"

Tyg didn't have an answer and fell silent.

Inside Antyn instructed the maid to find Tyg a room for the night as he explained to Tyg that he would send someone to collect some of her belongings first thing in the morning so they were there for her when she woke up. The maid curtsied then she stepped up the stairs to the second floor with Tyg following.

"Tyg." Antyn called out making Tyg pause and look back. "I assure you, Lev did nothing to you tonight. Kissing him is wholly on you." Antyn turned away and walked off down the hall, leaving Tyg staring after him.

Antyn found Leviathan in the drawing room sitting in a large leather chair, having a whisky.

"Calmed down now?" Antyn said as he sat in a chair opposite with an amused expression.

Leviathan fixed Antyn with a glare. "Why does everyone suddenly think humour is okay to throw at me?"

Antyn coughed and shifted in his chair uncomfortably. "Sorry, Lev."

"So, is she going to try and blame me of using my power to coerce her into everything now?"

"Probably."

"Can't I just lock her in that room until it's time to go back?"

Antyn laughed. "You know she can obviously pick locks and scale walls, so I don't think that would be very effective."

"Shame this place doesn't have a dungeon."

"Lev, seriously."

"Every step closer seems to throw us ten steps back again, it's frustrating. I can't tell her what she is, yet she is so close to unlocking her power, but I can't risk that happening here. I need to get her home, but I need that fucking iron ore."

"I don't know if it's a good idea telling her what she is at all?" Leviathan looked at Antyn questioningly. "If she knows, she's going to want to be taught. That could be dangerous for us."

"Good point..." Leviathan said taking a sip of his whisky. "...but, if she unlocks it without knowing what it is, it could be extremely dangerous for her."

"Let's just decide to cross that bridge when we get to it." Antyn said casually. "So what happened tonight?"

"I just realised something that's all."

"Realised what?"

"She is mine." Antyn stared at Leviathan as Leviathan fixed his gaze on his brother. "No one will call her theirs ever again, and no one will touch her, understand little brother...no one."

Antyn swallowed hard and looked away. "Of course, Lev."

"Of course, who?" Leviathan's eyes were intense and glowing, Antyn looked back at him startled then scowled.

"Yes, my Liege." Antyn scratched his jaw as Leviathan seemed satisfied and leaned back in his chair. There was a moment of silence before Antyn spoke again.

"So, you want to leave for Landau tomorrow?"

"Yes, the sooner our business here is done, the better. I hate this fucking place." Leviathan said, his knuckles going white round the glass. "This is why Kingdoms work and these 'governments' do not. They're all pompous jackasses who spend all their time vying for position and more riches, poisoning and killing each other, spying on each other...it's pathetic." Leviathan took another sip of his whisky. "I could come in here with fewer than a thousand trained and battle hardened troops and take over this place easy."

"Maybe later, Lev. Let's just get the iron ore in our possession for now."

"And Tygarya."

"Yes."

46

The next morning Tyg woke to find herself in a grand bedroom. Tyg had never stayed in such a bedroom, she had only seen bedrooms like this when doing her job and sneaking into them, she had enjoyed the soft downy bed with its luxurious covers, she could get used to this. She noticed her clothes had been brought to her room from her house just like Antyn had said. Grateful she didn't have to dress in the white dress again, she quickly put on her soft leather pants, singlet and white linen shirt. She raked her fingers through her hair roughly, getting the tangles out, then decided to pull it all up in a high ponytail. She asked the maid to find a hair tie she could use and the maid took her own ribbon out of her hair from under her white lace cap and gave it to Tyg.

"I can't take this." Tyg said as she looked at the fine satin ribbon, it was a delicate pink colour and would have been expensive for someone on a maid's earnings.

"Please, it would be an honour if you wore it." The maid was so nervous Tyg felt sorry for her. She hadn't been nervous like this before the brothers got here.

"Okay, but I'm borrowing it, I'll get it back to you I promise." Tyg said as she tied her hair up with it.

"I'm sure you will, my Lady."

"No need for the 'my Lady', I'm not, just call me Tyg. I've told you before."

"Oh no, I can't do that, I was explicitly told."

Tyg frowned annoyed. "By whom?"

"Lord Leviathan, my Lady."

"Really..." Tyg said, rolling her eyes. She got up and went over to the doors that opened up to the balcony, she could hear the commotion going on and knew Leviathan was just out there. As she stepped out Tyg looked down at the lawn. She could see Leviathan was doing some sort of soldier inspection. They were all lined up standing to attention and Leviathan was walking up the line looking and speaking to every one of them. Tyg counted twenty five, plus an officer.

As Tyg leaned on the railing watching, Leviathan suddenly stopped and pivoted round to look up at her. She was surprised, could he sense her? Could this connection thing he spoke about actually be real?

He raised an arm and indicated for her to come down. Tyg looked at the ground below the balcony, then stepped over the railing and doing a forward turn she did a flip in the air and landed on the ground. All the soldiers gasped as she straightened, dusted her pants off and walked nonchalantly over. Leviathan was standing with his arms folded.

"I meant to come down the stairs, Tygarya." He said to her unamused. "You have now ruined the focus of my men and given the maid a heart attack."

Tyg suddenly looked up at the balcony to see the maid looking at her pale and shaking.

"Sorry!" Tyg called out and turned back to Leviathan, who was still standing with his arms folded looking anything but impressed. "What?"

"Not very lady like, Tygarya."

"Well, actually that's what I need to talk to you about."

"Is that right?" Leviathan said as he put his hand in the air, made a strange gesture and all the soldiers suddenly came to attention, turned as one and marched off.

"Neat trick." Tyg said.

"So, what do you want to say?"

"Can you stop going around telling people I'm a lady, I'm not and I could go to jail for impersonating an aristocrat, you know."

"How do you know you're not?"

Tyg just gave Leviathan a long look, then noticed more commotion going on.

"Are you leaving?" She asked as they started walking down the side of the manor.

"Heading to Landau."

"Today? Is this because of what you said last night?"

"Pretty much. " Leviathan said as he stopped and faced Tyg. "I want you to come with me."

Tyg baulked at the idea. "No way, I can't leave."

Leviathan scowled. "Because of your Boss?"

"It's not quite that simple. What's so important about Landau, anyway?"

"You haven't been told? It's no secret, really."

"Told what? I gather information, they don't tell me anything." Tyg looked away as she realised she had let something slip. Leviathan studied her a moment.

"Lord Karon has a rather large mine on his land."

"A mine? Like, for what, gold?"

"Iron ore." Leviathan watched her with his vulture gaze.

"Don't you have iron mines?"

"Yes, but I need more. Better quality."

Tyg's eyes went wide. "For weapons?"

"Yes."

"For war?"

"Yes."

"Here?"

"No, not here...not yet anyway." Leviathan said with finality. "Tygarya, I really want you with me."

Tyg fidgeted under his gaze. "Geeze, is this what it's always going to be like with you?"

"What do you mean?"

"This intensity, do you ever relax?"

"When people do what they are told to do, yes." Leviathan said amused.

"Great, so I guess I have to look forward to a life time of this then?"

"Just obey, Tygarya."

Tyg looked into his eyes. "You see..." She pointed at his chest. "...right there...that's the problem."

"Why? You seem to obey the orders of your Boss, don't you...what's the difference? Besides, you come from Tylandria. I'm the Emperor of Tylandria. So, technically you are one of my subjects. I'm the only man alive you SHOULD be obeying."

Tyg stared at him her eyes blazing, pressed her mouth shut, folded her arms, turned and walked off.

Leviathan rubbed his fingers across his forehead a moment, then turned and followed Tyg as she walked into the Manor through the open doors and into the kitchen.

Antyn stopped Leviathan before he could reach the kitchen, he scowled, but turned to discuss the travel arrangements.

A few minutes later, Tyg emerged out of the front of the Manor, munching on some fresh bread and cheese.

Leviathan and Antyn turned towards her.

"Did Leviathan tell you?"

"Tell me what?" Antyn looked confused as Leviathan scowled and folded his arms again.

Tyg looked at Leviathan. "Stop that." She indicated his folded arms, then turned to Antyn. "I'm not coming with you, I can't...I have things to do here."

"Really? He hadn't even told me you were coming?" Antyn flicked a look at Leviathan.

"Oh, good then...progress." Tyg said as Leviathan unfolded his arms and went to say something. "No...my turn...I have a compromise for you." Leviathan's jaw clenched as he bit back his words but his eyes were blazing. Tyg suddenly wondered how far she should go with this, the look on Antyn's face told her not to continue, but too late to back out now. "Since I won't be going to Landau...but you seem to want to keep me where you can keep an eye on me....we'll discuss that at a later time but I know that's why you brought me here instead of taking me home last night...how about I just stay right here, in Lord Karon's...no...your Manor, with your soldiers here keeping an eye on me for you?"

Antyn raked a hand through his hair and shook his head, his eyes troubled as he looked from Tyg to Leviathan and back.

"I want nothing to do with this, I'm busy." He said, throwing his hands up and walking off.

Tyg looked at Leviathan with an eyebrow raised as a slow smirk crossed his face.

"You won't promise to stay here the whole time though, will you?"

"No, sorry, I can't do that...I have work to do."

"Don't you get it, Tygarya, you don't have to work. You don't have to do what your Boss wants, anymore. You don't need anything from these people!"

"All I need is you...is that it?" Tyg said sarcastically.

Leviathan blinked at her, taken aback. "Not quite." He muttered and rubbed his fingers on his forehead. "Fine, Tygarya, I agree. You stay here until I get back. My soldiers will accompany you into the city too though."

"No."

"Yes. Or, I have you thrown in jail while I'm gone. For impersonating an aristocrat, was it?"

"You fucking wouldn't?" Her eyes flashed

Leviathan smiled viciously. "Try me." His eyes glowed.

"Argh, by the Gods, you're so frustrating. Okay, I agree." Tyg said exasperated.

Leviathan's smile changed to a softer and adoring smile.

"Pleasure doing business with you." He said as he mimicked doffing his cap and walked off to find his brother.

Tyg stood watching him go, her hands on her hips. She turned away with a satisfied grin. 'Too easy.' She thought to herself and wandered back inside to explore more of the manor, realising now that Lord Karon had gone. Gone where? That was still not known.

Leviathan found Tyg, half an hour later, in the library. Tyg had wandered in there and become fascinated by the books.

She was lying on a couch, reading. A bowl of grapes on the side table half eaten. As Leviathan entered she lowered the book and sat up.

"We're ready to leave."

"Oh, okay." Tyg said in a nonchalant tone that made Leviathan frown.

"Made yourself at home quick enough." He snorted. "For someone who said their not influenced by finery and riches."

"Where is Lord Karon?" Tyg asked straight back as she looked at Leviathan unblinking, she smiled smugly as she saw that comment throw him off balance.

He looked down on her then with that vulture gaze. "He's already in Landau."

"Is he...really?"

"Yes." Leviathan seemed confused. "Why, where do you think he is?" He asked folding his arms.

"So, he's not lying in a ditch somewhere?" Tyg asked with an arched eyebrow.

"No. What would be the purpose of that?"

"No idea, just checking." Tyg said flippantly.

"Why?" Leviathan's voice becoming commanding.

Tyg regarded him with a cool look, looking up the way she was, she slowly blinked and then looked back up through her long lashes and shrugged.

Leviathan stiffened as she gave him that look, then his eyes darkened dangerously. Tyg stood up and stepped over to him.

"You're a dangerous individual, so I just needed to make sure."

"I'm dangerous...says the assassin." Leviathan said smugly. He grinned when he saw Tyg falter and freeze, her eyes coming up to his looking shocked, then Tyg frowned.

"Yes, you're very dangerous." She scowled.

"What's the matter, Tygarya, not used to being out witted?"

Tyg gave Leviathan a look then that took his breath away, as she stepped around him, holding his gaze. Her eyes hooded and dark.

"No, I'm not, but that's not it exactly."

Leviathan grabbed her by the upper arm as she past him and drew her to him. As her shoulder touched his chest he saw her eyes change to that intense ice blue fire.

"No, it's not...you like the challenge." Leviathan breathed as he smouldered down at her.

"No." Tyg said as she turned and placed her hands on his chest, not breaking the eye contact. Leviathan didn't want to move, didn't want to break whatever this was happening.

"I find myself actually liking being out witted by you." She said disarmingly sultry. There was no mistaking it now.

Leviathan wrapped his arms around her then, lowering his head, as she lifted hers to meet him. They kissed then, slowly and passionately. Tyg's hands slid up his chest and around his neck as he lifted her off her feet by his embrace pressing her body against him.

"Lev, it's time to go!" Antyn suddenly called out from beyond the doors just as he opened them and wandered in. He froze.

Spell broken, Tyg broke off the kiss and stepped back out of Leviathan's embrace, looking at Antyn surprised. Leviathan turned his head to Antyn with a look that could easily have killed him if Leviathan chose to and at that moment he had been close to it.

"Never heard of knocking?" Leviathan growled.

"I am so sorry, brother...Tyg. Forgive me...I'll leave."

"No need...we're done here." Tyg said as she grabbed a grape from the bowl by the couch and sat down again grabbing her book.

Antyn stood stunned as Leviathan turned to look at her, his eyes going dangerously dark. She had turned sideways on the couch, her back leaning up against the arm, her knees pulled up, with the book resting on them. His eyes suddenly blazed to light. Antyn was suddenly sent from the room by a blast of energy and the doors slammed shut. Tyg looked up shocked and suddenly felt fear as she looked at Leviathan's face as he stepped over, grabbed the book and threw it down the other end of the couch. He grabbed her chin as he sat by her hip and leaned over her like a predator and kissed her again. Tyg's hands went to the sides of his face, as he forcibly kissed her, she couldn't resist kissing him back. Her eyes went wide with shock as he trickled power into the kiss, then she closed her eyes and kissed him eagerly.

Leviathan broke the kiss off then, a smug look on his face, his eyes hooded but shining. He looked at her, as she was left breathless.

"Nothing is ever over until *I* say it is." Leviathan growled huskily. He grinned as he bopped her with a finger on the nose, then stood up. Tyg was shocked, that was what Stills used to always do...

"What was that?" Tyg asked breathless, touching her lips.

"A taste of a sorcerer." Leviathan said smugly. Tyg looked at him in awe. "You'll miss me now, Tyg." He said to her softly.

"You called me Tyg." She whispered.

Leviathan looked at her a moment as he leaned down and stroked her cheek with the back of his hand, turned and stalked from the room. The doors opening by themselves.

Speechless, Tyg watched him go. She sat there contemplating things for a long while, then determined she got up and made her way out to the main entrance.

The small convoy had already set off and was halfway up the pathway. Tyg folded her arms and leaned on a large column, watching dismayed. Suddenly the large black figure of Leviathan on his equally large black stallion, turned from the front of the convoy and galloped across the grass back towards her.

Tyg stood up, unfolding her arms, surprised. He did sense her. Tyg watched with admiration at the fine figure he posed on the horse. He was a very competent rider. As he reined in his horse at the bottom of the steps he looked at Tyg with blazing eyes.

"Changed your mind about coming?"

Tyg smiled and shook her head. "I was just hoping to give you a final wave goodbye." She said as she watched him jump off his horse and stalk up the stairs his eyes fixed on her like a predator. "I don't want to leave things like that...in the library." Tyg faltered and went quiet.

Leviathan had reached her. He pushed her gently against the column and kissed her again using that same trickle of power. He then broke off the kiss, breathless himself, needing to contain his desire for her. He rested his forehead on hers as she looked at him, panting.

"It's going to be a long few days, I fear this will be lost on my return." He kissed her lips again, then breathed.

"Well, you'll just have to do your best to remind me when you get back."

Leviathan smiled, kissed her again chastely, and gave her a very smouldering look, then turned and vaulted onto his horse, and galloped off to catch up to the convoy.

Tyg watched them go until they were out of sight, then turned and walked inside, heading to the study to find some paper...she had messages to write.

47

It was no more than an hour after the convoy was gone and Tyg was sitting back in the library with another book, there was a polite knock on the door and the soldier who had been left in charge came in, striding up to where Tyg was lying on the couch.

"Excuse me, my Lady?"

Tyg scowled but let it slide, she had given up on the 'my lady's'

"Hello, who are you then?" She looked up at a stern but youthful face with dark brown hair and hazel eyes.

"Lieutenant Corvyn, my Lady."

"Okay, so you're in charge I take it?"

"Yes, my Lady."

"Geeze, too many my Lady's for me. You're very formal aren't you?"

Corvyn smiled. "I have news concerning the staff, my Lady."

Tyg frowned at him. "Is there nothing else you can call me?"

"Not that would be proper."

"Bugger proper." Tyg scowled. "So, what's the news?"

Corvyn looked taken aback, but continued.

"The staff have packed their belongings and are wishing to leave."

"What? Why?" Tyg got up. "Where are they?"

"Outside, my Lady, we have detained them awaiting your instruction."

"My instruction...?" Tyg shook her head. "Fuck's sake, I wasn't aware I had any authority here...." She muttered as she walked past Corvyn, who blanched at her language and followed her out.

She found the butler and his wife, the groundsman and the stableman all standing nervously on the pathway circled by five soldiers.

"Well, I don't think holding them like hostages is really necessary, is it, Corvyn?"

Corvyn looked surprised at Tyg, then waved his hand and sent the soldiers away, to the vast relief of the staff.

"What's going on? You want to leave?" Tyg asked them.

"Yes...miss, we are taking this opportunity to get out of here." The butler said. Tyg could see they were still terrified.

"Okay, well no one can actually stop you, but where will you go? What will you do for a job? For money?"

"We're going to Annul, try and find work there."

"And, if you can't?"

The staff all looked at each other. "We don't know, but we can't stay here." The Stableman said.

"I still don't understand why?" Tyg said shaking her head.

"Because they...they're not..." He stammered as he looked at Corvyn nervously. None of the others would even look at Tyg. Tyg turned to Corvyn.

"Go away." She said to him. He planted his feet and stuck his thumbs into his belt.

"I can't do that, my Lady."

Tyg stepped up to him unafraid. She knew they would have had explicit orders to not touch her, not that she would have been afraid anyway. She spoke very quietly at him, her eyes blazing ice blue, only inches from his face.

"I suggest, Corvyn that you back up away from me and these people so I can converse with them out of your hearing. I'm asking nicely, Corvyn, next time I won't be."

Corvyn baulked at Tyg's eyes blazing and at her snarling mouth, showing her long canines like some sort of wild animal. He suddenly realised the power in her and the Adramelech brothers' interest in her suddenly made sense to him. He backed up and bowed. Tyg looked at him strangely for a moment.

"At once, my Lady. I apologise." He said as he stepped away several yards and stood watching.

Tyg turned back to the staff, who were all staring at her in awe. "Talk to me, please."

It was the Stableman that continued. "They're not human."

"Not human? Who aren't human?" Tyg asked confused.

"Those brothers, especially the giant one. They use magic."

"Oh, I get it now...you've seen them using their power."

"You know!" The Butler suddenly injected. "How can you stay here young lady?"

"I'm sure it's nothing to be scared of." Tyg thought she sounded like she was trying to convince herself. "As long as you don't cross them."

"Well, we don't want any part of it, please let us go."

Tyg looked at them hard for a moment. "You know you can't go telling anyone about what you've witnessed here, right?"

"Yes, miss. We all agree...if we can go."

"Okay, but wait here a minute." Tyg turned and walked over to Corvyn, who snapped to attention as she approached.

"Don't do that." She berated him. "I'm not an officer or anything. Look, did Leviathan leave any money here?"

"Yes, my Lady. It's in the study, in a lockbox."

"Do you have a key?"

"Yes, my Lady."

"Then can you go and get enough money out to pay these people some sort of severance pay."

"But..."

Tyg's eyes blazed, cutting him short. "I'll take responsibility for it, Corvyn, and make it generous."

"Yes, my Lady." Corvyn bowed, turned on his heel and went inside, making a strange gesture to one of the soldiers nearby, who came over and took up Corvyn's position. Tyg rolled her eyes.

"For fuck's sake, Corvyn." She muttered, then turned back and wandered back over to the staff. "Where is the maid girl?" Tyg asked then, noting she wasn't among them.

"She chose to stay, stupid girl." The cook muttered.

Tyg smiled, glad the young girl wasn't being unreasonable like these idiots in front of her, leaving perfectly good jobs because of scary bedtime stories about witches.

"What are we waiting for?" The butler asked, nervously.

"Severance pay." Tyg said with a smile. "You do want to be paid what you're owed, don't you?"

They all stared at her. "Thank you, miss. We are very grateful."

"Well, the Adramelechs aren't unreasonable from what I've seen, when it comes to this sort of thing. You could have just talked to them...at least Antyn anyway." Tyg said it in earnest but even she felt she was perhaps taking liberties a bit far when it came to Leviathan, he was after all by her own evaluation a narcissistic, possessive tyrant.

"Perhaps..." The butler muttered unconvinced as Corvyn came back, carrying a large purse full of coins. Tyg indicated for him to hand it to the butler.

"Thank you so much, miss." The butler said smiling with surprise at the weight of the purse, as the others crowded around him.

"Well hopefully it will keep you all fed at least until you can find work, good luck."

"The Gods' bless you, young lady." Tyg baulked at that and walked back inside without turning back, with Corvyn hard on her heels.

"Was that wise, my Lady."

"Why? You can't keep them here against their will."

"But, they know…"

"And they said they wouldn't say anything…have a bit of faith, they're simple folk."

Corvyn blinked, this young woman was complex. "What are we going to do about finding more staff?" Corvyn asked then.

Tyg turned and regarded him. "It's all sorted, Corvyn, just get some horses ready, I need to go into the city and collect someone."

"Who, exactly?"

"Don't worry yourself about it, Corvyn, just organise the horses."

"Yes, my Lady." Corvyn replied grumpily, turned on his heel and walked off.

Tyg went to the window and watched the staff walking off up the pathway. Things couldn't have worked out better for Tyg, now she planned to employ her friends as the new staff of Karon Manor.

48

As Tyg cantered through the streets, heading for Barion's house, she noticed the stares of the people and drew up her hood. Corvyn had insisted on two more soldiers accompanying them, so now they caused a scene, as four riders in black and armed to the teeth are want to do. Tyg didn't like this unwanted attention, especially when she hadn't even been able to get word to Palin yet as to where she was staying and why. She knew word would reach him now, but the information wasn't going to please him very much. She had got herself into a bit of a bind, that was going to have to be sorted sooner rather than later, before the gossip train reached full momentum.

When they pulled up in front of Barion's house, Tyg jumped down and went to go inside. She noticed Corvyn doing those strange gestures and the soldiers take up positions. One held the horses, one went to stand at the entrance and Corvyn obviously intended to follow her inside.

"Is this really necessary?" Tyg asked. "Anyone would think my life was in danger."

"Our lives are the ones in danger, my Lady, if we don't. Please, just let us do our jobs."

Tyg was surprised at that. She appraised Corvyn, then smiled and went inside. Both Mae and Tess were there.

"Tyg! Oh, thank the gods, you're alright."

"The gods had nothing to do with it." Tyg muttered, causing Corvyn to glance to her. Mae stared in horror at the uniformed soldier standing behind Tyg.

"Who is this?"

Tyg grimaced. "Lieutenant Corvyn. Tess can you show him into the front room, please." Tyg turned to Corvyn. "Wait in the front room, I'm going upstairs for some of my things, got it."

"My Lady, I don't..."

"You are NOT following me upstairs." Corvyn blinked as Tyg's eyes blazed again. He gave a curt nod and followed Tess. Mae was staring at Tyg.

"What on earth have you gotten yourself into now?" She asked, wondering if Tyg was now courting this handsome young officer.

Tyg snorted. "You wouldn't believe me if I told you." Tyg walked up the stairs. "Come on, I'll try and explain some of it at least."

"So, you're taking Tess with you?" Mae asked after Tyg had explained she was going to be staying at the Karon Manor for a while.

"Yes, sorry to leave you in the lurch, but I did employ her..."

"Its fine, Tyg. I just worry what Barion and Palin are going to make of all of this."

"Well, I don't much care what Barion has to say...sorry...but I don't. As for Palin, as soon as I can lull these damn overzealous soldiers into thinking I'm an easy watch, I can get the hell out of the Manor undetected and get over to see him.

"Please be careful, you're playing with fire."

Tyg rubbed her temples as her head ached. "I know but it's more than one fire and that's the problem."

"How dangerous are these men...these brothers?"

"Potentially? Extremely dangerous, that's why I have to placate the situation." Tyg laughed. "Call me a peace keeper if you like, because that's all I'm trying to do at present is keep the peace, and as you know it's not my forte."

"Okay, just take care, dear one." Mae said then smiling sadly. "I'll go get Tess and organise her things."

"Okay, I need to get word to Dane also, I want him and Pete to come to the Manor too." Tyg held out the message she had written for him.

Mae looked at Tyg for a moment then took the note. "Okay, leave that with me. Barion will know how to reach him."

"Of course, thanks Mae."

Tyg entered the front room, where Corvyn was waiting and found Tess there serving him a glass of water.

"Tess, just the person. I have need of your services."

"Sure, Tyg, how can I help?"

"You're getting a promotion. Gather up your stuff, you're coming with me back to the Karon Manor."

"What?" Tess was stunned. Tyg noticed Corvyn watching intently.

"Mae is helping collect your belongings up...I'll explain on the way."

Just then one of the soldiers came storming in. "Trouble Lieutenant." He growled in their language

Corvyn stood up and went to the window. "What is it?"

"There are several City Watch standing outside, their Captain is asking to speak to Lady Tygarya, Sir."

"That will be Tom." Tyg said sweetly when Corvyn translated it, to the surprise of Corvyn. "Stay calm, Corvyn and show him in."

"Yes, my Lady...you heard her...show him in...only him!"

"Sir!" The soldier clipped his heels and turned and left the room.

Tyg turned to Tess. "Go, Mae's waiting for you."

Tess fled as Tom came striding in. He looked very formal in his bright red uniform. He didn't look very happy to see Corvyn standing in the room.

"Tyg, we need to talk...privately."

Tyg looked at Thomas a moment, then turned to Corvyn, who had taken up that defiant stance again. "Corvyn?"

"No way, my Lady, he's armed."

"My Lady?" Thomas looked at Tyg, who wiped a hand over her eyes wearily.

"Ah...ignore it, Tom, it's their strange sensibilities and formality." Now she had both men looking at her with grumpy expressions. "Under different circumstances you guys would probably like each other." Tyg smiled coyly.

Thomas appraised Corvyn. "I doubt that." He said but he removed his sword belt and handed it to Corvyn, who smiled, bowed his head to Tyg then left the room.

"Gods Tyg! Are you alright? When I got news of soldiers coming into the city and stopping here I had to come."

Tyg smiled. "I'm fine, Tom, really. They're an escort is all?" Tyg's lip curled up in a sneer.

"An escort? So, you are with the Adramelechs now? I had heard you were being held at the Manor."

"I don't know what the rumours are saying, but trust me, Tom. There are bigger things at stake than my virtue."

"Like what?"

Tyg sighed. "You better sit down."

Tyg filled Tom in on the Adramelech's business in Arial and Landau and the fact that they gave her proof of coming from Tylandria, and wanting her to return with them to her homeland.

"Typical, Lord Karon just thinks of himself getting richer by any means possible, stuff everyone else." Tom scoffs. "So what are you planning to do?"

"I really don't know." Tyg said rubbing her chin as an idea came to her. "But you can do me a huge favour."

Once Tyg returned to the Manor she introduced Tess to the maid, whose name was Neeki. The two girls went off to the kitchen together to start preparing the evening meal for the soldiers still at the manor. Tyg made her way into the library, her favourite room in the house, with Corvyn behind her.

"Nice work." Corvyn said to Tyg, standing with his arms folded.

Tyg looked at him with an eyebrow raised. "You're casual all of a sudden?"

Corvyn shrugged. "I need to adapt to my surroundings."

Tyg smiled. "Glad to hear it." She went over to the drinks cabinet and poured herself a whisky from the decanter. She looked at him and raised the decanter at him.

"No, thank you. I'm working."

"But, when do you ever not work?"

Corvyn chuckled, lifting a thumb and scratching his jaw. "When I sleep."

"So, you're telling me you never get down time?"

"Once we are back home, I will."

Tyg sat down on the couch. "For how long?"

"Probably a week, it's the standard time off."

"Do you have family?"

Corvyn chuckled and scratched his chin again. "I'm a bit young to settle down yet."

"Really? How old are you?"

Corvyn stared at her a moment, then sighed. "I'm twenty four."

"That's not too young to settle down?" Tyg said confused.

"It is in my line of work."

"Why is that?" Tyg asked. Corvyn looked uncomfortable and a bit annoyed with the questions. "Look, I'm just trying to understand you a little better." Tyg laughed. "You don't have to answer."

"It's just that it's not really spoken about, just something that happens. As soldiers we don't really think about settling down and starting families until we've lived through at least three battles, once we know we can survive, and aren't going to leave people behind us, we can think about the future...maybe."

Tyg looked at him surprised. "Wow, okay...makes sense I suppose. How many battles have you been in?"

"Two."

"Hmm...okay. I'm finished with the questions for now." Tyg smiled at him.

"Very well, I shall leave you and go attend to my duties then." Corvyn bowed his head to her and left the room, closing the doors behind him.

Tyg smiled slightly to herself, she liked Corvyn, and not because he was somewhat good looking with his dark hair and hazel eyes a bit like Stills, but he was smart. She grimaced then, she wondered how much trouble Corvyn would get into once her plan took effect.

Late afternoon Corvyn once again came looking for her. She was stretched out still in the library, devouring the books. As he walked in and saw her still reading he smiled. "Like to read?" He asked as Tyg put the book down and looked up at him.

"Yes, actually. I never got the chance growing up, but I find books fascinating. What do you need, Corvyn?"

"There are two men here saying you sent for them?"

"Yes!" Tyg got up and sprinted for the door. Shocked Corvyn ran to catch up. By the time he reached the front entrance he found Tyg hugging the young man with brown hair, then hugged the man with black hair. She turned to Corvyn.

"Here is our new Stableman, Dane." Tyg introduced Dane to Corvyn. "And, our new Groundsman, Pete." Tyg introduced Pete to Corvyn. He inclined his head to the two of them.

"Is Tess here too?" Dane asked.

"Why, yes she is." Tyg said with a smirk. "You like her?"

Dane blushed as Corvyn smiled with relief.

Tyg clapped Dane on the back and laughed. "I'll see what I can do, my friend. Come on, I'll show you to your rooms."

Dane looked at Corvyn following them down the hall. "What's with that?"

"Oh, I know...annoying but hopefully Tom, my friend in the City Watch, is coming tomorrow to get me out of here so I can go see Palin." Tyg whispered.

"Good, Barion wasn't at all happy when he came and found us."

49

The next day Tyg entered the kitchen to find Dane and Pete being fed breakfast by Tess and Neeki. Tyg smiled to herself.

"Tyg! Good Morning." Tess said as Dane and Pete indicated the same thing, their mouths full. Neeki looked shy, but Tyg was hopeful with the others here she would come out of herself.

"Good morning, everyone's settled in I see?"

Tyg went over to Neeki and held her ribbon out to her. "Sorry it took me so long to get it back to you, I actually forgot...you should have reminded me."

"Oh, thank you, milady." Neeki said bashful.

"Milady?" Dane spat his bread out.

Tyg rolled her eyes and smiled. It was nice to have these rogues around her again, it made the events of eight months ago almost bearable. "Shut up, Dane." Tyg said in good humour. She looked around and didn't see any soldiers. "Now, don't react badly when the City Watch turn up, okay." She said it to all of them.

"The City Watch?" Pete asked as they all looked at each other.

"Yeah, Tyg's found a way to get to Palin, using them."

"Oh okay.'

"Just watch what you say." Tyg warned as she glanced at Neeki.

"Okay, sorry, Tyg." Dane answered looking down.

Tyg reached across and grabbed a chunk of bread and went over to the pot and poured herself a coffee, then walked off outside.

She saw the soldiers were going through their inspection. No wonder they weren't following her around. She leaned on a column, chewing her bread, watching them. The discipline was tight, she had to give them that. She had never actually seen soldiers before, and now here were real, scarred, battle hardened ones.

She looked at Corvyn as he walked up to each soldier, just like Leviathan had. Corvyn was young for a lieutenant, she thought, but she could see he had a commanding presence that even the soldiers clearly older than him seemed to respect.

He finished up and sent them off to their posts, he turned and saw Tyg watching. He came over.

"Professional curiosity?" He asked with a grin.

Tyg couldn't resist the opportunity to tease him a little. "No, appreciation of the male form."

Corvyn faltered and stared at her for a second, then he grimaced as he saw her wry smile. "Are you teasing me, my Lady?"

Tyg chuckled. "Yes, Corvyn, of course..." She turned away as if to leave. "...maybe."

"My Lady!" Corvyn said surprised.

Tyg turned back. "Relax, Corvyn. Gods, you're so uptight."

"The things you say...they're not proper." Corvyn stammered.

Tyg returned to leaning on the column. "Proper for whom?" She asked as she took a sip of coffee.

"For a young lady, such as yourself."

Tyg spat her coffee out. Corvyn stepped back surprised. "Do I look like a young lady to you?" Tyg indicated her clothing. "Besides, I could beat any of your soldiers in any weapon, hands down."

Corvyn baulked at that and straightened with pride. "No." He said stiffly.

Tyg grinned as she took another sip of coffee. "Care for a wager on that?"

Corvyn's jaw clenched and he settled a calm stare on her. 'Battle hardened for sure, he's not going to allow himself to be goaded into anything.' She thought to herself.

"No." Corvyn said again and strode off across the lawn, heading for the stables.

Tyg laughed to herself. "Too bad!" She called out. It was too bad actually, she felt like she needed to do something...to train. Just then Dane and Pete came out.

"What ya doin'?" Dane asked.

"Nothing, I'm extremely bored...and you?"

"Got to meet the Lieutenant at the stables."

"Huh, right...he's already gone over there." Tyg said grinning.

"Shit, I better go." Dane said as he hurried off after Corvyn.

"What about you, Pete?"

"I don't know, what does a groundsman do exactly?"

Tyg shrugged. "Keep the bushes trimmed and the lawns short?"

"Great." Pete rolled his eyes.

"How about some practise with me..?"

"You serious? No way, I'm not crazy."

"No, I didn't mean combat. How about shooting arrows?"

"Yeah, okay."

"Great, I'll go get...ah...my bow." Tyg felt a lump in her throat and turned away.

In her room Tyg took the bow out of her weapons bag and put it together, stringing it. It was a beautiful piece of craftsmanship and she loved looking at it. She ran her hand over it, tracing the decorative etchings along the flat surfaces as they curved away. She grabbed six arrows and went back to find Pete, who was standing out on the lawn with a large wooden shield that he was putting up as a target.

As he walked back to her, she handed him the bow. He looked at it appreciatively. "Wow, nice."

"You first." Tyg said. "Three shots each, we'll go shot for shot."

"I'm not that good." Pete grumbled.

"That's okay, that's why people practise."

"Okay." Pete said as he took his first shot, which missed the target completely. "See, I told you."

"Positivity, Pete...don't worry about it." Tyg said as she took the bow back, grabbed an arrow and shot it. It landed dead centre of the shield. Just as Corvyn came back round the house, he froze and watched from a distance, as Pete stepped up to take his next shot. Tyg gave him a few pointers and helped him with his stance. He managed to make the shot hit the shield, just on the edge.

"See!" Tyg said encouragingly. She took her second shot and pierced the first arrow, splintering it.

"Not fair, Tyg, bloody hell." Pete grumbled. "Just take your third shot, I forfeit."

Tyg laughed and took her third shot, again splintering the arrow already in the centre of the shield.

"Fuck!"

Tyg heard the voice behind her and turned her eyes flashing, grabbing the last arrow and raising it, to find Corvyn standing behind them.

"Professional curiosity?" Tyg said to Corvyn as she lowered the bow, grinning. He was looking at her with a worried frown.

"Where does someone like you learn to shoot like that?"

Tyg shrugged. "Someone like me?"

Just then a soldier came striding over. Tyg turned and in one fluid motion pulled the string back and shot the arrow into the centre of the shield once again. The soldier faltered while Corvyn growled.

"Quit showing off!" He berated her. Tyg grinned at him as he turned to the soldier. "What is it?"

"There are some City Watch guards arrived, they say they are here looking for Lady Tygarya."

"What the hell?" Corvyn growled. "Stay here." He said to Tyg as he strode off.

"Like hell." Tyg said, playing her part, as she handed her bow back to Pete. "Make sure this gets put back in my room, please."

"Sure, Tyg." Pete said as he winked.

When Tyg got round the front, there was a standoff. Corvyn was standing in front of Thomas and both were frowning at each other. When Thomas saw Tyg he turned and pointed. "There she is."

The City Watch went to move towards her but Corvyn's soldiers all drew their weapons and Corvyn himself stepped in front of her.

"What's going on?" Tyg asked innocently.

"You are under arrest, Tyg." Thomas said then, taking out a piece of paper and holding it out.

Corvyn snatched the paper and read it. "Fuck's sake, is this right?"

Tyg took the paper. It was an arrest warrant for assault on a Lord. Tyg had decided to play on something that actually had happened, it made the lie easier to maintain.

"Yes, actually. At Lord Ranor's banquet, Lord Kor said something to me I didn't like. So I slapped him across the face. Leviathan actually witnessed it, but he's not here."

"Shit." Corvyn said wiping a hand over his face.

"Don't worry, Lieutenant, I'm sure Captain Thomas will take good charge of me, and I'm sure I can get this sorted. Let me go with him."

Before Corvyn could answer Tyg stepped round him and walked up to Tom, holding her wrists out. He cuffed them and removed her daggers.

Tyg turned back to Corvyn as she heard him stepping over. "Leave it, Corvyn! I'll be fine, they don't mistreat women here in jail, do you Captain Thomas?"

"Certainly not!" He turned to Corvyn, "She will be questioned and probably fined then I will get her back....within a couple of hours."

Corvyn ground his teeth and folded his arms. "Better be back unharmed in less time than that."

Tyg smiled at him as she stepped up into the jail coach.

50

Once they were inside the city proper Thomas called a halt and dismounted, walking back to the jail coach and opening the door. He was surprised to find Tyg sitting there no longer handcuffed. She grinned at him as she got up, handed him the cuffs and jumped out.

"Thanks for this, Tom, I owe you big time."

"Sure do, Tyg." He said as he handed her weapons back to her. "Just make sure you're back in plenty of time, I don't want that man in my Precinct."

Tyg grinned. "I'll do my best, Tom, thanks again."

"Here, you may need this." Tom said throwing a cloak at her.

"Fantastic, Tom." Tyg laughed as she put it on then turned and took off up an alleyway as Tom got back on his horse and returned to his Precinct.

"Well, well, look what the cat finally dragged in?" Palin growled as Tyg wandered in to his hide.

"What do you mean? You're the one who disappeared for days. I told Dane to tell you where I was."

"Sending errand boys? What's next, Tyg? You going to start traveling with an entourage? Oh, wait..." Palin said sarcastically. "... An entourage of soldiers, wasn't it?"

"Very funny." Tyg said flatly as she sat down.

"No, it's not, Tyg. We've seen you being escorted around the city by Adramelech soldiers and we know you're staying at – what's now being called – the Adramelech Manor, so you better have some serious explanation."

"Sounds like you know everything already, why waste my breath?"

"So, you have moved in with them?" Palin asked surprised.

"It's not as simple as that, Leviathan made me agree to stay there."

"Made you? What are you his prisoner?"

"Might as well be." Tyg shrugged.

"Explain, Tyg." Palin wiped a weary hand over his face, he looked pale and worn.

"He's not just some Lord from some obscure county. He is Emperor of Tylandria."

"Emperor?" Palin muttered. A strange look came over Palin's face as he looked away with a dark frown.

"Yes, and as I come from Tylandria, apparently, I'm technically one of his subjects."

"Fucking hell." Palin breathed as he sat back in his chair. "He's playing that game?"

"Exactly, you see my predicament...besides, he threatened to throw me in jail while he was gone if I didn't agree to stay at the Manor and have his soldiers keep an eye on me."

"Really? Well, they're not doing such a great job of that."

Tyg grinned and shrugged again.

"So, do you intend to go back to Tylandria with them?" Palin asked his expression intense.

"It's looking that way, Palin. I don't know..." Tyg shrugged again and rubbed two fingers between her eyes.

"Well, that's where we have a problem." Palin growled. Tyg just looked at him. "Emperor or not, you belong to me."

"Palin..."

"Quiet!" Palin ordered.

Tyg sighed and fell silent, looking at the floor. She had great respect for Palin and all he had done for her, but for him to still think he owned her, irked.

"So, have you found out the reason they're even here?"

"Yeah, I thought you would already know. They are taking control of the iron ore mine on Lord Karon's lands up by Landau. That's where they are now."

"Yes, I had heard rumours, but it's nice to have them confirmed." Palin scratched his cheek. "Anything else about them we should concern ourselves with?" He looked at her intently.

Tyg looked up at Palin. 'Oh yeah, they're sorcerers.' Tyg thought to herself, but decided not to mention that. "They're not staying long, apparently. As soon as they have sorted out the mine production and started moving the ore back to Arial to be shipped they plan to leave. Leviathan doesn't like it here."

"Good to hear." Palin said glancing sideways at her. "Is your staying here going to cause problems with them?"

Tyg stared hard at Palin. "Yes. I believe it will."

"Damn it, Tyg."

"It's not my fault." Tyg said sullenly.

"What sort of trouble can we expect?" Palin asked looking hard at her. "Be honest, Tyg."

Tyg sighed again. "The worst kind...he will come at you with everything he's got."

"Why?" Palin said crossly. "No offense, Tyg, but what's so special about you. He's known you for what? Days? Are you saying he's fallen madly in love with you or something?"

Tyg grimaced as she remembered the kiss Leviathan had given her before he left and the statement he had made that she was his. She shivered. "Or something. He says I'm important to his Empire."

"What the fuck?" Palin stood up and paced the room looking pale and disturbed. "That's final. You're not going back, you're staying here!"

"Palin, I wouldn't..."

"Quiet! I've made my decision. Good luck to him, finding you in this city."

"Palin, listen. Leviathan's soldiers think I've been arrested by the City Watch. If I don't go back it could cause an international incident, because, trust me, they will storm the Precinct."

"You should have thought about that before getting others involved."

"I'm not going to let Tom take the blame for this. He'll lose his job, if he doesn't get killed. I won't have that on my conscience...I can't." Tyg's serious tone made Palin take pause.

Palin wiped a hand over his face, hearing the torment in her voice, Stills loss was still so raw with her. "Okay, Tyg, I will let you go back, but you need to come back here tomorrow."

"How exactly?"

"Sort it, Tyg. I'm sure you can get passed those guards if you really wanted to?" Palin grabbed her chin and looked down on her. "You had better want to, Tyg or I'll send a Squad to get you. I will not let that bastard take you from me."

Tyg's eyes flashed but she said nothing.

"You're special to me too, Tyg, you know that." Palin said softer.

Tyg's eyes faded back to pale blue as Palin let go of her chin. "I know." She muttered.

"So, are you with me, Tyg?" Palin held his fist out.

Tyg looked up at it, then at Palin's face. "Yes, Palin. I'm with you." Tyg said quietly as she touched his fist with hers. She stood up and wrapped her cloak around herself. She walked to the door, then paused and turned to look back at Palin, who glanced at her with a questioning look.

"It might be a good idea to send that Squad anyway, Palin."

"How so?" He growled.

"To send the right message."

"Hmm, I see where you're going with this..." Palin scratched his chin in thought. "When are the brothers due back?"

"I don't know? I expect they'll be gone at least a week. It's at least two day ride to Landau."

"Ok...stay at the Manor...I'll send word." Palin said dismissing her.

Tyg nodded and left, that at least gave her a couple of days.

Tyg walked back along the streets deep in thought. She really had no idea what the hell she was going to do. Caught between Palin and Leviathan was not a position she wanted to be in, she knew it wasn't going to end well for anyone as she had absolutely no idea how to appease the situation for all parties. Someone was inevitably going to be left bitter and vengeful. Problem was for her, one of them was a Sorcerer, and she did not look forward to seeing him vengeful. She shivered as she got a vision of the streets she was walking devastated and on fire. Letting Palin down was going to be the lesser evil for everyone, but would she be able to do it? She owed him her life. And, now she had commissioned a Squad to come after her. She grit her teeth and stared at the ground as she walked on, heading back to the City Watch Precinct, where Tom was.

As she came around the last corner she froze.

"Fuck." She growled. In front of the steps to the precinct were Adramelech soldiers on horses, which meant only one thing. Corvyn was inside causing trouble. No doubt calling for her release. "Oh well, it worked just long enough." Tyg muttered as she dropped her hood and walked up the street.

When the soldiers saw her they all looked surprised and looked at the doors leading inside with worry.

Tyg smiled at them. "I hope Corvyn hasn't killed anyone, I have friends in there."

"My Lady, you're probably just in time to prevent that." One of the soldiers said going pale. His accent was rough but at least he could speak the language.

Tyg pinched her nose, staving off the dull ache in her head. "Alright, someone go tell him I'm here."

A soldier dropped off his horse and ran inside as Tyg stood surrounded by the rest of them. A crowd was gathering which was not good.

After a few moments the doors banged open and Corvyn strode out of the Precinct with Tom, the soldier and a few of Tom's city watch trailing behind him. The look on Corvyn's face said it all. Tyg grimaced, there goes the civility. It looked like the squad was the only way she was getting out of the Manor now.

"Tygarya! Where the hell have you been?" Corvyn yelled as he strode up to her. He actually looked quite impressive in all his black battle armour and helm, but Tyg thought he had over reacted.

"I told you I would be fine and to stay at the Manor." Tyg said calmly.

"You set this up?" He glanced at Tom who was standing on the steps looking very overwhelmed by what was going on.

"Yeah, I did, Corvyn, I'm sorry." Tyg said genuinely apologetic. "Can we go?" Indicating the crowd.

"You've got a lot of explaining to do." Corvyn yelled.

Tyg calmly walked past him and up to Tom. She took one of his hands in both of hers. "Sorry, Tom. I hope this isn't going to implode on you?"

"No, Tyg, just get him and his soldiers the fuck out of the city." Tom said barely holding back his anger as well. Tyg wondered what had gone on inside. The city watch guards standing behind Tom all seemed pale as ghosts.

"Okay." Tyg said and turned. Tom grabbed her arm then stopping her in her tracks, causing Corvyn to place a hand on the hilt of his sword and release it an inch from its scabbard.

"Are you sure you are still okay?" Tom asked seriously as he flicked a glance at Corvyn warily.

"Yes, Tom, they can't hurt me." Tyg smiled and rolled her eyes as she stepped out of Tom's grasp.

Tom looked hard at Corvyn as Tyg went back to him. Corvyn was staring back, his hand relaxed from his sword as Tyg reached his side.

"Oh, for fuck's sake, Corvyn, relax damn it. You're causing a scene." Tyg muttered to him in ire.

Corvyn flicked his head and slid his gaze to her. Tyg faltered as she saw something in his eyes. Did they just flash with light? Surely not?

"Corvyn, get on your fucking horse." Tyg said as her eyes flashed too and she stepped up to him, her hand going to her own weapons.

Corvyn baulked and blinked. "Tygarya?" He said stunned.

"Yes, Corvyn?" Tyg said back through gritted teeth.

He looked at her hands on her daggers and dutifully removed his, then went and grabbed the reins of his horse. He turned to her questioning. Tyg folded her arms and smiled.

"Yes, I know." She laughed. "What are you going to do now, Corvyn? No horse for me."

Corvyn grit his teeth and straightened up. "Get up, my Lady!" He growled at her. Tyg raised an eyebrow at him and smiled wider.

"Exciting." She said as she put her foot in the stirrup and swung her other leg over, holding onto the pommel. She shuffled forward on the saddle and looked down on Corvyn, smiling sweetly, kicking her foot out of the stirrup. He ground his teeth together and put his own foot in the stirrup, vaulting up onto the horse behind Tyg, his arms coming round her as he grabbed the reins. Tyg chuckled to herself as she leaned back into him, feeling the hardness of his chest plate. The other soldiers were all avoiding Corvyn's gaze. He kicked his horse into a gallop and his soldiers followed him as he took off down the street.

"Easy, Corvyn, there are pedestrians." Tyg muttered.

He rounded a corner and then slowed to a canter.

"Just tell me why?" Corvyn muttered in her ear as he finally started to calm down slightly.

"Come on now, this is exactly the sort of thing you were warned of by Leviathan, wasn't it? I was never going to stay in the Manor and be escorted everywhere by you. I have people to see and things to do."

"Fucking hell." Corvyn muttered. "Yes, I was warned, but I thought..." He trailed off. "I won't make the same mistake trusting you again."

"No, I know you won't." Tyg said back to him solemnly, glancing over her shoulder at him.

He glanced across at her and slowed to a walk. He shook his head.

"No, I'm not going to let you out of my sight."

"I'm sorry, Corvyn, it was necessary."

"Who the hell are you?" He stared at her. Tyg returned the look calmly, searching his eyes.

"Not a question I find myself able to answer, to be honest."

Corvyn's eyes darkened slightly and he shook his head again. "You're going to be the death of me. I actually can't wait for Emperor Leviathan to return, and that's saying something."

Tyg looked straight ahead, but placed a hand on his thigh, next to hers.

"No, Corvyn, that won't happen, I won't have your death on my conscience." She heard him gasp as he took in a sharp breath.

She didn't know if it was the hand on his thigh or the words she spoke, but she smiled to herself. She patted his thigh and then removed her hand, wrapping her cloak around herself. "I promise you that, Corvyn, I can't have another on my conscience." She said as she pulled her hood up. She didn't want him to see her anguish. He stared at her a moment longer, she was so complex. His jaw ticked as he lifted up the reins and pushed the horse back into a gallop.

When they reached the yard and dismounted Dane was standing there watching. He looked surprised to see Tyg doubled on Corvyn's mount. She looked at him and winked. He smiled a knowing smile at her and flicked his head in acknowledgement. Corvyn caught the action and rounded on Tyg.

"He knew?"

"Knew what?" Tyg said coyly. "Drop it, Corvyn."

Corvyn sighed. "You do realise I have to make a report, don't you? So do I say you have staffed the Manor with people who work for your underground network?" He growled.

Tyg looked at Corvyn in surprise. "Just what did Leviathan tell you before he left?"

"Everything I needed to know to prepare me for you." His eyes were intense and his anger was still palpable.

"Yet you still let me be taken away by the City Watch? Surely Leviathan told you Thomas was a friend, and you even met him at my home? I don't think writing a report would be in your best interest, do you? Relax!"

Tyg walked off, leaving Corvyn shame faced and glaring after her. All he wanted to do right now was drag her over his knee and spank the sassy little minx.

"Damn it! Why did he leave me here in charge of that?" He muttered and stalked off after her, giving Dane a baleful look as he past him, as Dane walked over to take the reins of his horse and lead it to the stables.

51

Inside, Corvyn found Tyg in the kitchen with Tess. Tyg was standing next to the bench, leaning on it with her hip, her arms folded, watching Tess cutting up vegetables. Like a good girl, Corvyn thought.

"Why can't you be more like her?" Corvyn spat out as he entered.

Tyg looked at him with genuine surprise, then she laughed musically. Corvyn shuddered at the sound and shook his head slightly. Tyg caught the movement and frowned. She moved to a cupboard and opening it, took out a bottle. She grabbed two glasses off the side and walked over to the small breakfast table. She motioned for Corvyn to sit and sat down herself. She poured out two glasses of the fiery volka drink and pushed one over to an empty seat and looked at Corvyn, waiting.

Corvyn sighed and sat down, taking off his helm, combing back his unruly chocolate coloured hair. Taking the volka he downed it in one gulp and placed the glass back on the table in front of Tyg. He folded his arms.

Tyg sighed, at least he had drunk her peace offering. She rubbed her fingers between her eyes a moment, then looked up at him. He was watching her, waiting with a resigned look on his face.

"Yes, there are people in my life that are very secretive people, very dangerous people and I had to let them know what was happening, that I was okay. Check in, so to speak. I couldn't go there with an escort of soldiers, they would have killed the lot of you."

Corvyn snorted. "You underestimate me and my men."

Tyg regarded him. "I don't think so...you're rash."

Corvyn grimaced at that and stared hard at her.

"So, you've been called that before? So, why do you think Leviathan left you in charge? To prove yourself?"

"Perhaps."

"Well, I'm truly sorry then, I won't leave the Manor without you again."

"That is one thing we can agree on, my Lady." Corvyn got up, bowed curtly and stalked from the room. He was replaced by a soldier in a matter of minutes. As Tyg sat at the table drinking, the soldier stationed himself at the door.

Tess came over and sat down, making Tyg look at her with an eyebrow raised.

"Is everything alright?" She asked Tyg.

"No, Tess, everything is far from alright, but don't you worry yourself about it. Actually, you're quite good with figures aren't you? Haven't you been helping Mae? With the household accounts?"

"Yes, Mae says I'm a quick learner and have a very logical mind, whatever that means?"

"Good."

"Ah...why?" Tess asked a little timid.

"Because Tess, I didn't bring you over here to cook meals and clean up after soldiers. I brought you over here to take control of the running of this entire household...can you do it?"

Tess looked surprised, this was a promotion she never expected would ever happen in her entire life.

"Yes...I think so...thank you."

"Well, don't thank me yet. I still have to get this round Corvyn and he's a little bit pissed with me right now."

"A little bit?" Tess said smiling. "Well, that's never stopped you before..."

Tyg glanced at the soldier, who glanced at her. Tyg smiled and put a finger to her lips and shushed him. The soldier's lips twitched slightly, like he was holding back a grin and went back to staring at the wall. So he understood...

"Now, the other thing I wanted to talk to you about..." Tyg turned back to Tess.

"Another thing?" Tess asked surprised.

"You like Dane, yes?" Tess blushed furiously and stared at her hands, stammering.

"Well....I...he..."

"I'll take that as a yes." Tyg smiled as Tess blushed further. "Would you like me to act as your mediatory?'

"Would you take no for an answer?"

"Nope." Tyg grinned and stood up. "I'm off to find Pete."

As Tyg walked out of the kitchen and made her way outside, the soldier followed along a couple of yards behind. Tyg grimaced at the noise of his armour. She found Pete turning the soil in a large vegetable patch at the back of the grounds. As she approached, he saw her and stopped, leaning on the shovel. Tyg looked off for a moment at the small tent city of the soldiers not far away.

"Pete, I have a need of you."

"Sure thing, I was getting bored doing this."

"Come on then. Wash up and meet me in the library."

"No problem."

As Tyg turned and walked back the way she had come, she past the soldier and grinned at him. He scowled at having to walk all the way over here and now walk all the way back.

"It's a hard life." She muttered at him.

He grunted as he turned and dutifully followed her back to the house.

As Tyg approached the manor, she saw Corvyn standing on the paving outside the main side entrance doors. His arms folded as he was clearly watching her and what she was up to.

Tyg sneered as she passed him and headed back inside, he pivoted on his heels as she passed and watched her head through the lounge room and towards the library.

"Watch her carefully." Corvyn said to the soldier as he followed along. The soldier grunted and rolled his eyes. "I mean it." Corvyn growled. "She has power...she might not know how to use it, but she's extremely well trained in other fields and she's as sneaky as hell. Do not treat her like a human girl."

"Sir." The soldier nodded his head curtly and continued as Corvyn also followed him in.

They both saw her standing at the door to the library, one hand on her hip and the other on the doorknob. "Do hurry up, I would hate for you to lose sight of me." Tyg grinned and opened the doors and went inside.

"She's up to something." Corvyn said to the soldier, grimacing. "Bloody hell, I don't think I have the strength for this." The soldier looked at his officer with pity but said nothing.

Just then Pete came in and walked passed them and into the library, and with a grin Tyg closed the doors.

"Shit!" Corvyn spat as he strode over and opened the doors to find Tyg and Pete about to sit down on the couch. Tyg grinned as she collapsed into the couch and crossed her legs.

"My soldier stays in the room." Corvyn growled as the soldier entered and took up position by the door.

"Whatever makes you happy, Corvyn?" Tyg replied pleasantly as Pete also sat and made himself comfortable. "It's just a boring staff meeting is all...about vegetables...since you seem to have passed the household over to me to sort out...are you sure you don't want to attend this meeting? Oh, and you can start handing the household accounts over to Tess as well."

Corvyn grit his teeth and slammed the door shut.

"I guess not, huh?" Tyg said to Pete, who was smiling broadly.

"No, guess not." He said.

"Okay, Pete." Tyg said as she got up and went to a table with paper and pen on it. "We need to discuss what things to plant in that garden of yours. I'll make a list, give you some coin and then you can go into the market and get what's needed. Sound like a plan?" Tyg winked at him.

"Yep, sounds good to me." He grinned. "Okay, what are some good winter vege? Put down cabbage, broad beans, turnips, peas, carrots, potatoes..."

As he rattled off vegetables, Tyg was writing on the paper, not his list, but a note to Palin explaining what happened at the Precinct and the fact that she now had a permanent detail set to follow her every move. So she was completely unable to leave without outside assistance and Palin needed to be a hundred percent sure that he wanted/needed her out right now, because there would be bloodshed. She hesitated, and she was really starting to like Corvyn. She added, bloodshed not an option for me! Tyg also wrote a quick list of vegetables on another piece of paper and hid the note underneath it.

"Okay, is that it?" Tyg said to Pete.

"Yep, pretty sure."

"Okay." Tyg went to a drawer and pulled out a bag of coins she had put in there previously. If Corvyn was going to take over the study, this library was going to become her office. She chucked the bag at Pete. "This should cover it and here's the list." She said folding the list and the note and handing it to Pete who put it in his pocket, standing up.

"Right, I'll be off then." He smiled and left. Tyg looked at the soldier as Pete walked straight passed him out the door. Tyg smiled to herself and sat down on the couch, grabbing the book she was reading off the side table.

About ten minutes later Corvyn stormed into the room. Tyg smiled slyly and put the book down.

"Where is that man going?" Corvyn was looking at the soldier.

"To the market, Sir, for vegetable plants."

"Really?" He looked at Tyg, who blinked at him.

"What's the problem now, Corvyn?" Tyg asked sounding slightly annoyed.

"He seemed to leave in a bloody hurry, galloped out of here like wolves were chasing him. The gate guard said the same thing about vegetables. Showed a list, said he had to make it before market closed."

"So, what's the problem?"

"You're up to something....again"

Tyg sighed. "Corvyn, this really isn't going to work."

"What isn't?" Corvyn's voice had taken on that husky growl again.

"Your suspicions of my every move...it's going to get tiresome very quickly." Tyg's eyes flashed. The soldier on guard saw and placed his hand on his sword. Tyg frowned. "Really, Corvyn...get a grip on this."

"Tell me where that man really went." Corvyn folded his arms, staring down at her.

"Why don't you just put me in chains for the rest of the time the Adramelechs are gone and then you can explain all this to them when they return. I'm sure they will see that you handled the situation in the correct manner and be happy with your services."

Corvyn grimaced again and wiped a hand over his face. He turned to the soldier. "Leave. Stand outside for a moment, I need a private word with her Ladyship."

Tyg sat up. This was a turn she didn't expect. As the soldier left Corvyn removed his helm, his coat and his gauntlets, throwing them all on the table, then sat down in the armchair. Tyg was watching him intently as he looked at her with that same glint in his eye as earlier. He raked a hand through his unruly hair.

"I don't know where that man has really gone and I don't much care, to be honest. It is you I have been charged with minding." At the word minding Tyg's eyes went dark, that word reminded her of Stills and how they had first met. She looked at Corvyn.

"And, like I said I'm not going anywhere."

"Can you promise me?"

"Sure, if you can believe the word of a thief and a brigand."

Corvyn sighed. "You have a very bitter tongue, Tygarya." Tyg smiled at him

"I had a very bitter upbringing."

"Can we at least find some common ground here, I can't keep this up."

"What exactly are you suggesting, Corvyn?"

"Run whatever you like out of this Manor, I don't care. I will turn a blind eye....as long as you go nowhere."

Tyg looked surprised for a moment. "Tell me, honestly Corvyn. If I wasn't here when Leviathan gets back, what would happen to you?"

Corvyn blanched and went deathly pale. "Death would be a welcome respite to what the Emperor would do to me."

Tyg grimaced and looked away at the shelves of books. This was all getting out of her control, simple men were simple to work with, but Sorcerers were something completely new.

"Please, Tygarya, tell me...for the sake of everyone in this house, you're not planning on leaving again."

"For all in this house?" Tyg baulked.

Corvyn sat forward intensely. "The Emperor is a Sorcerer, you know that! Why the fuck do you play with fire like this? This is not a fucking game. This is life and death for everyone! He has the power to lay waste to this entire city not just this house! Stop playing around at trying to outwit everyone, grow up and realise we are all following orders just to stay alive! If you disappear he will literally, not figuratively, tear this entire city apart to look for you! He has made it abundantly clear that now he has found you he doesn't intend for you to ever leave his sight again."

"Fuck..." Tyg muttered. Perhaps he should have just hauled her off to Landau with him, things would be a lot easier on her...so that was it...terror...Leviathan ruled by terror. She knew she couldn't have Palin try and get her out, Leviathan would kill everyone. "Do you know why I'm so important to him?"

Corvyn's eyes glinted with that look of power again. "I am not privy to the Emperor's plans."

Tyg sighed and buried her face in her hands for a moment. Corvyn watched her hoping he had gotten through to her. She leaned back looking defeated and curled her legs up on the couch as she looked at Corvyn and held his gaze.

"I have no intention of going anywhere, Corvyn, I promise you that."

Corvyn relaxed slightly but still felt there was more. "But?"

"There are people who will not let me leave this city with Leviathan."

"Fuck's sake." Corvyn blanched again. "Can't you stop them, it will be a slaughter."

Tyg shook her head. "Their determination is the same as Leviathan's obviously is."

"They don't know what they're going to bring down upon themselves and we can't tell them. The fact the Adramelechs are both Sorcerers is one thing we have all sworn to keep secret while we are here, we can't even warn them." Corvyn wiped a hand over his face. "But I can try and make their plans of getting to you impossible."

"Just let me go, Corvyn, I can stop this."

"Are you mad? No fucking way, I have to send a message to the Emperor and get him back here as soon as possible."

"Shit, is that the only other option?" Tyg didn't like that idea.

"I see no other, I don't have enough soldiers to patrol this place fully, and you are not going anywhere...I know you won't come back and that will mean my death."

Tyg sighed heavily and wiped her hands over her face "Okay...what if you got help?"

"From who?"

Tyg shrugged "The City Watch?"

Corvyn looked hard at her. "They are not soldiers, they prance around looking like prats in fancy uniforms. They would run at the first signs of a battle."

"We're not talking about a battle." Tyg said then, causing Corvyn to narrow his eyes at her. "Besides, sending a message to Leviathan is still going to take two days to reach him then another two days to get back. Please, at least talk to my friend, Thomas."

Corvyn regarded her a moment, she looked genuinely concerned.

"Okay, as a thank you for being honest with me, I'll talk to your friend, but I doubt very much he will be willing to talk to me."

"Why, what did you do in that Precinct?"

"It doesn't matter." Corvyn looked coy. "What matters is I doubt he will want to help."

"Well, thank you for being reasonable. We can only try, and if nothing else their bolstered numbers may make people hesitate in their actions."

"Let's hope so..."

Tyg tried to get Thomas to help but he refused to have anything to do with Corvyn, the Adramelechs or what was going on in Karon's Manor. He was now engaged and wanted to focus on being a Lord's son rather than a Captain of the City Watch anymore.

Pete returned with a message saying Palin was giving her two days to sort herself out or a Squad would be coming that night. Corvyn shut the place down tight, no one was going in or out after that. She didn't dare risk trying to get a message back out to Palin to stop him, but at least the Squad would come for her before Leviathan got back. And if a Squad came at least Corvyn couldn't get blamed for simple incompetence, which he would if she just left in the dead of night.

52

Two days later, shortly after noon, Corvyn went looking for Tyg in her usual place.

"Tygarya, you are wanted outside." Corvyn said as he entered the library and bowed his head to her. She noticed a smug look on his face.

"What is it, Corvyn?"

"Come and look, my Lady." Corvyn said openly smiling.

Tyg was instantly suspicious as she got up and walked with Corvyn to the main entrance. As she walked out the front doors her knees just about buckled. She looked at Corvyn with shock on her face.

"How is this possible?" She asked him as her eyes went back to the approaching man on horseback, cantering down the path with four soldiers flanking him. There was no mistaking the imposing form of Leviathan on his black stallion, but how the hell was he here? Corvyn had only sent word two days ago.

"Magic can be a very resourceful tool, my Lady." Corvyn said smugly.

"Fucking hell." Tyg muttered. "And you accused me of trying to outwit people."

Corvyn shrugged. "I do what is best for all involved and that was contacting the Emperor about your fears. The fact that you thought that meant sending a horseman with a message was your assumption."

Tyg looked back at him, glaring. Her eyes blazing. "I hate you!" She growled at him. "Do you realise what you've done!"

Corvyn chuckled, then straightened at attention as Leviathan jumped from his horse and strode up the steps two at a time and came to stand directly in front of Tyg. She couldn't even bring herself to look up at him.

"Tygarya, looking as lovely as ever...demure is a nice look on you." Leviathan said coarsely as he stood in front of her. "I have to say, I am not surprised to find myself back here earlier than expected."

"Well, I am." Tyg said, flashing another look at Corvyn.

Leviathan chuckled as he looked at Corvyn. "Yes, the Lieutenant has excelled himself."

Leviathan put a hand on Tyg's shoulder and turned her around, then put his hand on her back and pushed her forward. "Come, we have much to discuss. Captain, you come too."

"Yes, my Liege. Thank you, my Liege." Corvyn flushed at the sudden promotion as he bowed, then fell in behind Leviathan.

They walked into the library and Leviathan steered Tyg to sit on the couch. He looked down on her with that vulture gaze for a moment then sat next to her. He deliberately put his arm up over the back of the couch behind her. So Tyg curled her feet up between them and leaned on the arm, folding her arms defiantly. Leviathan smiled and indicated for Corvyn to sit in the armchair.

"So, Tygarya, please tell me that the Captain here was exaggerating when he told me that there was an urgent risk of you being removed from the Manor, by force?"

Tyg looked at Corvyn. She could feel Leviathan looking down on her from beside her. Why was he acting so bemused by the whole thing? "All I said was that certain people will not let me leave the city with you when you go home."

"Is that so?" Leviathan said in a voice low and controlled. "And, who exactly are these people?"

Tyg shifted in her seat to turn and look up at him finally, she swallowed hard. His voice may have sounded controlled and amused but his eyes were glowing with ire.

"You know exactly who." Tyg muttered.

"Hmm, your Boss?" Leviathan growled.

"Like I told you before, I owe him."

"You owe him nothing, Tygarya, he thinks he owns you." Tyg baulked and stared at Leviathan in shock. "I think it's about time I had a chat with your Boss."

Tyg grimaced at the sound of Leviathan's voice, but her eyes flashed.

"Why? So you can pay him gold and own me too?" Tyg sprang up from the couch and ran from the room. Corvyn stared after her shocked, he had no idea the extent of her abuse here. He started to feel sorry for her.

"Don't feel sorry for her." Leviathan growled at Corvyn as he stood up. "She made her choices and she's just using them as an excuse."

Corvyn stared after Leviathan as he stalked from the room. He couldn't help but still feel sorry for the girl, even after everything she had put him through over the last few days.

Tyg wasn't upset, she was angry. She ran to her room upstairs and slammed the door shut. How fucking dare he? How the hell did he find out all this information? Her mind was spinning, and her head was hurting. She sat down on the bed and cradled her head in her hands. She reached up and undid the braid, releasing her hair, trying to relieve some of the pressure. She collapsed back and stared at the ceiling.

The door flew open and Leviathan stood in the doorway. He faltered for a second, the light going out of his eyes as he took in the sight of her, half lying back on the bed, her hair fanned out around her head like a halo. He smiled and leaned on the doorframe with one shoulder as he hooked his toes over his other foot. He took up the whole doorway, his head skimming the top.

Tyg sat up startled, and stared at him.

"Well, that's a sight I can't stay angry at." Leviathan said as he just looked at her from the doorway. Tyg tore her eyes away from his and looked out the glass doors of the balcony.

"I don't know why you're angry at me for all this at all?" Tyg said back to him, not able to look at him, every time she looked at him all she could think of was those last kisses they had shared before he left. "All I've been trying to do is NOT get people killed, over something so stupid."

"You're not stupid, Tygarya." Leviathan said softly.

Tyg shook her head. "I don't get it, I'm really not worth other people's lives and I hate the way it makes me feel to think anyone like Corvyn or Dane or Tess might die because of me. I've already lost..." Tyg took a deep breath and couldn't continue.

Leviathan was still leaning in the doorway. He scratched his chin. "What makes you think any of them would lose their lives?"

Tyg turned her head and looked at him with surprise, but still wouldn't look him in the eye, instead she looked at his feet. "I...well, it was looking that way, before you showed up."

"Tell me what was planned?" Leviathan asked in that low authoritative voice.

Tyg sighed. "A Squad."

"What the fuck is a Squad?"

"A Squad is four assassins that go in, in the dead of night to acquire a target, usually used in situations where multiple threats will need to be taken out...they were coming tonight."

"Fucking hell, Tyg." Leviathan growled. Tyg looked up at him as he called her Tyg. Their eyes locked and they stared at each other for a long moment. It was Leviathan that blinked and looked away.

"Well I'm here now, and that won't be happening, you're mine now."

"How can you stop it?"

"If you want me to explain, let me in?" Leviathan said amused again.

"What?"

"I won't enter your bedroom unless you say I can." His eyes darkened.

"Oh." Tyg fell silent in thought for a minute, then stood up. "I think perhaps we should go somewhere else then?"

Leviathan laughed and rubbed his eyes as he stood up and stepped back out of the doorway. "Fair enough, lead the way." As Tyg walked past him he muttered to her. "See, you're far from stupid."

"I didn't mean it like that." Tyg snapped as she past.

"No, because you're sneaky and manipulative. That's why I like you." Leviathan said pivoting round to keep her in his eye line as she walked into the hallway. Tyg stopped in the middle of the hall and turned to look at him with an eyebrow raised. "What? Is it so hard to believe?"

"How do you know so much about me all of a sudden?" Tyg countered back.

Leviathan chuckled and leaned back on the doorframe, facing the hallway. "Because I know how to ask the right questions. What I can't find out is the name of who you work for?"

"Hmm." Tyg grunted with smug relief.

"I can't help you get away from him if you're not going to help me."

"How did you know he owned me?"

Leviathan shrugged. "I didn't...it was a hunch. Tell me, why did you put my Lieutenant in that list of people you care about?"

"What?"

"When you said you didn't want certain people to die you put Corvyn in that list."

"Did I? I just feel sorry for having to deceive him."

"But, you don't feel sorry for deceiving me?"

"When did I ever deceive you?" Tyg's eyes went flat.

"You agreed for my soldiers to escort you into the city."

"That's not deception." Tyg smiled at him. "That is just a lie."

"You define a difference, interesting." Leviathan muttered.

"Besides, you threatened me with jail, remember? What else was I supposed to do?"

"Perhaps, right now, jail or maybe a dungeon would be the best place for you." Leviathan growled.

Tyg stared at him then squeezed her eyes shut. "I can't do this right now." She grabbed the sides of her head.

"Tyg?"

Tyg looked up at him using the short form of her name again. "My head is pounding..."

Leviathan stood up and stepped over. "Hmm? Take my hand."

"What?"

"Take my hand, I can make it go away."

"I just need to train or something..."

"Training relieves your headaches?"

"Yeah."

"And do you get many of these headaches?"

Tyg shrugged and leaned her head back on the opposite wall.

"Hmm, interesting." Leviathan said as he scratched thoughtfully at his chin.

"Glad you find me so fucking fascinating." Tyg growled staring at the ceiling.

"Oh, but you are..." Leviathan grabbed her hand and held it as his eyes glowed, he shivered and closed his eyes. Tyg noticed her headache was gone. He opened his eyes and looked at her intensely. Tyg stopped breathing. Leviathan suddenly pushed her back against the wall again placing a finger under her chin he tilted her head back so they were face to face and kissed her. She kissed him back, bringing her arms up round his neck. He lashed his tongue into her mouth possessively as she was held enthralled. He stopped and shuddered as he dropped her chin and stepped back.

The power swirling in his system right now made her intoxicating. He shook his head and looked at her. His eyes dark and smouldering. Tyg was still leaning on the wall, watching him, panting out of breath. She frowned.

"I should have stayed in my room."

Leviathan smirked. "I'm glad you didn't."

"Would you have seriously not come in?

Leviathan shrugged. "I'm used to getting what I want, and right now all I want is for you to trust me."

"Did you take my headache away with your magic?" Tyg asked breathless, she found it hard to look at him when he was looking at her like that.

Leviathan shrugged again. "I suppose."

"Thank you."

Leviathan laughed then. "No, Tyg...thank you." He took her hand again and pulled her to him and put his arm around her as he walked her down the hall.

"For having a headache?" Tyg was confused at that last statement.

Leviathan laughed again and squeezed her tighter to his side. "No, for being you."

As they walked back down the stairs they saw Corvyn standing there with a soldier, he looked up as the soldier snapped his heels, bowed his head, turned and left. He frowned as he saw Leviathan's arm around Tyg and Tyg once again saw that flash in his eyes.

"Are you and Antyn the only Sorcerers?" Tyg suddenly asked Leviathan. He looked down on her surprised.

"No, there are others."

"But not here?"

"No, why do you ask?"

Tyg flicked another glance at Corvyn. "No reason..."

Leviathan looked down at her curious for a moment, but Corvyn interrupted.

"My Liege, we need to sort the wards."

"Wards?" Tyg asked.

"Come... watch...wards are magic. They will stop anyone trying to enter this property." Leviathan explained.

"Oh." Tyg said in awe.

53

As they walked outside Corvyn fell in beside Leviathan. "I have put out the talismans around the boundary, my Liege, and the runes are inscribed."

"Good, Captain. What wards have you used?"

"The outer ones are simple Confusion and Disorientation wards. The inner ones are binding spells. I thought if they got that far you would probably like to be able to meet them."

Leviathan laughed, and it wasn't pleasant. "Quite, make sure those binding spells have barbs in them, I want them to scream."

Tyg looked up at Leviathan in shock as Corvyn calmly answered. "Of course, my Liege."

As they reached outside she could see the soldiers were walking around something etched in the grass, holding torches on long poles and were pushing them into the ground around it. The torches weren't lit yet. Leviathan let go of Tyg and walked up to the runes written on the ground. Tyg could see they were contained within a circle and the torches were being put around the outside of the circle. Leviathan was studying the runes and looking at a stone that was in the centre. He was watching carefully as Corvyn seemed to adjust and add something. The barbs, Tyg guessed, completely confused as to what was going on. How did Corvyn know all this stuff?

As Corvyn stepped back Leviathan turned to Tyg.

"No one is coming in or out of this place once these wards go up, is that clear?"

Tyg nodded, she saw Dane, Pete, Tess and Neeki out of the corner of her eye, standing together. How long had they been standing there? Tyg looked at Dane and locked eyes with him. He frowned at her and she shrugged. There was nothing she could do about things now. With Leviathan back everything was completely out of her control. She folded her arms as she suddenly felt cold.

Suddenly a strange purple line of light came from Leviathan's palm and hit the rock on the centre of the circle, it erupted in purple light sending a beam shooting up to the sky and arching out over the house. It forked out and hit the talismans Corvyn had set around the boundary and formed a dome. It glowed there for several seconds then seemed to disappear, but Tyg had the feeling it just couldn't be seen. Then Leviathan did it again, only this time the light from his hand wasn't light, but an inky blackness that spread across the sky like the last one making the whole area inside go pitch black, the torches suddenly ignited, and Tyg could see that it was Corvyn that had ignited them with a flourish of his own hand. What the fuck was going on here? Then the inky blackness slowly ebbed away from the top of the dome down, slowly letting the light back in.

"As long as those torches burn the wards hold." Leviathan said as he turned and walked back to Tyg. "Well?"

Tyg didn't know what to say, but she wasn't going to let him think she was impressed. She snorted. "You must be fun at parties." Leviathan looked at her shocked and then laughed, running a hand up her cheek and into her hair, he yanked her face to him and kissed her forcibly on the lips. "Fucking hell, Tyg, what does it take for a guy to impress you?"

"You wanted to impress me?"

Leviathan shrugged. "Sure why not? It's your arse I'm saving."

"And I thank you, but you had me impressed the moment you told me you liked me."

Leviathan looked at her perplexed for a moment, then put his arm around her shoulders. "Come on..." He led her inside as she looked back at Corvyn who was standing with his arms folded watching the soldiers standing guard at the torches. He turned and caught her glance, his eyes were glowing golden in the light.

"So, what happens now?" Tyg asked as Leviathan led her inside.

"Firstly, you better talk to your friends and let them know what they just saw is strictly secret for now."

"Huh, okay, but then what?"

"Then we wait and see if your Boss decides to play with us..." Leviathan growled in that low commanding voice. "...and sends that Squad to spring our traps."

"What will happen to them if they do?"

Leviathan looked sideways at her, gauging her responses. "They will encounter the first wards...Confuse, will make them forget why they're here...Disorientate, they won't know where here is or what direction to go in to escape. Then my men will locate them and kill them."

"Oh..." Tyg felt so helpless to avoid the inevitable.

"And..." Leviathan continued. "...If any of them manage to keep their focus enough to get through those wards they will run into a binding spell, which wraps around them like a net, but the more they struggle the tighter it becomes and with barbs it will feel like every inch of their body is being pierced by needles."

"Fuck, that's a bit extreme isn't it?"

Leviathan looked at her. "No, I'm not playing around with these guys, you said they were trained assassins."

Tyg sighed feeling out of her depth with all this magic talk. "Okay, let me go talk to Dane..." Tyg said quietly as she stepped out from Leviathan's arm, turned and headed for the kitchen and servant quarters at the back of the house.

Leviathan watched her go as he slowly folded his arms, his eyes lost in thought.

She found all of them in the servants quarters common room. They all stopped speaking when she walked in. Tess and Neeki were seated on a small couch and Pete was sitting at the table they ate at. Dane was pacing.

"Fucking hell, Tyg, what the hell was that? Magic?!"

"Yes, Dane, it was magic." Tyg said wearily.

Tyg heard the two girls muttering at each other, it sounded like Neeki was saying 'I told you so'.

"Leviathan is a Sorcerer" Tyg continued. "That's why he is so damned dangerous."

"Why the fuck haven't you told anyone! This is like a fucking dream...no, a nightmare." Dane paced again.

"I..." Tyg faltered. Why hadn't she? If only she had...but would anyone have actually believed her if she had? She collapsed in a chair at the table and buried her face in her hands. "I know I should have. I've completely fucked up, I have no idea how Leviathan managed to get back here so fast and now these wards things are up there is no way we can get a message out to warn anyone. Whatever happens tonight it's going to be all my fault."

"Shit, Tyg..." Dane put his hand on her shoulder. "I'm sorry."

Tyg sighed again, resting her forearms on the table and hanging her head. "You guys can't say anything about the magic."

"Well, we can't get out to tell anyone."

"Even after...you have to stay quiet on it." Tyg looked up at Dane.

He looked at her a moment then nodded. "Sure thing, Tyg."

"Thank you, Dane."

"So, what's really going on between you and the big guy?"

Tyg rubbed her eyes with one hand and grimaced. "Argh, I have no idea. I've never been so damned confused about anything in my life. With..." Tyg faltered, but was determined to get it out...his name. "...with Stills it was so normal, so natural, but this is so intense. I can't think straight, and right now I really need to be able to focus on keeping everyone alive and getting out of this situation."

"Yeah, you're really stuck between a rock and a hard place." Dane said sitting down next to her. Tyg looked sideways at him as he continued. "Follow your heart, Tyg."

"What the hell has this got to do with my heart?"

"I know Pa...ah...Boss is like a father to you." Dane said purposely avoiding Palin's name. "But you know deep down you're destined to want to go back to your homeland. Whether it's with the big guy or not, you have to follow your heart. Boss can't stand in your way if you want to go home Tyg, he has no right."

"But, I took an Oath."

"So what? You're not abandoning that Oath, just because you want to follow your dreams."

Tyg looked at Dane amazed, then smiled and grabbed his hand and squeezed it. "Thanks Dane."

"But, what happens tonight?" Pete grumbled, having sat there listening to the two of them.

"I don't know, this magic thing is completely out of my control."

"Are they going to die?" Pete asked intensely.

Tyg looked at the table. "Probably, there's nothing I can do to stop it now. If only Corvyn had told me Leviathan would be arriving here today...damn it!" Tyg lay her head on her arms on the table. "These are my people...my Guild!"

"You can't blame yourself, Tyg." Dane said. "You gave Boss the decision. He chose to not trust you and send the Squad anyway, their deaths should be on him."

"If only that were true." Tyg muttered. "I better go..."

"No, stay with us, have something to eat." Tess got up and came over.

"I'm not hungry." Tyg muttered again, she was just lying her head into her elbows, her forearms curled up over her head.

"You need to keep your strength up." Tess said concerned. She knew that Tyg hadn't eaten anything since yesterday.

"I said I'm not hungry." Tyg closed her eyes and just hid her face under her arms.

They all looked at each other concerned, none of them had ever seen Tyg like this.

A soldier suddenly appeared in the doorway, causing them all to look round startled, except Tyg who didn't move.

"His Imperial Majesty requires you to attend him, my Lady."

"I don't care." Tyg muttered from underneath her arms.

The soldier baulked, and looked at the others for a moment. "Is she okay?" He asked them.

"What do you bloody think?" Dane answered as he got up and placed himself between the soldier and Tyg's back.

Tyg just groaned. "Leave it, Dane." She said as she lifted her head and turned to look at the soldier. "I'm disobeying your Emperor's orders, got it, now go away." The soldier baulked again, as Tyg covered her head again, trying to shut the world out. She heard him turn and leave with a huff.

"Was that wise?" Dane asked as he turned back to her, placing a hand on her back.

"I don't care."

"Yeah, you already said." Dane grimaced. They all stared at Tyg not knowing what to do.

After only a minute, Captain Corvyn appeared, striding into the room. "What the hell is going on now?" He growled but then saw Tyg crumpled over the table, hiding her head. "Tygarya?"

"Go away, Corvyn." Tyg muttered in a muffled voice.

Corvyn clenched his jaw and came up beside Tyg, pushing Dane aside with one hand easily and leaning over the table, banging his other fist down on it to get Tyg's attention. He was surprised when she just calmly blinked up at him and sneered. "Tygarya! It's lucky for you that Russo, that soldier, came to me instead of the Emperor. Do you really want him crashing in here and pushing your friends aside?"

Tyg blinked at him. "No, of course not." She sighed.

"Then go to him when he fucking requests it. We've been through this..."

"Yeah, but you've kept something from me, Corvyn." Tyg's voice suddenly made everyone's blood curdle. As she raised her head, her face was only inches from his. Her eyes flashed. "Haven't you?"

As if to confirm what she was saying Tyg clearly saw Corvyn's eyes flash as he tried to keep his temper under control. Tyg grinned when she saw it, a vicious animalistic grin. "Back off, Corvyn."

"Tygarya, I don't think now is the time..."

Suddenly Tyg stood up, grabbing Corvyn and flipping him on his back. She had Corvyn pinned to the table, a dagger at his throat, the other hand firmly pressing down on his chest, one knee was between his legs and her other foot was on the table beside his hip as she crouched over him. Corvyn was surprised by how fast she moved. Like a cat. He lay there calm, his hands held out.

"Tyg, what the fuck!" Dane and Pete both yelled as they backed up away from the table. The two maids both crouched in fear on the couch together.

"Next time, I'll kill you, if you ever come near me again!" Tyg said to Corvyn as she leaned over him further, her body pressed against his bringing her face only inches from his, her eyes were black. "I trusted you Corvyn, now people I probably know are going to die tonight. You're right, this is no game."

Tyg jumped off him and stood up, sheathed her dagger and stalked from the room. Corvyn sat up staring after her. Dane and

Pete just stood watching him. He grimaced to himself as he stood up. Shaking his head he walked from the room.

"That girl is going to get us all killed." He muttered. He had deep concerns about what he just witnessed, her eyes going black, that wasn't normal, even from their land, what the hell was she?

54

Tyg wandered back through the house and found Leviathan in the library talking to two soldiers. She walked in and collapsed on the couch, lying down with her head on the arm, pulling her knees up and folding her arms. Leviathan watched her as she walked through and frowned. He dismissed the soldiers and walked up to her.

"What's wrong?" He asked her, standing over her and looking down on her with that vulture gaze.

"What's bloody right?" Tyg muttered.

Just then Corvyn appeared in the doorway, panting slightly from running. Leviathan turned and looked at him, and raised an eyebrow at him. Corvyn saw that Tyg was there and smiled. "Just making sure Lady Tygarya had got your message, my Liege." Corvyn bowed and quickly left.

Leviathan turned back to Tyg. "What the fuck was that about?"

Tyg looked up at him, her eyes a cool ice blue. "I don't like being summoned."

Leviathan laughed. "Is that all! Tygarya, I just want you next to me, where you're safe."

"Can't you just send me to my room instead?" Tyg said coolly.

Leviathan frowned. "No, I don't think so...I want you right beside me tonight...all night...until this is over."

"Fine, whatever."

Tyg sat moodily in the library for the rest of the afternoon while Leviathan conducted his business from the desk against the wall.

At one point Tess and Neeki came in with a food platter and put it on the table in front of Tyg. Leviathan snacked from it from time to time but Tyg just lay on the couch with an arm over her eyes. Leviathan had decided earlier on to just ignore her. As long as she was lying there being dramatic she wasn't causing any trouble elsewhere.

"Eat." Leviathan said at one point, causing Tyg to remove her arm and look at him as he stood there chewing on a slice of ham.

"Bite me." Tyg said and returned her arm to her eyes.

"Fine, starve, whatever..." Leviathan replied and went back to his endless amounts of paper work and request forms. Owning a mine and keeping these soldiers here was making him drown in bureaucracy from the Council. Everyday more paperwork seemed to arrive at the gates for him to fill in. He wished Antyn was here, he was much better at all this bureaucratic nonsense.

Tyg eventually fell asleep on the couch as it got late. Leviathan stood over her staring down at her while she slept. Captain Corvyn knocked and entered, he froze as Leviathan put a hand up for silence, as he grabbed a throw from the back of the couch and placed it gently over Tyg, trying not to wake her. Corvyn was staring at Leviathan, he had never seen him like this, but when he looked at Tyg's sleeping face he shivered.

Leviathan turned and walked up to Corvyn in the doorway.

"She's pleasant, isn't she?" Leviathan said smiling.

"My Liege, was that humour?" Corvyn asked surprised.

Leviathan scowled and rubbed his forehead. "Quite, she has that effect even on me it seems."

"Well, it is nice, my Liege, yes."

"Perhaps I can just make her sleep until we get back home." Leviathan muttered almost to himself.

"It would make things a lot easier, my Liege." Corvyn snorted. "But seriously can she at least be unarmed."

Leviathan came out of his reverie. "What?"

"She literally attacked me earlier today, held a dagger at my throat."

"She held a dagger at your throat? Perhaps your promotion was unwarranted, Captain."

"She's been highly trained, my Liege, she's dangerous and fast. So fast, it's unnatural."

"Well of course it's unnatural, Captain, what did you expect, she's not human?"

Corvyn swallowed hard.

"What? You hadn't worked that much out on your own?" Leviathan asked amused.

"Yes...but...what is she?" Corvyn breathed, hardly even wanting to know the answer.

"Oh, I think you know." Leviathan said cryptically with a slight smirk.

"How is that even possible?" Corvyn asked frowning, disturbed.

Leviathan looked at him intently for a moment. "You understand my reluctance to let her go then..."

Corvyn looked up at Leviathan and swallowed hard. "Yes, my Liege."

"Good."

Suddenly the wards triggered with a howling sound and great flashes of purple light streaked across the sky. Leviathan turned and saw Tyg had sat up and was looking around.

"Go Captain!" Leviathan ordered him and Corvyn took off.

"What is it?" Tyg asked bewildered.

"It's the wards, your friends are here." Leviathan said menacingly.

"What!" Tyg stood up shocked, she had hoped against hope that they wouldn't come.

Just then they heard a blood curdling scream and the shouts of combat along with the sounds of weapons striking each other, echoed through the still night.

Tyg raced up to the door, but Leviathan caught her round the waist. "No, Tygarya!" He grabbed her hand and walked with her outside towards where the circle on the ground was glowing, purple streaks from the ward stones that were being crossed raked across the sky, but Tyg saw one line of inky blackness. Someone had reached the Binding spell, she tried to cover her ears from the screams she could hear. She knew what it meant.

"Stop it!" Tyg begged. Leviathan ignored her and just stood watching the circle and the wards like he could follow the action through them. The look of satisfaction on his face was chilling. Tyg was trying to wrench his fingers off her wrist, to no avail because he was stronger than her.

The screams went silent and the fighting stopped. It had obviously been brutal and short.

Corvyn came running up. Tyg noticed blood splashed across his chest plate. She growled and her eyes flashed. She suddenly found the strength to wrench free of Leviathan's grip and launched herself at Corvyn.

"This is all your fault!" She screamed at him. Once again, however, Leviathan's arm wrapped around her waist, this time he lifted her off her feet as she fought against him, trying in vain to reach Corvyn who was standing there with a look of abject horror on his face, one arm up shielding himself. He stood up when he realised Leviathan had her and frowned as Tyg's onslaught continued.

"You sanctimonious piece of shit! You have the nerve to tell me off about mind games yet you're the one that's devious!" Tyg grabbed a dagger off her belt as she struggled against Leviathan who was actually surprised he was having difficulty holding her back, and threw it at Corvyn. He saw it coming and dodged it but the look on his face as his eyes flashed was pure anger.

Leviathan turned around so they weren't in eye sight of Corvyn anymore and he placed a hand on Tyg's head. "Calm the fuck down!" He ordered her in that same calm low voice. She shuddered as all the fight seemed to suddenly evaporate out of her. He held her tight as she panted for breath from the exertion.

"Leave, Captain." Leviathan ordered. "It's over now, Tygarya, got it." He said once Corvyn had stormed off. "It's all finished, you can't change the outcome now."

Tyg breathed in a deep breath. "I'll go back to my room now."

55

Neeki walked into Tyg's room to tidy the bed, swap out the water jug and clean the chamber pot, but Tyg was still in there lying on the bed reading yet another book.

"Milady." Neeki said quietly as she walked in.

Tyg glanced around the book and smiled at her. "Hi, Neeki."

"You seem to be spending a lot of time in here, are you unwell? You still haven't eaten anything."

Tyg chuckled. "No, actually, it's the one room that I get to myself without Leviathan breathing down my neck and after last night...I just can't eat."

"Oh, I see." Neeki blushed. "He is very besotted, isn't he?"

Tyg lowered the book and sat up, looking at Neeki. 'Is that the way people see it?' She thought. "There's nothing 'besotted' about it." Tyg muttered.

Neeki glanced at her, water jug in hand. "Oh?"

"He won't let me out of his sight because he doesn't trust me." Tyg explained.

Neeki looked at the ground as she walked to the door. "I can understand that."

"What?" Tyg said smiling, finally some spark out of the shy girl. "Come on, be free with your words, Neeki, no need to fear."

Neeki stopped at the door and hugged the water jug. "Well, Milady, I don't mean to cause offense but you're not like any other woman I have ever met."

Tyg smirked amused. "No, I suppose I'm not. I guess I have managed to cause quite a bit of drama since I've been here, huh?"

"It's not my place to say, Milady." Neeki smiled as she looked up at Tyg, she hovered in the doorway, then turned and walked down the hall, placing the water jug with the other one from Leviathan's room in the dumbwaiter. Tyg could see two soldiers standing in the hall. As she came back in for the chamber pot Tyg waved a hand dismissing her. "It's not used." Tyg muttered from where she had gone back to reading.

Neeki hung around, fidgeting with her hands. Tyg lowered the book and looked at her questioningly.

"Something else?"

"I was wondering, Milady, what was going to happen here when all these men go back to where they came from?"

Tyg stared at her, then grimaced. "You're worried about your job?"

"Yes, Milady."

"Don't worry. I'll go talk to Leviathan and sort it out for you, okay?"

"Thank you so much, Milady. I knew, from what the others say about you, that you wouldn't let us down." Neeki curtsied and left the room.

Tyg rubbed her eyes with the fingers of one hand. "Fucking hell." She muttered. Now she had this to worry about as well. She put the book down and got up.

She found Leviathan in the drawing room, sitting in a leather arm chair in front of the fireplace, one foot resting on the thigh of his other leg with papers resting on them as he was reading through them. As soon as Tyg entered he threw the papers onto a side table and looked up at her smiling.

"Tygarya! What a pleasant surprise, I thought you were going to hide in your room all day." His eyes sparkled as he watched her walk over and sit in the other arm chair angled across from him.

She tucked her legs underneath her in the comfy chair and met his eyes. She frowned at his statement.

"Is that why you said that?"

"Said what?" He asked amused.

Tyg sniffed and one side of her mouth twitched in a smirk. "And you call me sneaky and manipulative."

Leviathan shrugged as he chuckled. "Whatever keeps you where I know exactly where you are?"

Tyg continued to frown at him but said nothing.

"So, what can I help you with, my dear?" Leviathan asked. He was in a good mood Tyg thought. After last night's events she thought he wouldn't be. She wondered what was happening to the guy they caught from the Squad attack. She hoped she didn't know him. Tyg was so deep in thought she hadn't even noticed his term of endearment.

"Tyg?" Leviathan prompted her out of her thoughts.

"Yes, what? Oh, I was just wondering when you all leave what happens to this house?"

Leviathan shrugged. "I sell it."

"Sell it?"

"Well, it's not like I'm going to need it and this trip is already causing me to haemorrhage money."

"So Lord Karon's not coming back?"

"No, once he's finished in Landau he intends to retire to some place called the Paradise Isles." Leviathan got up and went over to the drinks trolley and poured himself a whisky and one for Tyg.

"Why do you ask?" He said as he stood over her holding the glass out. Tyg took it with a smile and balanced it on the arm of the chair with one hand as Leviathan sat down again.

"The staff are wanting to know."

"Your friends are wanting to know, you mean."

"I won't leave them jobless, not after everything..." Tyg stopped and changed tact. "How much do you want for it?"

Leviathan raised his eyebrows. "Why? You think you can afford it?"

"Hardly." Tyg sneered as she stared at the whisky glass, swirling it round.

"I really can't keep it, Tyg, I'm sorry." Leviathan said causing Tyg to lift her eyes to his, had he ever said sorry to anyone? She wondered. "The costs of running a place I will never return to, it's not feasible."

"I know..." Tyg muttered. "I just hoped...I'll have to come up with something else."

Leviathan watched her, he could see the wheels turning in her mind as she sought to come up with a solution. She really did have a clever mind and he found himself forever intrigued with what she would come up with next. She was definitely someone who thrived with keeping their mind busy and she seemed to love taking on these pity parties and trying to make everyone happy all the time, usually at the expense of her own happiness, he mused.

"Sometimes you have to just let people live their own lives and sort things out for themselves, Tygarya. You can't fix every situation for others otherwise they come to expect it and end up doing nothing for themselves."

Tyg had gone back to swirling the whisky in the glass. She sighed and then took a large sip. "I know, but I owe it to them, I dragged them over here in the first place."

"Because we needed staff, not because you promised them a better life or anything more."

"Perhaps, but they're my friends."

Leviathan snorted. "Friends! That's why friends are a waste of time and energy."

Tyg looked up at him surprised. "You don't have any friends?"

"I have enough hangers-on and enough people to be responsible for, let alone having *friends* hanging around mooching off me."

"Friends don't mooch." Tyg said shocked.

"Really? Seems all you've done for these people is lift them up out of the gutters and whorehouses, have you not?"

"What's wrong with that?"

"Now, they expect more..." Leviathan snorted. "...and will expect more...they wouldn't have moved out of their dreary lives on their own."

Tyg fell silent. Was he right? She did reconnect with Dane only days ago and found him still working for Barion in the Hut. If she hadn't met up with him again he would definitely still be there. Leviathan was watching her amused as she glanced up at him.

"Well, I still don't agree with you." She said quietly then drank some more whisky. "Also, Tess needs to go to the city proper."

"Really?" Leviathan raised an eyebrow. "What for?"

"To collect the rest of my things from home, so she'll need a cart and some help. She also wants to buy some fabric and stuff, she's a dressmaker."

"Your dressmaker?" Leviathan grinned as he remembered Tyg in the white dress. "You should wear dresses more often."

"Not very practical, but yes she is. She says she's working on a surprise for my birthday."

"Your birthday!" Leviathan sat up and Tyg rolled her eyes grimacing.

"Well, you're the one to blame for that, getting my documents from the orphanage."

"Quite." Leviathan rubbed his chin. "Okay, I will arrange it."

"Thank you." Tyg said and took another mouthful of whisky. "There's one more thing."

"Only one?" He chuckled.

"For now." Tyg grinned, she actually enjoyed conversing with Leviathan like this, it was normal. "I am wanting to bathe, so if you can please ensure no one..." Tyg saw the smile creeping across Leviathan's face. "...NO ONE! Comes near the bathhouse while I'm in there, it would be much appreciated."

"Of course...although the image that puts in my mind is going to keep me distracted for the rest of the day." Leviathan was grinning widely now. "You will like the castle back home, we have a bathhouse in the lower levels, fed by a natural hot spring."

"Wow!" Tyg was stunned.

"And we have internal plumbing."

"What's that?"

"Running water...everything inside. Plus the hot spring actually heats the castle in the winter. I'm not above saying that we are far more advanced back home than here."

"Okay, so now I'm impressed." Tyg said with a smile. Leviathan grinned back proudly causing Tyg to screw her face up at him. Leviathan laughed as she downed the last of her whisky, put it on the side table and stood up.

Leviathan stood up at the exact same moment and caught her up in his arms. One of his hands going to the middle of her back and the other around the back of her neck as he tilted her head back and kissed her, twining his fingers into her hair. Her hands were on his chest and she could feel the defined muscles. She remembered the day she saw his chest when he was coming across the lawn changing his shirt. She was going to have to admit to herself sooner or later that she was definitely physically attracted to this Adonis of a man, and she definitely enjoyed kissing him. It was just way too complicated between them right now with everything going on with Palin.

She tried pushing away, finally breaking off the kiss and getting her breath.

"You really enjoy springing that on me, don't you?"

Leviathan smiled as he held her still, not letting her go yet. His forehead bowed and pressed against hers. "You don't fight it and I know you're more than capable of it, besides it's the first chance I've even had today." He chuckled as he put a finger under her chin and raised her mouth back to his.

They heard the jingle of armour and a coughing sound from the doorway. Leviathan dropped Tyg's chin and looked up over her head. Tyg heard a slight growl in his throat at his annoyance.

"My Liege, the horses are ready." It was Corvyn's voice.

Tyg turned to face him. "What's this?"

"Nothing." Leviathan said, tightening his arm around her, his hand now on her stomach as he pressed her back against his chest. Tyg wasn't sure if he was holding her protectively or offensively from Corvyn. "I'm heading to the docks to sort ships."

"You don't own ships?"

"No, I've never had use of my own ships before and probably won't again so I'm commissioning some sea captains, like the ones who brought us here, to take the ore." Leviathan said as he breathed deliberately on her neck and ear making her shiver. He looked up at Corvyn. "We'll need to take a horse and cart and an extra soldier with us along with the maid Tess, she has to collect the rest of Tygarya's things from that house and she's got a couple of errands as well I have approved. Organise that and let me know when you're ready."

Corvyn hadn't taken his eyes off Tyg the whole time Leviathan was talking to him, but he clipped his heels and bowed his head. "Yes, my Liege." He answered, pivoted on his heels and left the room.

"I'm really going to have to start locking doors." Leviathan breathed on her neck again as he nuzzled into her hair. "I love your hair down and it always smells divine." He said as he inhaled deeply.

He grabbed her hair and pulled it aside and kissed her neck, trailing his tongue up towards her ear.

Tyg pulled away out of his grasp and turned to face him. He could see she was blushing.

"Too much..." She breathed.

"Fair enough, I understand." Leviathan said straightening up, although she could see his eyes had gone dark. He was used to getting what he wanted, she figured that included women.

"It's only been days since meeting each other, this is really intense." Tyg explained, but she stepped into him and put her arms around his waist laying her head on his chest. He looked down on her surprised by the action then smiled and wrapped his arms around her, resting his cheek on top of her head, as he was easily a foot taller than her. He had to keep reminding himself she was only eighteen, although she acted far older than her years.

"Okay, slow then." He muttered, smiling to himself. "But, don't think I didn't notice Corvyn only had eyes for you just now."

"What?" Tyg said incredulously as she tried to push away, but Leviathan held her tight. He was extremely strong more than a match for her. She knew why Corvyn was staring at her, so did Leviathan, and it wasn't for that reason.

"It's alright, it seems you steal every young man's heart."

"What do you mean by that?" Tyg suddenly felt like she was suffocating and tried again to push away. This time he let her, but kept hold of her hand and played with her hair with the other.

"You just have a way about you Tygarya." Leviathan chuckled. "Don't be offended, I'm not going to take it out of Corvyn's hide...although I should..."

"No, you shouldn't."

"...it is something I need to adjust to, I know you are mostly unaware of it."

Tyg stared at him. "Who else?"

"Hmm?" He said distractedly, lifting her hair to his face.

"You're being evasive." Tyg growled.

"Am I?" Leviathan grinned like the devil.

"You can't say things like that implying something and then not expand on it."

"Can't I?"

"No, you can't. What did you mean every young man's heart, who else?"

"Who else indeed." Leviathan said cryptically as he looked into her eyes. She noticed his eyes darken again. She gasped as she suddenly realised what he meant. He grinned viciously as she stepped backwards away from him until she hit the armchair and fell back into it. She looked up at his face as he stepped over and put his hands on the arms of the chair and leaned over her. That vulture gaze hard in his eyes as he crowded over her with his dominance, his mood swiftly changing to dangerous levels. Tyg held her breath, she couldn't get a clear footing with him, Leviathan was so mercurial and hard to read.

"Have you guessed, my dear?" Leviathan whispered, his eyes looking into hers. "Have you guessed which young man is ready to die for you?"

Tyg's mouth went dry and she croaked. "The Squad..."

"Indeed." Leviathan's voice had turned cold. He watched her battling back tears.

"Fuck...I know him?"

"I don't know, but he knows you...and won't give up any information on your Boss...but he will or he will die."

"No..." Tyg breathed.

"So tell me his name, save the young man's life."

Tyg looked at Leviathan in horror. "I can't...he can't...we took an Oath."

Leviathan stood up straightening the cuffs of his shirt. "Then he dies...slowly...and brutally."

Tears fell down Tyg's cheeks, another death caused because of her. She buried her face in her hands as Leviathan walked off and closed the door behind him.

56

Tyg got up and raced after Leviathan, banging the door open. Leviathan stopped and turned surprised.

"I want to see him." Tyg demanded her eyes blazing.

Leviathan looked shocked. "No." He said calmly and turned away.

Tyg looked at the doors leading to outside, she guessed they were probably keeping him somewhere over where the soldiers had their tents. She glanced back at Leviathan's back as he was walking away, then bolted for the doors. Yanking them open she ran outside. Her plan was to run to the encampment and find which tent they were holding him in. But, as soon as she stepped through the doors she found she couldn't move. All her muscles were screaming at her as she tried to move them but it was like they were bound in stone.

"Tygarya, stop resisting and calm down." Leviathan said as he stepped around her and looked at her face. So it was him using magic on her again! Tyg took a deep breath and calmed herself. She suddenly collapsed to her hands and knees as Leviathan let her go.

"How..." Tyg said getting her breath. "How fucking dare you!" She breathed as she came quickly to her feet, dagger in hand and launched herself at him. He calmly looked at her as he flicked his wrist almost unperceptively and she went flying backwards across the floor. Pain suddenly exploded in her head and she dropped the dagger, grabbing both sides of her head as she grit her teeth against the immense pain.

"Emperor! Stop! I beg of you!" A voice called out.

The pain immediately stopped and Tyg looked up to see Leviathan standing over her. Corvyn standing beside him. Leviathan's vulture gaze was blazing as he stared at her. It had been Corvyn returning that had saved her.

Tyg lifted a hand to her face, it came away red, her nose was bleeding. She went to stand up and Corvyn came over to help her.

"Get the fuck away from me!" Tyg growled at him. Corvyn looked hard at her and pressed his lips together but stepped away as Tyg stood up on her own. Corvyn was surprised she wasn't injured more. Leviathan was standing with his arms folded and smiling at her tenacity.

Tyg chuckled, which caused Corvyn to baulk at the sound and Leviathan to raise an eyebrow.

"So, finally I find out what all the fuss is about?"

Leviathan snorted. "Fuss?"

"Why everyone keeps telling me to just toe the line, do what you ask."

"Hmm." Leviathan grunted. "You still won't though, will you?" He asked, an amused grin spreading across his face, he was almost hoping she would say no.

"I've been hurt worse." Tyg said calmly, rearranging and smoothing her hair. Leviathan looked shocked, then narrowed his eyes.

"You have the Captain to thank for that." Leviathan muttered as he glanced at Corvyn, who dutifully looked at his feet and said nothing. "It's normally my brother that stays my hand when I get angry, but he's not here, so you're lucky Captain Corvyn came when he did, young lady, even after you wanted to kill him last night."

Tyg met Leviathan's gaze, she was faking it and he knew it. The pain she had felt in her head was indescribable and to think he would have let her continue to suffer that...

"Don't raise a weapon at me, Tygarya, I already warned you once remember?"

Tyg grinned. "How could I forget...I...?" Tyg suddenly didn't feel well, she felt like she was drifting.

Tyg came to in Leviathan's arms, he had caught her as she had collapsed in a faint. The concern on his face was the polar opposite of just a few minutes ago. She looked around. He was carrying her into the library so she hadn't been out for long. He looked down at her and smiled. She was so confused. Hadn't he just tried to kill her?

"Put me down." Tyg croaked, her mouth dry.

"I am, just wait." Leviathan lay her down on the couch and kneeled next to her.

Tyg noticed Tess was standing behind him, a glass of water in her hand which Leviathan took and handed to Tyg.

"Tess says you haven't been eating?"

Tyg sat up and took the water, taking a sip to moisten her dry mouth. "I'm not able to eat."

"You must." Leviathan said it in that low commanding voice.

"Why must I? I was nearly dead a few minutes ago. You were going to kill me, so what do you care?"

Leviathan's eyes went wide and he stood up. His jaw clenched and he sighed wiping a hand over his face. "I wouldn't have."

"Really? Might take a bit more convincing of that one?" Tyg sneered.

Leviathan gave her a look then that perplexed her. He turned and left the room. "Take care of her and don't let her out of your sight." Leviathan ordered.

It was then that Tyg noticed Corvyn was standing by the doors, he didn't look at all happy with the order.

"Great!" Tyg muttered as Tess started fussing over her. "Stop, Tess, I'm fine."

"Fine!" Tess said surprised. "Hardly, look at you."

Tyg realised, as she felt the tightness of the dried blood on her face that she must look a fright.

"It's nothing, I'm fine." Tyg said again as she remembered the excruciating pain in her head that had caused her nose to start bleeding. She almost felt faint again thinking about the power Leviathan wielded against her.

"Go get her some food, she needs to eat." Corvyn ordered as he came over and sat down heavily, running a hand through his hair, in the arm chair next to her. Tess curtsied at Corvyn and hurried away.

"Just shut up, Corvyn, I don't need to hear it." Tyg growled at him before he could start telling her off again.

"You must have a bloody death wish." Corvyn muttered as he put Tyg's dagger on the table.

"What of it? What do you care? What are you anyway?"

Corvyn smiled faintly. "I'm an officer in the Tylandrian Army, Special Royal Guard."

"You know what I mean." Tyg sneered at him.

"That's classified." Corvyn said simply. "Enough with the questions."

"Why, what's wrong with questions?"

"I know the reason *you* ask questions is to store the answers away to use them to some advantage, you're very calculating and like people have said before, sneaky."

"Rubbish, there's nothing wrong with trying to know all you can about the situation you're in...it's called survival."

Corvyn regarded her a moment. "Is that why you read all these books as well? Trying to find some advantage by reading fairy tales?" Corvyn chuckled to himself.

Tyg's expression went flat. "Knowledge is power, Corvyn, I would have thought you would have known that?"

Corvyn stopped chuckling and stared at her. "Stop it, Tygarya." He raked a hand through his hair. "Gods, I can't wait for Lord Anytn to get back."

Tyg looked at him with an odd expression, as Corvyn glanced at her. "Fuck's sake, why do I always find myself talking to you?"

Tyg smiled and looked at a cushion, grabbing it, she hugged her arms around it. "Maybe you just need to talk?"

Corvyn scowled at her and stood up. "Well, this conversation is over."

"But, where are you going? You can't leave...remember?"

Corvyn grimaced. "Damn it, why me?" He rolled his eyes and went over to the desk that was against the wall. He sat down over there and put his booted feet up on the desk with his back to Tyg.

"You know exactly why you." Tyg said.

"Stop." Corvyn growled.

Neeki came in then and Tyg noticed there was a soldier stationed outside the door that let her in. She brought some food and more water in a bowl with a cloth for Tyg to clean the blood off her face.

"Tess has gone into the city." She mumbled, that meant Leviathan had gone too. She put it all on the low table in front of Tyg, curtsied and almost ran out the door. Tyg glanced at Corvyn who had turned slightly to watch, he was looking very amused.

"What's so funny?" She asked as she shuffled forward and dipped the cloth into the water and wiped her face, she looked at him when he didn't answer.

"Seems it's your turn to terrify the staff." Corvyn laughed to himself.

"Oh, yeah, very fucking funny." Tyg chucked the cloth at him, he ducked and avoided it as it hit the desk. He laughed harder. Tyg smiled in spite of herself and grabbed a piece of apple off the plate of food and sat back further into the couch again.

"You can go back to your room if you want?" Corvyn said then.

"You can't keep an eye on me in my room." Tyg sneered.

"True enough, but I can lock you in."

"Fuck you." Tyg muttered as she lay down and started reading a book. Corvyn just laughed and stood up, and started looking around the books on the shelves.

57

After an hour Tyg threw her book down and stretched out. "This is so boring, there's only so much reading I can do." She sat up and looked at Corvyn. "What are you reading?"

Corvyn had his feet back up on the desk. "Stories about Vampires and Werewolves, they are hilarious."

"Hilarious? They're supposed to be scary."

Corvyn snorted. "Hardly."

"Not for someone like you I guess?" Tyg said slyly.

Corvyn put the book down and swung his legs off the desk onto the floor and stood up. "Stop fishing for information, it's tiresome." He took a pocket watch out and looked at the time.

"You have a pocket watch?' Tyg asked surprised.

"Of course, how else do I know when my shift is over?" Corvyn said amused. "Come on, you can do my rounds with me, since the Emperor isn't back yet."

"Fuck, how boring." Tyg grumbled as she got up.

"At least you'll get to stretch your legs and get some fresh air...put a coat on though."

"A coat? Why?"

"Can't you just do something someone asks you to do, please?"

"Sure, but it's upstairs."

"Fine, let's go then." Corvyn rolled his eyes and raked his hand through his hair.

When Tyg entered her room she was surprised to see the balcony doors had been chained and padlocked shut, from the outside and there was a soldier standing outside on the balcony.

"What the fuck is that all about?" Tyg turned to Corvyn as he stood in the doorway. "Am I officially a prisoner now?"

"No, but you've proven to be a rather dangerous commodity."

"Really?" Tyg said caustically.

"Well, you have tried to attack me twice and even tried to attack the Emperor, so, yes."

Tyg grinned viciously causing Corvyn to frown. "It's no joke, Tygarya. Back home you would be executed for that."

"I wasn't ever joking, Corvyn." Tyg said in a deadly voice as she grabbed a thick woollen coat with buttons up the front, off the chest in her room.

"That's our concern." Corvyn muttered back darkly. She grabbed her hair and put it up in a ponytail, then put the coat on, stuffing her hands in the pockets. Corvyn was hoping putting on a coat would detract from her looks, but it didn't and the ponytail just made her eyes look huge. Corvyn wiped a hand over his face, it was stupid to feel jealous of the Emperor when he clearly knew the Emperor was probably the only man in the world who could handle this young woman – that radiated power like a bonfire.

"Ready?" He asked.

"Yes, if I have to?"

"You can just stay here?" Corvyn said hopefully.

Tyg laughed as she walked past him, patting his cheek. "Not a chance."

Corvyn's knees almost buckled and he shook his head and grumbled, then turned and followed her down the stairs, passing the soldier that was following them everywhere. He growled at him as the soldier was clearly finding this all very amusing.

"So when is Antyn due back?" Tyg asked as she wandered along next to Corvyn as he walked the perimeter of the property checking his soldiers were all alert and doing their jobs.

Corvyn shrugged. "Couple of days at least."

"Hmm." Tyg muttered as she picked a flower from a garden as they passed it and sniffed it. "Where's the other Captain?"

"Asleep no doubt."

"Asleep?"

"It's his regiment that does the night shift."

"Oh. I see...that's why you're always stuck with me?" Tyg guessed. "Cause you can speak our language, your soldiers can't, not very well.

"Knock it off, Tygarya." Corvyn growled. "Just enjoy the walk."

Tyg chuckled. "You call me 'my Lady' when Leviathan is around, but Tygarya when he isn't, why not just call me Tyg and be done with it?"

"Because it wouldn't be proper."

"What's proper got to do with what you call me, if I'm telling you...?"

Corvyn stopped and looked at her. "Because shortened names, nicknames etcetera are for people close to you...friends, family, lovers..." Corvyn's voice caught in his throat. Tyg actually giggled, hiding her mouth behind the flower. Corvyn coughed and started walking again. "Are you here on earth just to torment me?" He shook his head disdainfully.

"What a horrid thing to say?" Tyg teased, laughing, she saw him squeeze his eyes shut and clenched his jaw at the sound. "I don't seriously torment you, do I?"

"You have no idea." He muttered.

Tyg just laughed again, the fresh air had lifted her mood considerably, but then she stopped dead in her tracks and stared at the ground. Corvyn stopped and turned as Tyg crouched down and placed her hand on the earth.

"Fuck." Corvyn groaned as he stepped over to Tyg. "Leave it be, Tygarya, for fuck's sake."

Tyg was looking at a patch of blood on the grass. She stood up and searched the ground finding another one, she stepped over to it and crouched. Corvyn bit his lip as he saw her eyes glowing and the power in her was building.

"This was a mistake, I think we should go back."

Tyg moved again, Corvyn wondered how she was even seeing it all. She stood up and turned to him.

"How many died?"

"What?"

"How many died?"

"Four." Corvyn replied nervous where this was going.

"Four? So, two soldiers died too?" Tyg asked, she had already learnt that they had let one assassin go to tell of what happened.

"Yes."

Tyg pressed her lips together and looked around.

"Tygarya, don't be stupid." Corvyn put his hand in the air and made a series of those obscure gestures. The soldier that was following plus two others from the sentry posts all drew their swords and circled her. Tyg glanced around her, stuffed her hands in her pockets and smiled at Corvyn.

"Seems we're even."

"What?" Corvyn said confused.

"Two for two." Tyg explained, her eyes blazing at him. He looked at her then remembered what she had said when Leviathan had held her back. His eyes started glowing as well as he started to get angry at her. "My two are on me, I acknowledge that, but your two are on you...you should have told me, Corvyn, I could have prevented it all." Tyg walked past him heading back to the house. "You should have warned me instead of trying to teach me some sort of fucking moral lesson." She muttered to him as she past.

Corvyn looked after her, his mood darkening as he saw Leviathan's quick rise to violence in her as well, from zero to a hundred in seconds. He calmed himself and followed her back to the house as the soldiers sheathed their weapons. "Gods, help us if these two actually get together for real, they'll bring the fucking world down around us with just their love spats." He muttered to himself as he raked a hand through his hair. He was just thankful she hadn't been armed just now.

When they got to the house, much to the relief of Corvyn, Tyg went to her room and slammed the door shut.

58

When her door opened an hour later, Tyg froze. She had been doing crunches on the floor at the end of the bed which was facing the door. There was only one person who opened her door without knocking. She rested her head back on her hands and looked over.

"What the fuck is this?" Leviathan demanded, holding up a small wicker basket. He looked shocked at seeing Tyg on the floor but was even more shocked when she scampered over on all fours and knelt before him. He settled a very amused but alluring look on her.

"Puddy!" Tyg exclaimed, completely oblivious, as she opened the basket and pulled her cat out of it, hugging the tabby cat and kissing its head.

Leviathan was still staring down at her on her knees. He smiled wily, still smouldering and leaned against the doorframe crossing his feet the same as before.

"Well, this is new!" He chuckled to himself.

"What you've never seen a cat before?" Tyg looked up at him. She realised leaning diagonally across the doorframe was actually the only way Leviathan could fit.

"Yes, we have plenty of cats running around at home, that's not what I meant." He scratched his chin as he continued to smile to himself at her innocence.

Tyg frowned confused, but stood up and walked back to the bed, depositing the cat on it. Then she walked back to Leviathan and grabbed the cage. She stopped suddenly as she reached for it.

Her eyes went wide and she bit her lip, Leviathan was sure she even blushed a little. He chuckled.

"Oh! I get it...me on my knees before you....rude!" Tyg sneered and wrenched the cage from his hand and skipped and pirouetted away as Leviathan tried to grab her. "Ha! Not this time." She grinned self-congratulatory.

Leviathan smiled and folded his arms. "So, you send us all the way to the house for a cat?"

"Not all...you were passing anyway...and other stuff...where's the other stuff?"

"Oh, it's here..." Leviathan stepped back out of the doorway and two soldiers, each carry a chest, came in and deposited them on the floor, bowed and left.

"Thank you." Tyg said to them.

"So, does this mean you're coming with me?" Leviathan asked as he leaned in the doorway again.

"What? Where?"

Leviathan just looked at her with a deadpanned expression.

"Oh, there...well, you seem hell bent on destroying any possibility of me being able to remain living here..." Tyg muttered bitterly.

"What does that mean?" Leviathan growled.

"You know what it means..."

Leviathan rubbed his chin again and looked around the room. "Why are your drapes closed?"

"Bloody Corvyn, that's why." Tyg said as she went over and opened one to reveal the padlock and the soldier standing on the balcony. She let the drape drop back. Leviathan laughed.

"Congrats to him...yes, I heard you've been annoying my Captain again." Leviathan grumbled. "You really need to leave the poor man alone."

"Well, that's a bit hard when he keeps getting in my way...and that's your fault."

Tyg sat on the end of the bed and folded her arms.

"Back on this track again, Tygarya? It's getting boring." Leviathan growled.

"The little snitch, I can't believe he keeps telling you everything..." Tyg sulked.

"He's doing his fucking job, Tygarya, grow up!" He growled deeply.

Tyg looked at Leviathan shocked for a moment then blinked and downcast her eyes. "Still doesn't mean I have to like it."

"Fuck's sake, Tyg. I came to ask you something."

Tyg looked up at him shortening her name again. "Really? Okay..."

"Tell me what to do?"

"What to do?"

"To fix this stalemate, I don't want to be ambushed every time I go to the docks."

"What! What happened?" Tyg stood up. He was glad she looked surprised.

"Nothing, but I was expecting it."

"Oh...you were testing me...that's nice." Tyg said bitterly and sat down again.

"Tygarya, we need to sort this out."

"No, WE don't...I do...and I can if you would just let me."

"We're just going round in circles." Leviathan said fatigued and stood up turning away, he took a step to leave.

"So the assassin isn't forth coming then? Is he still alive?"

Leviathan turned thinking she was being smug and coy, but instead he found her hugging the cat with her head down actually looking miserable.

"Why do you ask if the answer will only upset you?"

Tyg shrugged. "Because I need to know."

"I don't think you do. Have you eaten anything yet?"

Tyg flinched which was a certain no to Leviathan. "I had some fruit...but don't change the subject."

"Yes, he's still hanging in there."

Tyg flinched again and squeezed her eyes shut. "Please, just kill him, I can't bare it"

She looked up at him then, imploring him with her eyes. Leviathan clenched his jaw and curled his fists. "Just tell me the name."

Tyg blinked and looked back down again. Leviathan growled in frustration and stormed off slamming the door.

Tyg got up and opened the door. "Okay!" She yelled at him.

Leviathan froze and pivoted around. "Okay what?" He regarded her with that vulture gaze.

Tyg chewed her lip as he stalked back to stand directly in front of her. "Okay what, Tygarya?" He growled.

Tyg looked at the floor. "If you let me see the assassin, I'll tell you what you want to know."

Leviathan grabbed her chin and lifted it. "Look at me!" Tyg lifted her eyes to his, his were glowing. "Say it again!"

"Let me see the assassin and I'll tell you my Boss's name and where to find him."

Leviathan dropped her chin and stepped away from her, his eyes did not leave her face however and Tyg stood in the doorway calmly looking back.

"Why now? All of a sudden?"

Tyg blinked and looked down. "I want his misery and suffering to end, I can't bare it anymore! Knowing he's out there because of me."

"That's why you won't eat?"

"I can't eat! I feel sick." Tyg groaned. "Sick with guilt." Tyg looked back up at Leviathan. He hadn't moved and hadn't taken his eyes off of her. "Please, Leviathan, I beg of you."

Leviathan growled and his eyes blazed. "Damn you, woman!" He said as he turned and stormed off.

Tyg screamed at him and went to follow but the soldiers stood in the way. "Leviathan! Please!"

Tyg hung her head and went back in her room and closed the door. As soon as she was out of sight she smiled. She went to one of her chests and grabbed one of her throwing daggers out of it, and playing it over and under her hand and spinning it through her fingers, she went to the bed and petted the cat with the other hand, very happy with her performance.

59

It was the next morning before her door flew open again.
Leviathan startled, as he seemed to every time he came to her
room. This time she was on the bed, lying on her stomach, her legs
bent from the knee with her feet in the air, her ankles crossed and
her head resting on the palm of one hand, her long braid hooked
over her shoulder, as she was tickling the cat's stomach with it as the
cat lounged on its back, purring audibly.

"Gods Tyg, I've never wanted to be a cat more in my entire
life!" Leviathan breathed.

Tyg was looking up at him through her long lashes, she noticed
Corvyn was behind him as well as another two soldiers. She smiled
at him, just like the cat was smiling, he thought. But she made no
move to change her position. Instead she started swinging her feet
back and forth and smiled at him wider. Corvyn turned away and
shoved the soldiers back from view. Leviathan squeezed his eyes
shut and shook his head. He levelled a dark smoulder at her.

"I know I said I wouldn't enter your room, so don't *make* me!"
Leviathan growled.

"Oh, fine." Tyg huffed as she sat up. 'Distraction affective.' She
thought. "What can I help you with?"

"You wanted to go see your friend?"

"What?" Tyg said surprised. "Are you serious?"

"No, I think I'm a fool making a huge mistake, but anyway..."

Tyg got up and grabbed the same coat she was wearing
yesterday. It was starting to get cold with winter round the corner
and frosts had started to form on the grass at sunrise.

"Hang on!" Leviathan grabbed the coat and checked the pockets, then handed it back to her as he glanced down at her, not seeing any weapons he let her continue out into the hall as she smiled and put the coat on. Tyg smiled at Corvyn, who was frowning at her as he turned and led the way down the stairs.

Leviathan put his arm around her shoulders. "You stay with me, got it? Any stupid heroic behaviour and I will not be responsible for the outcome."

"Sure thing." Tyg said as she put her hand inside his unbuttoned coat and wrapped her arm around his torso. She looked up at him. He was smiling down on her, but his eyes were in conflict.

As they crossed the main room Tyg stopped. "Hang on." She said and hurried over to where there was a bottle of red wine, grabbed it and pulled the cork out. She drank it back like it was water.

"Tygarya!" Leviathan growled. She lowered the bottle, now half empty and wiped her mouth with her hand.

"Okay, I'm ready now." She said smiling as she walked back to Leviathan. Corvyn, she noticed, was standing with his thumbs in his belt, smiling and shaking his head. Leviathan looked at her and reached out and wiped a drop of wine from her chin with his thumb, then grabbed her shoulder and pulled her into him.

"Come on!"

They walked across the lawns out to the soldier's tent encampment. They walked briskly through it towards the back. One tent caught Tyg's attention as it was the only one with soldiers posted around it guarding something inside and the posts were of a solid beam construction. To take the weight of someone hanging, Tyg mused bitterly. Tyg was surprised to see the other Captain was there waiting for them. As they approached he straightened and bowed his head. "My Liege." He said in a clear crisp voice.

"So, he survived the night?" Leviathan asked.

"Yes, My Liege, he is very strong of will."

Tyg grit her teeth and tensed, Leviathan felt it and tightened his grip on her. "Don't." Was all he said as the Captain made a gesture and one of the soldiers standing by the opening pulled back the flap as he bowed his head.

Leviathan went in with Tyg firmly in his grasp, followed by Corvyn and the other Captain. Leviathan ran his hand down her arm and moved it to her stomach as he pulled her in front of him and held her firmly.

"Take a good look, this is as close as you get."

Tyg gasped, she had seen tortured men before, but this guy seemed to be completely covered in blood. In the smoky light of the torches it was hard to see, Leviathan was keeping her a good ten yards away from the wretched figure that was strung up by his wrists. No wait, not strung up, hooked up. Tyg could see he had a butcher's hook through his wrists. Tyg ground her teeth. Corvyn and the other Captain had gone around Leviathan and her and were standing on either side of the tent about five yards from her on either side. Both were watching her, as Tyg's eyes started to glow. Corvyn coughed causing Leviathan to tighten his grip and bring his other arm around her.

"Tyg, don't be stupid." Leviathan growled in her ear.

At the mention of her name the figure stirred and their head lifted. Tyg went numb and felt like she was going to be sick. She suddenly realised the man wasn't just covered in blood, he had been skinned. She started shaking.

"Tyg..." The man groaned as he saw her.

Tyg shook her head. "I don't know you..."

He coughed which seemed to cause him excruciating pain. "Matters not..." He croaked.

"Enough of this!" Leviathan said. "Tell me what I want and I'll have Captain Eskel here, kill him fast."

Tyg's eyes went black and she snarled showing her teeth.

"My Liege!" Corvyn called out, causing Leviathan to react instantly and turned Tyg away from the man and face him by grabbing her shoulders. She could feel his power holding her still. She stared at him. He studied her face for a moment, gauging how far gone she was.

"Fuck, Tyg. I warned you!"

Tyg raised a hand to her neck, rubbing it as she stared at Leviathan. "And, I told you, I took an Oath!" Tyg growled, sounding like an animal. She broke through Leviathan's power hold on her and turned, taking the throwing dagger out of her braid and throwing it all in one fluid motion – those two seconds was all she needed, she grinned.

But then she found herself flung sideways, crashing to the ground, then lifted up off her feet, her back slammed into one of the large wooden beams supporting the tent. It felt like a hand was around her throat but no one was touching her. Leviathan, however, was standing directly in front of her, looking up at her as he choked her with his power.

"You fucking stupid bitch!" He yelled. Corvyn had run to the assassin. He looked up with a sick expression.

"He's dead, she got him right in the eye."

"Fuck!" Leviathan growled as he stared at her. Her eyes were still black and she felt nothing, she laughed as she choked.

"I was aiming for his heart."

That made Leviathan lose his mind and Tyg saw his eyes go golden green like a dragon's. He dropped her to the ground and sent her flying over to the other side of the tent, crashing into the table of torture implements, sending everything flying. Then he stepped over to her and grabbed her by her braid.

"I should have your fucking hair cut off!" He picked her up by her hair and looked at her, she looked back and smiled. He dropped her then and suddenly the pain in her head ignited as she grabbed the sides of her head and grit her teeth, she was curled up on her knees. Leviathan kicked her over onto her side and crouched down as she was trying hard not to scream from the pain.

"I should have known you weren't going to tell me, but I'm more irate at the fact that you did finally deceive me with this whole plan of yours." The pain increased and Tyg had no choice but to scream out in pain as her body just did it with no thought from her. She could feel the copper taste of blood in her throat and knew her nose was bleeding again.

"Tell me his name, Tygarya and I'll stop this." Leviathan's voice was cold and empty.

Tyg was screaming again as she curled into a tight ball. Corvyn had come over and was standing beside Leviathan. He clenched his jaw at the sight and against protocols he placed a hand on Leviathan's shoulder. He was sent flying backwards, but he got to his feet again and shouted at Leviathan.

"You're killing her, Emperor! Blood is coming out of her ears! Stop! You told me to tell you..."

Corvyn reached him again and stepped in front of Leviathan, kneeling over Tyg sheltering her. "You told me to tell you if you went too far. Stop! I beg of you, my Liege! Stop!"

Leviathan blinked and Tyg stopped screaming. Leviathan stood up and stepped away, his eyes guttering out and returning to blue. "I am a fucking fool." Leviathan muttered and staggered from the tent.

Corvyn looked at Tyg. She was unconscious. He lifted her up, surprised at how little she weighed and carried her out.

Halfway back to the house Tyg's eyes flickered open. Corvyn was relieved to see the pretty sky blue colour of them.

"Put me down." Tyg breathed.

"I don't think so."

"I'm going to be sick, put me down!" Corvyn stopped and lowered her to the grass, she got on all fours and wretched. She sat back on her legs, her hand going to her head. Then she dry wretched again. With her stomach being empty for a couple of days there wasn't anything to vomit. She spat bile on the grass and sat up again.

"How are you even awake?" Corvyn asked as he crouched next to her.

She looked at him and wiped her face of the blood and bile. "Help me up."

"I'll carry you."

"I don't need to be carried!" Tyg said doggedly. "I'm fine!"

"You should be fucking brain damaged." Corvyn said shocked.

"Well, I'm not." Tyg said as she staggered to her feet. Corvyn grabbed her arm and put it round his neck and helped her walk the rest of the way to the house.

"You seriously are trying to get yourself killed."

"No, just stop a man's suffering at my expense." Tyg chuckled, but then coughed and wretched again as Corvyn held her.

"You must have known what your actions would cause?" Corvyn was completely perplexed by her.

"To me it was worth it."

"You're insane!"

"Maybe..." Tyg admitted as they reached the house. Tyg pushed Corvyn away and grabbed the door frame. Corvyn watched completely dumbfounded as Tyg staggered off towards the back of the house.

"Where the fuck are you going?"

Tyg stopped, turned and smiled. "I'm suddenly starving."

"What the fuck? What the hell are you? You shouldn't even be able to walk...in all theory you should be dead!" Corvyn growled.

Tyg squinted. "Please stop yelling at me, I heal fast is all, okay." Although she knew she was far from fine. Her eyes were blurry, her ears were squealing and she felt like she was on a boat in rough seas. Corvyn followed her to the kitchen where Neeki was starting to prepare the midday meal. She turned in horror.

"Milady, what's happened?" Neeki went to her and helped her sit down. Corvyn stood behind her chair.

"Nothing's happened." Tyg chuckled to herself. Corvyn baulked at her comment.

"Nothing! You call that nothing?"

Tyg pushed Neeki's hands away from her face. "Just get me some bread or something please."

Neeki rushed to the bench and started cutting slices off the fresh loaf she had baked that morning.

Tyg turned to Corvyn. "My hero...why did you do that?"

"He would have killed you...He spoke to me earlier, told me if things went south the only way to subdue you was to let him handle it. A stand up fight wasn't how to stop you." Corvyn sat down wiping his face. He stared at her in awe. "The Emperor must know you can take that power and it not kill you."

Tyg flinched. "I certainly hope not." Tyg muttered as Neeki put the bread in front of her with a glass of water and a wet cloth.

"What?"

"I don't want him thinking he can do that to me all the time." Tyg shivered at the thought.

"Fucking hell." Corvyn breathed as he got her meaning. "I'm really glad I'm not you."

Tyg snorted at that remark. "Please don't report it to him, Corvyn, I beg of you, he's going to figure it out eventually but..." She looked into his eyes

"No, Tygarya...I won't." Corvyn said as he looked back.

Tyg blinked and looked at her plate as she pulled bits off her bread and stuck them in her mouth. Corvyn blinked too and shook his head. He stared at her.

"Would you like anything, Captain?" Neeki asked him.

"No, thank you."

Tyg picked up the cloth and wiped her face, she was actually surprised at the amount of blood there was on the cloth, she looked down at her coat, saw it was covered. She struggled out of it and threw it on the floor.

"Neeki...can you draw me a bath? I was supposed to have one yesterday..."

"Sure, Milady."

"A bath? Seriously?" Corvyn asked as Tyg slumped her head onto her arms on the table.

"Shush, Corvyn." Tyg breathed then fell asleep.

Tyg woke no more than twenty minutes later to voices. She raised her head and looked around at the door. Corvyn was talking to one of his men in their language.

Tess was sitting beside her and someone had draped a blanket over her shoulders.

"Tyg!" Tess smiled. "How are you feeling?'

"Like my head has been trampled by a stampeding herd of horses." Tyg said but smiled.

"Well, you woke just at the right time, your bath is ready if you still want it?"

"I do, yes. Thank you."

"I took the liberty of going into your room and getting the oils you like."

Tyg looked at Tess. "Thanks." Tyg stood up causing Corvyn to spin round. Tyg levelled a flat look at him. "Settle, I'm going for a soak in a hot bath."

Tyg could hear a commotion going on upstairs. She looked at the ceiling, frowning.

"What's that?"

"That is his Imperial Majesty." Corvyn snorted, causing Tyg to look at him with an eyebrow raised.

"Why the contempt?"

"Seems you've really managed to get under his skin, he's been smashing stuff, yelling and cursing for the last half hour. He can't have much stuff left to break in that room he's locked himself in."

Tyg's eyes widened, then narrowed as she smiled. "Do you want me to go talk to him?"

Corvyn choked. "No!" He coughed. "No way, I suggest you just stay the hell out of his way for the next couple of days." He thought about it. "At least."

Tyg smile was weak. "I was joking, I have no intention of going near him."

"Good, don't scare me like that, you're so unpredictable, I seriously can't stand much more of this. Give me a straight forward battle any day." Tyg stepped over to him and placed a hand on his shoulder.

"I owe you one, Corvyn, thank you."

Corvyn was surprised. "Don't mention it." He looked down at the table with a strange look.

60

Tyg decided to not get out of bed the next day. She was trapped in her room anyway so what was the point. Tess brought her breakfast and Neeki did her usual chores and let the cat outside, so what else was there to do but lie in bed all day, besides she had a nauseating headache.

However, she was interrupted in her laziness in the early afternoon by a knock on the door.

"Who is it?"

"Captain Corvyn, my Lady." Corvyn said in a coarse whisper.

Tyg frowned at his formality. "What do you want? I'm still in bed."

"Can you come to the door?"

Tyg sighed and got up, wrapping a silk robe around herself. She heard the door unlock and she opened it. Corvyn immediately averted his eyes, coughing and shuffling awkwardly on his feet which made Tyg smirk.

"Why are you whispering?" She asked with a whisper of her own.

"Shush, I don't want to disturb the Emperor."

"What? Is still in his room too?"

"Yes." Corvyn's disapproving scowl was obvious.

"Wow, and he tells me to grow up. What's his problem? I thought he would be stomping around the place making himself feel better."

"Ah..." Corvyn said a bit stunned by her comment and surprised by how well she looked. No one would have guessed at all about yesterday's events looking at her now. "Well, I think he's a bit regretful about yesterday."

"Damn right he should be."

"However, he doesn't know that you're perfectly fine...obviously."

"Well, he knows I'm alive at least. So, I don't get what his problem is...I'm the one who should be sulking."

"He doesn't know if you're alive or dead...he hasn't been out and won't let anyone in to find out."

"He knows, trust me." Tyg said snarky.

"Okay? That was snarky...could you explain that to me, please?" Corvyn stuck his thumbs in his belt.

"He seems to be able to sense when I'm nearby. As we are actually just across the hall from each other it's a fair bet that he knows I'm alive."

"Oh, I see." Corvyn said understanding.

"Although..." Tyg said deep in thought.

Corvyn groaned. "Although what? No, wait...do I want to know this?"

"Depends on if you want your Emperor to come out of his room?" Tyg sneered.

"Okay smartarse, what's your theory?" Corvyn crossed his arms.

"Well, if he can sense when I'm close by then he'll probably have guessed I haven't left my room all day." Tyg looked at Corvyn like he should know what she meant.

"And?" He prompted.

"And, because I haven't left my room he won't know I'm okay will he? He probably thinks I'm laid up in bed injured or near death or something. Good for him!"

"Tygarya!" Corvyn hissed under his breath.

"What? He deserves to feel guilty about it." Tyg sneered "It makes me feel better."

Corvyn looked at her. "You're both acting like goddamn children, if you ask me...and he's old enough to know better."

Tyg laughed. "I bet you wouldn't say that to his face." Corvyn baulked. "Didn't think so. So what do you actually want?"

"Well, since the Emperor won't come out, I thought you might like to, since you are feeling better."

"You like my company?" Tyg smiled genuinely.

Corvyn flushed. "Just keeping you separate."

"So if he wasn't locked in his room I still would be?"

"Absolutely!" Corvyn folded his arms.

Tyg gave him a look to say she didn't believe it and smiled. "Okay, let me get dressed." Tyg closed the door.

After a few minutes she re-emerged dressed as usual but with her hair pulled back in a ponytail at the nape of her neck. Corvyn thought it made her look very sedate, which she was anything but.

"So, am I allowed to go outside?"

"Sure, with me."

"Of course, people will start thinking we're courting...." Corvyn coughed and flushed again as Tyg chuckled. "I wouldn't have it any other way." She said cryptically making Corvyn frown at her. "What the fuck is that noise?" Tyg had kept hearing a thud, smash, pause repeatedly all day.

Corvyn rolled his eyes. "It's the Emperor. I think he's smashing a vase against the wall over and over."

"Huh?"

"Putting it back together and re-smashing it..."

"Oh, he can do that?" Tyg caught Corvyn's expression. "Yes, of course he can...he's a Sorcerer." Tyg said snarky again.

"Yes, not something you like to remember is it?" Corvyn retorted savagely.

Tyg looked at him taken aback. "Wow, who's the snarky one now?"

Tyg looked down the hall at the door to Leviathan's room, which was the master suite of course, Lord Karon's old room.

"Tygarya..." Corvyn warned, looking at the faraway expression on her face.

"What? No harm no foul." Tyg walked down the hall as Corvyn whispered to her to come back.

She stopped at Leviathan's door and put her finger to her lips to shush Corvyn. He raked a hand through his hair, frustrated, as Tyg put an ear to the door.

It all went quiet which disappointed her slightly, she was just about to walk back when the door swung open. Tyg straightened with shock and looked in to see Leviathan standing by the massive four poster bed, wearing only leather pants. His hair was down and he looked a wreck. 'An amazingly handsome wreck.' Tyg thought, with all those muscles out on display. He was staring at her with that vulture gaze but with an intensity she hadn't seen before. It made her hold her breath and her heart start thumping like a jack rabbit...

"What are you doing?" He asked, his voice dripping with venom. "How are you standing there looking...fine?"

"Ah...well..." Tyg said quite nervously. "Corvyn there was getting worried." Tyg pointed down the hall to where Corvyn was shaking his head and mouthing to stop. "How did you know I was at the door?" She knew she had made no sound...she was a professional after all.

"Your scent." Leviathan growled. "Captain!"

Tyg looked up the hall to where Corvyn was mouthing swear words and strode up the hallway. "My Liege?" He bowed his head low in the doorway.

"Get this woman out of here."

"Now wait a minute!" Tyg fumed. "You've been sulking in here all day because you didn't want to know how badly injured I was and so I just wanted to let you know I'm fine, so you can stop smashing things like a child, giving me a headache, and go back to being an Emperor."

Leviathan turned away from her, visibly shaking with rage. Tyg's eyes widened as she saw for the first time the massive life like tattoo of a dragon's head on Leviathan's back. Its eyes seemed to pierce into her soul. "Oh, wow!" She breathed. "Didn't expect that?"

Leviathan spun back round. "Captain! If you don't get this bloody woman out of my sight now I'll have you stripped back to private!"

"Yes, my Liege." Corvyn grabbed Tyg by the shoulders and started trying to drag her away.

"I'm sorry, Leviathan." Tyg called back to him. "There was no other way to end his suffering."

Leviathan stared at her. "This is not about him...or you."

The door slammed shut again.

Corvyn got help from his men to drag Tyg back down the hall.

"Alright...alright...I'm going!" Tyg said as she brushed them off and walked by herself down the stairs.

"I'm right, you actually want to die!" Corvyn said next to her.

"Don't be so dramatic, that's all your problems, you're scared of him." Tyg said again stunning Corvyn speechless. "He said it wasn't about me, but I know it was." Tyg said smugly.

"What makes you so damn cocksure about it?"

"Because, my dear Corvyn, he has said from the beginning that I'm important to his Empire, so he knows he nearly fucked up by going too far and nearly killing me." Tyg explained so matter-of-factly about her own demise that Corvyn just stared at her. "But now he knows I'm recovered and completely fine he'll be out of that room shortly..." Tyg glanced sideways at Corvyn. "...Wager on it?"

"You think you've got him all sorted out, huh?"

"Not by far." Tyg snorted. "But on this...yes."

Corvyn didn't look convinced. "You're sociopathic, aren't you?"

Tyg's eyes widened then narrowed sceptically. "Others have called me that before..."

"Figures." Corvyn said rolling his eyes and walking off.

61

As they wandered around the property, Tyg saw that her balcony was now empty, a ladder was up against it and the soldier was standing on the ground. She smiled.

"At least that soldier gets a break." Tyg said laughing.

"Quite." Corvyn replied, still thinking about what she had said before.

"Don't worry about it." Tyg said encouragingly.

"Fine for you, you're not under his orders."

"Well, actually I am kind of...I am 'one of his subjects'" Tyg said emphasising it drolly.

"Ha! You've got no idea."

"I know what it means to be aligned to someone or something and have complete loyalty to them and their cause." Tyg muttered.

Corvyn looked stunned, again, there was no end to the fascinating dialogue this woman could spout. "That's right you do..." Corvyn said bitterly. "That's what's causing all the problem."

"Hmm." Tyg grunted as they came around to the other side of the house. Corvyn stopped to talk to one of the soldiers in their language, while Tyg hung back and stretched her back out, reaching up and looking at the sky. They walked on to the next sentry and Tyg did a casual cart wheel making Corvyn look at her with a frown.

"Cut it out!" He growled at her.

"You're no fun." Tyg said pouting, folding her arms.

"You're being watched, smartarse!" Corvyn said. "I thought you had better sense of your surroundings." He quipped as Tyg suddenly looked up at the balcony of Leviathan's room.

"By the Gods, would you look at that!" Tyg exclaimed as she saw Leviathan standing with his hands on the railing watching her. He had put a shirt on, but it was unbuttoned and wafting in the breeze, as was his hair which was still down. "He is very handsome, isn't he?" Tyg breathed.

"I wouldn't know." Corvyn muttered.

Tyg waved at Leviathan, which made him stand up straight.

"What are you doing?" Corvyn growled, then groaned as Leviathan raised an arm and signalled for Tyg to go closer. "Fuck's sake, you're on your own." Corvyn said and stuck his thumbs into his belt and planted his feet.

Tyg smiled at him and walked off over to the balcony. As she approached Corvyn saw Leviathan lean on the balustrade, resting his forearms on the railing and look down on her.

"Tygarya." Leviathan said as she approached.

"Yes, Leviathan?"

"Thank you for letting me know you're alright." He said with a smile.

"That's okay, clearly no one else was going to, they're all too scared of you."

"Quite, but you're not...still?"

"Are you asking me or telling me?"

Leviathan looked up at the horizon for a moment smirking, then he looked back down.

"Meet me downstairs?"

"Are you still angry?"

"With you? No."

Tyg regarded him a moment, squinting slightly in the light. She was quite liking the view from here but thought it best not to say that. "Okay then." She said finally and turned away.

As Leviathan disappeared inside Tyg wandered back to Corvyn.

"I have to go back inside."

"Alright." He said with no question as it was clearly an instruction from Leviathan.

"Yes, he wants to meet me downstairs." Tyg grinned and winked as she wandered back the way they had come.

"Fuck." Corvyn said as he turned and followed. "Glad I didn't take that wager."

Tyg laughed that musical laughter of genuine pleasure she had, causing Corvyn to shudder and shake his head. There was power in that laugh, a strong persuasive power.

As Tyg re-entered the house through the side doors into the main living area Leviathan was standing there watching her. He shook his head and smiled. "How the hell are you okay?"

"Is that some sort of attempt at an apology?" Tyg said, but smiled.

"It's as much of one as you're going to get." Leviathan growled.

"Okay, I'll take it." Tyg said as she came up to him and put her arms around him and hugged him, putting her head on his chest. "I'm sorry too."

Leviathan looked at her, she was always surprising him. Her complete lack of fear was unprecedented and always left him stunned, but grateful, anyone else would have been too terrified to do any of what she had just done to diffuse the tension between them. She was a marvel to behold, he thought as he put his arms around her.

Corvyn's jaw clenched when he saw Tyg walk into Leviathan's arms. Like a mouse to a lion, he thought, no...like a viper to a lion, he revised.

"You can go, Captain." Leviathan said dismissively.

"My Liege." Corvyn bowed his head and left.

Leviathan grabbed Tyg's shoulders and pulled her away from him and looked at her. "Don't ever do that again."

Tyg regarded him with a soft smile but didn't say anything, she couldn't say that she wouldn't if given the same circumstances.

Leviathan grabbed the hair tie at the back of her head and gently pulled it out of her hair, then grabbed her hair with both hands and shook it free. "Much better." He said, then hooked her chin with one finger as he lifted her head and bent to kiss her. After seeing him on the balcony and shirtless in his room, Tyg was only too happy to be kissing him again – she hated conflict.

62

"What the fuck is going on here?" Corvyn came in to find Tyg and his soldier both kneeling on either side of the low table, their hands locked together. The soldier tried to pull away but Tyg held him in place.

"Sorry, Sir!" The soldier mumbled.

"You're losing an arm wrestle with a girl?"

"She's not...she's strong...Sir."

"Obviously..." Corvyn turned to regard Tyg and switched to her language. "Is there no end to your screwing around?"

Tyg shrugged. "Just because your soldier lost, don't get bitter at me."

"What's going on in here now?" Leviathan asked as he strode into the room. Tyg let go of the soldiers hand and sat up on the couch behind her. Leviathan grinned when he saw what was happening. The soldier stood up and came to attention as did Corvyn.

"Tell me, Tygarya, have you ever lost?"

Tyg thought about it. "Sure, when I was younger."

"Perhaps you would like to test your strength against me?"

Both Corvyn and Tyg baulked and the soldier made a quick exit from the room, as Leviathan levelled that vulture gaze at her. He noticed a sneaky smile creep over her lips. He folded his arms and waited for the inevitable twist from her.

"I don't get into matches or wagers I know I can't win, I'm not the risk taker people think I am. I know my odds." Tyg looked up at Leviathan casually appraising him. "I'd go head to head with you in a sword fight though."

Corvyn actually choked on that one.

"Like bloody hell that's ever going to happen!" It was Antyn, as he walked casually into the room, full of smiles. Leviathan looked at Tyg a moment longer, his head cocked sideways and his eyes glowing faintly.

"Antyn! You're back." Tyg said actually happy to see the younger brother. "Do you not want to wager on it then?"

Leviathan laughed and turned to his brother. "See what I've had to put up with? And, the poor Captain here is probably the most pleased man on the planet to see you." Corvyn smiled but said nothing.

"Quite...I have heard of your exploits while here, Tyg. I knew you for a hell cat the first day I met you and from what I hear you have far excelled that description." Antyn took Tyg's hand and kissed it formally.

"What makes you think your reappearance makes any difference to that?" Tyg said a bit defensively.

Leviathan chuckled and held his hands out as if to say 'See.'

"Because, Tyg..." Antyn replied calmly. "...two sorcerers are better than one."

"But, Corvyn here..." Tyg went to say.

"Is not a Sorcerer and is somewhat underqualified to deal with you it seems."

Tyg noticed Corvyn press his lips together and curl his hands into fists. "Don't insult the Captain!" Tyg growled. "How dare you, he's right here."

Corvyn and Leviathan looked shocked. "You defend him now?" Leviathan asked confused.

Antyn was still calm and sat down relaxing back into the comfy chair. "Always the champion for the underdog and down trodden."

Leviathan slid his gaze to Antyn as if that meant something. They looked at each other for a moment.

"I'm glad you're back." Leviathan muttered to Antyn.

"So is everyone, I'm guessing." Antyn said with a knowing look.

Tyg was looking at Antyn with a curious look on her face. Somehow Antyn already knew everything, but how? Antyn saw it and smiled, his eyes sparkling. "Is it not accurate?" He asked her.

Tyg chuckled and shrugged. "You're the wordsmith."

Antyn raised an eyebrow. "Indeed, I suppose I am."

"Well, Captain, you'll be glad to hear that you are now relieved of the duty of watching over our dear Lady Tygarya, now Antyn is back we can share the load between us." Leviathan said.

Corvyn bowed his head. "My Liege." He turned to Antyn. "My Lord." Turned and left the room closing the doors.

"Share the load?" Tyg snorted. "That's a bit rude."

"Is it really?" Leviathan said as he went and poured them all a drink.

"So, you were arm wrestling with the soldiers?" Antyn asked amused.

Tyg regarded him coolly. "Yes, that's the extent that my boredom has transcended too, being kept cooped up in this bloody house."

Leviathan placed the drinks on the table in front of the couch and slid one across the surface to Antyn who caught it deftly. Leviathan sat down on the couch next to Tyg.

"You've only got yourself to blame for that, Tygarya." Leviathan growled.

"Quite..." Antyn agreed as he sipped his drink.

"Oh, I see, so now there's two of you you're going to gang up on me...the poor young girl caught in the middle of all this." Tyg tried to sound as dramatic as possible. "Like it's all my fault."

Antyn almost spat his drink out.

"You've been reading too many of those fairy tales, Tygarya, they've gone to your head." Leviathan chuckled as the brothers looked at each other again and Tyg saw Leviathan nod slightly.

"Let's lay the cards on the table shall we, Tyg?" Antyn began. "You are a trained assassin, an exceptional warrior in every field, you have the reflexes of a cat, you're super strong and...I am guessing here...but you have accelerated healing? Yes?"

Tyg stared at him, her eyes blazing. "What the fuck is this?" She growled, curling up like she was about to pounce. "You've only just arrived back and see fit to start an interrogation?"

Leviathan placed a hand casually on her shoulder and pushed her back down. "Calm down, Tygarya, please. I don't want to hurt you anymore." Tyg looked at him, her eyes going wide, but she took a deep breath and uncoiled her legs and sat down. "Much better, thank you." Leviathan said, causing his brother to look at him in wonder. Leviathan caught the look and scowled.

"Shut up, Antyn...I already know how much this woman is influencing me. Don't for one minute think you're going to start getting pleases and thank yous."

Tyg grinned, as Antyn sat up. "Well, that's one for the books I have to say, I'm amazed, Brother."

"Just get back to the point."

Tyg was watching the pair of them carefully. She was starting to feel like Leviathan had just been waiting for Antyn to get back before throwing the chains on her.

"Right...my point, Tyg, is that you're special..."

Tyg scowled and buried her face in her hands. "Not this again?"

"Shush." Leviathan ordered as he put his arm around her shoulders. She tried to shrug him off but he growled. "I'll put you over my knee instead?"

Tyg's eyes flashed as she looked up at him horrified.

"Okay, enough of the insatiable flirting for fuck's sake. Geeze, no wonder the men around here are all walking around like they're on egg shells, with you two hellions going head to head all the time."

"Flirting! Hellions!" Tyg growled, but Leviathan just laughed.

"Shut up, Brother and get back to the point, before we all degenerate down to another fight, like you say."

"Hmm." Tyg grunted as she leant forward and grabbed her drink and sculled it back in one go. Then she sat back, folding her arms. As she sat back Leviathan managed to steer her so she leaned back into him, he tucked her into his side, under his armpit, his hand coming round her to rest on her hip.

"That's better." Leviathan said with a smile.

"Okay..." Antyn continued with a frown, seeing Tyg suddenly not wanting to struggle out of Leviathan's embrace, but relaxed and seemed to want to be there. He shook his head. "What was I saying?" He thought. "Oh yes. You're special, Tyg, because we think you are the last of your kind."

"What?"

"We believe, after watching you and learning about you..."

"Studying me like some lab rat, you mean."

"Tygarya!" Leviathan admonished.

"...that you must be an Elvian."

"What the fuck is an Elvian?"

"A race of people from our land that disappeared about forty years ago, there are the rare half breeds still, but nothing like what you are."

"And, these people were like me?"

"Yes, natural warriors, they could pick up any weapon and excel at it in a matter of a day."

"Hmm, took me longer than a day." Tyg seemed challenged by that.

"But, you are probably a half breed, but the difference between you and the rest of them is we think you may have Royal blood."

"No way?" Tyg said incredulous, as she pushed away and looked up at Leviathan, her hand on his chest.

"See, I told you, you're a Lady." He said amused and hooked a finger around a stray strand of her hair and flicked it back behind her ear. His gaze smouldered and he traced the finger down her cheek as she locked eyes with him. He smiled and then, as she leaned forward bringing her face towards his, he ran his hand back around her head, running his fingers into her hair as she kissed him, initiating the kiss for the first time. She ran her hands up his chest and around his neck as their kissing got more passionate fuelled by their mutual desire for each other.

"Ah...brother in the room." Antyn said, breaking the moment and ending the kiss. Tyg smiled shyly and looked down. "You're a regular ebb and flow of emotions aren't you? No wonder you've got my brother so confused."

"You're confused?" Tyg asked Leviathan, an eyebrow raised, more making a challenge of Antyn's statement than anything.

"No, not at all, my brother talks rubbish." Leviathan laughed and kissed Tyg on the lips.

"Oh, ganging up on me now...nice one." Antyn said as he fell back into his chair and took a large sip of his drink. "Anyway, so you can see Tyg why it's so important that you return to your homeland."

"Perhaps...things are starting to steer more and more in that direction." Tyg agreed.

"So you agree, that's good, however there is still one thing apparently standing in the way of that, yes?"

Tyg looked at him with her eyes flashing again. 'Yes, very quick to mood swing.' Antyn thought. 'Volatile, like Leviathan.'

"Yes." Tyg said sounding suspicious, suddenly she stood up, too fast for Leviathan to stop her. "Wait...I see where you're going with this...fuck the both of you!"

Tyg walked to the door and turned. "I'm leaving now, going for a walk, don't either of you dare try to stop me." Tyg turned and opened the door, grabbing the hand of the startled soldier that was there, dragging him behind her as she walked off. "I'll take him with me...don't worry...I'll be fine." She said without a backwards glance, hoping against hope she wasn't subjected to Leviathan's power again, but nothing happened.

Leviathan's eyes went dark seeing Tyg grab the soldier's hand and he went to stand up.

"Leave it." Antyn said quietly. "She doesn't know, and you can't blame him."

Leviathan wiped a weary hand over his eyes then looked at his brother, who was staring into his whisky glass. "I told you she was too clever for that to work."

"Indeed, she was almost there though."

Leviathan snorted. "You don't know her like I've come to know her."

"Have you thought about questioning that stableman, he seems to know her quite well, you say?"

"If I start torturing her friends I might as well just chain her up and torture her."

"Hmm, why not open the gates and let them journey into the city again without escorts, act like the trouble has past."

"You think she'll use them to get word out?"

"We can only hope." Antyn calculated. "It's either that or set her free, Lev, maybe she's right and she is the only one that can sort this."

"Not going to happen, she's mine. The minute I let her out of those gates will be the last I see of her, I know her boss's type...wouldn't surprise me if he knew exactly what she was. Stakes are high here. We aren't the first country to travel here from the Continent." Leviathan growled like an animal as he stood up. "I think we may have use of Captain Corvyn still though."

"You think that's wise, you don't want her becoming attached to him. She crusades everyone that she gets close to."

"Too late for that, you saw it." Leviathan grimaced. "Besides, it amuses me, she keeps trying to find out what he is."

"What? She doesn't know? Why keep that a secret when you clearly told her we're Sorcerers?"

"Weren't you listening? It amuses me." Leviathan growled at Antyn. "Now, I'll go give the good news to the Captain and tell him to go save his private from her clutches." Leviathan chuckled as he walked off.

Antyn watched his brother go then breathed like he had been holding his breath the whole time. "Fucking hell, it's worse than I thought." He muttered to himself and pondered the intricacies of toxic relationships.

Tyg was lying out in the rose garden on the marble seat, the soldier standing off to one side. The roses had all but finished now, a few browned and dying ones still clinging to the stems. She was looking at the clouds, as Corvyn strode up in a foul mood.

"Go!" Corvyn ordered the soldier, who bowed his head and left hurriedly. Tyg glanced up at him. "Just when I thought I was rid of you, you have the audacity to tell, not one, but TWO sorcerers to fuck off! And, they just listen and let you speak to them like that?" Corvyn was pacing, raking a hand through his hair.

"Calm down, Captain." Tyg said with an authority she had never spoken to him before. He halted pacing and turned to her wide eyed. She was looking at him from where she was lying. Her eyes sheltered from the sun by one hand held up. He suddenly knew then that he would follow her into a maelstrom if she wanted him to.

"What have you done to me?"

Tyg actually looked perplexed. "Me? Nothing...what do you mean?"

"Never mind." Corvyn raked his hand through his hair again. Tyg sat up and motioned for him to sit. He looked at her a moment then sat down next to her.

"I'm sorry...I didn't realise my actions of walking out on Leviathan and Antyn would mean they would make you come out here as nursemaid."

"It's fine." Corvyn said with a smile.

"Are you sure...you just said you were glad to get rid of me."

"Hmm." Corvyn grunted.

"Tell me, Corvyn, why should I go back with Leviathan when he leaves?"

Corvyn quailed at the question. "I can't answer that question for you, Tygarya."

"I'm going to be all alone over there."

"I doubt that."

Tyg looked at him with an eyebrow raised.

"There's lots of people in the Emperor's court who will relish getting to befriend you."

Tyg snorted. "To get to Leviathan...no thanks, I'd rather stick a knife in their ribs, I don't do well in those situations."

Corvyn chuckled. "No, I imagine you are going to cause quite a stir."

"Thanks." Tyg said dryly. "I want at least one person in my corner, Corvyn, that's not Leviathan or Antyn."

Corvyn turned to look at her. "I am in service to his Imperial Majesty, Tygarya."

"I know that, but...I'm asking you to look out for me...I know I'm instinctual, hot headed and quick to violence, a hellion...but that's me, I've been made that way...I think you're someone I can trust to tell me the truth of a situation, when I have it wrong. I respect you, Corvyn, and that respect doesn't come lightly from me."

"Hmm." Corvyn was speechless. He felt like falling on his knees and devoting his loyalty to her. He sighed a deep breath. "I can tell you that Emperor Leviathan is a harsh but fair ruler, Tygarya. He makes sure no one is hungry or jobless."

"What?" Tyg was stunned. "You mean you have no one like me...like I was growing up?"

"Yes, we still have thieves and crime, but it's their choice to be there. The Emperor provides work for anyone willing to do an honest day's work for an honest day's pay, is what I'm saying. Whether it's building roads or harvesting fields or joining the army, he has work on offer for all who want it."

"That's amazing?" Tyg thought about how different her life might have been if she had been able to go to work in the fields. "No wonder they were so shocked by me." She laughed a short self-loathing laugh.

"Indeed." Corvyn frowned, battling his own inner demons.

63

Tyg was sitting in the kitchen having her morning coffee when Dane came through from the servant's quarters.

"Hey, Tyg. Did you hear? Lord Antyn has said we are allowed to come and go from the Manor freely now he's back."

"What the hell? When did he say that?"

"This morning, so we're heading in to the market."

"Huh? I suppose since Leviathan didn't get attacked when he went to the docks they think everything is alright? They don't realise Boss doesn't work that way." Tyg said in a hushed tone, checking the door to the kitchen was closed, so the soldier posted outside didn't hear. She paused then. "Who's 'we'?" She asked.

"Yeah...Tess and Neeki are coming with."

"What about Pete?"

"Bah! He's obsessed with that bloody garden these days."

"Ha! Who would have thought it?" Tyg said amused.

"Yeah...so?" Dane looked at her questioningly.

"What?"

Dane leaned in conspirator like. "Do you want me to get a message out?"

"No." Tyg looked at Dane with a raised eyebrow.

"Really? I thought..."

"You're not thinking Dane....you really think you won't be watched where ever you go and with who you talk to? Forget it. It's too risky."

"So, what are you going to do? You can't stay here forever...or are you going to try and sneak out of Arial on their ships?"

Tyg looked at Dane. "Why not? Like you said, I'm not breaking my Oath if I just leave and I'm sick of people thinking they own me."

"So, you've completely given up on trying to stop your Boss from extracting you?"

"If he wants to keep this fight going with Leviathan and Antyn, that's his decision, all the conflict between me and Leviathan has been caused by him and the Guild alliances. I'm sick of it, Dane I want to go with Leviathan."

"You have feelings for him?"

"Yeah, I think I do...at least enough to want to pursue it."

"I understand, Tyg."

"Thanks, what about you and Tess?"

"Ah...well..."

"Seriously, Dane, you're hopeless, she likes you...just step up."

"Sure, just like that..." Dane grumbled as he flushed.

"Yes, Dane, just like that...buy her something at the market...I'll even give you the money too."

"No need, I got paid yesterday." Dane beamed with pride. "Sure is strange getting paid for honest work."

Tyg regarded him. "Do you like it though, looking after the horses?"

"Yeah."

"That's good. I'm trying to figure out a way for you to stay here, Dane."

"I know." He smiled at her kindly. "Neeki said. It's okay. Tyg, now that I've done it I can find work somewhere else, don't worry too much about me...or the others."

Tyg smiled at Dane, her faith was restored. She just wished Leviathan had been around to hear it.

"Well, better be off..."

"See ya, Dane...and remember...buy something for Tess, okay."

"Will do." Dane grinned as he left.

Tyg got up and wandered through to the main living areas. She glanced at the closed doors leading through to the drawing room. She could hear a raised voice, not in anger but it sounded like frustration, and she knew whose voice it was.

She walked over and smiled at the guards at the door. "Am I allowed in?" She asked when they looked at her. Their helms covered their foreheads and cheeks and made them look serious all the time. She was glad Corvyn hardly wore his. She made the gesture of wanting to go in, since they didn't know the language – or acted like they didn't. One nodded his head.

Tyg opened the door and walked in to see Leviathan standing by the fireplace and Antyn sitting in an armchair, they both turned when she entered.

Antyn gave her a beaming smile. "Tyg! Just the person..."

"For what?" Tyg asked suspiciously as she walked over to them.

"To make Lev relax, he's a bit wound up."

Tyg looked at Leviathan as he glowered at his brother, but he raised an arm towards Tyg so she could step into him, which she did, and he put his arm around her. "What's the problem?" Tyg asked. "Maybe I can help?"

"I doubt that." Leviathan muttered.

"Why? If it's anything to do with this city, I know a lot of people, so tell me."

Leviathan looked at her a long moment but it was Antyn that spoke.

"We're having trouble getting ships."

"Ships? But didn't you go to the docks the other day?"

"Hmm." Leviathan growled.

"It seems that the sailors here aren't too keen to sail with someone named after the demon god of the sea."

"So, don't tell them your name." Tyg shrugged.

"If it were that easy, Tygarya my dearest." Leviathan said as he twisted a strand of her hair around a finger. "I'm already too well known."

"Ah, yeah...well...you aren't easily forgettable." Tyg muttered causing Leviathan to chuckle at her and tighten his grip on her. Tyg thought about it a moment then suddenly knew what to do for everyone. "I've got it! See, I can help...and not only help with ships but probably get this house sold for you too, as payment for the hire of them." Tyg grinned.

"What the fuck? How?" Leviathan grumbled.

"Well, by the Gods, I'm impressed." Antyn said raking his hand through his hair.

"It's really rather simple, but it's going to take a bit of persuasion and I'm going to need to leave the manor."

"No." Leviathan growled.

Tyg rolled her eyes. "Wait...not to go into the city proper, but over to Lord Doven's Manor, but I'll have to write a letter of intent first, he's very proper and likes every protocol to be followed."

"Wait...isn't your friend Lord Doven's son?" Leviathan growled, pulling her closer to him.

"Yes, actually he is..." Tyg looked up at Leviathan amused. "Did you know my friend, Thomas, is engaged?"

"No, why would I?"

"Exactly, so before you start trying to act jealous and possessive at the mention of the Dovens, know the facts."

Antyn baulked and coughed.

"Hmm." Leviathan growled again. "I'm going to need to hear more about this plan first."

"Okay, well I need to sit down." Tyg went for the other armchair but Leviathan quickly side stepped and sat down in it first.

"Really?" Tyg said shocked.

"You can still sit..." Leviathan indicated his lap and smiled wickedly.

"Seriously? That's hardly taking things slow."

"It's hardly taking things fast either....Antyn's here, so I can't do anything untoward."

"Like he could stop you."

"Well, his presence would stop me." Leviathan levelled a serious gaze at her. "Trust me."

Tyg looked at Antyn who shrugged amused. She looked back at Leviathan, shrugged and sat down on the floor in front of the fire.

"Here..." Leviathan muttered and stood up, giving Tyg the seat. As she got up and sat in it smiling Leviathan sat down on the arm and leaned his arm over the back of the chair around her. Antyn watched conflicted and felt more than a little awkward.

"Finished playing you two?" He asked as Tyg curled her legs up and leaned towards Leviathan, into the chair, under his arm. Leviathan looked very satisfied with the outcome and dropped his arm off the back of the chair and onto Tyg's shoulder. He then gave Tyg a very smouldering look as she looked up at him.

"Stop that." She said, like she was telling off a small child, making Leviathan chuckle, as their eyes locked and Leviathan ran the back of his fingers up and down her arm.

Antyn raked a hand through his hair. "Fuck's sake, can we continue before this all descends into depravity."

"Antyn!" Tyg scowled.

He took a long hard look at her, his power of foreshadowing suddenly kicked in.

She's not the hard nut she tries to make everyone think she is. She likes the feeling of protection being in his arms gives her. It's calming for her, but she has no idea it's because he is the perfect strong alpha male. She's strong when she has to be, but doesn't actually want to be...it's purely out of necessity. She's an Empath, but not for the whole of humanity. Dangerous to get on the wrong side of because she will do anything for those she chooses to protect, but she'll be borderline sociopathic to those she opposes...yes...very dangerous...very volatile...hopefully if I can keep the peace between them her feelings for him will grow to where he will be the one she would die for...then we will have her exactly where we need her.

"Antyn!" Leviathan growled. Antyn blinked and wiped his eyes. He looked at Leviathan who was staring at him. They shared a long look.

"Are you okay?" Tyg asked.

"Yes, I'm fine...I day dream sometimes when a thought hits me..." Antyn muttered as he sat up and raked a hand through his hair. "Sorry...continue Tyg, I can't wait to hear your plan." He glanced at Leviathan, who was still glaring at him, and winked, causing Leviathan to frown.

"Well, its simple really...Lord Doven owns a shipping company and a fleet of fishing vessels as well. That's how his family made their money and became land owners generations ago."

"Interesting, and you think he will let us use his ships in exchange for this house?"

"Maybe, but that's the part that will take some persuasion. You see, with Thomas engaged to young Lady Belmont he's going to have to come up with lands of his own before her father will let her marry him. It's a win, win situation, don't you think?"

"Simply astounding..." Antyn said impressed.

"And, by doing this you guarantee your friends stay employed, right?" Leviathan growled.

Tyg sat up and looked at him. "Yes, got a problem with that?"

"No...it's not my problem to solve...but..."

"No buts, just leave it." Tyg growled back.

Leviathan regarded her a moment, then slipped his arm up and encircled her head with his hand and pulled her head back to his chest. "Fine...I'm not after an argument today."

"Glad to hear it." Tyg muttered.

"Okay, draft the letter and I'll have someone deliver it for you." Leviathan said then. "But, not right now..." He tightened his hold on her as she smiled.

"You know, you can actually be a nice guy when you put your mind to it."

Antyn choked and coughed as Leviathan looked down on her with a raised eyebrow. "Rubbish." He denied the comment. "I'm purely being possessive of you, Tygarya."

Antyn's eyes went wide at Leviathan's candour, it also caused Tyg to sit up and stare at him. He regarded her calmly with a faint smile.

"Why would you say that?" Tyg demanded. Leviathan put a hand on her shoulder.

He shrugged. "It's the truth."

"Let me up! Damn you." Tyg swatted away Leviathan's hands and stood up. Leviathan just smiled and didn't stop her as she stalked out of the room. He dropped into the seat and crossed his legs and chuckled.

"Everything was going so well, why did you do that?" Antyn asked once Tyg had left.

Leviathan fixed Antyn with a blazing stare. "Tell me what you saw!"

64

Tyg avoided Leviathan after that. How dare he...she was so sick of other people thinking they had some sort of claim over her. Important to his Empire or not, she didn't care one iota.

Tyg walked outside and stood on the terrace, looking off at the distance. Her eyes fell on the distant figure of Pete toiling in his garden. She smiled and walked over to see him. She heard the soldier following. She grinned to herself...she felt just like doing some training and seeing what she could get to come out and play.

As she approached Pete he stood up and dusted the dirt off his knees.

"Hey Tyg."

"Hi Pete, so gardening isn't that boring after all, huh?"

Pete scratched the back of his neck. "Nah, it's not bad...nice when your hard work pays off and your plants start to grow...I guess...can't wait for spring, but I have to do this hard toil now, before the ground freezes."

"Cool, I'm glad." Tyg smiled. "Can I use your rake?"

"What? Sure, I suppose." Pete walked over to where the rake was and then handed it to Tyg. She put her foot on the side of it by the head and snapped the head off it.

"I'll buy you another one." She laughed at Pete's distraught cry and then twirled it round. The soldier backed up a step and put his hand on his sword as Tyg went through a flurry of movements, twirling the stick round her back and jumping and flipping and throwing the stick in the air. She stopped, tucking the stick into her armpit and grinned at the soldier. She walked over to the wooden fence boundary between the Manor and the paddocks beyond and jumped up onto the fence post.

The soldier and Pete stood watching her for several minutes. Pete even sat down on the grass, as she walked skilfully backwards and forwards along the fence while spinning the stick.

She saw out of the corner of her eye a familiar figure striding across the lawn, one hand resting on the pommel of his sword. His black cape billowing out behind his left shoulder. She smiled to herself, he was just the person she had hoped would come out of the wood work once word reached him about what she was up to. As he reached them he came up beside the soldier and stuck his thumb into his belt as he regarded Tyg coolly.

"Okay, you can get down now." He said unamused.

Tyg did a side twist somersault and landed on the ground, going to one knee as she drove the stick into the ground. She stood up and walked over.

"I just needed to clear my head."

"Sure." Corvyn said unconvinced.

"Why aren't I allowed to train? Your men train every day?"

"Because it's been decided that it's too dangerous...you're a berserker."

"No, I'm not." Tyg said indignantly.

Corvyn stared at her. "Gods! You're not even aware of it, that's worse."

Tyg smiled as she stepped up to Corvyn. "Okay, maybe I am." She grabbed his arm and turned him around. "Walk with me." She said as she hooked his arm with hers. His eyes just about popped out of his head.

"Tygarya!" Corvyn tried to extract his arm from Tyg's "This is not proper."

"Rubbish! It is proper to escort a lady in such a fashion, you are an officer....I looked it up."

Corvyn grit his teeth. "Damn you and your reading...I'm dead if the Emperor sees, you know that."

"No, I won't let him do anything to you, I've told you that already."

"Still think you have any sway over the Emperor..."

"I do all the while he's trying to get me on a ship and home with him."

"You would resort to black mail...of an Emperor? Who's a Sorcerer...and the most powerful Sorcerer ever known?"

"Well, I wouldn't go that far..." Tyg chuckled and walked on a few steps. "Look, like I said before, Corvyn, I need you to help me make sense of stuff. I rely on your honesty."

Corvyn sighed and rubbed his eyes with his other hand as Tyg continued to lead him across the lawn.

"What has the Emperor done now?"

Tyg grimaced. "I told him he could actually be nice when he wants to be at which he turned round and said he was just being possessive of me..."

"So, you're pissed off?"

"Yeah, a little...but that's not why I wanted to see you."

"You wanted to see me? Is that why you were playing with sticks?" Corvyn growled. "I do actually have work to do besides looking after you..."

"I need a favour, Corvyn."

"You're already over on that score..."

"So, I'll owe you two...tell me what you want from me then?"

"Nothing." Corvyn grimaced. "What do you want?"

"I want you to carry a letter to Lord Doven at his Manor. It's about a mile or so up the road."

Corvyn looked at Tyg stopping their walk. "What's the catch?"

Tyg grinned. "Lord Doven is Thomas's father."

"The Captain of the city watch?" Corvyn growled.

"Yes, and it's all good now...you're a Captain...he doesn't out rank you now..."

"He never out ranked me, Tygarya." Corvyn exclaimed his eyes glowing faintly. "Any army ranked officer would out rank that jumped up Lord's son!"

"Okay...okay...I'm sorry. I just thought that was the problem between you, but now I see it's to do with class not rank."

Corvyn clenched his jaw but said nothing and continued their walk.

"So you will deliver my message?"

"Yes, of course I will...Fuck!" Corvyn muttered then as Leviathan walked out onto the terrace and stood staring at them as they approached. He folded his arms and settled his vulture gaze on Tyg.

"Why the fuck are you touching my Captain?"

"He is being a gentleman and escorting me back to the house." Tyg said it so sweetly that Corvyn baulked and almost stumbled.

"How nice of him..." Leviathan said as Corvyn finally managed to get his arm back from Tyg.

"My Liege." He bowed low.

"At ease Captain." Leviathan muttered.

However Tyg continued. "...Yes, it was nice of him...as he did so at my request. So, if you've got a problem with it you'll have to talk to me." Leviathan's gaze never faltered. "Oh and by the way, I have also requested Corvyn take my letter to Lord Doven, since he seems to have the right knowledge of class etiquette to appease the Earl."

"You don't think it wise to ask my permission before accosting my men for your own errands?" Leviathan asked with a growl.

"Well, it's actually an errand for your betterment, I didn't think you would mind?"

"Well, I do mind." He stood in front of her like a stone wall.

Tyg sighed and glanced at Corvyn, who was standing in front of them both with a look of thunder at Tyg. She looked back to Leviathan with a look of completely feigned sincerity.

"My Imperial Majesty, Emperor Leviathan Adramelech of Tylandria..." She paused and bowed her head. "My Liege...I do solemnly propose that Captain Corvyn of the Tylandrian Army, Special Royal Company, be given the duty of delivering the very important message to his Lordship Earl Doven at the Doven manor in the hopes of securing ships for your voyage home, are you agreeable?"

Corvyn just about fainted on the spot, he was surprised Tyg had even listened when he had told her that...Leviathan stared at her, the corner of his mouth twitching as he suppressed a grin.

"Fine." He said simply.

"Thank you...I shall go and write it then..." Tyg smiled, her eyes glowing with mirth as she walked off into the house.

Leviathan turned to Corvyn. "Be very careful with that one, Captain, she's mine."

"My Liege!" Corvyn stated with shock as he fell to one knee. "I would never!"

"Mind you don't." Leviathan growled as he turned and strode off into the house after Tyg.

Corvyn stood, shaking. "That bloody woman!"

"Captain?" The soldier that had dutifully followed along behind Tyg came up concerned.

"Shut it, Private." Corvyn muttered. "Get back to your duties." Corvyn stalked off muttering to himself.

Tyg was in the library and had just sat down at the desk to write the letter requesting an audience with Lord Doven and son, when Leviathan walked in and the doors closed behind him. Tyg turned to look at him and bit her lip seeing his dark expression.

"I know...too far." She muttered.

"What the fuck, Tygarya! Don't you dare try to undermine me to my soldiers ever again!"

"What? No...I didn't mean to do that..." Tyg looked down at the desk. "I'm sorry."

"I did like that you called me your liege, however."

"What?" Tyg turned and looked up in shock. She found Leviathan smiling at her. Tyg grinned back but lowered her gaze.

"It was very manipulative but effective." He almost purred when he said it and gave Tyg a very smouldering look as he stepped up beside the chair and put his hand under her upper arm and pulled her up to stand in front of him. "I could have been very angry, but like I said before I'm not in the mood for an argument." He hooked Tyg's chin with a finger and lifted it as he stroked her hair back from her face with the other hand. Tyg just looked at him, biting her lip, remembering what Palin had said about keeping her mouth shut. Leviathan ran his thumb along her bottom lip pulling it from her teeth. "I have to get back to Antyn....you're lucky this time, Tygarya...but stop provoking me, you know what I'm capable of." Leviathan lowered his head and kissed her on the lips then let her go. "Write your letter, send Corvyn off with it and come to me in the drawing room when you've finished." He said as he walked out of the library, the doors opening and closing on their own. Tyg swallowed hard but smiled.

Once the letter was finished she rolled it up and put a red ribbon around it then went to find Corvyn. He was just coming out of the stables with his horse saddled ready to go. He had his full formal uniform on and his helm was hanging on the pommel of his saddle. Tyg thought he looked very dashing.

As he approached he looked crossly at her. "Walk with me to the gate."

"What?" Tyg was surprised. "You're not going to tell me off too?"

"Just walk." Corvyn muttered as he passed her and continued up the pathway.

Tyg caught up and walked beside Corvyn, glancing sideways at him waiting for him to speak.

"I cannot be your confidant on returning to Tylandria, Tygarya."

"What? Why not?"

"I have received orders that as soon as we get into port we are to march across to Enyana, which we have already conquered, move straight through to the border of Kolastan and meet up with the army there."

"You're going straight back to battle?" Tyg was surprised. "But, what about your week off you said you were getting?"

"Orders are orders." Corvyn shrugged but he looked bitter.

"This isn't because of what I did before?"

"No, this is business, Tygarya...the Emperor has always been planning this and now he has the ore he can progress."

"Oh, I see." Tyg was genuinely upset to know she was going to lose contact with Corvyn once he returned to Tylandria.

Corvyn stopped at the gates as the guard opened them. "The letter..." He held his hand out.

Tyg handed it to him, not even looking at him. He took it and placed it inside his breastplate. "How will I know which estate is Lord Doven's?" He asked as he put his helm on.

"It has large wrought iron gates with the insignia of D and S for Doven Shipping on each gate overlaid with gold. Just follow this road to a smaller lane on the right and travel down that about half a mile. You can't miss it...it's much bigger than this place."

"Thank you, Tygarya...and I'm sorry."

"Whatever." Tyg said as she turned away from him. She hadn't even lifted her eyes once while talking to him.

He watched her as she walked off back down the pathway and grit his teeth. "Bloody woman!" He muttered to himself as he felt how much she was under his skin. He mounted his horse and coaxed it out the gates. He looked down the road and saw the horse and cart of Tyg's friends returning, cantering along. Good, at least her friends are back, he thought as he turned the opposite way and nudged his horse into a gallop.

Tyg walked back along the pathway, then turned and walked down the side of the house instead of going through the main doors.

"Damn!" She growled actually biting back tears. She stuffed her hands in her pockets and was scuffing her feet slowly along the grass, when she heard her name.

"Tyg!" Dane ran up, breathless.

"What is it?" Tyg spun round surprised at the panic in his voice.

"This strange guy...came up to us..."

"What strange guy?" Tyg asked immediately suspicious.

"One of your lot...I'm guessing...he gave me this..." Dane handed Tyg a letter sealed with a black wax mark imprinted with the symbol of the crossed swords over a hooded skull. The symbol of the Assassin's Guild.

Tyg went pale. "What the fuck." She breathed.

"He was dressed in black, he didn't show his face. He wore a coat with a high collar buckled up over his face and a hood pulled down. I could only see his eyes."

"What did he say, Dane?"

"Said this was for...ah..."

"The exact words, Dane." Tyg growled.

"He said...this is for that black haired giant bastard at the Manor where Tyg is being kept."

"Fuck." Tyg pinched the bridge of her nose and squeezed her eyes shut.

"I can't give it to him, Tyg..."

"It's okay, Dane." Tyg tapped the letter on the palm of her other hand. "I'll give it to him."

"What do you think it is?"

Tyg stared at the seal on the letter. "It can only be one thing...carrying that seal."

Tyg sighed and started to walk across the lawn towards the house.

"What?" Dane said as he fell in beside her.

"A challenge."

"No way!" Dane exclaimed, Tyg glanced at him but said nothing. "Aren't you scared to give this to the big guy?"

Tyg snorted. "Have you known me to be scared of anything?"

"Ha! No, guess not...that's why I brought it to you."

Tyg laughed an unpleasant chuckle.

65

She strode into the drawing room, where Leviathan and Antyn were looking over a large map. They both looked up surprised as she walked up and threw the letter on the table, on top of the map, in Leviathan's direction.

"This ought to make you happy." Tyg said her eyes blazing as Dane hovered in the doorway. She turned to him. "Come in here, Dane."

"What is it?" Leviathan looked at the seal and frowned.

"That is the seal of the Assassin's Guild, they have sent you a message."

"What the fuck!" Leviathan snatched up the letter and tore it open. He read it and threw it back down in disgust. "That son of a bitch!" He muttered under his breath.

Tyg folded her arms. "It's a challenge isn't it?"

Leviathan settled that vulture gaze on her. "How did you come by this?"

"Dane got approached at the market and given it."

Leviathan's gaze slid to Dane then back to Tyg. "You expected this?"

"No, I didn't think he was that stupid."

Antyn had picked up the letter and read it. He placed it back down on the table and tapped his knuckles on it. "Well, this just got serious."

"What the fuck do you mean *just* got serious?" Tyg's eyes flared brighter and she took a step towards him. "People have already been killed over this stupid shit!"

"Tygarya, calm down." Leviathan growled as Antyn regarded her surprised, he hadn't seen her rage since he had left for Landau and he had forgotten the power that flowed around her. Leviathan turned to Dane. "Leave, I'll speak to you later."

Dane hovered a moment, but Tyg turned to him. "Go Dane...I'm fine."

"You always say that, but..."

"Just go."

As Dane left he noticed the soldiers on the doors all had their hands on their swords and Captain Eskel was now standing outside the drawing room.

"What's going on?" He asked Dane.

As Dane filled him in they heard a crash come from the drawing room.

Leviathan stepped over to Tyg and tried to reach out to her, but she had stepped away.

"What does it say? This is your fault. Get the fuck away from me!"

"Tyg, please calm down." Antyn implored but Leviathan raised a hand to silence him, then flicked his wrist and sent Tyg flying backwards into one of the armchairs in front of the fire. As she did she crashed into it and sent a vase on the table next to it crashing to the floor, smashing into pieces. She found herself unable to move.

"Fuck you." Tyg growled at Leviathan. She hated him being able to use his power against her, she felt defenceless against it and defenceless was one thing she hated feeling.

"If you calm the fuck down, I'll let you read it." Leviathan said his voice still low and calm. He grabbed the letter up and walked over to her.

Tyg breathed in and out several times and managed to calm down. Her eyes flickering. Leviathan held his hand out with the letter and Tyg found she could move again.

"You need to stop doing that to me." Tyg said through gritted teeth as she snatched the letter.

"You need to stop overreacting all the time." Leviathan said folding his arms.

"How can you be so calm?" Tyg demanded.

"What's there to get worked up about?"

Tyg stared at him for a moment then looked down and read the message.

MEET ME, WITH TYG, DAY FROM TOMORROW
10AM, NO ONE ELSE
TYG KNOWS WHERE

ꝑꝕꝝ∷·

TYG GRIT HER TEETH. "The fucking fool." She muttered.

"What's these symbols?" Antyn asked.

"It's proof he wrote it."

"I think you can drop the subterfuge now, Tygarya, and tell me his name." Leviathan growled. "And, where he wants to meet."

Tyg sighed and looked up at Leviathan. "I am not going to let this happen."

"Tyg..." Antyn said from behind Leviathan.

"Shut it, Antyn." Leviathan growled causing Antyn to walk back over to the table, raking a hand through his hair.

"You can't stop it now, Tygarya, so don't try, because I'll take you with me in chains if I have too."

"This is ridiculous!" Tyg said fed up.

"A challenge has been issued, you think I should ignore it?"

"Just let me go by myself."

"No."

"Fuck's sake, so you go and win and kill him or whatever...so what? What does it get you?" Tyg's eyes were blazing again. "Because don't you fucking dare say it gets you ownership of ME!"

Leviathan straightened and glared down at her with that vulture gaze. "It gets *you* your freedom."

Tyg was stunned. The light went out of her eyes and she blinked and looked away.

"I can fight for myself." She muttered.

Antyn collapsed in a chair in the back ground with an exasperated groan. She looked at him with an eyebrow raised, then back to Leviathan who was still standing with his arms folded looking at her amused.

"I'm sure you could, Tygarya, but that's not how this works."

"Am I missing something?"

"Your Boss is giving you a way out. If I kill him...he's being extremely honourable."

"Keeping my Oath to him intact you mean, so I won't have the rest of the Guild on my back."

"Exactly."

"But you will kill him, won't you?" Tyg asked quietly. She wasn't sure she could handle another death on her conscience again so soon, especially not Palin's. Why was he being so stupid, he would know by now that Leviathan was a wielder of magic...what was he thinking?

"I'll do my best to avoid that, if that is your wish?" Leviathan said quietly. Tyg saw the look on Antyn's astonished face and knew this was rare.

"Are you serious?" Tyg asked.

"Absolutely, but if he won't accept anything but death, that's not my doing."

"Thank you." Tyg got up and hugged him. He smiled and stroked a hand down her hair, feeling the power she had built up absorb into him. Antyn grimaced and looked away as Leviathan's eyes glowed softly.

"Of course, he might actually win…" Antyn muttered crossly.

Leviathan regarded his brother tersely. "Don't be stupid."

Tyg looked up at Leviathan. "Don't for fuck's sake underestimate him, he taught me all I know."

Leviathan looked at Tyg thoughtfully. "Very well."

"Fine, so we have another day and a half left before we have to worry about that, can we get back to this?" Antyn said changing the subject back to their war plans and tapping the map impatiently.

Tyg looked over at the table they had, had moved into the drawing room and the map on it.

"Is that Tylandria?" Tyg asked in wonder as she walked over to stare at the map.

"Actually, it's the whole continent of Tylan." Antyn said, pointing to a spot in the middle. "This is Tylandria and this…" Antyn ran a large circle around the middle. "…is the stretch of the Empire at this moment."

"But, you're moving into Kolastan as soon as you get back." Tyg stated looking at the map.

"How the fuck do you know that?" Leviathan asked as he moved over to beside her.

Tyg looked up at him. "You know it's unfair to cancel leave for these soldiers on their return…why?"

Leviathan placed his hands on the table and turned his head to look at her, his eyes glowing.

"Are you trying to tell me how to run my Empire now, Tygarya?"

"No! Not at all…sorry…forget I mentioned it." Tyg backed away from the table and went over to the armchairs by the fire again and sat in one. Leviathan had watched her, unmoving. He looked up at Antyn.

"You ask her because I'd like to go at least one day without arguing with the woman." Leviathan growled shaking his head, looking towards the table.

Tyg overheard. "Well, you can't argue with me tomorrow, because it's my birthday." She said smugly.

Leviathan closed his eyes and smiled as he bowed his head to the table. "Oh, Tygarya, do not worry, I had not forgotten." He stood up and pivoted around to look at her, sitting lightly on the table's edge and folding his arms.

Tyg laughed, that musical laugh that made both Sorcerers shudder. "I was only kidding. What's a birthday anyway? I've gone eighteen years without one. I just wish I could convince Tess I don't need any fuss."

"Quite." Leviathan said amused as he glanced at Antyn again. "Well?"

Antyn coughed. "How did you know about Kolastan, Tyg?"

Tyg looked over at them both. "Why? Is it classified?" She sneered.

Leviathan laughed loudly doubling over, then rubbed his forehead. "Fucking Captain Corvyn, you know I really should be stripping him of his rank and giving him ten lashes."

Antyn regarded Leviathan surprised, he could feel a 'but' coming, which would never have even been in his vocabulary before meeting Tyg.

"But, I feel very strongly that it's not his fault...it's yours...I should be giving you the lashes."

Tyg looked at him stunned, then shuddered horrified, hugging herself, remembering. "You wouldn't..."

Leviathan and Antyn looked at each other when they saw her strange reaction. Leviathan's jaw clenched and his eyes brightened to even think someone might have actually whipped her. Antyn shook his head slightly. Leviathan sighed. "No...I wouldn't...but like I said, stop provoking me and stop spending time with Captain Corvyn. In fact, I will let him know he is to swap shifts with Captain Eskel from now on."

"Whatever." Tyg said shrugging causing Leviathan to frown and glance at Antyn again. Tyg saw the look. "I don't care...it doesn't change the fact they were supposed to get a week's leave on returning and now they're not...dissension in the ranks, Leviathan."

Leviathan looked at her astounded for a second then chuckled. "Fucking hell, Tygarya, can you stop championing every lost cause for one second? My men do as they're ordered, simple."

Tyg regarded him, then shrugged and turned away, curling up in the chair and staring at the fire. Leviathan rubbed his forehead again, closing his eyes, then went back to his discussion with Antyn.

66

About an hour later Tyg was in the kitchen sitting with Tess, she had got bored of listening to Leviathan and Antyn talking war strategies and said she was hungry. She wasn't but she was now happily on her third glass of volka when Captain Eskel walked in. Tyg turned and scowled when she saw the middle aged warrior with the scar down one cheek.

"Wow, he was serious then...not even a last word, fuck that is possessive." Tyg muttered as Captain Eskel bowed his head to her and smiled at the comment.

"Captain Corvyn has returned with an invitation from Earl Doven to attend him tomorrow evening." Captain Eskel handed Tyg a small envelope with the earl's seal on it.

"Thanks." Tyg said bitterly as she took the envelope.

Captain Eskel looked at Tyg. "I hope we're not going to have a problem, Lady Tygarya, with this shift change?"

"No, Captain, orders are orders...I get it...I know where to aim my displeasure at." Tyg's eyes flashed but she calmed herself. "Anything else?"

"No, my Lady."

"Fucking hell, back to this again, I had just got the last one trained out of the 'my lady's.'" Tyg grumbled "Did you let Leviathan know?"

"I have not, my Lady. Captain Corvyn told me to bring the message direct to you."

Tyg smiled. Sly, she thought.

"Oh, there is one thing you can do for me, Captain." Tyg said smiling at him. "My balcony, I would like it back...please...with

Antyn back I'm sure the chain could be removed, as it was Corvyn's decision you can reverse it surely?" Captain Eskel looked at her thoughtful. "It would go a ways to forming a good working relationship between us for the days we are still here..." Tyg cocked her head at him and blinked slowly. "Would it not?"

"Hmm, I suppose so, it was done before Lord Antyn arrived back, but has the reason gone away?"

"I haven't attacked anyone that didn't provoke it, Captain, so go ask your Emperor if you must but I would really like to be able to have coffee on my balcony in the morning."

"I will think on it, my Lady." Captain Eskel bowed his head then turned and left.

"What was that about?" Tess asked.

Tyg smiled. "Nothing to worry your pretty head about, now show me the necklace Dane bought you again." Tess gushed and pulled the little silver pendant out of her blouse and held it up.

"Lovely...I'm happy the two of you have finally acknowledged your feelings for each other." Tyg said with a smile. "Well I better go tell Leviathan and Antyn about this invitation."

"Are you going to need a dress?"

"Yes, actually, I am."

"Lucky it's your birthday tomorrow then." Tess grinned widely as Tyg scowled and left.

Leviathan and Antyn were still in the drawing room when Tyg came in.

"Message from Lord Doven." Tyg said holding up the invitation "I've been invited to attend him tomorrow evening for supper and drinks at 8pm to discuss my proposal with him and his son."

"That's good..." Antyn said then caught Leviathan's dark expression. "...isn't it?"

"Who gave you the message?" Leviathan asked.

Tyg smiled. "Relax, it was Eskel."

"Hmm, but you're still in a good mood?" Leviathan said smugly.

"Like I said, I don't care..." Tyg answered. "But what I do need is an escort tomorrow night, I can't attend two Lords without a chaperone either...he's that proper."

Leviathan scowled as Antyn smirked and looked up at her amazed. "How do you do it?"

"Do what?" Tyg asked confused.

Leviathan rubbed his eyes with one hand and shook his head. "There's no way she could have conspired this, surely?"

"You wouldn't think so..." Antyn said studying her.

"Can someone please explain...?" Tyg said annoyed.

"Drop the act, Tygarya, you knew full well that the only escort you can get tomorrow night is Captain fucking Corvyn! Now he has been changed to night shift."

"Well, that works well, because Earl Doven has already met him."

"I've a mind to go myself." Leviathan growled.

"Look, you can send anyone you like, but you are not going. It's important that the Earl is the most important man in the room. He's a class snob and likes people to have to kiss his arse to get favours out of him. I was actually thinking of Antyn going with me."

"So what are you going to be doing for him?" Leviathan growled again.

"Me?" Antyn said surprised.

"Shut it, Antyn, answer the question, Tygarya."

Tyg shrugged. "No doubt he'll ask me to sing for him."

"Of course..." Leviathan grumbled.

"Look, I'm doing this for you....remember."

"And, we are grateful, Tyg, and yes I think it best if I go with you as chaperone." Antyn answered, frowning at Leviathan, whose clenched jaw was ticking.

"Fine...I'm in your debt, Tygarya." Leviathan muttered.

"Well, not yet...but we'll see if I can pull this off."

"I have every faith that you will." Leviathan muttered remembering the last time she sang and the persuasive power it conjured.

Later that evening Tyg was sitting sideways on the couch in the library room, leaning back on the side of Leviathan's arm as he sat behind her, her knees pulled up with a book on them. Leviathan was reading also.

"This is quite pleasant." Tyg said with a smile. "I hope it's more like this if I go back with you."

"If?" Leviathan asked amused. He took a lock of her hair and held it up to his face as Tyg chuckled.

"Yeah, okay. " She said conceding the point. "Why are you always smelling my hair?"

"Because there is a scent there I cannot get."

"Oh, really?"

"Hmm, I get orange, vanilla, lily...even musk and sandalwood...but there's something nutty yet fruity and milky all at the same time that dominates the other fragrances, which I do not know."

"Really? You get all that from my hair?"

"I have a very keen sense of smell." Leviathan chuckled. "I suppose that's why it confounds me so much."

"Have you wondered that maybe it's because it comes from something you don't have back home?" Tyg asked him.

"Yes, it has...what is it?"

"Coconut oil. I soak my hair in it because it keeps it strong and healthy..." Tyg laughed to herself. "After years on the streets I guess I have become quite vain about my hair, but that's why it's so thick and shiny." Tyg smiled.

"And able to hide weapons." Leviathan growled as he picked a handful up and ran his fingers through it.

Tyg looked down at her book. "Now remember, no provoking."

"That's for you, not me...besides because it's so thick and strong means I can do this..." Leviathan grabbed a large handful up and twined it around his forearm then yanked back tilting Tyg's head back and up towards him, as he pulled the arm she was leaning on free and wrapped it around her. He planted a kiss on her lips, then smiled at her as she was arched back over his lap. "There's nothing you can do, is there? You're at my mercy..." He chuckled then kissed her again on the lips.

"Not fair, but maybe I don't want to do anything about it right now..." Tyg said as she leaned round, turning her body towards him and put her arms around his neck. Leviathan grinned then kissed her again, deeply this time.

"Brother in the room." Antyn mumbled from over at the desk where he had been filling in permit forms.

"Fuck off then." Leviathan growled.

Antyn turned and looked at them, just as Leviathan kissed Tyg again, his hand going to her stomach and slowly sliding up. Tyg broke the kiss off and tried to get up, but Leviathan wouldn't let her.

"Stay right there, Antyn." Tyg said panicking. "Let me up...let me up..."

Leviathan let Tyg up, his eyes looked startled at the sudden change in her. "Why do you do that?"

Tyg blushed. "I...I said take things slow." Tyg sat up putting her feet on the floor, she raked her fingers through her hair. Leviathan leaned his elbow on the arm of the couch and rested his fingers to his temple as he leaned his head down and looked at her sideways. He crossed an ankle up over the thigh of his other leg.

Antyn got up and went to the drinks cabinet and poured the two of them a drink each, he walked over and handed them to them.

"I'm going to the kitchen, I'm suddenly hungry for some supper."

Tyg took the drink and downed half of it in one gulp with a nervous action. Antyn looked surprised. "Okay, do you want the whole decanter?"

Leviathan snorted. "Yes, she does...she drinks like a fish."

Tyg turned to him and stared daggers at him.

"What? You do!" He laughed.

Antyn had gone back over and grabbed the decanter and placed it on the low table in front of them. "Enjoy." He turned and left as Tyg watched him, biting her lip nervously.

"Don't worry, Tyg...trust me" Leviathan said softly as he took up a lock of her hair again and smelt it. "What's a coconut?" He asked, changing the subject.

Later that night, when Tyg went to her room she noticed the chain and padlock was gone from the balcony. She grinned to herself and stepped out into the darkness. She stood out there, leaning on the railing for only a few minutes, waiting and listening. Finally she heard the jingle of armour and called down.

"I need to speak to Captain Corvyn." She could see the flash of metal in the light cast by the moon. The soldier moved away.

After another wait she heard the jingle of armour again, it came up directly underneath her and Tyg could just make out a figure in the darkness.

"Tygarya, what is it?" Corvyn's harsh whisper came up from the darkness.

Tyg smiled down at him. "I missed you."

"What the hell?"

"Don't get mad, we've spent a lot of time together over the past few days. Leviathan thinks he's so smart changing your shifts because he's jealous of nothing, but like I told you...I need you in my corner."

"Tygarya...you can't do this."

"Do what?" Tyg grinned down at him. "No one will know."

"My soldiers will know."

"So scare them a little, they'll stay quiet."

"It's not proper..."

"Pah, haven't you got it yet, Corvyn...nothing I do is proper...I wasn't raised that way." Tyg laughed.

"No, you were raised to cause trouble and break the law."

"Interesting...who have you been talking to?

"Was there a reason for calling me over here?"

"Just to hear your voice."

Corvyn sighed. "Goodnight, Tygarya." He muttered then stormed off.

"Goodnight, Captain." Tyg muttered smiling to herself.

67

Her morning had gone well, starting with a coffee delivered by Tess, so she could enjoy her newly unchained balcony again.

Then once Tess had persuaded her to go downstairs and into the servant's quarters, Tess had presented her with not one, but two dresses for her birthday. Apparently they had all chipped in the money for the fabrics, which Tyg could see would have been expensive.

One dress was a shimmering silver silk dress of classic simple lines and was sleeveless but came with a matching shawl to drape over her shoulders, which Tyg decided to wear to Lord Doven's later that night.

The other dress was a stunning black dress which Tess explained was to be put away and not worn until she was in Tylandria. Tyg was surprised Tess had finally made her a black dress. She hugged them all and thanked them from the bottom of her heart and had enjoyed a friendly breakfast with them. She decided that birthdays were nice after all.

The frost was thick today, snow would soon be here, so Tyg had taken up her usual residence in the library, curled up on the couch with a book, the fire roaring.

Antyn came up and handed Tyg a book. "For your birthday. It's a book of myths and legends, short stories from back home. It was part of my personal collection, I thought you would like it."

"Antyn…" Tyg said speechless as she sat up and gently took the book. "I don't know what to say…"

"Well, I thought you would like the stories, they all have morals behind them."

"Really..." Tyg was studying the fine leather embossed cover, then opened it and peeked inside. The illustrations were amazingly detailed and the writing was intricate.

"Of course, you'll have to learn our language to be able to read it, but think of it as incentive."

"Incentive?"

"Well, you're coming back? You're going to have to start learning our language."

"Oh, you're right." Tyg closed the book and stroked it. "Thank you, Antyn, this is the first book I have ever owned...I will treasure it."

"First book? Wow, okay...I didn't mean for it to be that big of a deal."

Tyg smiled as Antyn sat down in the armchair next to her. "Hey Tyg?" Antyn asked. "I was wondering, after Lev told me about those assassin squads...were you ever in one?" Tyg scowled at him. "Oh, come on, just a quick yes or no, is all I ask, it's not an interrogation and it's not divulging secrets about the Guild...I'm just curious."

Tyg scowled deeper at him. "Yes, for a short time." She muttered as she looked at her knees.

"A short time?"

Tyg looked up at him with a strange expression, it was a mix of mirth, anger and overwhelming grief. "It was decided I didn't work well in groups."

Antyn saw it clearly now. "You lost someone...someone dear to you..."

Tyg's eyes flashed. "Shut up, Antyn!" Tyg put the book on the table and stood up.

Antyn actually thought she was going to attack him. "Tyg, calm down, I'm just trying to understand you a bit better, I'm playing catch up after being in Landau."

"My life is not up for discussion." Tyg said as she stormed out of the library.

As she walked across the main room, Leviathan was coming in the doors from outside. He saw her expression.

"Tygarya." Leviathan said in that low commanding voice making her stop and turn.

"What?" She said more harshly than she intended.

"Something's wrong?" Leviathan said as he approached her. He could feel the power emanating from her.

"Just tell your brother to stop asking me bloody questions."

"Oh, I see." Leviathan said. "He's a scholar it's his nature to be curious and ask questions. I'll tell him to stop." Leviathan held his arm out to her. "Come here and calm down."

As Tyg walked into his embrace and muttered a Thank You, she suddenly felt much calmer. Leviathan's eyes flashed with the power he took from her.

He stepped back and grabbed her hand. "Come on, I have something planned for today." He walked through the main entrance with Tyg half walking half being dragged along by him as he held her hand firmly.

"What? Planned?" Tyg stammered as Leviathan had her out the doors and down the steps where Dane was standing holding two horses.

Dane was smiling at Tyg as Leviathan stopped and let go of her hand. Tyg noticed that one of the horses was Leviathan's big black stallion. The other a roan gelding.

"Where are we going?" Tyg asked Leviathan as she looked at him seeing him staring at her with that vulture gaze but with a sardonic smile.

"Is it not obvious?"

"Well, I see horses, but I thought I wasn't allowed away from the Manor?"

"No, Tygarya, you're not allowed out without me." Tyg's eyes went wide as Leviathan chuckled. "I figured you could do with a ride in the countryside...I'm sure since we're meeting with the Assassin's Guild tomorrow there will be no worries."

"A ride in the country?"

"If you want to?"

Tyg smiled. "Yes, I do...very much."

"Then let's go." Leviathan jumped up on his horse and waited for Tyg to mount in the saddle of the roan. Dane held its head as she did so.

"Have fun, Tyg."

"Ha, sure...thanks Dane." Tyg smiled and turned to Leviathan. "So, do you know where we're going?"

"Of course, try and keep up." He nudged his horse into a canter, then a full gallop as the guards at the gate opened it in anticipation. As he galloped off Tyg noticed a familiar bag of hers on the back of his horse.

"What the fuck?" She exclaimed and dug her heels into her horse in an attempt to catch up.

Tyg caught up to Leviathan once he slowed to a canter, but he nudged his horse back into a gallop again as she got near. Tyg smiled as she tucked herself behind her horse's neck and let its head loose so it had full extension. As she caught up to Leviathan he glanced sideways at her and laughed, then slowed his horse to a canter again. Tyg slowed her horse too and they cantered down the country lane for a couple of miles, then Leviathan took a left turn and followed that road heading towards the coast.

"Where are we going?" Tyg asked as they turned down another road.

"Somewhere secluded." Leviathan said cryptically and grinned.

"You're enjoying yourself." Tyg laughed

"And, you're not?"

"Yes I am, it's fantastic. I love fresh air." Tyg looked around at the meadows with their flocks of sheep. Leviathan suddenly turned his horse off the road and went down a farm's access road.

"Where are we going?" Tyg asked again.

They followed the grass track till its end at the end of a high craggy cliff. Leviathan jumped off his horse and strode right to the cliffs edge and stood staring out at the sea. Tyg dismounted and walked over to him. She followed his gaze out to the horizon.

"Are you homesick?" Tyg asked.

Leviathan turned and regarded her with a whimsical smile. He reached out his arm and she stepped into it as he embraced her. She hugged her arms around his waist and looked up at him.

"Why are we out here?"

He stared off at the horizon again, then looked down to face her, lifting her chin with one finger.

"I thought you might like to let out some energy and do some of your sword training."

"What? I thought I saw my weapon bag on your horse...so that's why the isolation."

Leviathan just smiled and stroked a lock of her hair that had come loose from her braid, away from her face as the breeze kept blowing it across the bridge of her nose. "So would you want to?"

"Gods! It's been so long."

"It's been just over a week..." Leviathan admonished her.

"When you're used to training every day for two hours at least a day...that seems like an eternity."

Leviathan chuckled. "I suppose so."

He turned and walked her back to his horse and handed her, her bag. She took it and crouched down opening it up. He was surprised at the array of weapons in there. She pulled out the sword she had been given by the Assassin's Guild and wiped the blade with her hand when she pulled it clear of its scabbard. She gave it an experimental twist of her wrist, sending it whistling round in an arc.

"So, you're just going to watch?"

Leviathan laughed. "Now is not the time for us to cross swords, Tygarya, so yes."

"Okay then." Tyg shrugged and walked off, circling her shoulders and arms warming them up. She jumped up onto a cropping of boulders and jumped from one to another getting higher and closer to the cliff edge. Once she was up high silhouetted against the sky she stood for a moment, taking in the calm and quiet and then started with the routine she always did back at the warehouse. Slashing, twirling, jabbing and somersaulting from rock to rock like she had done crate to crate.

Leviathan stood with his arms folded and watched silently. He was mesmerised by her movements, they came so easy and natural, fluid. Silhouetted up there he could see what she would become if allowed to. He clenched his jaw. "Like a fucking angel." He muttered and rubbed his chin with his thumb thoughtfully.

She paused at the pinnacle of rock, with her sword held out in front of her with two hands. Leviathan blinked as he saw her strike that pose from side on. He was glad no one else was there to see it. She could lead entire armies looking like that, Leviathan thought bitterly, then grinned to himself, he had only to get through tomorrow and she would be his.

Tyg eventually jumped down and walked back over and placed her sword back into its scabbard and sat cross legged down on the grass. Leviathan threw a water skin at her which she caught deftly and drank heavily from it.

"Thanks." She held it up to him but he shook his head and sat down on the grass next to her, folding one leg under him and the other was bent up so he could rest his elbow on his knee.

"Feel better?" He asked with an eyebrow raised.

"Yes, but now I'm all sweaty, so I'm going to have to bathe when we get back, before I head to the Dovens."

"Quite." Leviathan smiled wickedly.

Tyg just looked at him blankly, he chuckled and turned his head to look out at the sea again. Tyg appreciated the view of his side profile for a moment and then turned herself around and lay down in the grass, resting her head on his thigh as she grabbed a blade of grass and stuck it in her mouth.

Leviathan looked down on her surprised. She was so carefree with him, he was always so astounded by it. He was glad she had grown up here away from his continent and his reputation, not to mention the protocols of the Empire. She glanced up at him and smiled.

"This is by far the best birthday gift of the day, thank you."

Leviathan smiled. "Simple pleasures, huh?" He placed his hand on the grass beside her hip and leaned on it so he could look at her. With the arm that had been resting on his knee he grabbed her braid and started to slowly undo it.

Tyg chuckled. "You're obsessed with my hair."

"Hmm, now I know it can hide weapons..." Leviathan grunted as he nimbly worked his fingers through each crossing of hair until he finally had it all free and splayed out over his legs. Tyg silently watched his face while he did it. She suddenly sat up, crashing her lips into his, taking him by surprise. But he caught her in his arm and held her as she kissed him. He closed his eyes and kissed her back. When Tyg pulled her head away he looked at her with his sapphire blue eyes glittering.

"That was nice." He said truthfully.

Tyg actually blushed prettily making Leviathan frown, then she turned and rested her head on his chest and they both stared out to sea as he sat up and put both arms around her.

"I need to know which side you're on tomorrow, Tyg." Leviathan said to her quietly, as he kissed the top of her head. He felt her tense up, but she didn't move away.

"Is that why you brought me out here?"

"No."

"Good." Leviathan could hear the growl in her voice. "I can't support either one of you tomorrow, I think what you're doing is stupid and I don't condone it."

Leviathan stared out at the sea and remained silent for a while and he felt her relax into him again. He reached into his pocket and pulled out a ring and held it out in front of Tyg. It was a large gold dragon's head ring with sapphire eyes and silver teeth. It was jointed with two bands and went over the whole knuckle of one finger, so when bent its horns became formidable weapons in a punch.

Tyg gasped when she saw it and sat up, turning around to look at Leviathan as he spoke.

"I got this made for you."

"What the...?"

"I want to know that you're coming back with me, Tyg."

"I don't know what to say..."

"It's just a symbol of how serious I am about this...about you, you don't have to wear it yet, when you're ready too...but I just wanted to give it to you on your birthday."

"That dragon's head..."

"Yes, it's the symbol of the Adramelech Royal House, the same as my soldiers wear in their crest."

"And, what's tattooed on your back."

Leviathan chuckled. "Yes...you liked that?"

"It surprised me, but yes, it is exquisite." Tyg took the ring and held it in her hand. She was speechless. She had no clue that he was going to give her anything, let alone a ring of the symbol of his Royal House. "I will put it on a chain for now and wear it around my neck." Tyg whispered, still in shock.

"As you wish." Leviathan said smiling, his eyes glowing faintly.

Tyg looked up at those deep sapphire eyes and realised why the dragon eyes were blue sapphires.

"I will go back with you, Leviathan, regardless of tomorrow's outcome."

Leviathan gave her a strange look and reached out and pulled her into him, he lowered his head to rest on hers and embraced her. "Just call me Lev."

Tyg smiled a small contented smile. "Okay." She whispered.

Leviathan moved sideways then and pushed Tyg gently down to lie in the grass. He lay down next to her on his side, propping his head up on his crooked arm, looking at her. She looked up at him and blinked slowly. He leaned down and kissed her, just on the lips and propped his head up again.

Tyg rolled over onto her side and did the same, looking straight into his eyes. As they locked eyes together Leviathan just smiled and watched as Tyg moved her mouth to his to kiss him again. He embraced her then and kissed her fully and deeply. He wanted to just take her right there in the grass but he knew she wouldn't, so he contented himself with holding her and kissing her for several more minutes, then he sat up and looking once more out at sea he took a deep breath and stood up holding his hand out to her.

"We better head back."

"How did it go?" Antyn asked Leviathan later.

"She took it, hook, line and sinker...you were right, given the chance to expel some energy she is a lot more docile and easier to manipulate."

"And the ring?"

"She has it, but won't wear it yet."

"Give it time."

"Antyn, you should have seen it...when she was doing her training..." Leviathan shook his head. "...fuck me...if she was left to her own devices she would be the one ruling the world."

"Yeah, I figured."

"Gods, I need her under my control."

"And you will...and the prophecy will come to pass, don't worry."

Leviathan laughed causing Antyn to look at him, frowning. "What's so funny?"

"I'm just picturing my Generals' and Lord Chamberlain's faces when I arrive home with this silver haired Elvian on my arm."

"Ha! Yes. It's the castle steward I feel sorry for...he doesn't know what's coming in his direction. You might get some obstruction."

"Then they will burn for their insolence." Leviathan growled.

Antyn looked away at the flames, glad his ruthless brother was still in there, he had changed so much with Tyg around.

68

When Tyg came down the stairs later, dressed in the silver silk dress that Tess had made, Leviathan looked at Antyn and frowned.

"I definitely think I should be going."

"Nonsense, Lev...she'll be fine, with me and the Captain, nothing will go wrong."

Leviathan growled and his eyes blazed.

"Really, Lev, anyone would think you're actually starting to get real feelings for her."

"I am..." Antyn baulked and looked at Leviathan. "...the possessive kind." He said smugly.

"Oh...right." Antyn chuckled as Tyg reached the floor and Leviathan stepped over to her.

"Tygarya, you look beautiful...I don't want you to leave."

"What?" Tyg thought he was serious for a moment. "Oh, well, like I said I'm doing this for you."

"How can I ever repay you?" Leviathan's eyes smouldered with a smoky darkness.

Tyg smiled at him and put a hand on his chest. "Back up there, big boy. You might ruin my hair."

Leviathan went wide eyed, surprised and then frowned as she walked past him towards Antyn who was waiting at the door, laughing.

"Well, big brother? See, no need to worry about this young, beautiful hellion."

Tyg smiled sweetly at Antyn and reached out and patted his cheek as she past, trailing a finger along his jawline, causing Antyn to react the same as Leviathan just did. It was Leviathan's turn to laugh as he walked up and grabbed Antyn by the shoulder.

"Don't underestimate her, she's probably got a weapon concealed in that bodice somewhere and she's positively oozing power and confidence right now. Damn her, she knows how good she looks."

"Fucking hell, she doesn't need a weapon...she is one." Antyn agreed looking at the way her dress clung to her curvy bottom.

"Antyn!" Leviathan growled.

"Yeah, I know...she's yours...radda radda..." Antyn turned and followed Tyg out to the waiting carriage.

As Tyg had stepped out she saw Corvyn standing in all his Imperial Army glory, next to the open door of the carriage. She saw his jaw clench as he looked at her. "Lady Tygarya." He bowed his head to her, but smiled as he raised his head and met her eyes again.

"Captain Corvyn, nice to see you again." Tyg said with a cordial smile. She could feel Leviathan's stare and knew he was standing just behind her with Antyn, on the steps. But, she winked as she past Corvyn and stepped into the carriage. Corvyn grit his teeth as Antyn stepped into the carriage and closed the door.

"Tyg, my dear, you're looking as lovely as ever." Lord Doven said as he took her hand and kissed it. Tyg smiled at him, but discreetly wiped the back of her hand on her dress as she turned to introduce Antyn, but instead she saw Thomas scowling down at Corvyn, obviously noticing his change of rank. Corvyn was standing on the drive by the carriage in all his military regalia, his hand resting casually on his sword and grinning up at Thomas. Tyg frowned at him and Thomas also caught the look.

"Tyg, it's so nice to see you again." Thomas said as he also kissed her hand. Good, Tyg thought, he's obviously on his best behaviour in front of his father.

"This is Lord Antyn Adramelech, I think you have met before..." Tyg said as Antyn stepped up and bowed his head at Lord Doven.

"Yes, indeed, I must say your letter has quite peeked my curiosity, Tyg...Lord Antyn...please come through to the drawing room so we may discuss your proposal."

"Ah, I have one request, my Lord, before we go any further..." Antyn stepped forward.

"Yes, Lord Antyn, what is it I can help you with?"

"I humbly but rightfully request that you refer to Tygarya by her proper title when addressing her."

Tyg looked at Antyn stunned and gritted her teeth.

"I am sorry but I have to admit I am confused here." Lord Doven said. "I am not aware of ...Tygarya, you say...having any title?" Tyg heard the hint of a sneer, she groaned.

"Probably because, my Lord, you are not from Tylandria or aware of Tygarya's heritage."

"Indeed I am not, although, I must say..." Lord Doven turned to Tyg. "...and I hope you don't think me impertinent to say...but I always thought she looked like she should have come from good breeding."

"Good breeding?" Tyg's eyes went wide and blazed suddenly, but Antyn chuckled.

"Quite, my Lord."

"So, it is Lady Tygarya?"

"Lady Essyndyl, my Lord"

"Quite..." Lord Doven thought about it a moment and glanced at his son. "...and spoken for?"

Antyn smiled. "Yes." Tyg was starting to get to boiling point.

"Your brother, then the rumours going around are true?"

"Indeed, they are correct."

"For the sake of all the Lords and Ladies in the room can we just skip this protocol in the name of friendship and just use first names?" Thomas stepped in, seeing Tyg's discomfort at being talked about.

Antyn smiled at Thomas. "I concede if you agree, my Lord?"

"Indeed...Lady Essyndyl?"

"Absolutely." Tyg breathed as she scowled at Antyn, the conversation about her had thrown her off.

"Excellent, please follow me." Lord Doven said as he bowed his head graciously.

As they walked behind Lord Doven and Thomas Tyg grabbed Antyn's arm and pulled him back a bit.

"What the hell was that?"

Antyn shrugged. "Something Lev wanted stated, I didn't realise it would turn into a match making conversation."

"Wait till I see him..."

"Calm down, Tyg, it puts you on a level footing with the Lord, otherwise he would have spoken down to you."

"That's why you're here...besides I'm a woman..."

"It's your plan, so any advantage."

"Some warning next time..." Tyg said as she took a deep breath and gathered herself.

As they entered the drawing room Thomas was pouring wine and Lord Doven was seating himself behind a grand desk. Tyg and Antyn sat in very nice upholstered chairs in front of the desk and Thomas handed them each a glass as well as his father.

"So, Tygarya, you're in need of ships?"

"Indeed."

"So, you're planning on going back to Tylandria with these men?" Thomas blurted out causing his father to scowl at him. Thomas folded his arms and sat down in a chair off to one side.

"I must apologise for my son's outburst, he will not speak again until spoken to."

Tyg smiled. "Not to worry Edger, Thomas is a concerned friend and I love him dearly for it...also, I haven't had the chance to say congratulations on the engagement. Is there a date set for the wedding?"

"Thank you...no not yet." Thomas grumbled back.

"No..." Lord Doven interjected. "There will be no wedding until Thomas has quit the City Watch and taken his rightful place at Doven Shipping Company."

"I see." Tyg grinned, it was exactly as she had thought, snobbery.

"So, how many ships are you requiring?"

Tyg looked at Antyn. "Ten should do it." He answered with a shrug.

"Ten! I had no idea you were talking so many." Lord Doven choked. "And how do you intend to pay for ten ships fully manned taken for....how long?"

Again Tyg looked at Antyn. "They would be gone at least two months, it's just under a month each way in good weather and we are approaching winter here."

"Two months! Ten ships! I could be bankrupt having that many ships out of commission for that long."

"We are prepared to pay the sailors ourselves for their time, directly. Also, this sailing will open new territory for you to trade to, Leviathan is willing to negotiate permanent trading routes for your ships." Lord Doven's eyes went wide at the possibilities. "So, it's just a matter of what your ships are worth versus profit lost while they are out of your hands."

"Yes...quite...and your brother has the jurisdiction to promise such negotiations?"

Antyn laughed. "Oh yes, very much so." Tyg was surprised that most of the Lords still didn't know Leviathan was an Emperor.

"Well, I could make a hundred ounce weight pieces of gold a week off ten ships."

"So, you're saying eight hundred ounce bars?" Tyg asked frowning.

"Plus extra for ships worth in case any are lost at sea in storms." Lord Doven added slyly.

"Of course, let's say one thousand all up." Tyg said as she took a sip of her wine and locked eyes with Lord Doven. Antyn noticed her eyes were glowing slightly, he smiled to himself as he felt her power. "What worth do you then put on your son's marriage to Lady Belmont?" Tyg asked.

"What?" Lord Doven asked surprised. "What do you mean?" He held his hand up to Thomas to be silent.

"You said Thomas was being required to leave the City Watch and become part of the family business, but let's be honest...Lady Belmont isn't going to want to live here with her new husband, under your roof, is she?"

Thomas stood up. "What are you saying, Tyg?"

Tyg slid her eyes over to Thomas. "I'm right, aren't I?"

Thomas stammered and shoved his hands into his pockets.

"Yes, you are correct." Lord Doven said. "But, what's that got to do with our discussion concerning ships?" Antyn leaned back in his chair with his wine enjoying the show.

"Well, it just so happens that I have a Manor house available, fully furnished with staff and five acres of land for the reasonable rate of...oh...let's say..."

"Wait a minute!" Lord Doven interrupted. "How do you have a Manor house?"

"She doesn't." Antyn piped up. "But, I do...Lord Karon's old place, not two miles down the road, nice and close to the family residence."

Thomas gawked at Antyn and Tyg, then turned to his father. "Do it, Father!"

Tyg smiled a slow sardonic smile at the desperation in Thomas's voice...young love. Lord Doven stared hard at Tyg as she sipped her wine again, looking at him over the rim.

"Perhaps a few minutes with my son to discuss this." Lord Doven muttered.

"Certainly." Tyg and Antyn stood up and Antyn escorted Tyg out into the large living area.

"Remind me to have you present at all my negotiations." Antyn muttered to her under his breath.

"Hmm." Tyg grunted with a grin. "It hasn't worked yet. Do you have access to that sort of gold?"

"Hardly, not here."

"How much did you bring with you?"

"We've got maybe two hundred." Antyn shrugged again.

Tyg's eyes widened. "You're kidding?"

"Well, it's gone down with having to pay Lord Karon and the mine workers and such."

"Come down...fuck, how much gold did you bring with you?"

"Oh, you meant it as being a lot." Antyn laughed. "Leviathan owns a gold mine."

"You're serious?"

"Yes, he's Emperor, Tyg, he owns everything in his Empire."

"Fuck, I had no idea."

Antyn stepped closer to Tyg, his eyes bright and full of intent. "He is all powerful, Tyg, it's what Emperor means."

"Yeah, I'm slowly figuring that out."

"Figure it out faster, so we can all go home."

Tyg looked up at Antyn shocked, then scowled at him. "So tomorrow can't come soon enough for you then?" Her eyes blazed at him turning ice blue.

"Tyg, not here...I shouldn't have said that, sorry."

"Forget it." Tyg said as she wandered over to a grand piano and sat down, hitting a key.

"Do you play?" Antyn asked.

"No..." Tyg said as she hit two more keys like she was searching for a specific note. She hit another one and smiled. She hit it again and started humming at the key. Antyn looked at her as she started humming a song on a mournful tune, then she started singing it. A tragic love ballad about a poor boy in love with a Lord's daughter. Lord Doven and Thomas came out of the study at the sound and Thomas walked over to the piano, sat down next to Tyg and started playing the accompanying tune. Tyg stopped and smiled.

"You play the piano?"

"Yes, and I happen to know this one, start again." Thomas said smiling.

Tyg started again with Thomas playing the piano. Antyn watched amazed as Lord Doven came to stand beside him.

"Simply magnificent." He muttered.

Antyn looked at him and smiled...completely enthralled, he thought. As the song came to an end Lord Doven clapped. "Another, please." Tyg smiled and looked at Thomas.

"What else do you know?"

69

After a couple more songs Tyg had managed to congregate a whole audience of every person in the house. Lord Doven's wife and daughter and the servants had all quietly made their way towards the angelic sounds. Tyg stopped to a great round of applause.

"I need a drink." Tyg said with a smile.

"At once!" Lord Doven ordered snapping the servants out of their reverie. The butler poured Tyg a wine and brought it to her.

"Thank you." Tyg said as she glanced at Antyn, who was standing with his arms folded. She could see the family resemblance when he did that. He caught her look and winked at her making her smile.

"Gods, Tyg! We're going to miss that voice." Lord Doven said as he walked over to the piano.

"So, my Lord, what is your decision?" Tyg said with her eyes still blazing, locking eyes with him.

Lord Doven pouted in thought. "Eight hundred for the house and two hundred in gold."

"Nine hundred for the house and one hundred in gold." Tyg countered as she placed a discreet hand on Thomas's shoulder. Thomas looked at her, and she looked down on him smiling, then he looked back at his father.

"Sold! Agreed! Whatever...we take the deal." Thomas blurted out.

Lord Doven looked stunned at his son and grimaced as Tyg grinned. Antyn was amazed.

"Fine then, agreed." Lord Doven said and held his hand out to Tyg, who stood up and shook on the deal. "I'll have the papers drawn up for Lord Adramelech to sign tomorrow with the gold."

"Certainly." Antyn said stepping over and shaking Lord Doven's hand, they walked off to drink on it.

Tyg sat back down....tomorrow....she grimaced.

"Thanks Tyg." Thomas whispered to her.

"Quite alright, just make sure your lovely little wife treats the staff well...they're friends of mine."

Thomas laughed. "Of course they are."

"It's my parting gift to everyone." Tyg said smiling sadly.

"I'm going to miss you." Thomas said with an edge of regret.

"I'm going to miss you too." Tyg wrapped her arms around Thomas's neck hugging him and kissed him on the cheek. She caught Antyn's look of disapproval from across the room, and she stood up. "I think it's time to go."

That night on her balcony Tyg was looking at the moon when she heard the jingle of armour below her in the darkness. She smiled and went to the railing, leaning on it and looking down.

"Corvyn." She said quietly.

"Tygarya...was that you singing tonight?"

Tyg laughed. "Is that why you looked weirdly at me when we got in the carriage?"

"Sorry...I was...your voice is..."

"Thank you, Corvyn." Tyg let him off the hook. She looked back up at the moon. "Corvyn..."

"Yes?"

"Has either brother said anything to you about tomorrow?"

"Tomorrow?" Corvyn's voice sounded genuinely naïve.

"Hmm, tomorrow is going to be a big day...for everyone...be prepared."

"Why? What's happening?"

"Someone is going to die tomorrow and I can't stop it." The sadness in Tyg's voice tore at Corvyn. "Would you like me to sing a song for you?"

"Tygarya, I could never ask such a thing of you."

Tyg laughed a short sharp chortle. "Oh, Corvyn, you are more proper than Lord Doven."

Tyg started humming a wordless lament, then let her voice go souring and dipping sadly. Corvyn stood looking up at her silhouette, her hair glowing in the moonlight, her arms folded on the railing as she sang to the moon. He swallowed hard and shuddered, his eyes glowing faintly. She turned and slid down the balustrade then to sit on the ground, disappearing from Corvyn's view as her song got sadder, he knew she was crying and wished he could go up there. He bit his lip and walked away muttering. "That bloody woman."

Both Antyn and Leviathan came out of their rooms at the sound. Leviathan strode up to Tyg's door but Antyn put a hand on his arm and shook his head. Leviathan pressed his hands on either side of the door frame and bent his head, pressing his forehead against the door, listening to Tyg's singing.

"She's sad about tomorrow, she knows the outcome before it's even happened." Leviathan growled.

"It would seem that's what it is about yes." Antyn agreed scratching his chin. "Tomorrow was mentioned at the Doven's and she has been melancholy ever since...it is what it is, Lev."

Leviathan growled. "It could jeopardise everything we've done here."

The singing stopped. "You need to eliminate him, he's the only reason she has for staying now, she's secured all her friends positions, amazingly."

"I know, but what's going to be the cost?' Leviathan turned to regard his brother. "Damn her upbringing to hell, I am going to make him pay dearly for it." He stalked back to his room and slammed the door.

70

As they walked into the gloom of the warehouse Tyg instantly noticed Palin standing in the middle of the large open space, two assassins flanked him, their faces covered and their arms folded. Tyg was surprised there didn't seem to be anyone else.

Leviathan gripped her shoulder tightly causing her to grimace as he stopped her from walking any further.

"Introductions are in order." Leviathan growled.

"Of course...I'm Palin, head of the Assassin's Guild here in Arial."

Leviathan smiled to finally have his name. "Palin." He said in an icy voice.

"First things first, I need Tyg to put these on." Palin instructed as he threw some manacles into the dirt at her feet. "We all know how unpredictable you can be, I don't want you thinking you can involve yourself in any of this."

"What the fuck! No way is anyone getting those things on me!" Tyg growled as she stepped away from everyone.

"I actually have to agree with him." Leviathan said smiling and lowering his head. He glanced at his brother. "Put them on her."

Antyn stepped over and picked them up, noticing the key was sitting in the lock of one, as Tyg stepped backwards again, wary.

"Like fuck, Leviathan!" Tyg growled, then she saw the look on his face as he turned to face her. "You fucking wouldn't? I'll never forgive you!"

"Wouldn't I? There is no other way..." Leviathan grinned as he sent pain into Tyg's head. She collapsed to her knees but tried to fight the pain as Leviathan only increased it. Tyg grabbed the sides of her head. Antyn stepped up behind Tyg and grabbed one of her arms twisting it round and clapping the manacle on her wrist. He then grabbed her other hand but Tyg fought against him pulling her arm back not letting him twist it round behind her back.

Leviathan increased the pain making Tyg yield and Antyn was able to fix the manacle round her wrist. As soon as the manacles were on her wrists the pain stopped, but not before Tyg's nose had begun to bleed.

Palin looked shocked as Tyg lifted her head and glared at all of them. "So that's how you've been able to control her."

She looked at Palin and sneered at him her eyes blazing. "Fuck you!"

"Keep her on her knees too." Palin said grimacing at her. "That's a neat trick Sorcerer."

"You seem to know a lot about what's going on here...interesting." Leviathan said.

"Well, what people don't know about me is I originally come from Gardonia and I know all about you, Emperor Leviathan Adramelech of Tylandria. You see I was there in Gardonia when you pushed through and took half of Gardonia for yourself because you wanted a sea port on that side of the continent."

"Very interesting." Leviathan said his eyes blazing.

"What the fuck, Palin." Tyg growled.

"So you have known exactly what Tygarya is from the very beginning...it all makes sense now." Leviathan grinned viciously.

"I'm no expert on magic but I know my history." Palin shrugged.

"What the fuck is going on here?" Tyg muttered.

"It seems you've been groomed for a purpose right from the start, Tygarya. Palin here, knew you for an Elvian the first time he saw you and that's why he took you in and made you his own personal killing machine...isn't that right?"

Tyg's head was in turmoil.

"Correct." Palin said with no hint of remorse.

Antyn was standing behind Tyg a hand on her shoulder, keeping her from rising, but she was getting more and more worked up. Antyn put both hands on her shoulders and sent a wave of calm through her. She shuddered and looked over her shoulder at him.

He was surprised at her eyes blazing. "Get the fuck off me, Antyn." Tyg said calmly.

He realised then that calmness wouldn't work on her because she wasn't feeling any anger emotions right now, she had passed through that and was deadly calm. He purposely stood on the chain between her wrists to prevent her from getting away from him. She growled.

Leviathan glanced over. "Do you have her, brother?"

Antyn looked at Leviathan but said nothing.

"Quite the handful, isn't she?" Palin laughed.

Leviathan slid his gaze back to Palin. The look on his face was enough to cause the two assassins to both reach for their swords.

"Shut the fuck up." Leviathan said to Palin, taking off his coat and rolling his shoulders. He blamed Palin for Tyg's dangerous headstrong personality.

"Oh, gods, don't tell me you've fallen for her unusual charms too?" Palin laughed again.

"Let's get this over with." Leviathan growled and placed a hand on his sword.

"Whoa there, ground rules first...Emperor." Palin said, drawing out the title facetiously.

"Yeah, let me guess...no magic...fine by me. Let's go!" Leviathan drew his sword and flicked his wrist round sending the sword arcing round in a circle. Leviathan held it low and with confidant purpose. Tyg suddenly noticed movement to her left, she glanced over and saw a bowmen with an arrow aimed at her. "What the fuck?"

Leviathan turned and saw the bowman kneeling up on a shipping crate. Palin smiled.

"You use magic, she gets an arrow."

"Fuck you, Palin." Tyg growled, straining against Antyn's weight on the chain.

"I don't need magic." Leviathan snorted as he stepped closer. Tyg knew Leviathan had a right to be cocky, he wasn't an emperor raised in riches. He was an emperor raised as a warrior on the battlefield and his muscle tone showed it, but Palin was also an expert swordsman. However, although strong and bullish he wouldn't have Leviathan's stamina. Tyg knew Palin's plan would be to strike hard and fast and try to end this quickly.

Leviathan struck first, the ring of steel on steel reverberated around the empty warehouse as Leviathan locked swords with Palin as the two assassins dived out of the way. Leviathan leaned in as Palin tried to push back, and grinned viciously at him. "I'm going to take great pleasure in destroying you."

"Talk's cheap." Palin said back as he finally pushed Leviathan back freeing his sword.

There followed a flurry of strikes back and forth all seemingly well defended, when suddenly Palin grunted and moved away holding his arm. Tyg saw blood leaking through his fingers. Leviathan didn't give an inch and struck again. He was still calm and collected and hadn't even broken a sweat. Tyg couldn't fault his swordsmanship and had to admit he was probably the best she had ever seen. She had to re-evaluate what she had said about having a sword fight with him, he matched her on strength and he may even be better than her with a sword.

He jabbed and thrust and swung his sword round with astonishing speed and Tyg could see, although Palin had held his own, he was beginning to tire. Leviathan opened up Palin's cheek and grinned again.

"You have the opportunity to concede, Palin." Leviathan said then. "Tygarya has said to not kill you."

"Has she now..." Palin grimaced and lunged forward again. Leviathan easily blocked his sword stroke and countered opening a gash in Palin's thigh. Palin staggered backwards gritting his teeth. Leviathan stood tall and calm, he was standing sideways to Palin and his sword was low and outstretched towards him.

"So are you choosing death?'" Leviathan asked.

"Fuck you, you cocky son of a whore." Palin rushed forward again with renewed energy and after several passes of the two of them striking and parrying Palin managed to cut Leviathan across the ribs, ripping his shirt. Leviathan stepped back and laughed, ripping the shirt away. He struck the same pose as before.

"Oh, no." Tyg muttered, she knew the look Leviathan had on his face. It was the point at which he has had enough of playing...he had been holding back. "Fuck." Tyg whispered in awe.

"Nearly finished, Tyg...Leviathan finally gets to the point." Antyn muttered sounding bored.

Tyg turned to look up at him. "What the fuck, Antyn, can't you stop it?"

"Not me, but you heard him, he offered Palin a chance to concede...he did what you asked of him."

"But, I can't watch this..." Tyg lowered her head and let her hair fall around her.

"You must, Tyg." An assassin said a few yards away. He was standing calmly with his arms folded.

Tyg looked at him and snarled. "Jacob, is that you?"

He lowered his mask and smiled nastily at her.

"You fucking asshole...whoreson..."

"Tyg!" Antyn yelled crossly, he couldn't believe her language.

Jacob just laughed. "Nice to finally see someone can shut that smart arse mouth of yours. Bitch!"

Antyn levelled his gaze at Jacob. "Back off!"

Tyg was straining at the chains as Antyn knelt down and grabbed it in his hands. Tyg had started up again swearing worse than a fishmonger. Jacob took a step closer and Antyn suddenly had a fire ball on the palm of his hand.

"Lev can't use magic in his fight, but nothing says I can't, now back off!"

Tyg laughed. "Jacob thinks the Guild is his if Palin dies."

"Well, don't be too quick to die too, then." Antyn said to him. Jacob seemed to think about it for a moment.

Just then they all heard Palin cry out. Leviathan had cut his hand clean off, sending it and his sword flying out of reach. Leviathan had his sword at Palin's throat.

"On your fucking knees." Leviathan ordered him.

As Palin dropped to his knees Leviathan walked around him and crouched down behind him. He grabbed his hair pulling his head back.

"Did you know there are certain places a man can stick a sword through another man and not kill him?" Leviathan rammed his sword through Palin's back and it came through his stomach as he grit his teeth and groaned.

"Oh, shit." Antyn cursed.

"No!" Tyg screamed. "What are you doing?"

Leviathan pulled the sword out and stuck it in again on the other side. Tyg was screaming as Antyn grabbed her by the arms and started dragging her away.

"Where the fuck are you going?" Jacob asked stepping forward. Antyn had his hands full with Tyg and had to let her go to deal with Jacob, but the archer had also nocked an arrow and was aiming it at him.

"Leviathan! If you're done screwing around...a little help." Antyn yelled over Tyg's screams for Leviathan to stop.

He was enjoying treating Palin like a pin cushion after all the grief he had caused. He looked up and waved his wrist. The bowman slammed back against the wall and fell off the crate in a heap on the ground, his neck broken. Antyn threw a fire ball at Jacob, making him dance backwards. The other assassin was now advancing from the other side.

"Just leave her here and you can go." Jacob said

Leviathan stood up growling when he heard that. "Duck, brother." He said and sent a blast of fire over his and Tyg's heads but caught the two assassins alight. They both screamed as they flailed around burning.

Leviathan still had hold of Palin's hair and pulled his head up, blood gushed out of his mouth as he coughed, it bubbled and foamed. "Oops, looks like I punctured a lung by mistake, how careless of me."

"Lev!" Antyn yelled, he couldn't hold Tyg back any longer. Leviathan saw her eyes had completely dilated to black. He swiped his sword quickly over Palin's throat and threw him face down on the dirt. He stepped over him just in time to intercept Tyg and catch her as she ran for him. He scooped her up onto his shoulder.

"Let's go." Leviathan said to his brother and walked off, collecting his coat on the way, as Tyg was kicking and screaming against him.

Outside he put Tyg on her feet and turned her to face him.

"You can travel back the easy way or the hard way, which is it going to be?"

"Get these fucking chains off me!"

"Ah, no...I don't think that would be prudent right now." Leviathan said slightly amused. "Easy or hard?" Tyg screamed at him. "Okay, hard it is. Antyn hogtie her over the saddle of her horse." Leviathan instructed as he put his coat on.

Tyg blinked and sneered at him. "Fucking try it."

"Then get on the fucking horse, Tyg." Antyn said behind her.

Leviathan smiled at her. "Or easy, if you prefer to calm down."

"Fuck you." Tyg muttered at Leviathan as Antyn helped her on her horse and grabbed the reins then mounted his own horse and turned them both as Leviathan jumped on his horse and they made their way back to where Eskel and the soldiers were waiting for them.

Tyg uttered not a single word the whole way back, but tears flowed down her cheeks and she shook with rage.

"How is your wound?" Antyn asked Leviathan.

"Shallow." Was all Leviathan said as he too was silent most of the way. "You can heal it later."

Once they were back at the Manor Leviathan picked Tyg up and threw her over his shoulder again and walked up the stairs with her and took her to her room. He threw her down on the bed and grabbed the manacles. As he did they unlocked and came off her wrists. He turned and walked out.

"You're welcome." He muttered and closed the door, leaving Tyg breathless, voiceless and tears streaming down her face.

After that Tyg pushed the large dresser in front of the door and didn't let anyone in.

Later that night Tyg stepped out onto her balcony to find that there were several soldiers stationed on the ground around it. Tyg grimaced. Leviathan obviously thought she may run...but she noticed that one of them ran off. She smiled, no Corvyn had stationed them there. She leaned on the railing and waited.

Within minutes Corvyn appeared below her. "Tygarya! Bloody hell, your warning last night, it wasn't wrong was it? Are you okay?"

"No, Corvyn...I'm not."

"What can I do?"

Tyg looked down on him, he was holding a lantern and she could see him clearly. She stepped over the railing and jumped down to the ground. Corvyn stepped back surprised.

"I didn't mean that, Tygarya!"

"Send the soldiers away, Corvyn, please." Tyg pleaded with him as she stood there with her head down looking miserable. He regarded her a moment then made one of those obscure gestures and the soldiers all walked off. "Put the lantern out." Tyg said then.

Corvyn extinguished the lantern and put it down on the ground. Tyg suddenly crashed into him wrapping her arms around him and laying her head on his chest. He stumbled back a step with the unexpected force and looked at her surprised. When he realised she was crying he wrapped his arms around her and held her silently in the darkness.

He held her like that for a long time until he could feel she was just breathing and not crying anymore. He took her shoulders and slowly peeled her away.

"Tygarya, time to go to bed."

Tyg looked up at him in the darkness. "Thank you, Corvyn, I really needed that."

"I know." He said tenderly. "Now you need to go back..."

"Okay..." Tyg stepped away from him. "Give me a boost up?"

Tyg heard Corvyn chuckle slightly in the darkness. "Sure thing."

He held her foot as she leapt back up and grabbed the railing and pulled herself back up onto the balcony. She leaned back over it looking down and watched as Corvyn relit the lantern and held it up.

"Good night, Tygarya."

Tyg smiled at him. "Good night, Corvyn."

71

The next day dawned bleary and cold as autumn was starting to give way to winter. Tyg knew they would be sailing soon. She lay on her bed with her cat still miserable. She couldn't believe what Palin had said and admitted to, she refused to believe it...she wondered if he had said those things to steel her heart against his death, but she remembered the look in his eyes when he had said them. She shuddered.

Just then she saw her dresser across the door start to move of its own volition. Tyg grit her teeth as her door opened. She stood up expecting to face Leviathan, she was surprised when it was Antyn. She sat down relieved.

"Good morning, Tyg." He said.

"What do you want?" Tyg grumbled, causing Antyn to frown.

"You haven't eaten and everyone is worried."

"I bet Leviathan isn't." Tyg muttered.

"Actually, surprising to me, he seems the most worried."

Tyg looked at him frowning. "I don't believe you."

Antyn shrugged and smiled. "That's of no consequence...I speak the truth. Can I come in?"

Tyg collapsed back on the bed. "Whatever."

Antyn closed his eyes and shook his head. "Tygarya, don't do that please, show some decorum." Tyg sat up shocked blinking at him as he walked into the room and stood in front of her. "I may have to give you a few lessons on conduct before you get to the palace."

Tyg screwed her face up at him. "Palace? I thought it was a castle?"

"Well, it doesn't matter which you call it, it's a castle, but it's the palace so..." Antyn wandered over to the balcony doors and looked out, clasping his hands behind his back.

"Well, whatever you call it you can stick your conduct lessons where the sun doesn't shine."

Antyn turned and smiled at her. "Well, I know you can play nice, Tyg, I've seen you behave in social situations, so perhaps just a few lessons on the differences of culture?"

"Hmm, maybe, I'll let you know...I do want to learn your language."

"Well, perhaps we start there then."

"I'm not coming out of my room..."

Antyn raised an eyebrow at her. "You can't stay in here, Tyg, you're being juvenile."

"Don't think I have forgotten, Antyn, that you put me in fucking chains." Tyg's eyes blazed and she stood up.

Antyn glanced out the window then back to her. "Tyg, calm down, you know why...it was your boss that requested it." Antyn's eyes glowed slightly.

Tyg glanced out the window and saw Leviathan out there doing his soldier inspection. She grinned.

"Leviathan doesn't know you're in here, does he?" Tyg snarled at him.

Antyn smiled calmly at her. "Actually, no."

"Hmm, I figured as much, he doesn't give a fuck."

"Tyg, he wants to give you all the space you need to get over what happened."

Tyg laughed. "You must think I'm stupid...it's more like he's decided to just leave me here until I'm ready to go back to him."

Antyn's eyes narrowed, damn he thought, she's not stupid. Tyg smirked as she knew she had guessed right. "The sanctimonious asshole." She muttered and sat back on the bed. "Get out."

Antyn pressed his mouth together. "As you wish." He turned to leave. "But I will send someone in with food, please eat it. And we sail in two days."

Tyg rolled her eyes and picked up her cat, hugging it to her breast. Antyn smiled and left, closing the door.

She stood up still hugging the cat and walked to the balcony doors and looked out at Leviathan as he walked slowly past every soldier, stopping and talking to a few of them, getting some to adjust things. He turned then and looked up at her. Tyg turned her back and walked back to the bed. Leviathan's jaw clenched and he flicked his head irritated, then turned back and dismissed the soldiers and stalked off.

Leviathan caught Antyn coming down the stairs.

"Have you been talking to Tygarya?" Leviathan accused his eyes glowing.

"Ah, yes...trying to get her to eat."

Leviathan clenched his jaw. "I'll get her to fucking eat."

"No, you won't." Antyn said wearily. "Just persevere Lev, she will get over herself sooner or later."

"For how long, Antyn....she just turned her back on me at the window."

Antyn chuckled. "Did she now...she's calculating for sure."

Leviathan folded his arms. "Explain."

"She figured I was seeing her without you knowing, so it seems she let you know in a way without having to make contact with you."

"She can't have known..."

"That you would storm inside at the precise moment I was coming down the stairs?"

"...that I would turn around and see her." Leviathan's mouth twisted sardonically.

"A game of chance." Antyn smiled.

"I'm glad you're happy about this." Leviathan growled. "Gives you more time with her alone."

Antyn's eyes went wide as Leviathan stepped closer to him his eyes glowing brightly. "Lev? It's not like that...you know that..."

"Do I?" Leviathan growled again. "You play a long game, Antyn..."

Antyn stepped backwards. "Lev, I'm not...I assure you..."

"Hmm." Leviathan backed off. "Just get her on that damn ship."

"I'm sure she will be back in your arms before then."

"She hates me..." Leviathan muttered. "I told you that fucking boss of hers was going to ruin everything."

"Well you didn't have to torture him..."

Leviathan flashed his eyes at Antyn again and growled. Antyn stammered an apology as Leviathan stormed off to the drawing room.

72

"Hey Tyg, can you let me in?" Dane called out at Tyg's door. Tyg got up and unlocked the door and walked back to the bed and clambered back into it as Dane opened the door and walked in. He froze a moment seeing Tyg getting back into bed wearing only a satin chemise. His cheeks flamed as he shut the door. It was early afternoon of the next day and Tyg had still refused to leave her room in fear of bumping into Leviathan.

"What do you want, Dane?"

"I want to know how you are?"

"I'm fine."

"No you're not...you always say that!" Dane said frustrated.

"Okay, I'm not. What difference does it make? Did Leviathan send you?"

"Why do you not fight him, like you fight everyone else? You act so different with him. I don't get it." Dane asked.

"Because he's stronger than me. I've never had anyone stronger than me before. Plus, he's a fucking sorcerer...he can get into my head and in that moment..."

"Yeah, I've seen." Dane looked around awkwardly.

"But, there's something else...some driving force pushing me towards him...it's intense and confusing."

"His height? His muscles? His damned amazing good looks perhaps...that even a bloke like myself has to admit." Dane grinned.

Tyg laughed. "Maybe...maybe it's the hair?" Tyg laughed again.

"Ha! Well his hair is as black as yours is white, maybe it's an opposites attract thing." Dane joked, he liked making Tyg laugh.

Tyg shrugged. "I have no idea."

"Maybe it's simply destiny."

"Argh, don't say that word." Tyg groaned. "That's what he and his brother keep telling me."

"Well...maybe?"

"I hate the thought that I'm following some plan. It makes me think my life is not my own."

"Hmm, I can understand that." Dane shrugged.

Tyg looked over at the chests filled with her things. Dane followed her gaze.

"But, you're still going with him...even after what happened with Palin?" Dane asked seriously.

Tyg flinched. "I told him I would, no matter the outcome."

"Why the hell did you do that?"

Tyg shrugged. "And you know me, I can't go back on my word. I knew Palin would die, it's just..." Tyg choked back a mixture of tears and anger.

"What did he do?" Dane asked quietly, since no one had been able to get any real information out of anyone so far, only that Palin was dead along with three other assassins.

Tyg looked up at Dane with large luminous eyes. "He tortured him, deliberately, after agreeing to not even kill him if he submitted."

"Oh, I see..."

"But, Palin...he knew things...knew what I am...the bastard knew I was from Tylandria all along." Tyg growled her anger palpable.

"He did?"

"Yes and he purposely kept me like some sort of pet killing machine." Tyg grit her teeth.

"Fuck!" Dane rubbed the back of his neck. "I don't know what to even say about that."

"Ha!" Tyg laughed bitterly. "Neither do I..." Tyg looked at Dane. "...so, to answer my original question?"

"What was that?" Dane asked confused.

"Did Leviathan send you in here?"

"Actually, Antyn did...apparently your friend Thomas is coming this evening with his betrothed to view the house he just bought."

"Oh, I see...Antyn's check mated me..." Tyg grimaced. "Time to suck it up then, huh?"

"If you want to welcome Thomas to his new home." Dane smiled.

"You know you're going to have to start calling him Lord."

"Yeah, guess you're right..."

"Okay, can you let Tess know I'm going to need a bath then?"

"Okay..." Dane smiled and walked back towards the door. He stopped as he opened it. "If what you say about Palin is true, Tyg, don't grieve too long or too hard."

"I know, Dane...thanks."

"But, don't give the big guy a break either in a hurry." Dane beamed a grin at her. "He's suffering like a bear with a headache."

"Ha! Good to hear...thanks for cheering me up Dane, I'm going to miss our heart to hearts."

"Me too..." Dane smiled and left.

Tyg had managed to avoid Leviathan and Antyn when she snuck downstairs to her bath, but now she knew there was no way to avoid them as she walked down the stairs to greet Thomas and Lady Belmont. Tyg was wearing a pale blue simple sleeveless dress which tied up the back with a simple silver chain hung at her waist. She had decided to wear a dress for decorum, to show Antyn up, but kept it simple so Lady Belmont would shine. Tyg didn't even bother doing her hair and just left it in her usual braid.

Still Thomas's eyes shined as he watched her walk down the stairs. Tyg was grateful neither brother was there. However when she got half way down the stairs both brothers appeared out of the drawing room door across the large foyer and both stared at her with those same looks they had given her the first day they had laid eyes on her in the ballroom of this very house. Tyg stopped and stared at them both, causing Thomas to turn around and see them.

Antyn smiled and walked over to introduce himself as Leviathan merely stayed standing and folded his arms, staring at Tyg.

"Lord Doven, a pleasure, please make yourself comfortable, it's soon to be your house after all..."

"Lord Adramelech, pleasure...please meet my lovely wife to be, Marissa Belmont."

"A pleasure, my Lady." Antyn said as he kissed her hand.

"Thank you, Lord Adramelech." Marissa said shyly and glanced furtively to Leviathan then up to Tyg who was still standing on the stairs.

Antyn leaned in to Thomas and Marissa. "Excuse my brother and Lady Tygarya, they are in the midst of a lover's spat." He stood up and said louder. "Please follow me into the main living area..."

Marissa gasped in surprise but Thomas stared at Leviathan and frowned deeply then glanced up at Tyg.

"Are you coming, Tyg?" Thomas said to her, making her look down at him, snapping her out of her trance with Leviathan. He didn't want to leave her here with him.

"Sure, of course..." Tyg stammered and quickly walked down the remaining steps and Thomas offered her his other arm as Marissa was on one, he escorted them both to the large living area doors that were usually open but had been closed for dramatic effect. Marissa was obviously pleased as she muttered gleefully as she looked around the house.

"Oh it's lovely...I only got to see the ballroom last time I was here."

They all heard the doors to the drawing room slam shut as Leviathan obviously retreated. Tyg grinned and relaxed. Thomas turned to her.

"Are you okay, Tyg? And don't just say fine."

Tyg glanced sideways at him. "No, Tom, I'm not..."

Thomas grit his teeth. "I knew it!" He scowled. "What did he do?"

Tyg could hardly tell him, he would inform the authorities. "It's nothing, Tom, nothing for you to worry about...so do you have a date for the wedding yet?"

Thomas smiled. "Yes, and we are getting Mae to help with the organising along with Marissa's mother."

"Oh....great." Tyg said sarcastically. "So you'll be keeping a low profile then."

"Very funny." Thomas said. "But actually yes."

Tyg looked up. "Seems Miss Belmont has left us behind in her delight of the place."

"Well, perhaps we should just wait down here and talk?"

"Talk?" Tyg looked at Thomas with an eyebrow raised.

"I'm really worried for you Tyg, these guys...they...they aren't what they seem."

Tyg smiled. "I know exactly what they are."

"What? What are they, Tyg?"

"Leviathan is an Emperor, Tom."

"Emperor?"

Tyg watched that news tick over in his head for a minute. "And, he's a sorcerer."

"A fucking what?" Thomas looked at her. "You are making this up?"

"I wish...look Tom, I'm only telling you because I know you will keep your mouth shut until the ship sails."

"Fuck..." Thomas muttered. "You're serious?"

"Deadly, why do you think I have been playing it so cool...?"

"Tyg, I don't think you should go back with him."

"I have to, Tom..." Tyg grimaced, right now she really didn't want to.

"No, you don't." Thomas frowned and folded his arms.

"And how are you going to stop a fucking sorcerer from taking me, if that's his wish." Tyg muttered, looking around.

"Why are you so nervous? Tyg, I don't like seeing this side of you."

Tyg mouth twisted. "I can't explain it...it's just...look you know half of what I did here was illegal, don't you?"

"Yeah, I kinda figured..."

"Well, that means dealing with criminals, not nice people...right?"

"Right...that's why I was always worried about you."

"Yeah, thanks." Tyg smiled at him. "Well, Leviathan has...ah...cleared the way for me to leave..."

"What the fuck does that even mean...no...I don't want to know..." Thomas grimaced.

"Just understand Tom, what he's done for me, to get me out of that life and so..."

"So you are obligated to go with him?" Thomas scowled. "You know you're not, right?"

Tyg rubbed between her eyes, squeezing them shut. "I know...but it's where I come from, where my parents were from...I have to go back there."

Thomas smiled at her. "Okay, I get it...as long as it's not just because of him, because I fear, Tyg, he will end up hurting you."

Tyg stared at Thomas as he looked at her with a strange look. He blinked and looked away. "Oh, here they come..."

"Darling, I absolutely love it!" Marissa said as she swept into his arms and hugged him. Thomas smiled. "That's all that matters to me, my dear, your happiness."

Tyg folded her arms as Antyn came up beside her. "Get away from me, Antyn..." Tyg growled. He raised his eyebrows in shock. "You see that..." Tyg indicated Thomas and Marissa. "That is affection for one another...not this bullshit." Tyg muttered and walked off.

Thomas watched her go and turned to Antyn. "Please take care of her...she really isn't that strong..."

Marissa wandered off towards the front entrance, fussing over furnishings. Antyn stepped closer to Thomas.

"What do you mean?"

"Ask her about a guy called Stills...then you will see how fragile she really is." Thomas went to follow Marissa, then turned. "But be careful...she might just try and kill you just for mentioning his name." Thomas smiled and walked off.

Antyn frowned and rubbed his jaw contemplating Thomas's words. He knew that it must be Tyg's first love, the person close to her she had lost, he had already seen her react to that. He drew himself up and followed them out and saw them off. He noticed Tyg had vanished back into her room.

As he turned and walked back in the door, Leviathan was standing there with his arms folded. "Where is she?"

"You missed her, back in her room."

Leviathan's jaw muscles ticked as he ground his teeth and his eyes glowed. "Sort this, Antyn!"

"She's coming with us, what's the problem exactly?" Antyn didn't get why Leviathan was so upset.

Leviathan stared at him with a glare that made him back up. "I need her near me."

"What the fuck, Lev, listen to yourself...get a grip!"

Leviathan growled and shook his head in frustration, one hand threading into his hair. "What the fuck has she done to me?"

Antyn smirked. "Well, I would put a name to it, but you're likely to kill me if I do."

"Fuck up, Antyn." Leviathan muttered and stalked off back to the drawing room.

"Get some sleep, Lev...we sail tomorrow!" Antyn called out to him.

73

Tyg was sitting on the bed, cuddling her cat, watching as the soldiers carried her belongings out. She kissed the top of the cat's head. She was going to miss the rascal. She had decided it was best if he stayed here and became the Manor's resident mouser. Tess had promised to take good care of him.

Antyn walked up to the open door and stuck his head in.

"Can I come in?"

Tyg looked up at him and shrugged. "I guess."

Antyn walked in and sat down on the bed next to Tyg and reached out and patted the cat. "Tyg..."

"Don't say it, Antyn." Tyg growled at him.

Antyn sighed and looked away. He stood up and walked over to the balcony doors and looked out the window. "You can't keep this up..."

"Watch me."

Antyn turned back and stared at her. "Fuck's sake Tyg...what's it going to take to make you grow up and stop this petty behaviour...a month at sea in good weather is not going to be pleasant with you acting like this."

"Get him to apologise."

"What?" He looked startled.

"I know, it's never going to happen...and that's the problem." Tyg looked down at the cat. "I'm coming with you, what more do you want?"

Antyn sighed. "It's time to leave."

"Okay..." Tyg said and stood up, putting the cat on the bed. "Lead the way."

Antyn shook his head and walked out the door. As he walked down the stairs he glanced back.

"For fuck's sake, Tyg, this isn't right..."

"You're telling me."

"Argh, Tyg!" Antyn growled and stormed down the stairs and out the entrance doors. Tyg smiled to herself and wandered down the stairs and followed him out.

Outside she found her friends waiting for her. She gave Neeki, Tess and Pete quick hugs then turned to Dane.

"I only just got to find you again." He said to her.

"I hope you will be happy." Tyg answered with a smile and hugged him tight, he hugged her back and they held each other for what seemed to everyone else a long time.

"Tyg." Antyn prompted.

Tyg stood back and smiled at Dane. "Take care of Tess...I'm going to write...let you know where I am...I expect you to learn and write back one day, okay..."

"Okay, Tyg." Dane said. "Follow your heart, brave girl."

Tyg grimaced at that as she turned. Antyn frowned when he heard it. "Bye guys."

Tyg jumped up on her horse and waited as Antyn mounted on his. Most of the soldiers had already left early that morning.

"So where is he?"

"He went with the soldiers at first light." Antyn said grumpily. "He really can't deal with your angst, Tyg, he just wants things fixed between you."

"So why doesn't he fix it, damn him...he is so fucking conceited!" Tyg put her heels to her horse and cantered off leaving Antyn to ponder her words and the words of her friends.

They had almost reached the outskirts of town when Tyg stopped her horse and looked down a side road.

"I have to make a stop, Antyn."

"Tyg, we don't have time for your games." Antyn frowned suspicious that she may suddenly decide she wasn't going.

"No tricks, Antyn...there is just someone I have to say goodbye to..." Tyg's voice caught in her throat. Antyn heard it and frowned further.

"If you promise no tricks..."

Tyg nodded and turned her horse down the lane. It led down next to the river and Tyg got off her horse. "Wait here, I'll be back in a few minutes..."

"Tyg?" Antyn said cautiously.

"Trust me, Antyn...please."

Antyn watched as she walked off down through some bushes to the river bank. Antyn frowned when she disappeared from sight and jumped off his horse. He silently followed.

What he saw when he rounded the bushes halted him in his tracks. Tyg was sitting underneath a tree, leaning back on it and talking...to no one...then Antyn saw it. The wooden cross staked into the ground. He saw Tyg had ripped away some long grass from around it.

When he noticed the tears streaming down her face, he realised she *was* saying goodbye. He silently crept back to the horses to wait for her. This was obviously her first love, Stills. Antyn's jaw clenched and spasmed as he frowned darkly. She had seen too many things no young girl should have to see and dealt with even more. She was truly damaged and he doubted if anyone would ever be able to truly fix her...least of all Leviathan and himself, they had no intention of fixing her. He frowned deeply and scratched his jaw and pondered if they were really right in what they were doing. Was ultimate power worth what they had to do to her?

Tyg returned after a few more minutes. Antyn noticed her hair was wet around her face and figured she must have washed her face in the river to cool it from her tears.

"Are you okay?" Antyn asked as she got back on her horse.

"I'm fine." Tyg's usual flippant comment fell. He grimaced. 'No you're not.' He thought. 'Far from it.' But said no more.

☬

When they got to the wharf Tyg halted her horse in surprise. Flanking the dock was Luke, Jared and Brax. She slipped off her horse and Antyn jumped down.

"Tyg." Antyn said in warning.

"Don't worry..." Tyg said and smiled at them as she walked up to them.

As she got closer she started running and jumped into Luke's arms as he gave her a massive bear hug. He swung her round and Jared and Brax hugged her too.

"We're going to miss you, kitty cat." Brax said with a tear in his eye.

"I thought you guys would hate me."

"Never." Jared said. "And guess who the new leader of the guild is?"

"Who."

"Luke here."

Tyg looked at Luke with a beaming smile. "That's great!"

Luke shrugged. "That remains to be seen."

"Nah, he'll do great and so will you, kitty cat." Jared said as he scruffled her hair.

Tyg grinned at them all as tears welled in her eyes. "Gods, I'm going to miss you guys so much, this has all been such a whirlwind...thank you for coming and saying goodbye."

"Of course, we wouldn't miss it."

"You just take care, Tyg."

"Yeah and if that big bastard ever hurts you, you come back and let us know and we'll deal to him, okay." Brax said gruffly, causing Luke and Jared to both look at him weird, but Tyg just laughed.

"Okay Braxy..." Tyg laughed and hugged him again, kissing his cheek.

"Tyg!" Antyn called out in warning. Luke looked up and scowled.

"Looks like it's time for you to go, little cat."

Tyg followed his gaze and saw Leviathan was standing on the aft of the ship looking out at them with his arms folded. Brax dropped his arms from around her feeling suddenly like he shouldn't be touching her. Tyg scowled. She quickly hugged Luke and Jared again and wandered back to Antyn.

"Who the fuck are they?" Antyn asked.

"Friends. Why?" Tyg said snarkily.

"Good friends...?" Antyn muttered. "Fuck, Tyg, they were all over you, you're lucky Lev didn't kill them."

Tyg looked at him darkly her eyes changing colour. Antyn looked at her with an eyebrow raised. "Can we just get on board and get this over with." Tyg walked past him and up the wharf to the gang plank. She turned at the top and saw that Luke, Jared and Brax had melted into the shadows. She waved out once knowing they were probably still watching and stepped over onto the ship.

She was surprised at how flash it was, but then Lord Doven had given them his personal vessel to sail home on.

Antyn caught up to her, just as Leviathan started walking towards them.

"Show me to my room." Tyg asked Antyn.

"Your cabin."

"What?"

"It's called a cabin on a ship, not a room."

Leviathan stopped a few meters away as the Captain distracted him. He looked over the Captain's head at Tyg, his eyes glowing faintly, as she followed Antyn below decks.

"Cast off, Captain." Leviathan ordered.

END of Book 1
Tygarya's Saga is continued in Book 2
Loyalty Binds You
Out now!

GLOSSARY OF PRONUNCIATION

Tygarya – *Ti-gar-ya*

Vanarya – *Van-ar-ya*

Essyndyl – *Es-sin-dal*

Tylandria – *Ty-lan-dree-a (roll r)*

Antyn - *An-tin*

Adramelech – *A-dram-e-lek*

Corvyn – *Kor-vin*

Enyana – *En-yarn-a*

Arial – *Air-re-al*

Landau – *Lan-dau*

Annul – *An-nule*

Barion – *Ba-re-on*

Karon – *Kar-ron*

Irion – *I-ri-on*

Palin – *Pay-lin*

Enyana – *En-yarn-a*

BOOKS BY THIS AUTHOR

The Vampire in my Mirror
Tygarya Saga
Book 1 – Destiny Finds You
Book 2 – Loyalty Binds You
Book 3 – Betrayal Frees You
Book 4 – Destiny's Shadow Defines You
Redeemable Series
(Stand alone Mafia Suspense Dark Romance stories)
Caught in the Middle – Curry & Rice
Unwanted Attention – Mad Dog
Collateral Damage – Raven
To Love A Vampire Queen
Book 1 – Houses of Shadow and Wolf

ABOUT THE AUTHOR

ANNETTA LINCOLN

Annetta lives in New Zealand with her son in the lovely rural community of North Canterbury.

She loves walks on the local beaches and through the natural native bush that surrounds her little piece of paradise.

In 2019 Annetta was diagnosed with a rare SCC cancer and has battled with ongoing treatments, operations and scans. In 2023 she was told it had now traveled to her lungs at Stage 2, palliative care and more chemotherapy treatment would be needed.

Currently Annetta is living comfortably in a stable remission.

Annetta loves animals and owns two cats at present, barn rescue kittens they are brother and sister, Roman and Lily.

Annetta spends the rest of her spare time enjoying Anime and K-dramas, she is a great reader of fantasy and horror genres and loves listening to her son playing the guitar.

Annetta likes to spend her days writing in the hopes she brings a little joy to those who discover and read her books.

Instagram - annettalincolnauthor

Thank you for reading!